Meg Gardiner was born in Oklahoma and raised in Santa Barbara, California. After graduating from Stanford Law School, she practised law in Los Angeles, later teaching in the Writing Program at the University of California, Santa Barbara. She lives with her husband and three children in Cobham, Surrey.

Praise for Meg Gardiner:

'Ms Gardiner is a welcome addition to the ranks of American thriller writers.'

Sunday Telegraph

'From beginning to end *China Lake* is a book that no reader of thrillers will be able to put down. Great characters, dynamic plot, nail-biting action – Meg Gardiner gives us everything.'

Elizabeth George

'Fiction at its finest. There are so many nail-biting moments and hand-wringing twists that *Mission Canyon* makes exhausting reading. But that's a compliment.'

Peterborough Evening Telegraph

'Very well written, racy and witty.'   *Tangled Web*

Also by Meg Gardiner

China Lake
Mission Canyon
Jericho Point

MEG GARDINER

Crosscut

HODDER

First published in Great Britain in 2005 by Hodder and Stoughton
A division of Hodder Headline

A Hodder paperback

1 3 5 7 9 10 8 6 4 2

A CIP catalogue record for this title is
available from the British Library

ISBN 0 340 82940 0

Typeset in Plantin Light by
Palimpsest Book Production Limited,
Polmont, Stirlingshire

Printed and bound by
Clays Ltd, St Ives plc

Hodder Headline's policy is to use papers that are natural, renewable
and recyclable products and made from wood grown in sustainable
forests. The logging and manufacturing processes are expected to
conform to the environmental regulations of the country of origin.

Hodder and Stoughton Ltd
A division of Hodder Headline
338 Euston Road
London NW1 3BH

For my parents
To Sally, with love
To Frank, in loving memory

A number of people have helped with the creation of this novel. For their assistance, I thank my invaluable editor at Hodder & Stoughton, Sue Fletcher; Nancy Fraser, who knew that characters must go to the end of the line; and the writers' group, who never let up: Mary Albanese, Suzanne Davidovac, Adrienne Dines, Kelly Gerrard and Tammye Huf. My appreciation also goes to Sara Gardiner, MD, for her insight into post-traumatic stress disorder. And unbounded thanks, always, to Paul Shreve.

I

The breeze gusted through the wind chimes. They sang a jarring melody. Overhead a pair of fighter jets howled past, ripping silver across the sky above China Lake.

Kelly Colfax lugged a grocery bag from the trunk of her car. She had twelve things to do in the next two hours and she should have written them down. The desert heat was bad for her memory. Did Scotty say he was coming home early? She unstuck her skirt from the back of her thighs. She had to change and get to the night-club in time to set up. Tonight she meant to put things right.

She had forgotten her haircut, but that didn't matter. Gaining twenty pounds in fifteen years mattered, but tonight she could smile and say *See?* She had a good reason. It wasn't the pressure. She wasn't a screw-up. People couldn't blame her for all the things that had been going wrong. Couldn't call her the B-Team anymore, or Slacker or Space Cadet. Tonight they would apologize. They would congratulate and envy her. With a little smile forming on her lips, she opened the door and walked into the kitchen.

A stranger was standing by the sink.

She saw short hair, olive skin and eyes that seemed all pupil, deep and black. Dressed in utilities – working blues, like enlisted personnel wore. What was someone from the base doing in her kitchen? The stranger flexed both hands. Kelly saw them peripherally but couldn't break from that black gaze. A gold aura flared at the corner of her vision.

'So.' The stranger's voice was sharp and high-pitched. 'First question. Am I here?'

Kelly stared. On the counter were scissors and a funnel and a roll of electrical tape. And her high school yearbook.

'You think you're dreaming a sailor girl in your kitchen. You think I'm a nightmare.'

Kelly opened her mouth but couldn't form words. A girl? This freaky being flexing those weird fingers? Something wrong with them, like doll's fingers. And her face was expressionless.

'Question two,' she said. 'Can you run?'

Kelly looked at her feet. Fear curled around her chest like a thorny vine. She couldn't lift them. How could the stranger know that? *Was* this a nightmare?

'Also a no.' The stranger's lips drew back over her teeth. 'No flight. No fight.'

The fear pricked sharper. Kelly looked toward the front door. 'Scotty . . .'

The stranger reached for the answering machine on the kitchen counter and pressed Play. Kelly heard her husband's voice.

'Kell, I'm not going to make the party. I have to pull a double shift. Don't hate me.'

She dropped the groceries. A bottle broke and milk gushed across the linoleum. Scotty kept talking and Kelly's legs remained frozen. The stranger's freaky hands opened the high school yearbook and flipped through it.

'West. Skinner. Delaney. Colfax. Chang . . .' She stopped. 'Tell me about your classmates. How much do you know?'

Kelly felt saliva pooling in the back of her throat.

'Well?'

The stranger kept flipping through the yearbook and Kelly felt tears forming. She knew why those hands were freaky. The stranger was wearing latex gloves.

She looked at Kelly. A new voice roared from her throat, deep and booming. *'Tell me.'*

That voice unglued Kelly's foot. She moved it backward. Now the other. A sound was sliding from her mouth, a moan. This wasn't a waking nightmare. She had to run. She slid her foot another inch, turned and flung herself toward the door.

The darts from the Taser caught her between the shoulder blades. The electric shock made her drop instantly. Her face smacked the floor. She lay splayed, her arms and legs shivering like jelly. Saliva ran out of her mouth onto the cool tile beneath her cheek.

She saw the stranger walk to the knife rack. The sound of metal rang in the kitchen. The stranger pulled out the carving knife. Kelly felt her skirt turning wet and warm as she peed herself.

The stranger's boots appeared. She flipped Kelly onto her back as though she were a hunk of meat. The knife shone under the kitchen lights. Outside, the wind chimes rang.

The stranger leaned over and dogtags swung out from beneath her utility shirt. On the chain with the tags was a gnarled piece of metal. That wasn't Navy. Kelly saw a scar near her collarbone. Tracks, like an animal had mauled her.

'If you can't talk about it, we'll have to take a different tack. Let's see if you can feel it.'

She put down the knife, grabbed Kelly's wrist and pulled her toward the refrigerator. Her grip was like a wrench. She took the roll of electrical tape, whipped it around Kelly's wrists, and wound it around the handle of the refrigerator door, binding her there.

Kelly's juddering subsided into pins and needles. She could feel her muscles coming back under control, but when she moved her leg, it flailed like a frog jabbed with an electrode in biology lab. She heard the stranger, opening cabinets and pulling things out. She turned her head.

The stranger now held a bottle of Drano crystals. She walked to the spot where Kelly had fallen and poured the drain cleaner on the wet splotch of urine. It hissed and bubbled and filled the air with the caustic stink of lye and ammonia.

Reaching for the carving knife, she knelt and hitched Kelly's skirt up to her panties, revealing chunky thighs. She held the Drano above Kelly's leg and pressed the serrated edge of the knife to the inside of her thigh.

'Let's start over. Tell me when it hurts.'

2

The wind skipped over me. I stood in the parking lot, shielding my eyes from the setting sun. The heat was a wall against my face.

'This was a bad idea. Let's get out of here,' I said.

Out on the highway an eighteen-wheeler rumbled past. Dust spun in the air behind it, blowing across the razor wire that marked the edge of the naval base.

Jesse looked at me as if I'd blown a cylinder. 'Are you nuts? You can't back out now.'

I peered over the roof of the Mustang at the strip mall. 'Nuts isn't backing out. Nuts is going in there.'

He pulled off his sunglasses. 'Let me get this straight. Evan Delaney is chickening out of her high school reunion?'

The invitation read *China Lake's brightest nightspot hosts our festive gathering*. The nightclub sat between the adult bookstore and the auto wrecking yard. Beyond them stretched a million acres of absence: the Naval Air Warfare Center, where mirages hovered over the desert floor and the horizon flung itself up into mountains, purple and red against a huge sky.

Above the door of the club a banner batted in the wind. BASSETT HIGH 15TH – WELCOME BACK HOUNDS! Music banged through the windows. I could see the crowd packed inside.

'It's a set-up,' I said.

I handed Jesse the invitation, which specified *Dress: party casual*. In the high Mojave that means shoes optional, but the reunion committee had lied.

'They're dressed to the nines. I see sequins.'

'Damn, I should have gone with the ballgown and stilettos.'

I made a face at him. He looked perfectly presentable in jeans and a white button-down shirt. For that matter, I looked perfectly presentable in jeans and a white button-down shirt. How had I let that happen? God, we'd be voted cutest couple. They'd stick little cardboard crowns on our heads and ask whether we were engaged and why Jesse looked like he'd been smashed over a cliff. I'd say on and off, and because he had been. Then I'd stupidly mention that we were both lawyers, and spend the evening explaining that no, I didn't practice anymore and yes, their ex really could sue them for pouring sugar in the gas tank of the car. Why the hell had I come?

I pointed at the window. 'That's Ceci Lezak handing out nametags. She ran Student Council like it was the Reichstag.'

He looked. 'Explaining that funny little mustache. Come on, I want to meet her. Plus that guy who set his hair on fire at the talent show, and the girl who turned those four chickens loose, with numbers painted on their backs.'

'One, two, three and five. That was me.'

'And your mortal enemy could turn up.'

I groaned. 'Seeing Valerie is the last thing I need.'

I glanced north at mountains arrayed like saw blades. The Sierras and Panamints, and the Cosos, where Renegade Canyon cut deep through the rocks. One afternoon there, one debacle, had led to four years of rancor.

'We'll set up a steel cage and you can settle old scores,' he said. 'Grease up with Swedish meatball gravy and go at it.'

I stepped back. 'You need to cut down on the painkillers. And the satellite TV.'

He drummed his fingers on the trunk of the car. 'Last winter you fired a clip of ammunition at a homicidal maniac in your own house. You can't let a few snobs in shiny dresses send you packing.'

I sighed. He took my hand.

'Besides, don't you want to see your old boyfriend? What's his name, Tommy Chong?'

'Chang.'

He grinned. 'Thought so.'

He headed up the curb cut and toward the door of the club, nodding at the auto wrecking yard. 'Stay here and admire that giant heap of old tires. I'm going in.'

I put a hand on my hip. 'It isn't your reunion.'

His smile was wicked. 'Wanna bet?'

He pushed through the door.

Nobody was faster on his feet than Jesse, metaphorically speaking. Anything he thought up, he could undoubtedly pull off, despite being five years younger than everyone else here, and having grown up in Santa Barbara, and the fact that nobody in my graduating class had been anywhere as gifted and good looking, or paraplegic.

'Dammit.' I chased after him.

Inside, I found him beneath the strobing disco ball, at the sign-in table. Ceci Lezak was searching through a box of nametags. Her taffeta ruffles covered a build like a furnace. Her hair was sprayed into place with *pointilliste* exactitude. She looked harried.

'I can't seem to find it,' she said.

Jesse leaned an elbow on the table, smiling at her. 'Student Council was never better than when you ran it. I remember that cool campaign slogan . . .'

'Lift Off With Lezak.' She stopped hunting and beamed at him. 'Why don't I make you a new nametag?'

Oy. I walked up. 'Hey, Ceci.'

She clapped her hands together. 'Evan, wow. Look at you, all fit and tan and . . .' Eyes on my outfit. 'Spic and span.'

'You're very festive this evening.'

'And you're a writer and all.' She handed me my nametag and a welcome pack. 'You're not going to do an exposé about tonight, are you? Reveal our old high school secrets in print?'

'No. I won't blow your cover, I promise.' I stared at Jesse, tapping my index finger against my lips. 'You look so familiar.'

Ceci smiled. 'This is Jesse Blackburn. He was our foreign exchange student.'

'No, that's not it.' I snapped my fingers. 'Of course – Court TV, the trial. When did you make parole?'

The door opened and heat swarmed over us. In the doorway stood a suburban Brunhilde, blonde, ungainly and six feet tall.

'Oh my hell, you're really here.' Abbie Hankins laughed deep in her throat and engulfed me in a hug. 'I win the bet. Fork it over, Wally.'

Her husband lumbered through the door. He was taller and even rounder than Abbie, a St Bernard in a garish Hawaiian shirt. She passed me to him as if I were a rugby ball. He lugged me against his side, laughing.

'Thanks for costing me twenty bucks, Delaney.' He saw Jesse. 'Dude.'

He grabbed Jesse's hand and pumped it. At the table Ceci laced her fingers together, smiling expressively.

'You're looking debonair tonight, Dr Hankins.' She ran her gaze over Abbie's sundress. 'That's sweet. Wal-Mart does such fun fashions nowadays.'

A woman strode up wearing a reunion committee nametag and a dress that made her look like a spangled boar. Ceci waved her close, whispering and nodding at Jesse.

'There's no welcome pack for him, nothing. And I shouldn't be handling the table all by myself.'

'Should we call Kelly?'

'No. This is the last straw. I bet she had a few belts to loosen up before she came, and now she's home trying to put her lipstick on without running it up to her ears.'

Realizing that we were listening, they shut up and pasted on *Go Team!* smiles.

Ceci gestured to Jesse. 'You remember our exchange student?'

The boar wrinkled her forehead. 'Sure. Right . . . So good you could make it.'

They bit their tongues, staring at him. I knew they saw the wheelchair and little else. They hadn't seen the head-line *One Killed, One Critical after Hit and Run.* They hadn't watched Jesse spend these last years rebuilding his life. And they couldn't see that he looked better than he had in a long time. A deranged driver had blown him off his feet, but flashbacks, chronic pain, and grief at losing his best friend in the crash had kept him down. When finally he had sought help, he was diagnosed with post-traumatic stress disorder. Now, at last, he was on the mend.

Wally was suppressing a smile. 'How are things back in . . .'

'Manitoba. Good.' Jesse took the nametag from Ceci. 'And I was a political prisoner.' He turned and headed into the club.

Ceci held out a welcome pack to Wally. 'It has your fifteen-year commemorative pin, the *Dog Days Update* book and coupons for ten percent off at Krause's Auto Body.' She handed Abbie her pack. 'Discounts at Weight Watchers, too.'

Abbie smiled. 'How's their program working for you?'

Ceci colored. Abbie and I strolled after Jesse.

'What's with her?' I said.

'She's the dental hygienist for Wally's practice. She's an anal retentive neat freak who thinks she could run his life much better than a slob like me.' She pushed her glasses up her nose. 'She's been coming on to him for years.'

I managed not to gape. Abbie and Wally had three happy blond children and always seemed to make each other laugh. We should all be so lucky.

Above the bandstand hung strings of red lights shaped like chili peppers. The band was pumping out old pop rock, the jump juice of our youth. People crowded around the buffet table, their plates piled with coleslaw and weenies toothpicked to pineapples. Fusion cuisine, desert-style. The acreage of shiny Spandex on display could have covered the Hindenburg.

I smiled, suddenly glad to be back.

China Lake is the Navy's top weapons-testing facility. I was thirteen when the US Navy transferred my family here. It was not the California of my dreams, consisting instead of crystal skies, shrieking fighter jets, jackrabbits and blowing sand. When we drove into town my mother, who had weathered transfers from Norfolk to DC to Pearl Harbor, inhaled sharply.

My father, driving with one elbow cocked on the window frame, smiled and said, 'Welcome home, Angie. Again.'

She smoothed her hair against the wind and peered back at my brother and me. She had on her game face. *This is what we do. We're a Navy family. Chin up.* Right then, my stomach hurt. Twenty years later, this place was more or less my hometown.

Abbie stuck by my side. 'Man, look at Becky O'Keefe. Tell me my butt isn't that big.'

'Not by half.'

'You're a lousy liar.'

I stopped. 'Oh, no.'

On the wall behind the buffet hung a display of photos, blown up to poster size. Jesse was parked in front of it, shaking his head.

'Rock my world. Now I've seen everything,' he said.

The photo showed me standing on the football field at halftime of the Homecoming game, wearing a fake ermine stole and a cockeyed rhinestone tiara. I was clutching the arm of my escort, Tommy Chang, and looking surprised out of my head.

Jesse's mouth skewed to one side. 'Evan Delaney, Homecoming Queen.'

'Can I get a drink before you start in on me?' I said.

'And you never told me. All this time I'm thinking of you as the tomboy, the sprinter, the outsider . . .'

Abbie nodded. 'Dirt-biker, creative writer, girl gladiator . . .'

'He doesn't need any help,' I said.

'Talk about a cover story,' Jesse said. 'Did everybody in China Lake live a double life?'

'Yes. Like you.' I raised a fist. 'Fight the power. Free Canada.'

11

He gazed at the photo again. 'Who's that in the background?'

'Valerie Skinner.'

'Your mortal enemy?' He leaned forward. 'Why does she look blurry?'

'She lunged and knocked the tiara off.'

'She looks like a rottweiler. She really held the grudge that hard?'

Abbie grabbed a pineapple weenie. 'Like a vise grip.' She looked at the posters. 'I wish they'd put up the one of you getting the tiara back from her.'

Jesse looked at me.

'I tackled her,' I said.

'You speared her. It was majestic,' Abbie said.

I glanced around at the crowd.

'Don't worry. Last time anybody saw her was graduation. You're safe.' Abbie waved to a stout woman across the buffet table. 'Hey, Becky.' Under her breath she said, 'She's still making those appliqué shirts.'

Indeed, Becky O'Keefe was wearing a pink sweatshirt with bobbles and glitter. Abbie trotted over and hugged her.

Jesse leaned back, shaking his head at the photo. 'A coup attempt. Wild. Did you have Valerie flogged?'

'For your information, I made a damn fine Homecoming Queen.'

He laughed. 'My God. You liked being Queen. It wasn't an ironic act meant to subvert the high school social order. You actually liked it.'

'Yes. It was my glorious shining moment.' I pinched the bridge of my nose. 'And do not speak of my hair. If you compare me to Jon Bon Jovi I will dump you on your ass before you can shout.'

'I wouldn't dare.' He thought about it. 'Twisted Sister, maybe.'

I strode to the bar and asked for Chardonnay. He followed, ordered iced tea and sat tapping his thumb against his knee, wearing a cocky look.

'Tommy Chang isn't anything like you described him.'

'Not a word, Jesse. Nada. Zip it.'

He glanced at the photo. 'I pictured this ultra-cool rebel, Bruce Lee meets Clint Eastwood. But—'

'Tommy was *not* that short.'

His smile was dazzling to the point of infuriation. 'I think it's sweet. Frodo wins the hand of the queen.'

I took my Chardonnay. 'Don't you have cows that need milking back in Manitoba?'

'Right after the Justice for Blackburn rally at the parole board.'

I drank half my wine in one gulp.

A woman walked up to the bar. 'Evan?'

I set down my drink and shook her hand. 'Ms Shepard.'

'Shepard-Cantwell.'

She was in her early forties and looked ready for Woodstock. Her dress may have come down off the wall at the Guggenheim, considering that it mixed newspaper headlines with fake fur and glass eyeballs. She smiled at Jesse with the over-sweet gleam of the professionally condescending.

'Sorry that we never met when you were an exchange student.'

His tone was mordant. 'That's okay. My English is much better now.'

'It's wonderful that you were able to travel all this way, considering.' She turned back to me with a brittle smile. 'I

13

hear you're still writing. It's great that you found an outlet for your imagination.'

'Thanks.' Nitwit.

'How are your parents?'

'Good. Divorced.'

'Oh. Well. That's a shame.' She flipped her hair over her shoulder. 'Your dad had such panache. Even when he was raking us teachers over the coals, we couldn't help but be impressed. Give him my best, won't you?'

She swanned away. I downed the rest of my wine. *An outlet for my imagination.* Birdbrain.

Jesse said, 'Let me guess. Art teacher?'

'*The* art teacher. It was her class where Valerie stole my journal.'

China Lake was a place where you had to make your own entertainment, generally involving sports, garage bands and drinking. My hobby was writing. Valerie's was revenge.

In high school I scrawled my own world in a journal containing every poem and hissy fit and spasm of lust that spilled from my pubescent soul, and one day when Ms Shepard stepped out of the classroom Valerie took it from my backpack.

She denied it, vociferously. But she spent lunchtime reading sections aloud in the girls' room, including my fantasies about Tommy Chang and Keanu Reeves, and how I considered her a crude, skankfaced, butt-scratching diva.

'Ms Shepard asked the student teacher if he'd witnessed it. I can still see him, this prissy little guy going on like a howler monkey, telling her I was jumping to conclusions.'

'And Ms Shepard thought you had an active imagination?'

14

Ms Shepard saw surfaces, not subtext. First impressions were her thing, and she had drawn her first impression of me two weeks into my freshman year, the day our class took the field trip to Renegade Canyon.

'She called me an instigator.'

'So, on top of everything you were a troublemaker? What else are you hiding in your secret past? Animal sacrifice?'

'You really want to know?'

I stepped off the school bus that day into the heat, pulling a baseball cap low on my head. We were fifty miles down a deserted road on the far reaches of the naval base, on a field trip to study the petroglyphs, prehistoric art carved into the canyon walls.

Ms Shepard waved to us. 'Everybody over here. Bring your sketchpads.'

I shielded my eyes against the ferocious light, walking with my head down. The sunblock was hidden in my backpack, beneath my journal and a dog-eared copy of *Ender's Game*. Pale skin, pale poetry, science fiction: even I knew I was a geek.

The canyon gashed for miles through black rocks splattered crimson and yellow with lichen. Carvings covered the walls like graffiti. Snakes. Deer. Bighorn sheep. Weird human figures with spirals for faces and shock waves erupting from their heads, rising ghostly and vivid sixty feet above me. The light seemed to hum.

Ms Shepard trudged through the soft sand, waving. 'Imagine the young hunters hidden among the boulders. Picture the shaman carving these images to bring success to the hunt.'

I stared up at the figure of a horned human with feet

15

like talons. Someone pushed past, knocking my shoulder. Her voice came as small and sharp as a needle.

'Watch it, Nosebleed.'

My hand shot to my upper lip. Valerie snickered and walked on by.

Ms Shepard frowned. I found a wad of Kleenex in my pocket, but my nose wasn't bleeding. I felt a zinging sensation along my arms. Valerie had gotten me again.

Ms Shepard twirled in a circle. Her peasant skirt flared and her chandelier earrings danced in the sun. 'When shamans drew the prey animal, they gave the hunter power. Look. Can't you see it?'

I'll say. The walls were covered with bighorn sheep. And hunters spearing sheep, archers shooting sheep, dogs attacking sheep. Plus creepy sheep: two-headed ones, and big ones with little ones inside. It was mayhem.

'And these symbols. The snake represents fertility. And the spiral is the Mother Earth navel from which man emerged.'

There were snickers and audible *icks*. And behind me, whispering.

Valerie and Abbie and Tommy were inching back from the group. Shooting a surreptitious glance at Ms Shepard, Valerie slunk between two boulders and took off. Abbie looked around, checking that the coast was clear, and spied me.

She froze. Behind her glasses, her expression said: New girl, don't rat me out. Then she whispered, 'Want to come?'

Tommy nodded beside her. He was a wiry kid with powerful brown eyes and a convincing aura of cool, and whenever he looked my way my stomach hollowed. He mouthed *Come on* and slipped between the rocks. I followed.

Abbie took off like a rocket, blonde hair flying. Tommy and I sprinted behind. He shot me a smile. Exhilarated, I smiled back, thinking *I'm in.*

The break in the rocks led up a trail. After a hundred yards we caught up with Valerie. She was laughing. Until she saw me.

'What's she doing here?'

Valerie had hips and boobs, wore tight tops and her jeans slung low, and smelled of perfume and cigarettes. She was domineering, popular and cruel, and after two weeks of high school she ruled the freshman class like a hegemon. I couldn't figure a way around her, because wherever I turned she was in front of my face.

Like right now. 'Why are you tagging along?'

Abbie shoved her glasses up her nose. 'I said she could come.'

Valerie stepped up, inches from my face, and I felt myself shrinking. She tossed her brown hair over her shoulder. I was slow to recognize the deviousness behind her eyes.

'You can come on one condition. You answer this riddle.'

'Okay.'

'If you didn't have feet, would you wear shoes?'

'No.'

'Then how come you're wearing a bra?'

I blinked. A hot stone weighed on my stomach. Braying with laughter, Valerie ran ahead.

Abbie yelled, 'That's mean!' Taking my arm, she pulled me along. 'Come on.'

I complied, legs watery, climbing up the trail through

yellow light and a hot breeze. I hid my face from Tommy. Valerie said *bra*, she made him think about my . . . oh, God.

He called to her. 'Where is it?'

'Just ahead. My dad sets up targets out here.'

We squeezed through a crack between boulders and came out on the side of a hill, overlooking a valley. The sky was blue glass. Sand gleamed in the sun. Below, an access road ran to a complex of cinderblock buildings where Jeeps were parked.

Abbie put her hands on her hips. 'We came all the way for this? That's just, like, buildings. Where are the jets? There aren't even targets set up.'

Valerie scanned the horizon. 'I thought for sure . . .'

Soldiers in camouflage appeared outside the buildings. Some hopped into the Jeeps. One was talking on a radio. And one had a pair of binoculars to his eyes, sweeping the hills.

He called to his comrades and pointed. At us.

'Uh oh,' I said.

Heads swiveled to stare. They began pointing and shouting. There was a flurry of movement, men running toward the Jeeps or back to the buildings.

'I don't think we're supposed to be here,' I said.

The flash lit the desert floor. White light wound with orange, fireballs erupting from the buildings. The boom hit us and echoed off the rocks.

Valerie clapped her hands over her ears. Tommy dropped to the ground with his arms over his head. Abbie shouted, 'Oh, crap.'

Flames poured into the sky. The buildings disappeared, billowing black smoke. One of the Jeeps lay flipped upside down like a turtle, burning.

'I don't think that was supposed to happen,' I said.

Flames and smoke towered into the sky. After a second I caught an acrid whiff. Down on the valley floor, soldiers ran to and fro outside the ring of destruction.

'Something's wrong. Did they all get out okay?' I said.

One of the Jeeps swung around and began driving toward us, flinging up dust. The voice inside my head said, *This was secret. You weren't supposed to see.*

'Oh God.' Abbie sprinted away, back down the trail.

Tommy jumped up and ran after her. The Jeep lurched over the sandy ground below us and began to climb the incline.

I tugged on Valerie's arm. 'Come on.'

I ran. After a few seconds I heard her running behind me.

We pummeled back down the trail. The wind funneled between the rocks, blowing smoke over us. I breathed through my mouth to shut out the smell. The light smeared red and I glanced up to see smoke dimming the sun. And then I saw something worse. Cruising overhead was a military helicopter.

I was so dead. Ms Shepard was going to haul me away by the ear. And she'd call my parents. I streaked down the trail into the canyon, and stopped cold.

The helicopter sat on the ground, rotors blowing sand. Ms Shepard was herding my classmates onto the bus. Soldiers in camouflage had pulled Abbie and Tommy off to one side. Abbie looked ashamed.

Busted.

Valerie pounded into me from behind. She gasped at the sight of the helo. A soldier walked toward us.

We were totally busted. Unless I could talk us out of trouble. And man, was I good at talking.

'I can explain. I . . .'

I felt blood running down my nose and over my top lip. I wiped it off and my hand came away bright red. Valerie gulped, looked at Ms Shepard herding kids onto the bus, and pointed at me.

'Nosebleed said we'd see the best drawings if we followed her.'

My mouth fell open.

Heads turned. The soldier, Ms Shepard and my entire class stared at me. The rock in my stomach began to burn. Valerie hugged herself and started to cry.

'It's not my fault.' She turned to me, lips quivering. 'Why did you make me do it?'

My fist went into her face.

I swirled the wine in my glass. 'Valerie blamed me for the face she grew into.' The one that ended up carrying so much weight. 'Did I tell you she threatened to get a nose job and sue me to pay for it?'

Jesse looked wry. 'You could have claimed sovereign immunity.'

A wolf whistle cut through the music. Across the room, a man stood with his hands in his pockets, grinning at me.

'Here we go,' Jesse said.

I laughed and waved. 'Tommy.'

He was still a whippet. He was wearing a bowling shirt, the first time since graduation I had seen him in something besides motocross leathers. His brown eyes gleamed from beneath a ridiculous pork-pie hat. He tipped it back, cool as ever.

He sauntered over, chewing gum, and slapped my hand into a soul shake. 'Hey, Rocky.'

'You're looking smooth,' I said.

He pulled up his sleeve, revealing a nicotine patch. 'Dawning of a new era.'

'The tobacco companies are going to go bankrupt.' Smiling, I introduced Jesse. 'Freedom fighter or my boyfriend, depending on your point of view.'

Tommy shook his hand. 'Cool. What is it you do, exactly?'

'Take on The Man, mostly. You?'

'I *am* The Man.' He chewed his gum. 'Detective with the China Lake Police Department.'

Jesse's face was worth the drive.

At the far end of the club Ceci Lezak climbed up on the bandstand, shushed the band and stepped to the mike. 'All righty. Before the festivities get too lively, we have a few awards.'

Lively meant the football team was drinking Cuervo shots and we had less than an hour before chairs started flying. Ceci smoothed her ruffles into submission.

'We want to mark some milestones in our lives. All this is in the *Dog Days Update*, but I want to make special mention of a few people.'

Tommy leaned toward me. 'You punched anybody out tonight?'

I laughed. Jesse watched, his face enigmatic. He had nothing to be jealous of. Tommy had always been my crush, not vice versa. He never stuck with a girl for more than a few weeks.

Ceci read from a note card. 'Four couples have been married for thirteen years, so we had to get down to anniversary dates.' Her voice sounded tight. 'Congratulations to the longest married graduates, Wally and Abbie Hankins.'

In the center of the room Abbie whooped and thrust her arms in the air.

Ceci flipped to the next card. 'The award for the grad with the most children goes to Tommy Chang with five.'

The football team stomped on the floor and slapped their hands on tables, hooting, 'Yeah!' I turned to him in surprise.

He popped another stick of gum in his mouth. 'Two sets of twins. And two ex-wives. You see why I can't afford to smoke anymore.'

'The grad who still lives closest to campus is . . . me.' Awkward laughter from the crowd. 'And the award for the classmate who's come the farthest to the reunion?'

Beside me, I heard, 'Oh, shit.'

'Let's have a round of applause. All the way from Canada, Jesse Blackburn.'

By ten p.m. the pineapple weenies had given way to a cake the size of a sofa, topped with a plastic bassett hound and *Gone huntin'* written in green icing. Up on the bandstand a quartet of classmates had slung on electric guitars, and Stace Wilkins and Bo Krause were playing increasingly drunken guitar solos. When they launched into 'Pissing in the Wind', Abbie jumped up and pulled Wally onto the dance floor.

Off near the door, Ceci was wrestling a display into place on an easel. My gaze slid past her, but an odd tic of emotion drew my eye back to a woman who had just come in.

She was by herself, and she was sick. She seemed as frail as paper and carried herself with care, as though the slightest touch would bruise her. Under the disco ball her hair shone brassy brown. It was a wig. Her eyes were hot in an alabaster face. She gazed around the room expectantly, but nobody said hello to her.

People sometimes treated Jesse the same way, and few things made me angrier. I headed across the club. I might fumble for words, but that was better than ignoring her.

I extended my hand. 'Evan Delaney. You'll have to forgive me for not recognizing you.'

She was so pale that her skin was nearly translucent. I could see blue veins in her temples. Her hand was chilly.

'Hey, Nosebleed.'

My lips parted, but something had nailed my tongue to the floor of my mouth. I read her nametag. Valerie Skinner.

Her voice was a rasp, slurred at the edges. She pointed to her head. 'Brain thing. Messes up my speech.'

'Sorry to hear it,' I said. 'Really sorry.'

'Sure you are. You like my new look?' Turning her head, she showed me her profile. 'I'll send you the bill for the nose job. The weight loss has a downside, but at least I'll die thin.'

'You look . . .'

'Don't sweat it. Close your mouth, flies are getting stuck in your teeth.'

Luckily, I had laminated a smile to my face before coming over. Otherwise I would have looked like *The Scream*.

She gazed around. 'Time to get a drink and hold court. This is my last chance to get these rubes bowing at my feet.' Her smile was self-aware. 'Once a diva, always a diva.'

She walked off with the cautious gait of an octogenarian. I wanted to run straight to a Catholic church and confess my sins to a priest.

23

Ceci sidled up. At length she said, 'Is it a tumor?'

I frowned, galled that she would put it so baldly. 'I didn't see the x-rays.'

She twisted her hands together. 'I just thought, you've been talking to him all night, maybe he told you what's wrong.'

'Say again?'

She nodded across the room at Jesse. 'The wheelchair – does he have cancer?'

'Broken back. A car ran him down. Why would you think—'

'Good.' She relaxed. 'We don't need to add any more names to the list.'

But she continued twisting her hands, gazing at the display she had just set up. It was labeled Hound Heaven.

'Excuse me, Ceci.'

I walked over to it. Under the caption 'In Fond Memory', Ceci had tacked up photos, remembrances and newspaper obituaries. I gazed at them, feeling a tingling in my fingers.

Jesse rolled up beside me. 'Ev?'

I continued gazing at the display. After a moment he leaned back.

'Jesus,' he said. 'What happened, a sniper in the clock tower?'

Billy D'Amato. Car crash.

Shannon Gruber. Pneumonia.

Teddy Horowitz. Aircraft accident aboard the *USS Nimitz*.

Linda Garcia. Long illness.

Sharlayne Jackson. Complications of childbirth.

I put a hand to my head.

Marcy Yakulski. Auto accident. Pinned next to Marcy's

photo was an article from the *Cincinnati Enquirer.* 'Four Die in Fiery Crash.'

Cancer.

Long illness.

Exposure.

Jesse shot me a look. 'You may want to think about carrying a good luck charm.'

Light caromed off the disco ball, flickering over the names on the board. I read the last name and felt a sick headache spiraling up.

Dana West, RN. Surgical nurse. Died in a hospital fire.

'I have to get out of here.' I rushed for the door, queasy and desperate for fresh air.

The Mustang roared up Highway 395 heading north out of town, headlights swallowing the road. I kept the pedal down.

'I knew Dana West. The nurse who died,' I said.

I knew all the other names on the memorial board, but Dana West's face stayed with me. She had a warm smile, a laugh that cut through the lunch line in the cafeteria, and an ease about comforting anybody who was in pain. She lived three houses down from me. Jesse put his hand on the back of my neck.

'A hospital fire. She died on duty. This bitch universe, sometimes I . . .'

I ran the back of my hand across my eyes. Twelve classmates were gone. And Valerie Skinner was going to be next.

The desert night was radically still, the sky a black sail scooped full of stars. The road climbed over open country and, though it had been fifteen years, the rise and the twist in the road presented themselves to me as gifts. I pushed it up to the summit and found the turnout.

We were at the top of a natural amphitheater, looking west toward the Sierras. Far in the distance, the lights of Lone Pine clung to the flat. The silence was complete. I got out and walked around to Jesse's side.

He opened his door. 'Give me a hand? I left my hiking gear at home.'

He could walk a bit, but hadn't brought his crutches. I faced him and when he stood up in the doorway we locked forearms. Even bracing him, I savored the moment; I loved having him tall. He still had the lithe swimmer's frame that had brought him a couple of national titles and a spot on the US world championship team. He made it the two feet to the back of the car and pulled himself up to sit on the trunk.

The sky was spread with white fire. The dark wall of the Sierras soared above us. I leaned back against him.

'Dad brought me out here the day after I punched Valerie in the nose.'

I'd thought my life was ruined. I was suspended from school and my parents had grounded me. All I wanted to do was cringe in my room with the covers over my head. Instead, my father ordered me into the car, drove me up to this empty rise, and taught me how to shoot a gun.

Dad was a lean man with an Oklahoma drawl and cropped hair gone the color of ice, and he talked while he set up a row of tin cans and loaded Grandpa's old shotgun.

'There's anger, and then there's defending yourself. Yesterday was about anger, which is why you're suffering consequences.'

26

He showed me how to nestle the stock against my shoulder and to sight the target down the barrel.

'But don't ever kowtow to bullies. I'm proud that you stood up for yourself. You just went about it the wrong way. Both eyes open, Kit. And watch out for the kick.' ·

I aimed at the cans and fired. The sound rattled through my skull. We looked.

'You killed that cactus. Dead.' He took the shotgun and reloaded. 'When you go back to school, don't be ashamed. Take your licks and move on.'

'Can't I just be invisible? I'd settle for that.'

He stopped loading shells. 'Never settle. Not you, Kit. Not ever.'

Now I stared across the night. Jesse wrapped his arms around my waist.

'What happened?' he said.

'Everything turned around. When my suspension was up I went back to school and nobody messed with me.' I laughed, weakly. 'Except for Valerie. But I knew I could stand up to her, and I had friends who stood with me. I didn't settle for staying out of her way.'

'Settle isn't a word I connect with you. Surrender, give up – none of those words either.'

I wrapped my hands around his. Behind us the moon rose, shimmering and huge. Its light ghosted down the slope across the valley and hit the granite wall of the mountains. On the summits, snowcaps luminesced.

His voice went quiet. 'I know it's a blow, seeing how many of your classmates have died.'

'Chance makes me angry.'

'Nothing can grant you certainty. But I'll fight to make sure your life never becomes a compromise.'

It was more than reassurance. It was a promise and a

dare. And it was closer to a proposal than I was ready to hear. I turned around and laid my hands across his shoulders. His eyes were deep blue in the moonlight.

I gave him a non-answer. I pressed my mouth to his and gave him a kiss.

3

Ceci Lezak loaded posters and the Hound Heaven display into her CR-V. It was hot and the wind was blowing. She was beyond tired. Beyond pissed off. Her nylons had run, and she wasn't nearly drunk enough. Abbie Hankins had clung to Wally all night like a limpet. He hadn't even complimented her dress, and now the idiotic sequins had chafed her underarms.

And on top of it all, she'd had to do twice the work at the party, thanks to Kelly Colfax.

The wind blew sand across her face. This shitty little town.

She was supposed to get out of here. For Christ's sake, she'd been Student Council President. She wasn't supposed to spend fifteen years scraping dried food off people's teeth, feeling her life become as arid as China Lake with each passing year.

She shoved the last of the posters into the car and slammed the hatchback. She knew what to do with all this shit. Give it to Kelly.

It was one a.m. when she screeched into Kelly's driveway. Her headlights shone on the blue Miata parked inside the garage. The lights were on in the living room, behind closed blinds. The stereo too. Having her own private party. Well, piss on Kelly Let-It-Slide Colfax. She hauled the posters out of her CR-V, dumped them on the front porch and rang the bell.

Nobody answered. Her anger soured. She rang the bell again. Bitch, ignoring her. She walked to the front window. Kelly was in there, secretly laughing at her. Stumbling around drunk and disoriented, she bet, like at those last few reunion committee meetings. The blinds were clattering in the wind, and she could see slices of the inside of the house. Past the living room a corner of the kitchen was visible. A sack of groceries was spilled on the floor.

Wind chimes rattled and the bushes scritched. She had the eerie feeling that something was not right. She knocked again and opened the door.

'Kelly?'

A gallon bottle of milk had broken and run across the floor. It was mixed with something else, red wine probably.

This definitely wasn't right. She crept inside, heading for the kitchen. 'Kelly?'

Beyond the spilled milk, something was heaped on the kitchen floor. It looked like a coil of sausages but was too messy and too huge to have come from the butcher's. She smelled lye, and something worse. She took another step, peering around the end of the kitchen counter.

After that, she was screaming.

The moon was high when we drove back into town. Just past two a.m. we pulled into Hobo Joe's, where the neon sign of the tramp is always lit and truckers, cops and shift workers from the base can get hot coffee twenty-four hours a day. I grabbed my purse.

'Want coffee?'

Jesse spun the radio dial across long swathes of static. 'Please. Large.'

I was paying for two coffees when a police officer came through the door. His eyes were wary. He grabbed a coffee and stood behind me at the counter, sorting change in his palm. I nodded to him.

'You on your own this morning?' His mouth was tense, his tone astringent.

'No, my boyfriend's in the car.'

He glanced out at the Mustang. Slapping coins on the counter, he said, 'You take care.'

I followed him out, watching him walk to his patrol car. Jesse stuck an arm out the window and called to me, waving urgently. He looked back at the radio. I heard the news report.

At eleven that morning we pulled into the class picnic at the recreation center on the base. The place was packed, the mood restless and gossipy. In a small town, bad news travels faster than an explosion.

Jesse's voice was chill. 'My graduating class was twice as big as yours, and only two people have died since graduation. Now you're up to thirteen. What's wrong with this picture?'

A covered patio overlooked a playground and baseball fields. On one of the picnic tables Jesse found a copy of the *Dog Days Update*, which contained What-I've-been-up-to entries from a number of people, plus class notes and obituaries. After reading for a minute he ran a hand through his hair.

'It's random. Car accident. Long illness. Another long illness.' He looked up. 'What's that a euphemism for these days? Not cancer, probably not even AIDS. Alcoholism?'

'Within a few years of graduating high school? That would take intense effort.'

31

Too late, I shut my mouth. Jesse's younger brother had gone through detox at twenty-one.

'Ain't that the truth. Drugs?' he said.

'Plausible.'

'Exposure.' He looked at me, perplexed.

'Definitely drugs. Chad Reynolds went out in the desert and OD'ed on downers. They found his body a month later.'

'Childbirth.' He frowned. 'That's odd. I mean in this age, in the west.'

'I knew Sharlayne. She was a first grade teacher.' My eyes felt tired. I rubbed them. 'Excuse me.'

I headed to the counter for a soda. As I filled my cup I saw Valerie Skinner walk in.

In the daylight she looked papery. The weight loss emphasized her fragility. Her eyes were feverish and her chemo-porcelain skin gave her an ethereal look, as though she'd been transported from another time. Under the brassy wig she had a Renaissance face. She walked over.

'Quite a morning, huh? Looks like Kelly took cuts with the Reaper. Jumped the line ahead of me.'

I inhaled.

'Sorry, black humor doesn't go over with everybody.'

'That's not it.' I rubbed my eyes again, weary. 'Can we let the water go under the bridge?'

'Yeah.' She crossed her arms as if she was cold, though she was wearing long sleeves and it was ninety degrees. 'That's why I came. It's bygones-be-bygones time. You know, don't sweat the small stuff. Flush all your shit.'

'Amen.' We stared at each other. 'So it's a done deal?'

'Flushed.' She leaned toward me, smiling. 'How was it?'

'What?'

32

'Banging him.'

I blinked. She looked at Jesse, smirking.

'I saw you coming out of your room together. What did you do, hold chariot races? You give him the whip?'

Twenty years on, and I was still slow to spot the wily glint in her eyes. I colored. 'And here I was having trouble recognizing you. You haven't changed at all.'

'I can flush the shit and still yank your chain.' She cleared her throat. 'I have problems with my memory, but I know damn well that nobody in our class was that hot. Wheelchair or not. You brought him with you.'

She gave him another look. Her energy faded, from blue to wistful. 'Good for you. Enjoy each other.'

The Hankins kids came storming past, Abbie on their heels.

'Predator beat Alien,' Travis said. 'Totally.'

'Raptors could beat Predator,' Dulcie said. 'They're genetically engineered.'

Little Hayley followed them. 'What if Barbie fought Predator?'

Abbie shooed them ahead, saying 'Go get yourselves some food,' and hauled me into a hug.

'You run a science fiction household? I like it,' I said.

'Nothing makes you feel old and stupid like hearing about genetic engineering from an eight-year-old.' She smiled at Valerie. 'How you doing, woman?'

'I'm ready for my close-up, don't you think?' Valerie said.

Across the patio, a group of teachers was congregating. They looked plumper and dowdier than I recalled. Ms Shepard stood arm in arm with her husband, Dr Tully Cantwell. She was wearing a tie-dyed magenta skirt and a T-shirt emblazoned with petroglyph designs.

33

Abbie rolled her eyes. 'It's the center of the cosmos. Remember? Spirals are the Mother Earth navel . . .'

I put up my hand. 'Don't. That day alienated me from Mother Earth for good.'

'Heh.' She smiled and waved. 'Dr C.'

For frump, Dr Tully Cantwell had the teachers beat hands down. He had a ruddy face and an endearingly inept combover. He made his way through the crowd toward us. He was the official doctor for Bassett's sports teams and unofficial sounding board for kids at the school: jovial, sympathetic and matter of fact. With touching devotion, he was wearing a blue and green tie and a tie clip that said 'Go Hounds'.

Valerie turned away. 'I'm sick of doctors. And I don't need old smiley-face acting all caring about my health.'

She walked off. Dr Cantwell approached, extending his hand.

'Abbie. How's the knee?'

'It's craptastic, but I'm great. You're looking dapper.'

He smiled at me as well. 'Evan?'

'Got it in one.'

We chatted for a minute before I excused myself and headed to the hot food table. Jesse was getting a drink. Beside him, the Hankins kids were piling their plates with burgers and potato salad.

Dulcie looked sober. 'So what if Alien has acid blood. The Borg have shields.'

I got a plate. 'I'm with you on that one, girl.'

She stuck out her tongue at her brother.

Hayley stacked cookies on her plate. Barbecued beans slid onto the floor. 'If raptors fought the My Little Ponys, the ponies would win because they're magic.'

I grabbed her plate. When I handed her a pile of

napkins she squatted down and wiped the beans into a bigger mess. I took over for her, looking up at Jesse.

'Have you seen Tommy?'

He nodded at the far side of the patio. 'He's up to his elbows in the murder investigation. Looking a little stressed.'

Hayley poked a finger into her potato salad. 'Who would win if Infinity fought Googolplex?'

Jesse and I turned, staring at her.

'Infinity,' Jesse said.

She shook her head. 'Googolplex. Infinity's bigger, but it's just an eight on its side. Googolplex is ten times ten, ten to the hundredth times. It has *powers*.'

Jesse and I gaped at each other.

Hayley licked her finger. 'I have seven My Little Ponys.'

Two women walked up. 'I heard she was tortured. It was ritualistic.' They shook their heads. 'Drug addicts.'

Glaring at them, I ushered Hayley away from the table. Jesse took Dulcie and Travis to go find a seat. When I went back to finish cleaning up the spill, Tommy walked past. He was chewing gum, hard. His eyes were red around the edges.

'How you holding up?' I said.

He pulled up his sleeve, showing off two nicotine patches. 'Enough said?'

'Sorry.'

'Everybody here has a theory. It's drug-related. It's gang-related. It's Satanists. It's a lust killing. Two people have asked if we're arresting Kelly's husband, and Scotty was pulling a double shift on base when it happened.' He mashed his pork-pie hat down on his head. 'Ritual slaying, that's popular.'

'I heard that one.'

35

Across the patio, a group called to him. 'Chang. It true he wrote a message on the wall in her blood?'

'That's it. I'm out of here,' he said.

'They shouldn't have started serving beer so early.'

'Watch out for yourself, all right?' He winked as Valerie walked up. 'And Rocky, no tackling. Take care, Val.'

'Be good, Tommy,' she said.

She sipped water through a straw, watching him walk across the rec center. 'How'd a guy like him end up in such a creepy job?'

'Pardon?'

'Cop. Sometimes they wear a wire. They might be recording your conversation, you never know.' She sipped her water, and stopped. 'That sounded paranoid.'

'Slightly.' More than slightly.

'Must be time for more happy pills.' She shrugged, trying to laugh it off. 'At least I'm talking about somebody else kicking off. That's a change of pace.'

Her black humor was as heavy as a fireplace poker. I wondered if it was designed to keep people from getting too close.

I pushed it. 'Thirteen classmates – we're off the scale statistically, Valerie.'

'Curse of China Lake, some such shit.' She peered at me with mock suspicion. 'You're healthy, right?'

'As a herd of My Little Ponys.'

Laughter barked from a nearby table. Stace Wilkins and Bo Krause were hunched over, drinking beer and smoking. They had their backs to us. Bo tipped ash onto his empty plate.

' ''Tards' field trip. Little outing for him and chemo girl, but instead of Disneyland they bring him out here and let him get laid by the Homecoming Queen.'

Stace laughed. 'I could get with that.' He slapped his hand against his chest as though he was spastic. 'I have special needs.'

I saw black. As in that fireplace poker, swinging hard against the back of their knees. But I counted to ten, because this was anger, not self defense, and I didn't want to get sued by these pinheads.

Valerie set down her water. 'You jackholes aren't kidding.'

They turned around, startled.

'As I recall, you couldn't find your dicks with both hands and a compass. If there's retards around, I'm talking to them.'

She turned, her face shiny, and handed me a piece of paper with a phone number and email address. 'Keep in touch.'

Bo and Stace were glaring into their beers. I smiled at Valerie.

'Well done, crude diva. Thanks,' I said.

Her smile was snarky but winning. 'A compliment from you? My life's complete.'

Ceci Lezak sat in her car, watching from the parking lot as everybody went into the rec center for the picnic. She'd been sitting in her car since she left the police station. All night, wide awake. She couldn't make herself open the door and get out.

Everybody at the picnic would bombard her with questions. What was it like finding Kelly? How did she look? What did he do to her? Heat pressed in, squeezing her chest until she could barely breathe. If she told them, they would recoil. The sausage casings. Glistening tubes, stinking and bloody. She gagged, her eyes burning.

Wally's van was parked across the lot. When he pulled in her heart had spun faster. She'd been sure he would come over and comfort her, soothe her with his jolly, authoritative voice. Instead, the brood spilled out of the van, three little towheads whose white-blonde hair flickered in the breeze. They all looked like their mother. Abbie climbed out, talking too loud, and Wally waved them toward the rec center and took the backpack from Abbie, lightening *her* load, and threw his arm around her shoulder. He didn't even see Ceci.

She started the engine and squealed out of the parking lot. The road was a blur.

She saw Kelly again, sprawled on her back with her skirt pulled up to her waist and her blouse ripped open. The carving knife was shoved into her belly button. Entrails had exploded through the wound. Grey and bloody, intestines like glossy fat worms, bursting from her abdomen and slithering onto the kitchen floor. The smell of offal and excrement and corrosive chemicals had made her gag. But that's not what made her scream.

She couldn't go home, not alone. Pushing her foot to the floor, she drove to the office.

She felt calm at the office, organized and safe. It was Sunday so the place was cool and quiet, and it felt like Wally. She turned up the air conditioning and the sound system. The muzak soothed her. In Exam Room 1 a tray of dental implements sat on the counter. She straightened them into a perfect row an inch apart, arranged by size. The scalers, the little mirror, the curettes and hoes.

Kelly's legs had been spread, the insides of her thighs slashed. The pattern was orderly, beginning near her knees and growing deeper and longer as they ascended her legs. The slashes looked like claw marks.

38

The instruments on the tray were sterilized but didn't look clean. She found a piece of gauze and began polishing them, scrubbing, and scrubbing harder.

Claw marks, but no animal had poured Drano on Kelly's wounds and watched the lye burn into her shredded flesh. No animal had hacked at her genitals. No animal had jammed a funnel into the wound on her stomach and poured the rest of the drain cleaner into it.

The screaming was only in her head this time. She gagged and leaned over the sink, fighting off dry heaves.

In the outer office there was a knock on the door. 'Hello?'

A woman's voice, tentative. Ceci spat in the sink and walked out to the desk, holding the sickle scaler.

'May I help you?'

She stopped, brought up short. It wasn't a woman, but a man with a high-pitched voice. He was holding his palm against his cheek.

'Didn't mean to startle you,' he said. 'Dr Hankins said to come on over and he'd be right along.'

'I'm sorry?'

His voice was muffled, and she understood the strange pitch: toothache voice. He had on a *Go Hounds* baseball cap with little green paw prints, the kind they were passing out at the picnic.

'Cracked a filling,' he said. 'Hurts like hell.'

'You came from the rec center?' Ceci said.

'Yeah. Robin Klijsters.'

She frowned, trying to place him. 'I know you, don't I?'

'I was Antonia Shepard's student teacher. I'm here with Len Bradovich.'

Ceci unwound. Len Bradovich had played on the

39

basketball team. Six-foot-three with soft hands. He never gave her a look and he threw like a girl. Well, well. Robin Klijsters couldn't have topped five-five. He was soft and pouty and had a silly punk-rock haircut and those cheek-bones. Huh. She always wondered if Len played for the boy-on-boy team. And here was a girly little man he'd hooked up with.

His eyes were dark and wide, all pupil. Did pain do that to sissy boys? He dabbed the back of his hand to his forehead.

'Sorry, dentists' offices make me nervous. Think you could get me set up? I don't want to hang around longer than I have to.'

Ceci put on her professional smile, businesslike and wise. 'Let's wait for Dr Hankins. In fact, why don't I call him and see if he's—'

'Please.' Pain spun in his eyes. 'He said he'd be right here. And Len, I promised him I'd get back to the picnic soon as possible.'

Pussywhipped, and by another man. What a homo. He was even wearing a fanny pack. Heterosexual men didn't wear fanny packs, except maybe artists or academic types.

She waved him through. 'Come on back.'

In the exam room she gestured toward the chair, patting him on the shoulder, as she liked to do with nervous patients. He flinched. So did she. Under the baggy shirt he was rock hard. She put on her safety glasses, snapped on a pair of latex gloves and pulled over the implement tray. He had not sat down.

She gestured again to the chair and turned on the big examination light. 'Please, Mr Klijsters. The only way we'll repair that filling is if you open your mouth.'

She put a hand on his back, nudging him toward the

chair. He lurched, grabbed the examination light and swung it into her chin.

Ceci's head snapped back. What the hell? She put a hand to her mouth. She'd bitten her tongue. She stared at Klijsters, appalled.

'You freaking little wussie,' she said.

He swung his arm, backhanding her across the face. Her safety glasses flew off. She crashed into the implement tray. Oh, shit.

He stood absolutely still, staring at her with those black eyes.

She grabbed a curette from the implement tray. Before she could think twice, she stabbed him with it. She shoved it straight at his chest, impaling him through his shirt.

He jerked from the impact, but his eyes remained cool. 'Fight,' he said. 'Excellent.'

The curette protruded from his chest. Blood coursed down the front of his shirt. He let it run. He didn't flinch. He unzipped the fanny pack.

Ceci ran for the door.

The Taser darts struck the back of her blouse. She went rigid, hair to fingertips, vision streaking white with the electric shock. She saw the room tipping sideways, heard the noise as she hit the implement tray. She crashed to the floor.

She heard a sound. *Snap. Snap.* Klijsters was double gloving.

He hit the power button for the dentist's chair, raising it and tilting back the seat. The examination light hung above Ceci's face, surgically bright. Her hands and feet were bound to the chair with electrical tape.

Klijsters appeared above her. He was no longer

cringing with toothache. And he wasn't Robin Klijsters, she knew. He looked calm.

'Now.'

She heard the sound of metal implements tinging against each other. The sickle scaler appeared in his hand. The pick on the end was long and slightly curved and sharp at the tip. He leaned toward her.

'No,' she said.

She turned her head away. The Taser appeared in his other hand. It was shaped like a gun, but with electrical contacts instead of a muzzle at the end of a solid barrel. He pressed the contacts to her eyelids.

'Do not move.'

She smelled talc and latex. He touched the sickle scaler to her lips. She felt the raggedness of her tongue where she'd bitten it. Klijsters leaned closer. The sickle scaler teased her mouth and poked into her lower lip, pulling it open.

'Does it hurt?' he said.

'Stop. Don't.'

His eyes examined her face. He jammed the scaler all the way through her lip and pulled it up as though she was a trout hooked on a lure.

'Answer me. Does it hurt?'

She shrieked. He hit her with the Taser again. Her vision shot white and she jerked stiff.

He twisted the scaler through her lip and ripped, tearing her mouth open like a broken zipper. She felt a warm gush of blood, and gutted flesh and numbness.

He touched the bloody scaler to her cheek. His gaze was clinical. The scaler groped its way up her face, covered with the gore of her bottom lip. The sharp tip tugged her flesh like a talon.

His face was all business. The scaler clawed its way up her cheek. Deeper, cutting open her face, again and again.

He put his thumb and forefinger on either side of her left eye and spread the lid wide.

'Answer me. Does it hurt?'

His eyes were dispassionate, but more. Like the guys Wally talked about who should never have been admitted to dental school, the *Little Shop of Horrors* dentists who loved it too much. And then a great sob welled inside her chest, because she knew that Wally wasn't on his way over here. Nobody was.

Behind her ruined lip she worked her tongue to form the word. 'No.'

He drove the scaler into her eye.

4

When the patrolman appeared at the rec center flanked by two Shore Patrol officers, I was talking to Becky O'Keefe. She had a little photo album open on the picnic table, showing me pictures of her two-year-old son.

'He's a fireball.' She smiled broadly. 'You've really written three novels? That is so neat.'

'Thanks.'

'It's always awesome when you can find a way to make your passion work. Like me and crafts.'

Becky's appliqué T-shirt stretched mightily to cover her beer-barrel torso. It was chartreuse and featured tiny pom-poms and glitter paint. The cover of the photo album was decorated to match. Jesse was next to me, playing Hangman with Travis Hankins. He didn't look up, but he did smile. I took the pencil from him, drew lines for nine letters, and filled in *good sport*.

The Shore Patrol officers stopped a man in a *Go Hounds* cap, who pointed them toward the playground. They crossed the patio and walked out into the sun. Wally and Abbie were chatting while their girls climbed on the jungle gym.

Becky turned a page. 'Ryan's big for his age. Don't know if you can tell.'

'He's beautiful. He looks like . . .'

'Winston Churchill. I know.' She laughed good-naturedly. 'So do I.'

The patrolman spoke to Wally. Wally's face fell and Abbie grabbed his arm. He walked off the playground with the cop and Shore Patrol officers, head down, pale and grim.

Abbie watched him go, her blonde hair swirling in the wind. She caught my eye. Her hand went to her mouth and her shoulders began to shake.

I stood, grabbing Jesse's arm. He looked up, alarmed.

'Something bad's going on,' I said.

Five miles out of China Lake I pulled the Mustang off the highway at a truck stop. I couldn't wait to put 200 miles between myself and this town, but if I kept driving I would run the tank dry and there wasn't another gas station for sixty miles.

Back at the hotel, the parking lot had looked like a scene from a disaster movie, with people throwing luggage in their cars and hightailing it for the hills ahead of an avalanche. People who lived in China Lake, I knew, were stocking up on ammunition or attack dogs.

The wind ticked against the car and the sun burned gold in a shattering blue sky. I filled the tank and grabbed my purse.

'I'll get drinks.'

Jesse gave me a thumbs up.

The truck stop was a weary place with a café attached. The screen door griped open for me. Inside, an air conditioner struggled in the window, tassels flopping up and down. Behind the counter, the cook was watching a wrestling match on the TV.

'Getcha something, hon?' she said.

'Two bottled waters and a couple of burgers to go.'

She tossed hamburgers on the grill and I headed down

45

a creaking hallway to the women's room. The desolation on Abbie's face lingered in my mind. Ceci had been murdered in Wally's dental office, that's all I knew. I leaned over the sink and splashed cold water on my face. Straightening, I looked in the mirror.

A woman stood behind me, watching me over my shoulder.

I froze. I hadn't seen the door open, hadn't heard her boots on the groaning floor. She leaned back against the wall and blinked, slowly, like a Siamese cat.

'Go on, finish washing up. Don't mind me,' she said.

Cold water ran down my face and dripped onto the counter. She grabbed a paper towel from the dispenser and handed it to me.

I dried my hands and face. 'Hello, Jax.'

'Don't look so surprised.'

'Then don't be such a drama queen.'

'Honey, I'm forty-four years old. I've lived this long by knowing when to do dramatic things.'

I stared at her in the mirror. The sleeveless black T-shirt clung to her frame like high-gloss paint. The fatigue pants left more to the imagination, but there was no mistaking her ballerina's posture. Diamonds gleamed on her ears and left hand, six carats at least, set off against almond-brown skin.

Not many women would walk into in a fly-blown desert café wearing Caterpillar boots and $50,000 worth of jewelry, but Jax wasn't like other women. She wasn't wearing a holster, but I knew she was armed. Not that it mattered. Anybody who messed with her, I thought, she could kill barehanded.

No good could come out of seeing Jakarta Rivera here today.

She stared at me with the detachment of a runway model. Sidling over, she lifted my left hand and looked at my bare ring finger.

'You and your man ever going to tie the knot? The suspense is killing me.'

'Why are you here?'

'I brought a gift to your bridal shower. I expect performance. Heat those cold feet up, honey.'

'Please tell me Tim isn't out in the car having this same heart-to-heart with Jesse.' I glanced at the door, wondering if she had locked it. 'Is this about your dossiers?'

For nine months a fat envelope had lain in my safe deposit box. It contained documents that convinced me Jax and her husband Tim North were who they claimed to be, and had done the things they said they'd done. CIA, British Intelligence and, as they put it, private work. Contract assassination.

'No, this is something else,' she said.

They told me they wanted me to write their memoirs. In fact, they wanted something very different but, after everything was over, they delivered the envelope to me. I suspected they were using me as a dead drop – a place to park stolen and classified documents that they wanted for self-protection or blackmail. Possessing such documents, I knew, could put all of us in prison, but I couldn't return them. Jax and Tim had gone into the wind.

But the envelope was also a bargaining chip, for them and for me. I could sell it to their enemies, get them killed, and probably earn myself a hell of a payday. And they could, if they wished, torture me for the key to the safe deposit box, retrieve the dossiers and murder me.

Nice little balancing act they'd subjected me to.

'Shall we go out to the counter?' I said. 'Catch up on the family, watch the wrestling on the TV?'

'You need to talk to your buddy in the China Lake police department. Have him contact the FBI Behavioral Analysis Unit and get their profilers out here.'

The bathroom smelled of ammonia. My stomach was queasy.

'Shit,' I said. 'You think a serial killer committed the murders.'

'Murder doesn't describe these acts. Try butchery.'

I ran the back of my hand across my forehead. 'Two killings in twenty-four hours. You know the police already suspect that it's a serial killer. Why the hell are you here?'

'Because they don't suspect that the killer is ex-government.'

'Are you telling me you know who this is?'

'Yes and no.'

'What does that mean?'

She stepped forward. 'These murders aren't the killer's first. The locals will need federal muscle who can dig into government records and get the information they need.'

The heat was crippling. Sweat was running down my chest.

'What do you mean by government? Navy? Civil Service? CIA?'

'A clandestine service. That's all I know.'

'Do you know his name?'

'Coyote.'

The wind hissed against the walls. 'Is that a cover name?'

'Yes. I don't know his legal name.'

'How do you know that this guy is the killer?'

She blinked, cat-cool. 'In select circles, Coyote is a

legendary operative. The killings this weekend bear hall-marks of his style.'

The word *style* had never sounded so hair-raising.

'He hasn't been heard from in a long time. And if he's back at work, he's off the clock. No controllers, no restraints, just his own private blitzkrieg.'

'You're telling me that a trained killer has gone off the leash and started running amok?'

'I believe so.'

She waited a moment, and when I didn't mouth off again her voice cooled a few more degrees. 'This char-acter's a chameleon. You know Native American mythology?'

'Vaguely.'

'In tribal folklore Coyote is a trickster. That's who this guy is. He changes his appearance and behavior to suit the situation.'

'Can you describe him?'

'White, early forties, nondescript. That doesn't matter. What's important is that the police start unearthing this guy's trail and get on him, ASAP.'

'They're on this guy, you know that. Why would they listen to me?'

'The person who disemboweled Kelly Colfax with a carving knife also rammed a dental pick through Ceci Lezak's eye socket into her brain. Tell that to the police. It will convince them you know what you're talking about.'

I felt what can only be described as a stabbing pain in the center of my forehead. 'How do you know that?'

She gave me a flat stare, saying: don't be an idiot. I turned to the sink and washed my face again.

'They'll instantly consider me a suspect,' I said.

'You're smart. You'll finesse that.'

'Why do you care about catching this guy?'

'Homicide isn't a sport. Human beings shouldn't be taken like game animals.'

'Why don't you tell the police yourself?'

'I can't talk to them. Honey, I don't even exist.'

Jax Rivera, the world's only invisible drama queen.

'If I call Tommy Chang, I'm not going to hold back. I'll tell him who gave me this information,' I said.

'You can do that, but when he runs my name through VICAP he won't come up with anything except an expired Texas driver's license. But he will alert certain people to my proximity, and they would like to talk to me. On an extreme level. And to reach me, they'll come to you. On an extreme level.'

She turned toward the door. 'You have a webcam for your computer?'

'It isn't hooked up.' Jesse had been bugging me to set it up, but I suspected he wanted it for entertainment, not communication.

'Hook it up,' she said.

'Jax, why me?'

'Start looking, and you'll find out.'

I was heading for the café's screen door when the cook called to me.

'Hon, your burgers.'

I grabbed them, paid and walked out into the heat. Jesse had his door open and was pulling his gear from the back seat, about to get out.

'I was starting to think a scorpion got you,' he said.

I shoved the sack with the burgers into his hands and stood watching the café, hands on my hips.

He looked up. 'You know, PTSD is a bitch. But nothing compared to PMS.'

I gave him the death stare.

He raised his hands. 'No, of course that's not it. And I'll just be crawling under a rock now.'

A moment later I heard a motorcycle start up. Jax pulled out from behind the café and curved onto the highway. We watched her gun the throttle and accelerate into the distance.

'Is that . . . ?' Jesse said.

'None other.'

'Fuck me. With a flagpole.'

I got out my cellphone and called Tommy Chang.

The China Lake Police Department occupied a sleek glass and steel building in the Civic Center complex. The atmosphere in the station was crackling. Jesse and I waited at Tommy's desk. His pork-pie hat and an empty holster hung on a coat rack. Jesse gazed at framed photos of Tommy's five kids, and one of Tommy on a dirt bike, catching huge air. Outside was a white and red news van painted with the call letters of a Los Angeles television station. A cameraman was leaning against the back, sipping a Coke, talking to the reporter.

Tommy walked up, accompanied by his boss.

I stood and held out my hand. 'Detective McCracken.'

He was a walking side of beef, wearing scratched old eyeglasses. His red hair needed a good cut. His size made Tommy look like a ventriloquist's dummy.

He shook. 'It's Captain, nowadays. How's that little nephew of yours?'

I told him Luke was great, noticing that he didn't ask about my brother. McCracken and Brian nettled each other. But then McCracken had, at different times, placed both Brian and me under arrest, which we Delaneys find nettlesome.

He leaned against the edge of the desk. The metal creaked under his weight.

'Tell us more about this former government employee who provided the information about the murders,' he said.

Jax may have over-hyped the warning about giving her name to the police, but I knew that if I said the phrases 'CIA' or 'undercover operative', I would get laughed out of the station, put on an antiterrorist watch list or both. I put on my legal journalist's hat.

'This is a source. They've provided me with background for several stories I've written. That series on cybercrime, the criminal ring that infiltrated IT companies out on the coast.'

'What's his name?' McCracken said.

Thank you, bad grammar. 'That's confidential.'

He scratched his nose and huffed out a breath. 'Nothing's ever simple with you, is it?'

Tommy sat down behind the desk. 'I know your source wants to stay anonymous. But this is a murder investigation.'

'I'll give you any other information I have. But not the name.'

'Are you playing games?' McCracken said.

'No sir.'

'We're getting pounded with media attention over this. Local newspaper and radio. That Los Angeles TV news van outside with the dish antenna on top. And CNN's calling. It's going to be a circus.' He stood up. 'So what's your angle? Is this an ego trip? You want a scoop?'

Jesse rubbed his palm along his leg, which he did when

he was tense. Keeping quiet went against his grain, but this line drive was mine to field.

'No,' I said. 'I'm simply passing along the information.'

'Then give us the damn information. You tell us we have a killer nicknamed Coyote, but you won't help us contact the source who might give us something helpful.'

'That's all I know. If I learn more, I'll tell you.'

He shucked his slacks up by the belt, jiggling them over his belly. 'Fine. But expect a visit from the Bureau.' He eyed Tommy. 'Call the Resident Agent in Bakersfield. I'll phone Los Angeles. Behavioral Analysis and the Serial Murder group have units there.' He walked away shaking his head. 'Shit on a biscuit.'

Tommy rubbed his eyes. 'You'd never know it, but he's actually an engaging guy.'

'Tommy, I'm not trying to pull something. This information came at me like a broomstick being jammed into my spokes.'

'I believe you. But this is all so . . .' He looked up, frayed.

All so grisly, barbaric and overwhelming. And on his shoulders.

'You okay?' I said.

He gave a tight nod.

Jesse put a hand on the desk. 'What worries me? Those other names on the memorial board.'

Tommy looked at him, saying nothing. Outside a fighter jet curved into view and blinked past, trailing thunder.

'And so you know,' Jesse said, 'I have a Glock nine at home, and I keep it loaded. But since it's two hundred miles away, I'm going to tell Evan to put her foot to the floor and not pull over for anything, even a Highway

Patrol car with Jesus Christ behind the wheel. You okay with that?'

'Don't get stopped,' Tommy said. 'I've got no pull with Jesus.'

I stood up. 'Don't worry. Nothing can keep me from getting out of this town.'

5

The sun was dropping into the Pacific when I rounded the bend and we got our first glimpse of home. The ocean flared gold, as if it was an offering poured out below the peaks of the Santa Ynez mountains. The view never fails to thrill me. I wouldn't leave Santa Barbara for ten million bucks.

I dropped Jesse at his house on the beach. By the time I pulled onto my own street the sky had deepened to cobalt and stars were winking in the east. The live oaks and white oleander shimmered in the dusk. Near the corner, neighborhood kids were playing baseball. I pulled up in front of my place and my headlights caught the red Mazda convertible parked in the driveway.

For a second I sat idling the engine, my hand on the gearshift. I had a V-8 under the hood. I could be blazing up the street in a quarter of a second.

The Mazda convertible was empty. Shit on a biscuit. That meant my cousin Taylor was already inside my house.

I killed the engine, grabbed my things and got out. Pushing through the garden gate, I stalked along the flag-stone path toward my door. Across the lawn at my neighbors', the lights were off. Crud. Nikki and Carl Vincent could have helped me drive Taylor off. My little house was lit up like the Moulin Rouge. I heard the stereo blasting country music. Bad country. My-dog-died bad. Donny and Marie bad. The ivy on the fence was starting to curl.

I threw open the French doors, walked in and dropped my bags on the hardwood floor. Under the force of the music my shoelaces began untying. In the kitchen the refrigerator door was open. Sticking out behind it was my cousin's rear end. Her jeans were black-and-white cattleprint with a heart branded on the butt.

'Taylor.' Nothing. 'Taylor Boggs.'

I walked to the stereo. Saw the CD case. *Backseats and Backstreets: The World's Best Cheatin' Songs.* I turned it off.

Taylor pulled her face out of the fridge. A chicken leg protruded from her mouth. Her eyes went as round as pie and she pulled the drumstick from between her lips.

'Sweetie,' she said.

'How did you get in?'

Her contact lenses were the color of grape jam. Her T-shirt said MAKIN' HOLE. And beneath that 'Carnahan Drilling – we go all the way down.' She skipped toward me, arms outstretched.

'Where y'all been all weekend?'

All weekend – oh, God. How long had she been here? I glanced around.

She clenched me in a hug. 'What is going on with your hair? I like this longer length, but it needs some height.' She fussed with my toffee-colored locks. 'My gal at the salon can fix you up.'

Her blonde mane was hairsprayed to the size of a tumbleweed. I shooed her hands away from my head.

'I figure you took a house key the last time you were here,' I said. 'What I want to know is how you got my alarm code.'

'Don't be silly. I came by when the workmen were here, and told them I'd lock up.'

I ground my teeth. I was having the bathroom remodeled: new shower, sink, mirrors, window, paint and tile. I wanted to eradicate the memory of being attacked in there by a homicidal rock singer. Also, I'd shot the old shower to hell. I needed to tell Mr Martinez and his sons that Taylor was *persona non grata*. Let her in and she spread over the house like light sweet crude.

She was shaking her head. 'You should think twice about that black-and-white tile. It's awful sterile. I mean, you already have this rugged hiker thing going on in your living room.' She waved toward my Navajo rugs and framed prints of Yosemite. 'Your bathroom should say soft and fluffy. You know, feminine.'

'I'm familiar with the concept.' I walked to the living room, spreading my arms. 'Please explain this.'

'Don't get your undies in a bunch. I needed a quiet place to lay out my inventory.'

Draped across the furniture were bras and panties in countless colors and degrees of wickedness. Teddies, G-strings, and . . .

'Is that a codpiece?'

'Saucy, isn't it? It's Countess Zara Lingerie's new collection. His'n'hers underwear. It's called Fil/Fille.' She picked up another bit of male attire and jiggled it in front of me. 'Get it? *Feel-feel*?'

It was decorated to look like a stallion's head. I stepped back. 'Did you have to give it eyes and a mouth?' Then I stopped myself. 'Wait. Just wait. Why my house?'

'Ed Eugene's old fraternity brother's here and he didn't want my dainties fussing up their boys' weekend.'

I felt like chewing through an electrical cord and ending it all. 'Dainties?'

'Our new range – what do you think?' she said.

I turned to the playthings on my coffee table. 'That your dildoes look like a missile battery.'

She smiled. 'It's part of the couples theme. We call it Weekend Fireworks.'

'And is *she* part of the Weekend Fireworks?' I picked up the plastic inflatable doll that was lounging on the sofa.

'Suzie Sizemore. For my lingerie parties, you know, when some of the guests feel bashful about trying on our selections. Isn't she adorable?'

Suzie's vinyl grin indicated that she'd been getting gleeful with the missiles. I tossed her back on the sofa.

'Please tell me you didn't lay all this out in front of the Martinez boys.' The last thing I needed was my bathroom contractors seeing these things.

'Of course not.' She clapped her hands together. 'Now hold on. I'm mainly here to talk to you about my plans for the book.'

'*My* book?'

Hell, had she spent the weekend rewriting my novel-in-progress? I glanced at the computer. It was off. Thank God.

'Evan, it's not always about you.' She steepled her fingers in front of her lips. '*My* book.'

Lightheadedness was the only word to describe the feeling that came over me.

'See, I've developed my business talent. Which is more than just sales. It's my eye for beautiful lingerie as well as my second eye for making ladies feel exquisite, no matter what their figure flaws.'

Damn if she didn't look at my chest. Her eyes wandered as though lost on the Great Plains.

'But I haven't even begun to tap my writing talent,' she said.

The lightheadedness worsened. I wondered whether my face was expanding like a helium balloon.

'It must run in the family. Everybody who gets my Christmas letter tells me I've missed my calling. I should be an author.'

My eyes crossed. Taylor's Christmas letter was a three-page essay on Her Perfect Life. It omitted her husband's jealous streak and her taste for junk food and adultery, but did feature a photo of her riding bareback on one of Santa's reindeer. Taylor was dressed as an elf. Ed Eugene was the reindeer.

'Not that I would ever give up my job with Dazzling Delicates. Besides, that isn't truly a job, it's more of a gift.'

'You're going to write a book,' I said.

'A coffee table book. Along the lines of Madonna's *Sex*. It'll showcase photos of women looking sexy in Dazzling Delicates lingerie.'

I put my fingers to my temples. 'Taylor, that's called a catalog.'

'No, these are women on the beach, or riding motorcycles down the freeway.'

'The freeway. Sexy women.'

She clapped her hands together. 'That's where you come in.'

I blinked. Despite myself, I felt flattered. 'Really?'

'Of course. I wouldn't do this book without my cousin.'

Me, model lingerie? A giggle formed at the back of my throat. A silly, thrilled giggle.

Taylor gesticulated, saying she had to schedule the photo shoots and write the commentary to go with the pictures. She wondered about scheduling – how long did it take to write a book, a couple months?

'Count on six months to a year,' I said.

No, this was stupid. Me, getting my photo taken in sexy underwear? Dazzling Delicates underwear? The idea was ludicrous.

Black, I'd wear something black. Tight, and leather. And I'd throw on sunglasses like Trinity in *The Matrix*. And boots – Jesse would dig that. Thigh boots. Man, would he.

'A year? Honey, I can dictate a page in ten minutes, sending sales forecasts to Countess Zara headquarters. A book can't take that long. You sure?'

'Positive.'

I'd better buy some fake tan. And hit the gym. Tonight. Wow, Taylor really did know how to make women feel exquisite.

She patted my shoulder. 'But I know I can count on you. I mean, who else can do the proofreading?'

My helium-head felt a pinprick. 'Proofreading.'

'I need your expertise with adjectives. Fonts, too. And punctuation – I bet you're a demon with exclamation marks.'

I fizzled. 'Don't forget apostrophes. I'm lethal with those.'

'Aw. Hon, did you think I meant a photo spread? You live in hope, don't you.'

I counted to three. Picking up Suzie Sizemore, I pulled the plug between her shoulder blades. She whistled and began deflating. Taylor squeaked and reached for her. I folded her in half and squeezed.

'Evan, she doesn't like that.'

'Pack it up. I don't care if your husband has Francis of Assisi visiting for the weekend. The bathroom guys will be back tomorrow and I want this stuff out of here.'

'But I need to talk to you about that. I was chatting with them and I found the things you'd emptied out of the medicine cabinet.'

'What? Taylor, don't tell me you nosed through it.'

She pointed at the cardboard box by the television. When I left for the weekend, it had been in my closet. I felt queasy. She reached in, pulling out makeup, aspirin, and . . .

'Oh my God,' I said.

. . . my birth control pills.

She tapped her fingernails against them. 'The thing I noticed? This pack is six months old and hasn't even been opened.' She bit her lip and frowned at me. 'Darlin', you going natural?'

My lightheadedness morphed into a floating sensation, as if I was rising toward the ceiling. I grabbed the pills from Taylor, dumped bathroom stuff out of the cardboard box and began stuffing it with jockstraps and sex toys. Taylor told me to calm down. She understood if my biological clock was ticking like a nuclear bomb. I shoved Suzie Sizemore into the box with her crotch wrapped around her neck. Taylor said *How rude* and I shot back that Suzie looked more surprised than offended, what with her mouth open in that big round O. She tapped her foot. Well, she said, sounds like somebody's feeling *frustrated*. Did Jesse need to buy me some Weekend Fireworks? At which point I may have hissed at her, because she drew her arms up against her chest and jumped back from me. I think I was having an out-of-body experience.

I jammed the box into her hands, pushed her outside,

slammed and locked the door. She stood on the path, calling through the glass. She understood that I had needs. She could help. That's what Dazzling Delicates was about – helping those in need. I closed the shutters. Don't suffer with unmet needs, she shouted. It's unhealthy. You could develop a tic.

I walked to my bedroom, shut the door and flopped onto the bed.

This news would be all over the family within hours. That meant my aunts, cousins, Uncle Benny the priest, and my mother. I covered my face with a pillow.

Not in a million years did I want relatives yakking about my sex life. What went on between Jesse and me was off limits to anybody else. Yes, things were sometimes complicated. Not sex – sex was fine. Sex was a moon shot for me. It just took patience and imagination, by the truckload. But when a man had SCI, conceiving without fertility treatment was tough. The truth, which worried me more than I liked to admit, was that we didn't need contraception. I rolled over. If I strangled Taylor with a push-up bra, nobody would convict me. I could blame the tic.

I stood up, headed to the bathroom, flipped on the light and stopped short. Mr Martinez and his sons had been going to town. I had no shower, toilet or sink.

Jesse laughed when I called, and said he'd love a guest as long as I left Toby Keith and Patsy Cline at home. I packed up and was halfway out the door when the phone rang. I waited, hand on the knob, letting the machine pick it up. Jax's cool voice came on.

'Webcam.' She hung up.

Exhaling, I pulled the small camera from my desk drawer and wired it up to my laptop. Almost immediately the

62

video program beeped and a window opened. On screen I saw Jax, her face warm under a desk lamp, her diamonds afire.

'Good job. The chatter has escalated. People are paying attention,' she said.

'Is that how they taught you to talk back at Langley?'

In the background were a bed, hotel-quality artwork, drapes, a balcony. Outside, a man leaned against the railing, gazing at the dusk. A cigarette glowed red as he inhaled.

'Hello, Tim,' I said. 'How's the view there in Lone Pine? Or is it Palmdale?'

'Dubai, pet.' He blew smoke toward the sky.

'Jax, the China Lake police are calling in the FBI. They're annoyed at me but going all out.'

'Good. Because I have more information for you.' She adjusted the focus on her camera. Her image blurred and sharpened. 'Coyote was once attached to a project called South Star. It was black. Run out of China Lake.'

My pulse jumped. 'He's Navy?'

'No. And neither was South Star. It was DARPA-funded originally, but went dark. The research developed fast and weird. Big stuff.'

DARPA, the Defense Advanced Research Projects Agency, funded open research at universities and corporations. But sometimes projects turned hot and went classified.

'Coyote was a test subject for the project,' she said.

My thoughts adjusted. 'You're saying South Star wasn't a weapons system?'

'On the contrary. That's precisely what it was.'

China Lake was all about weaponry: missiles, bombs, anti-missile space defense. At the gate to the base a sign politely reminds drivers to phone for a police escort if they're delivering high explosives. But Jax was implying something quite different.

'Human weaponry,' I said.

'Precisely.'

'But you're saying this wasn't Navy research. Was it the Agency?'

'Could have been DIA or NSA, or any one of a dozen off-the-books pet projects of somebody with the ear of the brass.'

My mind was buzzing. 'If the killer was attached to this project, then there must be records. They'll have his name and can begin tracking him down.'

'Did you hear me? This project was black. It won't be like looking up names in the phone book. The Bureau will have to pry that information loose with a crowbar. If records even exist.'

'So? Ask around Langley.'

She smiled, showing ice-white teeth. 'For the longest time you refused to believe that I was with the Company. Now you refuse to believe that I'm not.'

Exactly. I didn't know what her real story was, who she worked for, whether she was freelance or still collecting a federal paycheck. And her smile told me she liked it that way.

She folded her arms. 'You have sources, I have sources. All mine know is that Coyote was once attached to South Star. You'll have to dig for the rest.'

'How am I supposed to do that?'

Her voice went quiet. 'Walk back the cat, Evan.'

Static rose on the line and the video pixelated. When it cleared, her feline eyes were dark and assessing.

'Explain,' I said.

'It's a metaphor for troubleshooting. When something

goes wrong, you analyze the situation to figure out why. Think of a cat unraveling a ball of string. You have to rewind the twisted yarn to find the flaw.'

Her voice lowered to a register that put me in mind of a Ferrari. Racing, smoothly and effortlessly, even though the engine was running at high revs.

'When you walk back the cat, your goal is to correct mistakes so they don't happen again. You reassess evidence and assumptions until you find the double agent, the false source or the analytic error. That's how you identify the real problem.'

'The obvious problem is that this person Coyote has killed two of my classmates. But you're suggesting that the real problem lies elsewhere.'

'Rumor has it that Project South Star was shut down because results ran ahead of the researchers' ability to control them. The question is, what happened to Coyote on that project?'

'If you want me to dig, give me a shovel. Tell me more about Coyote.'

Tim strolled in from the balcony. 'Very well.'

He had a mutt's face and the self-possession of a Buddha. His weathered eyes and haphazard English smile went with the working man's voice, though for all I knew he was the son of an earl.

'Coyote is adept as a trickster because he loves to play dress-up. He's airy-fairy. A little man over-butching it during the day and strapping himself into heels and Spandex at night.'

'He's a transvestite?' I said.

'She-male, mister sister, whatever you want to call it. His sexual identity has a certain fluidity that helps him blend into scenes, playing either gender.'

A wormy feeling passed through me. 'That's information I can give to the police. The rest of it, digging into this Project South Star, how am I supposed to do that? Give me some guidance.'

'Look at your connections.'

Connections meant China Lake. Static increased, brushing over the audio connection like sand.

'Be straight with me. Why are you telling me all this?'

'I'll tell you why,' Jax said. 'Because I have the training and the experience to know that I can turn anybody's lights out, and I'm damned good at it. But Coyote is flat-out petrifying.'

6

'She's playing with me. She's running a game,' I said.

Jesse didn't disagree. He watched me pacing back and forth along the edge of his deck. His blue eyes were dark in the night.

'If it's a game, that implies she wants to win,' he said. 'The question is, how does she do that?'

The night was cooling, a chill rolling off the ocean. Breakers shrugged up the beach. Behind Jesse the plate-glass windows shone with amber light from the house.

I turned and paced. 'Jax is trained to use disinformation as a tool. How do I sort truth from lie?'

'You took the first step by phoning this new information to Tommy. He'll investigate.'

I nodded. 'That still leaves me wondering what Jax wants from me.'

'Do you believe that Coyote frightens her?'

I slowed. 'Yes.' And that frightened me. Tremendously.

'In that case, presume she isn't sending you on a wild goose chase. Look at your connections. You know what she was getting at as well as I do.'

'China Lake.' I crossed my arms against my chest. 'But my connections are Navy. This defunct project was supposedly something else.'

The Navy doesn't have sole control over the base. In

its labyrinth of labs and million acres of test ranges, other entities run their own projects. Perhaps including South Star.

He scratched his head. 'At the reunion I was joking about cover stories and secret pasts. But—'

'Could it be real? No.' I put my hands up. 'Okay, I know China Lake's reputation. The military performs biowar experiments on convicts. Psy-ops types keep children in cages. Space aliens play pass the anal probe. It's all tinfoil hat stuff.'

'I'm not talking about UFOs.'

I reached the end of the deck and turned. He spun around and curved into my path, stopping me.

'You know what Jax has been hinting at. You're simply avoiding it.'

I looked at him, and the ocean, and up at the night sky. He touched my arm.

'Evan, call your father.'

It was late in Key West, but my dad was a nighthawk. He'd be watching the History Channel or reading a Patrick O'Brian novel if he wasn't working at the computer. I dialed on my cellphone and headed inside. As his phone rang I took up my pacing again, back and forth across the hardwood floor in the main room. Jesse came in and turned on the stereo. My dad's phone continued ringing.

The music spilled across the room, unfurling like a silk banner up to the cathedral ceiling. It was jazz and it was old. I looked at Jesse, surprised. Normally he preferred bands that had torched their guitars on stage circa 1969.

'Stress management,' he said. 'New tunes for a happier head.'

Walking past him, I rubbed his shoulder. Whatever

68

worked. Anything to pull him out from under the grief and survivor's guilt that had crushed his spirit to dust. Anything to stop the nightmares. To keep the sound of a siren or a gunning engine from igniting a flashback, putting him in Mission Canyon again, lying broken in the ravine, watching his best friend die. My hand lingered on his shoulder.

He shrugged. 'All part of the shrink wrap.'

That's what he called the recovery program he'd worked out with his doctors. It included drugs for neuropathic pain, antidepressants and anti-anxiety meds, and a group for survivors of violent crime. The rest was his own doing: throwing out the booze, swimming every day. And now switching from the Stones to Duke Ellington. It was a slow struggle to shore, but at least now when he drove away I didn't worry that he'd smash the car into a bridge abutment.

Now I had other worries.

In my ear the phone rang one more time and a message clicked on saying the call was being diverted. A new ringtone sounded. My father answered.

'Kit? What's up, honey?'

Four words and I felt safe. Time had added gravel to his voice and the prairie rhythms had deepened. Nobody made gruffness sound more welcome than Philip James Delaney, Captain USN, Retired.

'I've been hit with a wild pitch. The thing is, I think it's aimed at you.'

'Sounds serious. Does it involve your cousin Taylor?'

That made me smile. I hopped up to sit on the kitchen counter. 'You don't want to know about Taylor. This is something else.'

'Shoot.'

'Project South Star.'

On his end I heard a television burbling theme music. Four bars, six, eight.

'Dad?'

'Are you on a land line?'

Ting, I felt a cold drip on the back of my neck. 'My cell. At Jesse's.'

'Hang up.'

I set my phone on the granite counter, feeling the chill seep down my spine. He wanted me off the cell.

Jesse's phone rang. He turned toward it, but I jumped off the counter. 'That's Dad calling back.'

I picked it up from the coffee table in the living room. The brusqueness in my father's voice no longer sounded protective.

'Who's dredging up South Star?'

'Nobody you know.'

'Whoever it is has an agenda. Probably seeking publicity for himself. Whatever they've told you, just forget it. Drop the whole matter.'

'Publicity is not the issue.'

'Then why'd they throw this at a journalist? Who is it, a politician? Or one of those activists who thinks the government kills puppies for oil?'

'Dad, tell me about the project.'

'I can't. It's classified.'

I exhaled. Across the room Jesse watched me, trying to assess the conversation.

Dad's voice distilled. 'Somebody's yanking your chain, Evan. South Star is dead and you don't need to know any more than that.'

'Yes, I do. The murders in China Lake may relate back to South Star.'

A beat. 'Murders?'

'You don't know?'

Hesitation again. 'I've been traveling. Kit, what murders?'

'Two people from my graduating class, at the reunion this weekend. Kelly Colfax and Ceci Lezak.' I sat down on the sofa.

'Wait – *at* your reunion? You were in China Lake this weekend?'

'That's what I'm trying to tell you. Now will you listen to me?'

I summarized what Jax had told me about Project South Star: that it was a black project, outside the Navy's purview, possibly shut down when the research caused unpredictable results.

'Dad, what's the deal? A dead project from twenty years ago shouldn't make you concerned about cellphone interception.'

'What else have you been told?' he said.

'About Coyote.'

'What's that?'

'Not what. Who.' I pulled my feet up under me on the couch. I felt cold. 'He may be the killer.'

I filled him in. When I finished, he spoke slowly.

'Listen carefully. I don't know what's going on. But you need to back away from this, immediately.'

'I can't.'

'Kathleen Evan—' He caught himself. After a second he spoke with strained calm. 'If thirty-three years of being your father have taught me anything, it's that you will always question authority. But this once, please do exactly as I say without debate.'

The chill fingered down my back again.

'Don't talk about this to anybody else. Don't dig into

71

it. Will you be at home later?'

'I'm staying with Jesse for a few days.'

'Good. Keep that to yourself.'

That's when fear began bug-crawling across my skin. 'Dad, I've already talked to the China Lake police. And they're contacting the FBI.'

I could hear the TV behind him, applause and new music. 'Put Jesse on.'

Disconcerted, I stood and beckoned to him. When I held out the phone he looked wary. He'd met my dad once, talked to him maybe two other times. He put the phone to his ear.

'Mr Delaney?' A nod. 'All right – Phil.'

He listened, gazing past me. I bit my thumbnail.

'I do.' Nodding. 'Always.' He rubbed his leg. 'I understand.'

He handed the phone back to me. I scowled and mouthed 'What was that?' but he shook his head and angled around into the kitchen.

I got back on the line. 'What did you say to Jesse?'

'I explained about being careful right now.'

'Dad, what the hell does a government-trained killer want with two members of the Bassett High reunion committee?'

Jesse opened a kitchen drawer and began rustling around. I put a finger in my ear, but TV music was still coming from my dad's end.

Hang on. The TV music sounded familiar. 'Is that the Tonight Show?'

The Tonight Show came on at eleven-thirty, which meant it had long since finished in Key West, but was just starting here in California. I thought back to the way my call to him had been diverted before he picked up.

72

'Where are you?' I said.

'On travel, honey. I'm up north.'

'North as in San Francisco?' I pulled the phone from my ear to glance at the display. *Number withheld.* 'Are you at Mom's?'

'Where I am is beside the point. I'm going to doublecheck a couple of things. I want you to keep your head down.'

I heard metallic sounds in the kitchen. Glanced over. The Glock lay on the counter and in his hand Jesse held a box of 9 mm ammunition. Shit.

'Dad.'

'This may be absolutely nothing. A wild goose chase. But I want you to play things safe. Jesse knows what to do.'

'He's loading rounds in a spare clip.'

'Good.'

'Why? You think one clip won't be enough?'

His voice dropped another notch. 'Lay low. I mean it. I'll talk to you as soon as I know anything.'

I hung up. Jesse's eyes were cool. I watched him slide cartridges into the clip, feeling scared.

Also pissed off. My father was being evasive. Both he and Jesse were treating me as too fragile to watch out for myself. Of course, Jesse sometimes complained that this was how I treated him, and man, did this helping of my own medicine taste sour in my mouth.

He set the spare clip on the counter. 'I'm simply being cautious.'

'Right. I know drag racers who are more cautious than you.'

He picked up the Glock. 'Then consider this another form of stress management.'

'This is not reducing my anxiety. Not in the least.'

'Tomorrow we'll go to the firing range. Target practice is an excellent relaxation technique. Focus, breathe, fire. Very centering.'

'Blackburn, sometimes you seriously give me a stomach ache.'

'Cool down. You want an anti-anxiety mechanism, I've got the best.' He looked at the gun. 'Stopping power.'

7

By midnight the moon was up, conjuring white light on the Monterey Pines outside the plate-glass windows. I was wide awake, but Jesse turned off the table lamp and held out a hand.

'Let's try and get some sleep.'

I stood up. He went to the kitchen and took a couple of painkillers. I shut down the stereo, noticing that he planned to skip the Trazodone that fought his insomnia.

'Jess?'

'Not tonight.'

'Nothing's going to happen tonight. Don't mess with your meds.'

A few months back, messing with his meds had gotten him cruising toward a diazepam addiction.

'Call your doc in the morning, but tonight stick to the regimen. Please, babe.'

He scrunched his mouth. 'Yes, nurse.'

I tried to smile with relief, but he was watching me clench and unclench my hands. I relaxed my fingers and changed tack, sticking out a hip.

'To play nurse I need a little white uniform and those sexy medical tights.'

'No.' He mock-shivered. 'Hospitals and sexiness – in my mind those don't mix.'

I dropped the pose. 'Could you ever imagine me in photos? Dressed in lingerie?'

He was at the sink filling a water glass. He looked at me over his shoulder.

'Does this have to do with Cousin Tater?' he said.

'Glossy shots. Me, in lace and latex.'

His lips parted. The water reached the rim of the glass and spilled out, running over his hand.

'So that's a yes,' I said. 'What should I wear?'

'French maid.'

'No, seriously. I was thinking more a—'

'Dead serious. French maid.'

Hands on my hips. 'You mean with an apron and a micro-miniskirt and black stockings?'

'That go way up your thighs.' The water was running down his arm now. 'And stilettos.'

'Where is this coming from?'

'Four-inch stilettos. And yeah, red panties. Did I mention French maid?'

I walked toward him. 'Time out. Since when did you develop a cleaning fetish?'

'Petticoats. Garter belt. Those legs. So when you bend down to, like, polish something, ah, I mean stretching way way over, you—'

Finally noticing the water, he turned off the faucet.

I came closer. 'What if I was riding a motorcycle?'

'Stay on topic. Your hair's up but strands are falling in your face. You have a smudge on your cheek, near your lips . . .'

His gaze flowed over me. How that made me feel searing hot, I can't explain. I swear my jeans unzipped themselves. They shimmied down to my ankles and got kicked across the floor.

'A smudge,' I said.

He nodded. He was tan and his hair was halfway to the color of wheat from swimming. He looked so handsome that I was about to have a seizure.

'Because I've been getting dirty,' I said.

His voice dropped. 'Doing—'

'You.'

He was still holding the water glass. He splashed himself in the face with it.

I laughed. He shook his head, flinging water. And we both knew we were whistling past the graveyard, and didn't care.

I put my hands on his shoulders and he set down the glass, pulled me onto his lap and snaked his arms around me. My blouse had come unbuttoned, I realized. His hands ran across my bare skin and his mouth brushed my collarbone. I began working his shirt up his chest but he murmured 'You first,' and spun with me to wheel us into the living room. At the sofa he half-tossed me off his lap.

'On your back,' he said.

I lay down on the sofa and pulled one foot up. Then he was sitting between my knees and skating his hands up the inside of my legs. Way up, and I hupped a breath and tried to stop my foot from bouncing.

He traced the edge of my panties. 'This isn't scary. Why are your teeth chattering?'

'The hell it's not scary. I could burst into flame.'

His fingers teased past the lace and kept going. I looked at the ceiling. He leaned down and I felt his lips on my knee, and then on my thigh.

'Holy cow,' I said.

'*En français*, dirty maid.'

77

I felt his breath and his warm mouth on my hip, and on—

'God. Whoa. Jeepers creepers.'

That's a paraphrase. My actual words involved blasphemy and animal sounds.

So at two a.m. I was wide, wide awake.

Through the shutters I watched clouds shred across the Milky Way. Beside me Jesse lay deep asleep, one arm tossed over his eyes. He wouldn't stir unless I poked him with an icepick.

I got out of bed. In the living room I turned on the Sci Fi Channel and booted up my computer. I propped it on my lap and went online, looking for South Star.

I found everything except what I was looking for. South Star Plumbing. South Star Travel. Native American folklore: 'In Pawnee mythology South Star was the god of the underworld, magical and feared.'

Curious but not useful. Next I hit the big conspiracy-minded sites. The China Lake project wasn't even a whisper at trustnobody.com. I was going to have to look elsewhere. I slumped on the sofa, rubbing my eyes. Outside, the night sky closed in.

Hearing birds cawing overhead, I opened my eyes. Seagulls screeched outside in the sunrise, wheeling above the water. Getting up, I went to the kitchen, started the coffeepot and picked up the phone. I used the landline.

When I said hello, my mother beamed. 'Evan!'

Her voice sounded so much bigger than she was in real life. She was a hundred pounds dripping wet, with an elfin smile and a gunnery sergeant's mouth. The zest in her voice was perfect for shouting at passengers to evacuate the 747, *now*. She'd been a flight attendant for twenty years. She now worked in management for the airline, training new recruits.

'Honey, Lord, this is early for you.'

Six a.m. – yeah. The Glock stress-reduction method wasn't working. 'I'm too anxious to sleep.'

'Sweetheart, God. This bastard up in China Lake. I can't believe it. Ceci and Kelly, I remember both those girls.'

'Mom, I think the killer was part of Project South Star.'

Blank silence on her end. *Déjà vu.*

Far too late, she cleared her throat. 'Beg pardon?'

'The man who killed Kelly and Ceci may have worked on South Star. I've already talked to Dad about it.'

'Really.'

'Speaking of which, don't let him oversleep.'

'Phil?'

'I know he's in the Bay Area.'

'So you think he's here with me?' She let out an exasperated noise. 'That would violate our treaty.'

No overnights on American soil, apart from family weddings or the Oklahoma-Nebraska football game. I poured a cup of coffee.

'What did he tell you about South Star?' she said.

'Very little. I presume he's told you much more. That's why I'm calling.'

'And if he had, you think I would disclose it? You're out of luck.'

Angie and Phil Delaney: married twenty-two years, divorced thirteen, bound as tightly as barbs in fence wire. They lived 3000 miles apart, spoke each other's names with a dead chill, and every year took an exotic vacation together. Most recently they'd gone to South Africa. She could act ruthless toward my father, but God help anybody else who spoke ill of him.

'Phil would never break security to discuss a classified project. Not even with a priest in confession, much less with me.'

'So how did you get wind of South Star?' I said.

'I might ask you the same.'

'Why are you being evasive?'

Even as I said it, I had an inkling: fear. I was feeling it myself. Silence stretched across the phone line.

'Honey, I can't talk about this now. I have a breakfast meeting and I need to hit the road.'

'Then call me when you get home tonight.'

'Sure. Just lay low. Promise.'

I promised.

And I knew she'd been talking to Dad. *Lay low*. Sure, ma. It's as easy as sin.

Coyote folded the newspaper. The story had gone big: front section of the *Los Angeles Times*. But that was inevitable. Small town rocked by murders, it was tailor-made for news whores.

He sipped the Starbucks coffee. The sun was pleasant. Traffic on Sunset was heavy and the mini-mall was crowded. People were running into the dry cleaners or grabbing breakfast at Burger King. The Starbucks was busy with real estate agents talking deals and screenwriters worrying how to pitch their latest script. In a few minutes the kids from Hollywood High would come streaming in on their way to school. Caffeine rush. Go juice. Everybody trying to wake up, rev up, feeling the sharp end of the day stabbing them in the head. Everybody weak with the need to stay conscious.

The newspaper article contained bare facts mixed with rank speculation. A madman on the loose. Peasants in the town grabbing pitchforks and wanting to burn the creature. Indistinguishable from planned disinformation, really. But the story had drawn reporters like flies to a carcass, so it had been time to withdraw from China Lake.

Picking at a poppy-seed muffin, Coyote booted up the laptop. Camouflage was the craft of making people see what they expect to see. And today they were seeing a guy at the corner table wearing glasses and a baggy button-down shirt open over a T and khakis. An overgrown preppy with a baseball cap on his head and constipated anxiety on his face. Just another nebbish: a writer fretting over character arcs. Who notices writers on Sunset Boulevard?

The Starbucks had wireless, and Coyote logged on to the banking site. The account was flush. It was time to get a hotel room and regroup for the next stage. Someplace tall, a room on the top floor overlooking the city. Not that sleep would come, but heights assisted thought.

The Bassett High artifacts were locked in the toolbox in the back of the truck. The yearbook, the *Dog Days Update*, the biopsy samples; he had recovered a good haul. Collecting the samples had been delicate work, at odds with the ante-mortem aspects of the project. Remembering, Coyote's lips drew back. The sodium hydrochloride in the Drano had burned deeper into Kelly Colfax's thighs than expected. And he hadn't yet clarified his understanding of the results on her viscera. He had much to do. Scanning the Lezak x-ray into digital form and uploading it would take time as well, and required privacy. He glanced out: the truck was secure. He could see the amulet hanging from the rearview mirror. It gleamed in the sunshine, all its energy, his invincibility, stored within. He tugged at the collar of his shirt, pulling it up to cover the tip of the scar, the dregs of the claw mark.

He logged out of the bank site and logged on to Expedia, searching for hotels. Tall ones, with a view of the Hollywood hills. The busboy approached the table, asking if he could clear it. Coyote stared at the computer screen.

People grated on the nerves. On the skin. Civilians grated particularly. The unwashed. The untrained and unaware. The unworthy. Wanting their soft lives, their Prozac and bike paths and liposuction, never acknowledging the sacrifice and skill of the warriors who made their decadence possible.

Never recognizing the solitary hunter in their midst.

The busboy asked again. Without looking up, Coyote nudged the coffee mug across the table at him. It was merely a prop. Coyotes didn't need caffeine. The busboy took it and went away.

Expedia came back with a list of nearby hotels. Tall places. Good.

Coyote felt the juices start to flow. Things were clicking into place. Everything was tying together like a skein, one to the next. The two women in China Lake had been more than an opportunity. They had been proof. They validated the mission. They testified, and pointed the way.

Next.

8

I drove home at eight. Jesse followed in his truck, the slick black Toyota pickup he bought after I sweet-talked him into selling me the Mustang. He watched until I opened the garden gate, leaning an elbow on the window frame.

'Come down to the office and work later. I'll clear you a spot on my desk.'

I waved goodbye.

Inside, I checked my email and glanced at the phone, willing Dad to call. Men's voices came up the walk. It was my bathroom crew, Martinez and Sons. Mr Martinez entered, his watermelon belly preceding the rest of him. Behind him Carlos and Miguel maneuvered through the door, carting the big box that contained my new sink.

Miguel backed past me, smiling brilliantly. 'Ready to rock? You're going to love it when we get this thing in.'

Carlos edged around the dining table. 'Careful, bro.' He nodded to me. 'Morning.'

'Guys.' I followed them to the bathroom, making sure they had a clear path.

Okay, no. Admiring. They were twins, hometown heroes, former baseball stars at Santa Barbara High. Fine, they were gods. Twenty-three, bronzed and honed, identically beautiful and as distinct as mercury and marble.

They set down the box and ripped open the packaging.

I saw spotless porcelain. And Miguel's high-spirited smile. He called to his dad to turn on the boom box. Carlos ran his hand over the contours of the sink, checking the workmanship. He would have looked good carved in stone himself.

A knock on the front door spoiled my reverie. I poked my head around the doorjamb.

On the porch stood Tommy Chang. He was jingling coins in his pockets and working hard on a piece of gum. Next to him a sturdy man in a charcoal suit was examining the garden with an appraising eye.

I opened the door. 'Jeez, you must have been on the road since before sunup.'

'If you like me even a little bit, there'll be coffee,' Tommy said.

I waved them in. 'Black?'

'Milk, sugar, any stimulants you got.' He gestured to his companion. 'Special Agent Dan Heaney from the FBI's Behavioral Analysis Unit.'

Heaney had a calm face pitted with acne scars. He set a briefcase on the dining table while Tommy strolled around the living room, stretching after the drive. He nodded at one of my prints, El Capitan in winter.

'Love this one. There's some crazy dudes that climb that wall.'

I poured them coffee. Tommy took his gratefully.

'Awesome.'

Heaney took the mug, thanking me. 'To explain why I'm tagging along today, Detective Chang and his colleagues are running this investigation. The Bureau provides investigative and operational support. What my unit does is analyze crimes from a behavioral perspective and give him all the help we can.'

I glanced at the briefcase. 'Have you profiled the China Lake killer?'

'I have.'

Abruptly, I felt seasick. In the back of the house, the Martinez boys turned up the boom box and speed metal crashed out. The air felt close.

'Let's talk outside,' I said.

We went out to the wooden patio table under the live oaks. Tommy pulled a pack of cigarettes from his shirt pocket.

'Evan, here's the thing. The tip you gave us, the way it came in seems sketchy.'

'A source contacting a journalist? That's hardly strange,' I said.

'Most folks who know about a murder call the police direct.'

Heaney laced his fingers together. 'Unless the tipster has an ulterior motive.'

'Like having something to hide,' Tommy said.

I didn't comment on Jakarta Ulterior-Motive Rivera. 'I've told you everything I can.'

'No, you told us everything you want to.'

'Start with his name,' Heaney said.

'Anonymous means anonymous. It's privileged information,' I said.

His tie was stained with egg. I stared. I didn't think FBI agents made sartorial gaffes.

Tommy tapped a cigarette out of the pack. 'Reporters' privilege doesn't apply here. Journalists' shield law, either.'

Good one, Chang. The shield law protected journalists, though not necessarily freelancers like me, from disclosing the name of a source. But not unless they were threatened with contempt of court.

Heaney noticed me staring at the egg. Embarrassed, he tried to wipe it off.

'I believe you want to be helpful,' he said. 'But you should be aware that serial killers often insinuate themselves into the investigation of their crimes.'

Tommy held the unlit cigarette between his fingers. 'They hang with cops at bars, pumping them for information. Get themselves interviewed on the local news. And they dig on the media attention their crimes get.'

Heaney said, 'A lot of them are police wannabes. Security guards, night watchmen, academy washouts. They're ineffectual losers who fantasize about domination and control.'

My limbs felt heavy. My head was beginning to throb.

'My source isn't the killer,' I said.

'You sure?'

'Positive.' *A* killer, but not *the* killer.

Tommy ran the cigarette under his nose, sniffing it, and then distractedly shoved it behind his ear. On the inside of his wrist I saw a fresh nicotine patch.

'How about some pretzel sticks?' I said.

Jagged smile. 'Yeah, that'd be good.'

I brought him the bag. He rustled a handful out and stuck one between his teeth. I think if he could have, he would have sucked the salt into his lungs.

He looked at Heaney. 'Want to run her through the profile?'

Heaney nodded. 'We're looking for a white man in his thirties, possibly early forties. He's socially sophisticated. Confident, persuasive and convincing.'

'This is an ineffectual loser?'

'Some killers are socially adept. Guys with minimal social skills, your neighborhood weirdo, they can't charm their way into a victim's trust even for a second, so they blitz. Attack from the rear without warning. But this killer, Coyote you called him, he talked his way in to see Ceci Lezak. He gets his victims where he wants using words, not brute force.'

I nodded.

'He has above average intelligence and he's orderly and clean, almost regimented. He has a military background. And he keeps lists, writes journals, compulsively documents everything,' he said. 'Killing gives him such an ego boost that he may keep a diary or scrapbook of the media coverage.'

The scent of star jasmine hung on the air, sickeningly sweet. Heaney leaned over the table with his fingers laced together, like a mild-mannered pastor discussing plans for the church picnic.

'And Coyote is viscerally angry at women. He's sadistic and he's killing for one reason. To inflict pain.'

The breeze, flicking my hair across my face, felt like steel wool. Heaney's church-picnic placidity disturbed me.

'His intent is to murder and to inflict as much pain and terror beforehand as possible. The sexual component to the attack on Mrs Colfax indicates—'

'Dan.' Tommy eyed him.

My palms tingled. 'Sexual component?'

Tommy was sending Heaney a *zip it* vibe.

My throat was tightening. 'He tortured her sexually?'

Tommy put a hand on my forearm. Heaney leaned back. I wanted to hear, but I didn't want to hear. I rubbed my eyes.

'Why did he choose two women from our class?' I said.

'Serial killers feed on the thrill of the hunt. And if they can't find a victim who's in the wrong place at the wrong

87

time, they'll go back to a location where they've been successful. It helps them relive the thrill.'

Tommy ran a palm over his head. 'He may have been lurking nearby when Ceci found Kelly's body. He could have drawn a bead on her because of that.'

My throat was still dry. 'I thought these killers picked victims at random.'

Heaney said, 'There's always a victimology. Something draws the killer to the victim. Something he's seeking – brunettes, teenagers. Hitchhikers. Prostitutes.'

'Have you uncovered other victims?'

Tommy said, 'Looks like one up near Seattle last year. Whidbey Island, a woman named Carla Dearing. There were similarities.'

'A signature,' Heaney said. 'Cuttings. Almost like claw marks.'

'God.'

My eyes felt gritty. I knew that Heaney was basing his assessment on facts he hadn't revealed to me. Crime scene analysis, autopsy results, bestial acts inflicted on Kelly, degradation and mutilation and pain.

Sexual component. Holy God.

'This killer isn't typical, is he?' I said.

'Coyote fits what we call the assassin profile,' Heaney said.

The breeze sent the hairs creeping on the back of my neck. 'What's that mean?'

'Loner. Emotionally undemonstrative. Nocturnal, and into obsessive journal writing.' He hunched forward. 'This personality is more dangerous than most serial killers.'

'More?' Shit, just what we needed. 'How?'

'Most serial killers pick victims they know they can

handle, and they go to great lengths to keep from being caught. But assassins view their murders as a mission. They'll do anything to complete that mission. Even die.'

I breathed. 'Have you traced Coyote's code name back to Project South Star?'

'No comment.'

'My source asked me to pass this information along specifically so you'd get involved and bust through the national security thicket. Have you?'

Given the FBI's notorious rivalry with the intelligence agencies, I presumed Heaney would find satisfaction at catching them in a screw-up.

'Not yet,' he said. 'Coyote is a convenient shorthand right now. And whether or not it proves to be the code name for an operative trained by some defunct military program, it's accurate. Coyotes are solitary hunters. Night after night, same as serial killers.'

His demeanor didn't change, but his eyes were now anything but placid. They reflected the controlled calm of someone who has lifted the lid off hell and heard the howling.

Tommy said, 'Have you considered that there's another reason this source came to you, aside from you being a journalist?'

'I'm from China Lake. The victims were my classmates.'

'No. South Star, this super-secret project. Is it possible your dad worked on it?'

I really wasn't feeling well, I realized. My head was pounding, my limbs ached and my stomach felt uncertain.

'Dad was Nav Air. That was his life, US air superiority. Keeping our guys alive up there. My source said

South Star was not Navy and that means Dad wasn't involved.'

They didn't respond.

'You're alleging that my father was a spook,' I said. 'He wasn't. But even if he was, I'd never know and neither would you.'

Tommy held a handful of pretzel sticks tight in his fingers. 'Is your dad the source, Evan?'

That's why they were here. That's why they'd driven a hundred miles before sunrise.

'No.' I held his gaze. 'He's not, Tommy.'

Whether he saw it in my eyes, my demeanor or my tone of voice, he seemed to accept that. His shoulders relaxed a notch.

'In that case,' he said, 'you think he could provide some background to help us with the investigation?'

'Believe me, I've asked and he's looking.'

'Good. We need every ounce of help we can get,' he said. 'Because Coyote isn't finished. He's going to kill again.'

Ninety seconds after they left I was on the phone, calling my dad. He didn't answer. I left a message asking him to call back.

He was going to tell me what was at the bottom of this, but I wasn't going to wait for him. I had to take an alternate, intersecting route. I doublechecked my calendar. Friday I was scheduled to argue motions in court for Sanchez Marks, Jesse's firm. The rest of the week was flexible enough for me to scramble. I phoned Jesse and told him I wouldn't be sleeping at his place tonight.

'Give me forty-five minutes,' he said. 'I'll drive you to the airport.'

Still feeling crappy, I took two Tylenol, stuffed clean socks and underwear and a toothbrush in a backpack, grabbed my keys and computer case, headed across the lawn and knocked on Nikki Vincent's kitchen door.

She answered with the phone pressed between her ear and shoulder, carrying Thea on her hip. I followed her inside.

'Tell him the lighting's fine,' she said.

Play-Doh was blobbed on the butcher block table. And mushed in Thea's fingers and caught, bright blue, in Nikki's hair. Something creole was bubbling on the stove. Nikki set Thea in her high chair.

'Wine, yes. Vodka, in his dreams.'

It sounded like she was talking to her assistant. Nikki ran an art gallery but stayed home two mornings a week. She grabbed a dishtowel and ran it over Thea's hands and face. Held up a finger, indicating just a minute.

Nikki had been my college roommate, and living next door to her continued to anchor me. She was compact and voluptuous, African American, and today she was wearing shorts and a UCSB Volleyball T-shirt along with reams of silver jewelry. Her bracelets sang as she wiped her little girl's face. Thea squirmed and the phone squirted out from under Nikki's chin and fell to the floor.

'Sorry,' she shouted.

I took the dishtowel and finished wiping Thea's fingers. She was eighteen months old, sunny and curious and sturdy as a fence post. Coming into this homey chaos gave me a feeling of both longing and belonging, and I felt myself unwind. Even the smell of jambalaya on the stove didn't bother my stomach.

Nikki hung up. 'Sorry, the new exhibition. Temperamental artist, imagine that. What's up?'

'Road trip. I'll be back tomorrow. Will you lock up after the workmen and set the alarm for me?'

'No problem.'

'And if my cousin Taylor shows up, hit her with a rake.'

'With pleasure. Where are you off to?'

'Palo Alto.' I ruffled Thea's hair. 'Paying my mom a surprise visit.'

'You never pay your mom a surprise visit.'

Not since college, when I drove home and heard her down the hall in the bedroom, whooping, 'Phil, you *dog*!'

'I need to pick her memory about the bad old days in China Lake,' I said.

She shook her head and rolled her eyes.

'What's that for?' I said.

'You, Miss Military Industrial Complex. Your child-hood on the dark side is going to catch up with you.'

'Pinko.'

'Warmonger.'

She hugged me and kissed my cheek. 'Safe trip.'

Jesse stopped the truck in front of the terminal. 'You know what your father will say about this. You're not laying low.'

I grabbed my things from the back seat. 'Visiting Mom *is* laying low. I'm spending the afternoon airside past security, then airborne, then sequestered at a house only you and Nikki know about.'

'I can't take you to the firing range if you're in Palo Alto.'

Leaning across the cab, I hooked his red tie, pulled him to me and kissed him. 'Your ammo will keep for twenty-four hours. I'll be back tomorrow.'

I schlepped my things up the walk, past flowerbeds, and inside to the ticket desk, all of fifty feet. The Santa

92

Barbara terminal is less an airport than a hacienda plucked from *Man of La Mancha*, designed to show the happy tourist he has arrived in Fiesta Land. I showed my ID and paid the tax for the flight. This was the big perk in my life. As the daughter of an airline employee I essentially flew free, worldwide. The agent handed me my ticket and I hiked toward the metal detector.

An hour and a half later the small jet swooped off the runway and headed north. I leaned against the window and watched California scroll by. Special Agent Heaney's profile of Coyote hung in my mind, deeply unsettling.

Coyote, Heaney predicted, kept notes. A journal. Compulsively. It reminded me of Jax and Tim. In my safe deposit box I had twenty years of their notes and diaries and memos. Detailing, sometimes excruciatingly, covert ops they had run. Wet work, in the jargon of the trade.

I dismissed the possibility that either of them was Coyote. But I didn't dismiss the possibility that they were tasked with eliminating Coyote. Their masters at the CIA or NSA or Hits 'R' Us may have assigned them to kill this killer. If so, they might be using me to flush Coyote out of hiding. By pressuring me to pressure the cops and the feds, they could scare Coyote into making a mistake, and they could catch him. Sweat broke out on my forehead.

Forty minutes later we banked past the green coastal mountains and snarled freeways of Silicon Valley and bumped down onto the runway at San Jose, thrust reversers roaring. I caught the Super Shuttle to Mom's house, fifteen miles up the 101.

Arriving in Palo Alto, cruising along tree-lined Embarcadero Road, was like coming home. I went to law school at the sprawling campus up ahead, with its sandstone courtyards and red tile roofs. I'd loved it here, felt challenged by my classmates and professors, and coming back to this town made me feel sharper, prouder and bigger, if not younger.

And to hear my dad, I'd gone and blown my grand ivory tower legal education by kicking free from law practice after four years. For what – to turn myself into a legal journalist, brief doctor and science fiction novelist? Even now I heard him: girl, you're fixing to stay in debt your whole life.

But he knew why I did it. The black days when Jesse lay near death in the ICU taught me that you don't waste second chances. The day he came off the critical list, I quit my job.

My mom lived in a quaint and beautiful Spanish-style house with oaks shivering overhead in the breeze. The Shuttle dropped me off out front. The house was only four miles from where Mom grew up, though worth twenty times what my grandparents paid for their place. She bought it when she took the job in San Francisco. She had invested her modest divorce settlement in a stock portfolio that she cashed out at the right time, at the height of the boom. But then she was a stewardess. Her life revolved around knowing one truth: what goes up must come down. Angie Delaney was a wise woman. This was Palo Alto, and the house was now worth seven figures.

It was just after three p.m. and she was still at work, thirty miles up the freeway near the San Francisco airport. I let myself in and went out back to sit in the shade by the swimming pool. I sat down on a chaise longue to plan my ambush. It was simple.

Hug, laugh, eat, and hit her with hard questions about China Lake and Project South Star. Catching her off-balance was key. I couldn't give her time to plan her cover story. I put my feet up, listening to birdsong.

'Ev, sweetheart.'

I blinked. My mother stood above me, arms wide, beaming.

'Mom.'

She laughed and pulled me to my feet. 'My God, I don't believe it.'

Shoot, how long had I been asleep? I glanced at my watch: ninety minutes. I embraced her, smelling the fresh scent of her perfume.

'You look awesome,' I said.

She smoothed my hair, smiling as if a pot of gold had just dropped into her back yard. 'Flying up here to pull a commando raid on me, this is too much. What a hoot.'

She was fifty-seven and still a sprite, trim and tan. Her tailored gold suit stopped above her knees. Her heels were kicked off, dangling from one hand. Her hair was shorn to a spiky collage of silver mixed with Coca-Cola brown.

'What secrets were you going to squeeze out of me? Black projects? Secret weapons? What do you want to eat, a sandwich? Or I have soup.'

'South Star,' I said.

'I know, honey. Come inside.'

She gripped my hand and hauled me into the kitchen. It was photo central. The fridge was plastered with shots of me, my brother Brian, and especially my nephew Luke. The walls were a bright mosaic. Her postcard collection spanned thirty years and six continents. Alaska, Rome, Cape Town, the Grand Canyon. She sat me down at the kitchen table and opened the fridge.

'So.' She waved a hand. 'You satisfied that Phil isn't here?'

'Guess so.' Mostly I was satisfied that she spoke his name easily, without coldness or rancor. That indicated they were on the same wavelength at the moment.

'How's that man of yours?' she said.

'He sends his love.'

'Brian said he looked underweight. Are you cooking for him? Making him laugh?'

She took a pitcher from the fridge and poured two glasses of iced tea. I felt like a grouchy toddler roused too soon from the playpen.

'He's great. We're great. And it's status quo.'

'Just checking.' She smiled. 'He's still the cutest thing on—'

'Wheels. Yeah. You know how I like 'em. Tall, dark and paralyzed.'

She leaned against the kitchen counter, drank her tea, and rattled the ice cubes in the glass. 'Gee. I was going to say the west coast.'

Red heat climbed up my neck. She set down her tea. Taking a carton of orange juice from the fridge, she poured a glass and set it on the table in front of me along with a trio of pills.

'What's this?' I said.

'Vitamin C and Tylenol. You're coming down with something. You only get snotty when you're feeling punk.'

I found that I didn't have the energy to stick out my tongue at her. And the only reason I wanted to was because she'd gotten the jump on my slick-as-spit plan to ambush her.

'Sorry. Thanks.'

She put the back of her hand across my forehead. Her skin was cool. I felt soothed and safe and five years old.

'Well, you're not feverish.' She gestured to the juice, indicating *Drink, drink*.

I swallowed the pills. 'Achy and tired and a killer headache.'

'Is this PMS?'

'Why do people keep saying that?' I slumped, and conceded. 'It's PMS *extreme*. It's so bad it should be an event at the X Games.'

She turned back to the sink. 'Is that why you chased your cousin out of your house, hissing like a cobra?'

I pushed the heels of my hands against my eyes. 'I'm taking out a hit on Taylor.'

'You can't.' She turned around. 'Then who'd keep us posted on Kendall's divorce? Or Mackenzie quitting business school to make Vegan clothing?'

'True.'

Taylor spread useless information faster than a computer virus. The family counted on her for gossip.

She came over, stood behind me and wrapped her arms around my shoulders. 'Fine. I'll stop prying.'

'Excellent.'

'Once I'm dead. Then the Foundation takes over. It's in my will.'

I laughed, but felt the headache roaming around the back of my skull. She went and began taking things out of the fridge. I rubbed the muscles in my neck, rolling my head.

'Mom, I'm the one who's here to pry. I presume you've figured out that I flew three hundred miles because I need some straight answers.'

She set cherry tomatoes and a head of lettuce on the counter. 'I know. Let's make some dinner. I have a good Napa Valley red in the wine rack, we'll crack it open.'

'Please don't stonewall me.'

Her face was taut. 'I won't. This has been coming for a long time.'

'It has?'

'About twenty years.'

Coyote stood at the window. The view from the hotel room was panoramic. The sky was striated red, the skyscrapers downtown flecked orange with light. Smog provoked superlative sunsets, though they were increasingly rare. Pollution had decreased here. You could just taste it on your tongue, barely smell the hydrocarbons when you lifted your face to the breeze.

Down on Hollywood Boulevard, traffic droned. The sidewalks crawled with people. Tourists, players and whores, predators and prey. Wanting fame, wanting to get laid, selling themselves one way or another. They thought this was a hard town. Moneygrubbing and professional back-stabbing – in their world, that's what they considered hard.

He fingered the amulet, thinking.

The skull x-rays from the Lezak woman had been scanned and uploaded, along with his notes on the operation. He had documented everything. Lezak's response to the procedure had been textbook. Fight – stabbing him. Feebly, yes, but she made an attempt. Then screaming, squirming, attempting to flee – classic flight response. That, however, was not the exciting part. The exciting part occurred approximately ten seconds after he yanked the scaling implement through the flesh of her lip. She blanked. The look in her eyes, the way she fell still, told him everything. She went numb. The rest of the procedure was merely pushing and prodding. She did not respond. She didn't scream when he drove the sharp tip

98

of the scaler into her eye socket. Muzak and her ragged breathing didn't obscure the sound of the scaler penetrating her eye. Blood and aqueous humor ran out and poured down her cheek, but Ceci Lezak lay there perplexed, stunned and vacant.

The thirst began building. A dry taste on the tongue. The mission called to him.

Turning from the window, he removed his medical kit from the suitcase. He applied antiseptic ointment to the minor wound Lezak had inflicted with the curette. Then he injected: chemo first, the enzymes that ensured de-aggregation, so the wave didn't swamp him. Nandrolone after that. He would throw the disposable syringes in the hotel dumpster later. He checked that his other drugs were well stocked, those he kept in reserve for use on subjects. They were mainly tranquilizers – pentothal, ketamine and benzodiazepines. He closed the kit. In the bathroom he washed off the tan makeup and removed the green contact lenses. He never allowed the world to see the real eyes, Coyote eyes. The blown pupil spooked people, and it was memorable.

He returned his attention to the suitcase. The clothes, the shoes, the wigs, the cosmetics. Men's things on one side, women's on the other. Becoming female was occa-sionally necessary. Some targets responded more willingly to the anima than the animus. Still, that meant that he needed long sleeves to disguise his musculature. He clenched a fist, seeing the veins rise on his arm. He would wear a high collar, of course, to cover the scar.

His acting skills would cover his revulsion. As long as the mission was on track, he could stomach becoming a woman. Until the end, when the anima could be rele-gated to eternal shadow.

He ran his fingers over a black wig. The hair was coarse, shoulder length. With brown contacts, he could become suburban. A breeder. Yes, that's it.

Coyote flipped on the wig and looked in the mirror. She would wear conservative pink lipstick. She'd have a perky smile. Tight movements, thoughts of hubbie and kids. Menstruation, separation anxiety, PTA, scouts and ballet. Honey, have a brownie. I'm going to Pilates.

Soccer Mom, pathetic icon of the modern mythos.

Turning to the Tumi briefcase, he opened it and perused the weapons inside. Blades, C4, grenades. He took out a serrated knife. The five-inch blade shone bright. Coyote opened his palm and pushed the tip of the knife into his flesh, along his lifeline. A balloon of blood rose through the skin. He watched, dispassionate. The sensation of pain was nonexistent. A smile lifted his lips.

The blood pooled on his palm. It shone under the light coming through the window, pulsing in rhythm with his heartbeat. The sun hissed through the glass. It lit the blood to iridescent red and set it jumping off his palm, springing up like a tiny wet flame. He watched it writhe, fascinated, feeling no heat. But the wound was burning. The blood flame turned and beckoned to him. Telling him, giving him the answer.

A vacuum cleaner banged against the wall outside in the hallway, jerking him back. He blinked, feeling his head spin and settle. He looked at his hand. Blood was creasing along the lines of his palm. The knife had fallen to the floor.

That was a glitch.

Angry, he picked up the knife, cleaned the blade and returned it to the briefcase. This was the third time that had happened in the past six weeks. He had to get it under control. Did he require heavier chemo? He glanced at the medical kit. He had only three doses left.

The growl was in his head. He shut it off. He sat down at the desk with the *Dog Days Update*, the *Paw Prints* yearbook, the notes and journal, and began to cross reference. There were only a few left of these worthless unworthy people. These nothings, ignorant of the power that lay dormant inside them. Who failed to recognize it bursting to life, until the moments before death. That's why he had to take them. They were . . . glitches. He pored through the reunion book, finding the name he wanted. Mapquest gave him coordinates to the address, and he began to get a sense of the mission. It would require careful planning, because he had seen the end, in his dream vision.

Fire this time.

Mom sat down beside me at the kitchen table. Her face, with those wise eyes and that evergreen spark, looked apprehensive.

'That field trip your class took to Renegade Canyon. This has to be about what happened that day,' she said.

'The explosion.'

Again I saw the flash, felt the shudder in the air, and watched the cinderblock buildings disintegrate into flame. Saw the Jeep gunning up the hillside, coming after me and the others.

'Nobody would ever tell the parents. But I'd bet the farm that was South Star.'

'What happened?'

'An accident? An experiment gone wrong?' She shrugged. 'All I know is, you were treated reprehensibly.'

Even now I could hear the engines of the Navy

helicopter whumping off the canyon walls. The down-wash blew sand viciously in all directions. Valerie sat on the ground, her nose pouring blood from my punch. She was silent with shock. Me too. Ms Shepard came running to check on her.

The soldier came for me.

He smelled of dust and gun oil, and the barrel of his rifle had a dark gleam that scared me cold. He hauled me by the elbow onto the bus. My classmates stared at me with confusion and maybe fear.

The soldier glared at the driver. 'Go.'

The door wheezed closed and we lurched back toward the highway. Nobody spoke. The soldier stood in the door-well, rocking as the bus picked its way over stony ground.

Jeeps and a van raced past us going the other way. They screeched to a stop near the helicopter. The back doors of the van burst open and people jumped out.

'They wore biocontainment suits,' I said.

Olive-green, with hoods and faceplates. They handed the pilot a gas mask. They carried medical equipment cases like paramedics do. One climbed in the bay of the helicopter and bent over, going to work. The helo was carrying casualties.

Mom's eyes were hot. 'Later, we found out they took the school bus out of service. The Navy bought it and took it away, out on the base somewhere, to burn it.'

My voice felt croaky. 'What about us?'

'They sent everybody to the showers in the gym. Had all the kids wash and change into PE clothes to wear home. They took everyone's street clothes and sent them to the laundry on base.'

'I don't remember that.'

'Because they didn't take you with everybody else.'

I nodded. 'I had to wait for Dad. They put me in . . . I want to say an equipment room in the gym.'

'They talked to you separately. You four who had run off.' Her cheeks were burning. 'Do you have any *idea* how that incensed me? Taking a group of thirteen-year-old kids who were horsing around, and isolating you for interrogation. And they wouldn't let me in. You had been exposed to God knows what and they wouldn't let your mother in to see you. Those fucking security assholes.'

I took a breath. Mom always drew the line at the F-word.

'Jackboot SOBs. I feel sick just thinking about what it was like for you.'

'Mom, at the time I thought that was because I punched Valerie.'

'Oh my God. Evan, no.'

The equipment room was hot and dingy, a claustrophobic space with shelves stacked with athletic equipment. Blood was caked on my face and on the side of my hand. The air felt close, as if I had to breathe faster to get enough.

The police would be coming any minute, I knew it. They were going to arrest me for hitting Valerie. They'd put me in a lineup and she'd point me out. She'd cry and tell them I didn't even look *sorry* after I did it.

What if they sent me to Juvenile Hall? My throat tightened. Juvie was in Bakersfield. That was a two-hour drive from China Lake.

Then I heard my dad's voice in the hallway, rough and low, punctuated with remarks like cannon fire. He opened the door.

'Come with me, Kit.'

I rushed out like a cat freed from a box, taking big

breaths. Soldiers were in the hallway, and Mr Mickleson, the high school principal.

He pointed his finger at me. 'Two weeks' suspension, starting immediately. Are you listening, Miss Delaney?'

I stared at the linoleum, cold and lightheaded, trying not to pee my pants. My fingers felt numb. I wasn't under arrest, but Dad was furious. He said nothing, just led me down the hallway. He had my backpack in his hand.

Behind us came footsteps, three or four people. 'Captain Delaney.'

My father didn't stop.

A woman called to him. 'Phil.'

Dad pointed me at the gym. 'Go shower and change.' He handed me a brown paper bag. 'Put your street clothes in this. Wear your gym clothes home.'

He marched back up the hall, boots racking against the floor. A woman strode toward him. She had red hair and a strong voice.

'Strict protocol on this one, Phil. Don't think of violating it.'

'My daughter's coming home with me. You're out of bounds.'

The redhead glanced at me. 'Didn't you hear your father tell you to get going?'

Dad turned. His eyes were dark. 'Kit, now. Go.'

The words came fast and hard, like buckshot. They tore the air and I couldn't get a breath. The next thing I remember, I was sitting on the floor with cramps in my arms and legs, and Dad was holding the paper bag over my nose, telling me to breathe slowly.

Hyperventilation, one more embarrassment. I looked at Mom.

'What were we exposed to?'

'Corrosive chemicals. The high school told us they could cause skin blisters and asthma.'

'Didn't parents go ballistic?'

'Hell, yes. Then the base commander sent us a report from this woman Maureen Swayze, Director of Special Projects for some nebulous Office of Advanced Research. It said the explosion involved an experimental fuel. A new propellant, JP-5 mixed with caustic additives.'

'Did Swayze have red hair?'

'Like an oil well fire.'

'She was at the gym that day, arguing in the hall with Dad.'

An eyebrow rose. 'Arguing. Really.' She pursed her lips. 'Good.'

'Mom?'

Her eyes went sharp and broke from mine. She drew back from whatever she'd been about to unload.

'I used to see Swayze at the Officers' Club,' she said. 'She was a cold-faced bitch. She ran South Star.'

'How do you know that?'

'Not even black projects stayed totally dark. Rumors didn't spread, they floated around the place like perfume. We knew she was a project director. She had a vibe.'

She stood up. 'Her report assured us that any skin problems would be temporary, and that as a prophylactic measure they'd periodically test everyone who was on the field trip for breathing problems.'

'I remember that. Being called into the nurse's office and asked to blow into a tube to measure my lung strength.'

Her eyes looked acid. 'But then they asked parents to waive confidentiality on your medical records, so they could track your health.'

The Tylenol was not working. A hammer was thumping against the inside of my skull. 'Did you?'

'Turn you into a volunteer lab rat for Swayze and her Department of Weird Shit? No damn way. I ripped up the waiver form.'

'Thanks, Mom.'

'Think about it. Why would a fuel researcher need to have your medical records? She was a stone liar.'

She walked to the sink. 'Phil was taking it to her that day, huh?'

'Yeah. Why?'

'He tried to get to the bottom of what happened out in Renegade Canyon, but came back and told me it was classified. Swayze was off the scope, he said. Her working group was not Navy. He didn't have access to the channels that could give him the real information he needed.'

'Didn't he have contacts in all the labs at the base? Couldn't he—'

'She was doing top secret research.' Her voice sharpened. 'She was beyond the chain of command. He hit a dead end.'

We were drilling close to an old fight. I felt a hard nut in my stomach.

'You believed him, didn't you?'

'Of course I did. This involved you. But I . . .' She turned her back and stared out the kitchen window. 'I wanted him to keep pressing. He thought he couldn't.'

'You thought he had plenty of access to information about her project because . . .'

Tommy Chang's innuendo came flooding back, and Jax Rivera's pointed hints, and my boyfriend's jokes about secret lives. I groaned mentally, thinking: Jesse Blackburn, do you have to be right every stinking time?

'Was Dad in covert intelligence?'

'Probably.'

For a few seconds she leaned against the sink. Finally she turned around. Her gaze had lengthened.

'He used to empty the change from his pockets into a bowl on the dresser. One day I found Turkish coins there.' She looked reflective. 'He'd told me he was going to DC.'

'Oh.'

'And he kept a Canadian passport locked in his desk.'

I felt strangely detached. I reached for my glass of iced tea but it was empty. I went to the fridge for a refill.

'He never told you?' I said.

'No. And I never asked. He was Nav Air now and forever, and any intelligence work he did was related to that.' She shrugged and began slicing cherry tomatoes on the cutting board.

All at once I felt sad. I disliked being shown a wall within their marriage.

'So we never found out anything more about South Star. The parents, I mean. We pressed everywhere we could apply pressure. With the school. With the Navy. With every doctor in town. Especially Dr Cantwell – you remember him?'

'Doctor C, yeah. I saw him at the reunion.'

She nodded and gave a little *Huh, what do you know* look. Quiet pervaded the kitchen. Around us, postcards smiled and waved. I felt a slow welling, a shift, as if a beast was rousing itself from hibernation.

'Kelly Colfax and Ceci Lezak were on the field trip, weren't they?' I said.

A knowing look came my way. 'Yes.'

I got my backpack and pulled out the *Dog Days Update*.

Flipping it open to the obituaries, I set it on the counter in front of her.

'Help me remember,' I said.

The light was turning outside, the hot day cooling to a soft evening. She flipped a page, looking at photos of my dead classmates.

She ran her hand over a name. 'Teddy Horowitz.'

Aircraft accident aboard the *USS Nimitz*.

She turned the page. Shannon Gruber, pneumonia following a long illness. She shook her head.

'Aggressive breast cancer ran in her family.'

She turned the page. 'Linda Garcia.'

I put my hand on the book. 'Long illness. What's that mean?'

'I don't know.'

I tried to picture Linda back in school, recalling a torrent of brown hair, heavy makeup, heavier thighs. The sunlight coming through the window felt weirdly cold. Mom turned the page and we looked at the photo of Sharlayne Jackson.

'She was on the field trip,' I said. 'I remember.'

Complications of childbirth.

She shook her head. 'So many tragedies. But none of them connect, do they?' She flipped again. 'Phoebe Chadwick.' She let out a hard noise. '"Died suddenly". What a ridiculous euphemism. Who came up with this book?'

'Kelly Colfax and Ceci Lezak.'

'Crap.' She put both hands on the kitchen counter. 'What did Phoebe Chadwick die from?'

'Southern Comfort. With a barbiturate chaser.'

'Was China Lake really such a bad place to grow up?'

She was shaking her head. She flipped past several

more photos. When she came to Marcy Yakulski, she stopped. 'Auto accident?'

I recalled the newspaper headline on the board at the reunion. *Four Die in Fiery Crash.*

'Marcy was on the field trip,' she said. 'Her folks made a stink about the waivers.'

There was one name left. 'Dana West?'

She read the entry. Registered nurse, died in a hospital fire. She ran her fingers across her forehead.

'Mom. How many people do you think went on the field trip that day?'

She was pensive. 'You kids, your teacher . . . maybe twenty-five, twenty-six.'

I closed the book. We looked at each other, adding up names mentally. The hammer pounded a leaden rhythm inside my head.

'I count eight,' she said. 'Including Kelly and Ceci.'

So did I. A cold sweat broke out across my face and palms.

Almost a third of the people who went with me to Renegade Canyon were dead. My gag reflex kicked in. I ran for the bathroom and retched.

9

Parked at the far edge of the lot, Coyote watched the woman schlub her way out through the doors of the community center. The evening was hot, typical for Riverside. Dust, sage and agricultural fertilizer hinted on the wind. How curious that some members of the class would leave China Lake but cling to the desert lifestyle. Like Becky O'Keefe.

She clumped across the parking lot, stout, clumsy and all-too content, in love with the world of arts and crafts and homemaking. The hideous twinkly shirt and vacuous smile and rolls of fat on her upper arms testified to that. Taking Becky at the reunion had proved impossible. But tonight would be different. Tonight nobody would suspect and nobody would see.

Tonight Coyote was Soccer Mom, queen slut of the suburbs.

Soccer Mom's black wig was drawn back into a pony-tail, under a cap that said 'Walk for the Cure'. Workout pants and a long sleeved T-shirt hid her musculature. The shirt bore the photo of a little girl clutching a daisy. She had found it in the back of the van she stole in Pasadena, with the 'My kid is an honor student at El Rancho School' bumper sticker. The photo was a vomitous sentimentality but excellent camouflage. Soccer Mom, Princess Frigidity, she flaunted proof of her coitus via a photo on her chest.

Coyote lifted the tailgate of the van and opened the sports bag, looking toward the community center. It was a big place, well funded. It had aerobics classes and day care and Crafts for Beginners which, according to the *Dog Days Update*, was taught by Becky O'Keefe.

Coyote ran lipstick across dry lips. It felt repellent, this womaning process, weakening oneself with cosmetics. Even in the service of the hunt, it stained the spirit. Legend told of Coyote and Woman dueling to outsmart each other. But she had not yet met Woman. Only women.

The lipstick slid across Soccer Mom's lips. That's it, write with it like a hard slash. Draw your target and bring success to the hunt. Draw a woman, even if it's on your own face. Draw Becky O'Keefe right over here.

She threw the lipstick into the sports bag and put on a pair of weightlifting gloves. The flame tickled the edge of her vision and, from within the bag, a rough red towel unfurled and curled out like a six-foot tongue. It raised itself erect and swayed, a charmed snake, cool and lascivious. She heard it licking the air, a wet sound though the towel was dry. And it flicked out, searching for her.

Keys jangled. Next to the van, a car door opened.

Coyote snapped back. Becky O'Keefe stood by the Volvo station wagon, dumping crafts supplies into the back.

'Okey doke, pea pod,' she said. 'Time to load you in.'

The toddler was on her hip. About two years old, the age when heads were abnormally large and they defied their parents by screaming. A green river of snot ran out of its nose.

Now, there was no tongue lapping at Coyote from the sports bag. There was only this horselike woman next to her, shoveling her offspring into its car seat.

A glitch, now – this wouldn't stand. This could have jeopardized the mission. A sound began gathering deep in her throat. She forced it to stop. With supreme effort, she softened her voice to a womanly lilt.

'Excuse me.'

Becky turned with an unguarded look. Unprepared. Unaware of the most basic self defense measures. Stupid, worthless, unworthy woman.

'Hi,' Becky said.

She was infuriating. Dumb, like . . .

Red vision flared, ready to erupt. Coyote pulled back.

Becky just stood there smiling. The sound rolled in Coyote's throat. Even now Becky failed to sense danger. She had every chance in the world and she didn't take it.

She deserved everything that was coming.

Coyote shoved her hands into the gym bag and frowned with genuine frustration. 'I took off my glasses and now I can't find them. I'm blind as a bat without them, not even legal to drive. Could you help me look for them?'

Dead on the left, living on the right: Mom and I wrote down every name we could recall. Using my yearbook and the *Dog Days Update*, we cobbled together a list of two dozen kids who went on the petroglyph field trip. Then I sat out back under a red sunset and read it to Tommy Chang on the phone.

He took it stoically.

'You're getting sidetracked, Evan. Chad Reynolds OD'ed out in the desert. That's not spooky, it's sordid. And Billy D'Amato fell asleep at the wheel driving back from Lone Pine. He wasn't forced off the road and his truck didn't have some catastrophic breakdown. I know that because his wife made a huge stink, claiming it wasn't his fault. Problem was, his blood alcohol was point two-zero. He was drunk off his ass and rolled his pickup on the rim road. Period.'

'What about the rest of them?'

His voice edged uncharacteristically toward annoyance. 'Ted Horowitz. Yeah. Propeller hypnosis killed him.'

My throat tightened. 'Oh.'

'He was a deck crewman on a carrier. A plane handler, and he forgot Runway Safety 101.' His voice sharpened. 'It was a closed casket funeral.'

Propellers spin so fast that eventually you stop seeing them. My skin shrank as though flinching away from slicing blades.

I ran a hand through my hair. 'Tommy, I don't know what's going on. But something went wrong that day, and our classmates are dying because of it.'

'You want me to believe this killer is after kids who stumbled into some botched China Lake exercise, twenty years after the fact. You know how that sounds?'

'You have a better idea? Anyplace else to start hunting this guy?'

'I'm just looking for some reason why this would make any sense.'

'You're asking me to figure out the reasoning of a psychopath. I can't. But I'm telling you there's a connection.'

In the background I heard men talking. And noises, exhalations.

'Are you smoking?' I said.

'No. Sticking on a new patch.'

'You sure about that?'

'Well, no. I glommed the patches into a ball and stuck it in my cheek like a wad of chew.'

I wish he could have seen me smile, wan though that smile was. 'For dessert you could wrap a patch around a Tic Tac. Get that minty nicotine taste.'

He laughed. The sound quickly died. I gazed at the fading sky.

'Tommy, we need to warn people.'

Long silence. I think that's what they call a pregnant pause.

'Okay,' he said. 'Give me the names again.'

Relief ran across my skin. I read the list to him.

I heard him tapping his pen against his desk. 'You left a couple off.'

'Don't make me say them out loud.'

'Yeah. Bad joss.'

His pen scritched. I knew he was adding the last two names: his and mine.

'Keep your eyes open, Rocky.'

'You too.'

The oaks stood black against red twilight. Inside the house, under light warmed by the kaleidoscope kitchen, Mom was setting the table. I went in and started writing an email to Valerie Skinner. Halfway through, I paused.

Both something and somebody were eliminating my class. And Valerie was moving closer to eradication every day. How could I broach the topic without sounding ghoulish, nosy or plain lunatic? Finally, I just said it.

Twenty-six of us went on the petroglyph field trip. Eight are now dead.

Our class is dying. I think your illness might relate back to the explosion. I think that's why people are now being killed.

Call me.

I hit *Send*.

'Ev, it's food.' Mom waved me to the table.

'Great. One sec.' I took my phone into the living room and called Abbie. She took what I told her with atypical silence.

'I know this sounds off the wall,' I said.

'Yeah. But I don't think it is.'

'You okay?'

'Shit no.' She was speaking quietly. 'There's some things you should know. About Ceci. Stuff Wally saw at the office and the police confirmed.'

Her voice wavered.

'When the police found the body, they . . . God. The murderer – Evan, after he killed her, he x-rayed her. The machine was positioned next to her head, and film was missing.' Her voice broke. 'He took a snapshot of the damage he inflicted inside her skull. As a souvenir.'

My throat was dry. 'Do you own a gun?'

'No. The kids.'

'Have you thought about taking the kids and getting out of town?'

'You sound scared. That's bad.'

'I'm not scared. I'm goddamned terrified.'

My class wasn't unlucky. We were prey.

10

Becky O'Keefe hesitated, standing at the open door of the Volvo wagon with the two-year-old fussing in its car seat. Her beige stretch pants accentuated her haunches and paunchy stomach.

Coyote hid revulsion. To think of this woman thwarting the mission was intolerable, but Becky had become guarded, not buying the story of the lost glasses.

She had to buy it. The kid changed everything. The kid meant Coyote had to run the full op, here in the parking lot if necessary.

'Sorry, I know it's an imposition.' Coyote gave Becky a look of angst and expectation. 'But I have to pick up Madison from her playdate in ten minutes.'

Becky eyed the photo of the child on Coyote's T-shirt. Coyote smiled anxiously and glanced at her watch.

Becky came over to the van. 'What do the glasses look like?'

'Turquoise frames. They may have fallen down in the crack between the seats.'

Becky leaned into the van and peered around, running her hands along the edges of the folded seats.

'Unless they went in here,' Coyote said.

She pulled items from the gym bag. A sports bottle, a box of matches, a gym towel.

Becky looked over. 'Any luck?'

Her gaze caught on the neck of Coyote's shirt. The ragged tracks of the scar were visible. Coyote pulled the neck up but Becky was drawing back. In the Volvo, the child fussed. Becky turned toward him.

Coyote put a smile in her voice. 'Hey, what do you know? Here they are.'

Becky looked. Coyote raised the sports bottle and squeezed, spraying Becky in the face.

Becky blinked and spit. Coyote shot out an arm and punched her in the chest. Becky fell gasping against the back of the van.

Clutching her chest, she staggered to right herself. 'What are you—'

Coyote pressed the Taser to Becky's thigh and hit the switch.

Coyote bundled Becky into the back of the van. She was twitching and drooling, attempting to spit and blink away the liquid Coyote had sprayed on her face. It would be chill. It should sting. Ingested, it would render you blind. But the Taser strike had disrupted Becky's nervous system, and she was helpless. Her feet stuck out of the van like hooves. Coyote shoved them in.

She had to decide. Prudence said to shut the tailgate and drive the mare to an isolated spot. People were milling inside the lobby of the community center. But the mare's young was in the car seat in the Volvo wagon, kicking its legs. Soon it would cry. Transferring the child from the Volvo to the van would be risky. Time. It was all about time.

The she-horse stopped twitching as the Taser shock diminished, and began to moan. Coyote took a match from the box. They were windproof, waterproof matches, and they burned hot. She struck it against the box and held it up. Horsey looked at the flame. Its white glow reflected in her eyes.

Coyote flicked the match at Becky's face.

It landed on her cheek. The methanol from the spray bottle ignited.

Becky jerked. She shut her eyes and shook her head. Coyote grabbed her legs and pinned them. Becky flailed her hands, trying to raise them to her face, but her co-ordination remained disorganized. Coyote watched.

Methanol burns with a flame that's nearly colorless. Only the merest hint of blue rose from Becky's writhing skin, as if she were fighting a ghost. Though the alcohol fire, was charring her at 3450 degrees Fahrenheit, it seemed that a tiny aurora borealis had awakened, exquisite, inside the van.

Becky screamed.

Coyote snapped out of the reverie. If the mare inhaled flame and burned her airway, it would confuse the data for the experiment. She grabbed a real sports bottle, unscrewed the top and threw water on Becky's face. The fire died.

Becky twisted in the back of the van, her hands hovering above her face. Her eyebrows and eyelashes were burned away, her hair singed. Her eyes were swelling shut. Her skin was red and already blistered. Good. She tried to scream again but her mouth was burned, her lips slick and cherry red. The smell was intense.

Coyote pressed the Taser to her thigh. 'Hold still or you'll get another jolt. And then you'll never get out of here. Do you want to get out?'

Wheezing, Becky stilled.

Her face was mostly red, not black. The burn had gone

to the correct depth, down into the dermis, down to the hair follicles, blood vessels and nerve endings. Second degree. Much longer and the flame would have charred too deep, destroying the nerves in her face, preventing her from sensing pain. Second degree burns were always painful. Horrifyingly so.

At least they should be.

Coyote watched. Becky's face was degenerating. A few patches of skin were white, almost transparent, and she could see coagulated blood vessels beneath the surface. There was charring on her nose. Give her a few days more to live, and the nose would have to be cut away. She flailed, little sounds coming from her throat.

'Hold still,' Coyote said.

She seemed to be trying to look out the window at her car. Was she actually thinking of her offspring?

'Stay still for five seconds. That's all this will take.'

Coyote reached out with an index finger. The glove was going to blunt the sensation Becky experienced. A fingernail would have been better, but time was short. She poked at Becky's cheek, pushing her finger into a blister. Becky shrank back.

Coyote lowered her voice to the baritone register. '*Hold still, horse.*'

Becky had shriveled back against the side of the van. She could retreat no further. Coyote shoved the tip of her finger into the blister. It popped. Clearish liquid ran down Becky's cheek. Coyote pushed harder and scraped her finger down Becky's face. Becky wheezed like a dumb frightened mare but didn't move.

Coyote's lips drew back. She reached out with both hands, clawed her fingers into Becky's face and scored downward from her cheekbones to her jaw. Blisters ripped open and wept. Burned flesh sloughed onto Coyote's fingers. Becky held absolutely still.

It didn't hurt.

Coyote pulled back. She wiped the gobs of face from her fingers onto the mare's beige stretch pants.

'Get out of the van,' she said. 'Go.'

Whimpering, Becky fumbled to the edge of the tailgate and staggered out. Horses, stupid animals. Doing what they're told. Coyote grabbed her by the hair. The other hand swept out with the Ka-bar knife and slashed it across Becky's throat.

Arterial spray gushed across the parking lot. Becky's body dropped to the ground. Coyote tossed the knife away. Cheap knife, USMC spec, easily replaced.

She grabbed the gym bag. Gritting her teeth against the screaming of the kid, she walked to Becky's Volvo station wagon.

11

'Ev. Honey.' Mom's hand was gentle on my shoulder. 'It's six-thirty.'

I moaned at her and rumpled the covers up to my chin. Even without opening my eyes I could tell that it was a sunny morning. Teeth to toes, I felt as though I had been injected with glue.

Mom touched the back of her hand to my cheek. 'Still feeling puny?'

'Everything aches. My hair. My tongue. Even my thoughts.'

'Want to sleep in?'

'No, I want to catch a flight.' I sat up. 'Jesse's going to pick me up at LAX.'

My laptop rested on the pillow beside me. Forty pages of printouts spread across the covers, bedtime reading downloaded from the *Cincinnati Enquirer*, the *China Lake News*, Classmates.com, a personal site called *Sharlayne's Spirit*, and the website of Primacon Laboratories, Los Angeles.

I handed the Primacon page to Mom. 'Guess who I found.'

She flicked her index finger against the page. 'Well, what do you know. Director of Research and Development, Maureen Swayze, PhD.'

'I'm going to pay her a visit.'

'Excellent idea.'

I set my feet on the floor and my stomach swooped. I gripped the edge of the mattress, willing the wave to pass.

No good. I dashed to the bathroom.

Afterward, red-eyed, exhausted both physically and emotionally, I stood under the shower and let hot water pound the back of my neck.

Linda Garcia's obituaries were written in code. The *China Lake News* said she had died after a long struggle with illness. On the Classmates.com message board, her sister had posted about the tragedy of her illness, how 'this disease' wasn't limited to supermodels or rich teenagers, and of the speed with which it devoured her life following a series of personal heartbreaks. It had to be anorexia.

A couple of classmates replied with condolences, including Abbie. Reading them punched the oomph out of me.

The *Sharlayne's Spirit* website was even more depressing. A photo montage showed Sharlayne Jackson with her parents, with her husband Darryl and with the little kids in her school classroom. In every shot she smiled warmly, a comforting and reliable daughter, wife and teacher. Beneath the photos a caption read *Resting in the arms of our savior: Sharlayne June Jackson and Darryl Jackson, Junior*. Identical dates of death.

The site was set up to encourage donations to the Sharlayne Fund, which raised money for the NICU at Le Bonheur Children's Medical Center in Memphis. It wasn't just my classmate who died following childbirth. So did her baby.

I rolled my head, hoping for the hot water to do its work.

The *Cincinnati Enquirer* archives had several articles about the wreck that killed Marcy Yakulski and everyone else in her car. There was a blowout. The SUV ran off-road, flipped and hit an electrical transformer. The gas tank ruptured. The fire immolated Marcy, her husband, their four-year-old daughter, and her next door neighbor. The neighbor's husband later filed a lawsuit against the SUV manufacturer. How sad. How American. If I'd been him, sifting carbonized hunks of my wife from the smoking hulk of the vehicle, I might have done exactly the same. I grabbed the soap and scrubbed.

Something was hideously awry. I could feel it in the air, near and dangerous and as hypnotically insubstantial as the flying propeller that sliced Ted Horowitz to death. But there was nothing to pin it to, no common denominator to my classmates' deaths. Just the sense that this thing was spinning ever closer to me.

Mom knocked and called through the door. 'Phone. It's Valerie Skinner.'

I shut off the water. Wrangling a towel around myself, I stuck my arm out the door to grab the phone.

'Valerie.'

'Your email? Not funny.'

'It wasn't meant to be.'

Her voice was coarse. 'Plenty of people spout dumbass ideas about why I got sick, and offer me half-baked cures. But your conspiracy theory, that's a new one. And it hurts like hell that you're dumping it on me at a time like this.'

I wiped water from my eyes. 'I'm not loony, and I'm not playing emotional games with you. Call Tommy. He'll back me up.'

123

Quiet on the line.

'You there?' I said.

More quiet. 'You're serious, right? You swear to God there's something to this.'

'I swear.'

'Shit.' Her raspy voice began trembling. 'Okay. I was testing you. I had to make sure you weren't yanking my chain.'

I pulled the towel tighter around myself. 'Why would I do that?'

'Don't act like I'm paranoid. You aren't paranoid if they're really out to get you.'

Good point.

The tremor in her voice was worsening. 'I've been shitting bricks since I got back from China Lake. Thinking about all those pictures on the obituary board. And that day, remember how they took our clothes and made us shower? And afterward how they monitored us, like they knew something might happen?'

'I know.'

'What the hell is going on?'

'It seems to go back to a project at China Lake called South Star. Does that ring a bell?'

'No.'

'Maureen Swayze? Primacon Labs?'

'No.' Her voice faded. 'You think the Navy did something to us and they're trying to cover it up?'

'Not the Navy. And as far as I can tell this isn't a cover-up. I don't know why, but a serial killer has gotten it into his head that we're his prey.'

More ragged breathing. 'I'm truly fucking scared.'

My stomach tightened. 'You're not alone, are you?'

'Right now I am.'

'Why don't you call somebody to come over?'

'No.'

'Being alone doesn't sound like a good idea. How about a relative? A friend? Could—'

'There's nobody.'

The way she said it sent a pang through me. I searched for something to say, but she beat me to it. Her voice toughened.

'It's okay. The clinic's sending a van to bring me down for my appointment. I'll be surrounded by med techs.'

'Val, you're not going home by yourself after that, are you? I mean, I know chemo is awfully tough—'

'It's not cancer.'

That shut me up. 'What is it?'

'That's the jackpot question.'

'Don't you know?'

'Yeah. But—' Her voice drifted away. 'I have to go. Can I call you back?'

'Sure. Soon.'

A quiet came on her again. 'This thing in my head. It's digging holes in my brain.'

My stomach slithered. I bent over and hung my head between my knees.

'Just a little more tunneling and I'll be finished. Months, maybe,' she said. 'So how come this asshole wants to put more holes in me?'

At eight a.m. Mom and I were in her car crawling along in traffic on El Camino Real across from campus, on our way to San Francisco airport. The gold light and Mom's lime-green blouse and her silver hair felt too vivid against my eyes. I hid behind my sunglasses and sent a text message giving Jesse my flight number.

125

Mom glanced at the phone. 'He's terrific to drive down to Los Angeles and meet you.'

'Dad put the fear of God into him, about sticking close to me.'

'Ha. Jesse's one of the few people your father cannot easily intimidate.' Her smile was acerbic. 'He's a keeper, Ev.'

Guardedly I smiled back. She was making a joke at my dad's expense, but she was also giving me a nudge.

'Good to know,' I said.

'I mean it.'

'Also good to know.'

Her smirk faded. 'Honey, you don't ever need to defend your relationship to me. I knew you loved him from Day One.'

Unaccountably, I choked up. 'Thanks.'

'Sweetheart. Aw, hell.'

The ache still hit me, even now. Day One: I stood in the hospital corridor stammering to Mom on the phone. Jesse was shattered. A surgical team had spent the night piecing him back together with metal rods and bone screws. And God wasn't giving any sign that he heard my primal begging. *Undo this nightmare.*

She steered through the sluggish traffic. 'You've always been full of surprises. But you building something strong, after such an awful trauma – that didn't surprise me, it made me proud.'

My eyes were stinging. 'Now you're embarrassing me.'

'You found what counted. And it wasn't him breaking his back.'

Tears were welling. Dammit, I knew I was stressed out, but this was ridiculous. I pointed up the road at the Town and Country shopping center.

'Pull in. I need some stuff.' Like, to change the subject. 'Tissues and things.'

She flipped the turn signal. 'Yeah. And vitamins, and Saltines to settle your stomach.'

And a long nap, a pair of sexy Italian shoes, maybe two weeks at a spa in the Bahamas. She pulled up in front of the drugstore. I wiped my eyes and we got out.

Halfway along the sidewalk to the drugstore, my phone rang.

'Sweetie pie. Where you been?'

Mom saw my face. I held the phone out so she could hear Taylor's voice.

'I dropped off some photo layouts for you to look at, but I'm still working on the descriptions,' she said. 'Getting them right's a trick.'

We went into the drugstore, cruising past the check-stands. 'Yeah, that can be a tough part of writing a book. The words. What do you want?'

'The twins. Mind if I borrow them?'

'Carlos and Miguel?'

'I want to do a baseball spread. You know – get to third base, go all the way, watch the fireworks ignite.'

'No.'

'Just for a day or two. Evan, they're *twins*.'

'No.' Now I needed motion sickness pills. And mouth-wash. For my brain. 'If you want to work with them, do it after they finish the job at my place.'

Her voice turned pouty. 'Y'all can be such a stick in the mud.'

I mouthed *stick-in-the-mud* to Mom. 'It's how my parents raised me.'

She play-punched my arm and handed me a pack of tissues.

'Leave the Martinez brothers alone, Taylor. Now excuse me, but I'm heading into the Grammar Society punctuation seminar.'

'Wait, I have a proofreading question. Am I spelling this word right?'

She gave it to me letter by letter. My eyeballs rolled back so hard that they flipped all the way around.

'No. It's *ph*-antasmagoria. And it means a shifting medley of images, like in a dream. Not a fantastic orgy.'

Mom picked up a giant bottle of vitamins and we rounded the corner into No Man's land: feminine hygiene, girl-cootie central. A stockboy was shelving Tampax, staring at the floor to hide his shame. I glanced at the products on the shelf and stopped, feeling a jolt.

'Taylor, I have to go.' I hung up. 'Mom, I'll meet you at the checkstand.'

By the time she caught up I was outside. The traffic droned out on El Camino. I shoved the drugstore sack into my backpack, feeling glazed.

'You okay?' she said.

'Sure. Let's go. I don't want to miss the flight.'

She dropped me off in front of the terminal at SFO. Traffic was jumbled, cars swerving to the curb, passengers hauling luggage to the sidewalk. I fumbled in my backpack for my ticket and spilled things onto the floor of the car. I stuffed junk back in and climbed out.

Mom came around and hugged me goodbye. 'Call me tonight.'

'You bet.' She turned to go and I caught her hand. 'Thanks for what you said earlier. It means a lot.'

Her cherubic smile looked wry. 'Give my love to Jesse.' She squeezed my hand. 'Now hustle it. Security's a pig at this terminal. You're going to have to run for the gate.'

She blew me a kiss and drove away. After a moment I headed for check-in, full of free-floating anxiety. I ended up running for the gate.

The takeoff roll took longer than I expected. We bumped into the sky and arced over the city and across the coastline. The ocean glittered below. The 737 banked sharply to the south, thumping through the air. I grabbed an airsick bag and held it to my chest. The woman in the aisle seat glanced at me nervously. I felt as though I was rattling free of the plane, the day, things as I'd known them.

I glanced out the window at whitecaps on the ocean. The plane continued banking. I needed to get up but the seatbelt sign was lit. If we didn't reach cruising altitude real damn soon I was going to rip the armrests off my seat.

I crumpled the airsick bag in my hand, feeling the jet level out of the turn. I couldn't wait any longer. I unbuckled my seatbelt, grabbed my backpack and lurched to my feet. My seatmate jumped up to let me by. I banged down the aisle toward the lavatory, grabbing seatbacks for balance. A flight attendant raised her hand, about to tell me to sit down again. But she must have seen my pallor, because she stopped herself. I bumbled into the bathroom and locked the door.

I dumped out the sack from the drugstore and ripped through packaging, leaning back against the wall to steady myself. The engines roared in my ears.

I looked at myself in the mirror. 'Okay.'

Five minutes later by my watch, the flight attendant knocked on the door. 'Ma'am, are you all right in there?'

'Fine.'

Misstatement of the month. I wasn't fine. I was on

Saturn. I stared at the home test stick in my hand. The vertical blue line on the test strip was bright and definite.

I was pregnant.

12

I hiked toward the exit at LAX. The light in the terminal felt shiny. I seemed to be walking at an oblique angle to the walls and people, as if spacetime had momentarily uncoiled and spilled me sideways. A weird little melody droned in my head.

Pregnant. Holy mother of God. I had a graduate degree. Why did it take me so long to count past twenty-eight? A wild laugh skated through me, half whoop, half sob. I covered my mouth with my fist. This was inconceivable. The laugh skimmed past again, higher pitched.

I rounded the baggage carousels and saw the exit, the street outside, traffic sludging past the terminal in the Los Angeles sunshine. I saw people waiting to meet arriving passengers, watching us from behind a metal railing. I saw Jesse. He was resting an arm on the rail, tapping his thumb up and down in time to some unheard music. He was wearing his half-fingered gloves and a midnight-blue shirt and a pensive expression. He scanned the crowd, searching for me.

Joy.

Pure, abundant joy, that's what I felt. A baby. It was like having a star fall from the night sky into the palm of my hand. A blessing, a gift, God's grace. Sacred, and scary as hell.

I smiled a goofball smile and walked toward the big

unknowns. Telling him, for starters. Breathe deep, girl; get ready to blow him through the wall. I hitched my backpack higher on my shoulder and waved, striding toward him.

He spotted me and pushed off from the railing, looking puzzled. I was grinning like a clown and about to spew tears.

From my right a man approached. I saw a languorous stride and a head of cropped white hair.

'Kit.'

I stopped dead. It was my father.

He sauntered up, garment bag and computer case slung over his shoulder. His eyes were gunpowder black, restless and intent.

'Did you chase me down?' I said.

He set his things on the floor and cupped my face in his hands. 'This is not laying low.'

He looked great – tan and hale, in a rawhide sort of way. He was wearing his oldest cowboy boots and a baseball cap with the logo *USS Abraham Lincoln, CVN-72*, the carrier to which my brother's fighter squadron was attached. I felt blindsided.

'Mom told you which flight I was on.'

He kissed my forehead. 'You need to start listening to your old man.'

Grabbing his things, he swept me under his arm and pulled me toward the exit. Ahead, Jesse angled through the crowd and coasted to a stop, flummoxed.

He extended his hand. 'Phil.'

Dad shook it. 'Thought I mentioned keeping a close watch.'

'And here I am.' He peered at me quizzically. 'What is it?'

I leaned down and kissed him, running my fingers into his hair, letting my lips linger on his. He pulled back, wide-eyed.

'Tell me,' he said.

I wanted to leap on him, whisper it in his ear and have him hold me and tell me it was good, we were going to be fine. I was petrified and tongue-tied and my father was right there.

My mouth hovered close to his. 'Soon.'

Dad cleared his throat. When I straightened, he pressed me toward the door, boots knocking on the tile, and spoke to Jesse over his shoulder.

'You parked nearby?'

Jesse turned and pushed to catch up. 'Across the street.'

The automatic door opened and we headed outside into the sun. I said, 'Why the urgency?'

Dad adjusted his *Abraham Lincoln* cap. 'Things have changed.'

'What is it?'

He was holding me alarmingly tight. 'Darlin', I'm sorry. He killed Becky O'Keefe last night.'

The light went white and began to hum, drowning out the sound of traffic. Jesse's voice barely cut through the noise.

'That's not all. He stole her car, with her toddler inside. The little boy's still missing.'

We crossed the street to the parking garage, Dad gripping me against the sunlight and noise.

'Becky's husband was on the news, making a plea for the kidnapper to return the boy.' He shook his head. 'Godawful thing. It's your worst nightmare.'

'How did she die?' I said.

133

Dad didn't answer. I looked at Jesse.

'Her throat was cut,' he said.

The light hurt my eyes. 'Was she tortured?'

'I don't know.'

He was grim. Special Agent Heaney's statement came back to me: Coyote's aim was to inflict maximum pain on his victims before killing them. The humming in my head intensified.

'Ryan's only two years old,' I said.

The truck was parked near the entrance to the garage. Jesse unlocked it with the remote, the squelch echoing off the walls.

He touched my arm. 'I don't know that there's much chance we can help.'

'Not much chance is better than no chance. And every minute that goes by . . .'

He nodded. 'Right. Let's roll.'

He got in, popped the wheels off the chair and put them in the back seat. Normally he tossed the frame behind him as well, but add me and luggage back there and the fit got tight. He handed me a bungee cord. I lugged the frame into the truck's cargo bed and lashed it down. Dad watched as if we were performing brain surgery with knitting needles.

'You have this down to an art.'

He looked disconcerted and I couldn't spare any emotional energy to worry about it. 'Yeah. You ride shotgun.'

Jesse fired up the engine. I hopped in the back seat, Dad climbed in front and Jesse pulled out, spinning the wheel.

Dad buckled his seatbelt. 'Did you bring a weapon?'

'Repeat that when I pull up in front of the security

134

camera, please. Louder.' Sensing my father's glare, he nodded at the glove compartment. 'Locked in there.'

'Can you get much speed out of this truck?'

'Enough.'

I fought down a hoot. He could get speed out of a turnip. He glanced at me in the rearview mirror.

'Tell me?' he said.

Highwire trepidation pulsed through me again. I put my hand on his shoulder and shook my head. His mouth scrunched to one side. He paid and pulled into traffic.

'What are we going to get when we meet Maureen Swayze?' he said.

I got the Primacon Laboratories blurb from my backpack. 'A heavy hitter. Degrees in Electrical Engineering and Molecular Biophysics from Columbia. Doctorate from MIT. Worked in the pharmaceutical industry before spending a decade in government research. Her publications include *Nonlinear Protein Dynamics* and *Neurological Dysfunction: the Mathematics of the Random Walk.*'

He eyed me in the rearview mirror at that one.

'Chemistry term, I think.' I leaned toward Dad. 'She doesn't sound like a fuel researcher to me.'

'She wasn't. She was Director of Special Projects, and her office covered a number of operations.'

I nodded. 'I remember Swayze being at the high school after my class came back from Renegade Canyon. Red hair and a loud voice.'

'Your mom told me.'

'She remembers Swayze too. Says she's a cold-faced bitch.'

He turned. The surprise on his face was genuine. 'Your mother's a woman of strong opinions. Often black and white.'

'Is she right?'

'Maureen's a bulldozer and a pill, but that's as far as I'll go. Are you feeling all right?'

Jesse glanced in the mirror. 'Yeah, your eyes are shiny and you look kind of dazed. Like you've been whacked with a two-by-four.'

No, it was a different kind of wood.

A snerking sound came out of my throat, equal parts shriek and laugh. 'You aren't kidding. Hard enough to hit a home run.'

They both turned and looked at me.

I pressed a fist against my mouth and waited for my nerves to crawl back inside my skin. Outside, billboards and palm trees and hotels and airfreight offices and nudie bars blared past in the unbecoming sunshine. Cars switched lanes at speed, darting like blowflies. Jesse followed another pickup through a hole in traffic, jinking across two lanes to beat a light.

I forced my voice to a normal register. 'Will Swayze try to stonewall us?'

Dad frowned. 'She was always on the up-and-up. She may have her own agenda, but I have to think she'll tell us what she can.'

'There's a little boy on the line now. She'd damn well better.'

Two years old. Taken by a stranger whose hands were wet with Becky's blood. My God.

'Maureen isn't the issue, though. South Star is,' Dad said.

'And now you going to tell us about that?'

'Non-classified elements.' He poked up the brim of his hat with his index finger. 'South Star's mission was Peak Soldier Performance. Researching ways to keep soldiers

136

operating at top physical and mental levels under extreme conditions.'

'How?'

'Revving them up. Strengthening the immune system, increasing endurance and reducing the amount of sleep they need. Raising their pain threshold so they could keep going when they're wounded.'

Jesse swung up the onramp onto the 405 and accelerated into the freeway traffic. 'So it was about creating *über*-soldiers.'

'It was about keeping our men and women alive on the battlefield. When you get sleep-deprived, you make mistakes and people can die. But if you eliminate the need for sleep, you can operate twenty-four/seven without losing your edge. You can send fewer soldiers into battle and risk fewer lives.'

'Swayze was engineering insomnia,' Jesse said.

'Essentially.'

'And studying ways to increase pain tolerance?'

He changed lanes. It was archetypal Los Angeles traffic: huge SUVs and BMWs and low riders jockeying for primacy. Signs said 'Slower traffic keep right' but nobody obeyed, because no Angeleno will concede that another driver has a faster car than his. Ever.

'Not pain tolerance,' Dad said, 'pain threshold. Stopping soldiers from perceiving pain to begin with.'

'That's called morphine,' Jesse said.

'You bet. Morphine was a terrific painkiller for riflemen at Gettysburg, and it's terrific today, and it leaves you with a soldier who's incoherent and incapacitated. But say you could eliminate the sensation of pain while leaving soldiers clear-headed. What if you could inoculate people against pain beforehand, so soldiers could continue fighting when they're wounded?'

'South Star was developing a pain vaccine?' I said.

'Yes.'

Jesse shook his head. 'Redesigning soldiers to be sleepless and numb. Unbelievable.'

'That's a cheap crack,' Dad said.

'No, it's just my experience that those things don't tend to be so great.'

'It may sound cruel, keeping soldiers on the battlefield when they're wounded,' Dad said. 'But when you're torn up with shrapnel and fifty miles from a medic, having your comrades evacuate you isn't compassionate. It's dangerous and it jeopardizes the mission. If wounded men can defend themselves and help the unit, it's better all around.'

'Was this vaccine chemical, psychological, what?' I said.

'That was need-to-know. Best guess – neurobiological techniques, cognitive-behavioral psychology, cell regulation . . .' He shrugged. 'But I have to presume that whatever South Star was investigating, something went wrong. Very, very wrong.'

Jesse wrung his hand on the wheel. 'And instead of a supersoldier, it created a serial killer?'

'Or worse. Both.'

I leaned forward. 'I spoke to Valerie Skinner this morning. She doesn't have cancer. She says something's digging tunnels in her brain.'

Jesse's shoulders tightened. 'Shit.'

Dad stared at traffic. His face was weatherbeaten and his eyes remote.

'You don't look surprised,' I said.

'I've checked into why some of your classmates have died, and Valerie fits a pattern.'

'Whatever this thing is, it causes neurological malfunction, doesn't it?' I said.

He gave me a dark look. 'Hold on. This is hard to hear.'

Sliding the keycard into the door, Coyote entered the hotel room and stopped still. Anxiety pulsed beneath his skin. He drew sensory data: sights, sounds, smells. The suitcase stood in the corner, precisely parallel to the edge of the window. The filament ran from the handle of the weapons case to the leg of the desk chair. The chocolates rested on the open page of the journal, forming the points of a right triangle. Nobody had touched them. Touch chocolate, the scent gets on the fingers and travels around the room with you. But nothing had been disturbed.

He closed the door, booted the laptop, turned on the shower and stripped naked. Time was short. Unease was a metallic taste in his mouth.

The room was secure. But the mission was not.

He had chucked Soccer Mom halfway back to Hollywood, throwing her wig and clothing into a dumpster. He had sloughed off her anima and returned to himself. He had, per protocol, stopped at an Internet café to check his email and the news feeds before returning to base. When he did, he discovered that several tripwires had been set off.

Steam filled the bathroom. He stepped into the shower and the hot water began rinsing away the stench of the she-horse. Not cooked flesh, but the true stench of Becky O'Keefe, the odor of corpulence, of milk and meat and moistness.

The email was bad, the phone call worse. His contacts had given him trigger phrases. South Star. Explosion. Details of his project were beginning to leak out –

backstory, as they called it in Hollywood. Granted, his mission had become high-profile thanks to the news jackals. But the trigger phrases should not have seeped into the knowledge stream.

Someone knew too much.

He soaped up and scrubbed. Removing trace evidence from his body was crucial. He had to avoid arrest: arrest would derail the project. However, if it came to that, trace would be irrelevant. If the mission failed, he would suicide himself and take his captors with him. He ran the soap over his hair, lathering his scalp. The stench of the horse ran down the drain.

Someone knew too much and was talking about it. There was a leak. He needed to find it and plug it.

He slid the soap over his body, suppressing the urge to linger. Things were unfinished. The tripwires had prevented him from completing his work. The child remained.

He had much to do. He ran through the list in his head. Becky's car? Nobody was going to find it yet. He had given himself sufficient time.

The data? He would upload and cross-reference as soon as he finished washing.

The mother? The shower needled his chest and abdomen. He ran the soap across the raised tracks of the scar. And in a circle over his belly, feeling flat smooth skin. The mother, Becky the Mare, was drained of blood and stiff with rigor. She was gone.

The child?

Coyote circled the soap around his belly again and again. Steam cocooned him. The soap dropped from his slippery fingers. His hand continued circling his navel.

Cold water blurted through the showerhead. Coyote

blinked. Feeling the sensation of skin rubbing skin, he looked down. His hand was circling his umbilicus. His fingertips were wrinkled. How long had he been here?

He slammed the showerhead sideways and shut off the water. He had things to take care of. Wrapping a towel around his waist, he stalked out to the bedroom, running once more through his list.

The car. The data. The mother.

The mother, the mother, something went with the mother.

No – the mother went. The mother was gone. That was the truth of the world. Hollywood, outside his window, was where his mother had gone. *Stay here, K. I'll be back tonight.* In that hot bright apartment near the hills. But she never came back. He waited, and he burrowed into a corner of the apartment in a nest made of her clothes, until the building super found him and called Social Services. But her going was her gift to him. It forced him to learn how to struggle and fight. Need built strength. Lack built strength. He had been more than ready for boot camp, for everything the Army threw at him, for China Lake and the agencies he later served.

And now he was on his own again. Disavowed.

He rubbed the scar and picked up his amulet from the desk. The two were halves of a whole. The scar was born from the shrapnel in the amulet, as Coyote was born from South Star.

He felt a need growing, a thirst to latch on and nourish himself. A sound rose from deep in his throat.

He had a list, a schedule, but he was going to have to adjust it. He had to find the source of the leak. And he knew where to start looking.

He gazed out the window at the crawling gleam of Los

Angeles. The craving to draw sustenance intensified; the desire to eat and eat and nourish himself until he was gorged. He threw the towel in the corner. Tossing the suitcase on the bed, he began to dress.

The car. The data. The mother.

And now, a leak. He had to take steps.

He pulled on a T-shirt and khakis, a button-down shirt and baseball cap. Mr Hollywood Nebbish would serve today.

He was forgetting something. He could taste it on the air. Something about a child. A child seeking closeness to the mother. Becky's child? He paused. The thought eluded him. Slamming the suitcase, he turned to go.

13

The blue-green Santa Monica mountains cut the horizon ahead. Jesse closed on a gasoline tanker, doing eighty-five. Dad's voice was flat.

'Three deaths are particularly suspicious. Phoebe Chadwick, Linda Garcia and Shannon Gruber. In order: alcohol, anorexia and pneumonia. All of them atypical cases.'

'Define atypical,' I said.

'Phoebe was a party girl who stumbled off a curb during spring break and got hit by a bus. She'd had a couple of drinks, but according to the toxicology report she wasn't drunk. Turns out she'd been having tremors, her reflexes had gone haywire and she was slurring her speech. She also thought light sockets could talk and that Katie Couric was stalking her.'

'Yow.'

Jesse flipped a look in his wing mirror and yanked the pickup into the fast lane to pass the tanker.

'Wilshire exit's only half a mile ahead,' I said.

'I see it. You can stop clawing my shoulder.'

He swung the truck back across four lanes of traffic, swerved onto the offramp and braked sharply around the corner onto Wilshire Boulevard.

Dad braced himself against his door. 'And Linda Garcia, her anorexia came on like a fever and destroyed her in the space of months. Her father says it burned her from the inside out. By the time he carried her into the hospital she weighed sixty-nine pounds.'

'Damn.' I tried not to picture that. 'And Shannon? Her obit reads pneumonia following a long illness, and Mom said aggressive breast cancer ran in her family.'

'It wasn't cancer. They don't know what it was.'

'How—'

He turned sharply. 'I've spoken to all their parents in the past thirty-six hours. People I served with, worked side by side with, every one of whom has buried a child.'

My gaze broke from his.

Jesse beat the light at Sepulveda and we passed the Federal Building, towering on its lonely plot like a pillar of salt. Dad's voice dropped back to flat calm.

'Shannon's life turned into one solid panic attack. Her folks found her hiding in a closet wrapped in wet towels because she was terrified of dust mites. They nearly had her committed, until a psychiatrist shot her full of Thorazine and strapped her down so they could MRI her. They found massive abnormalities in her thalamus.'

'A brain tumor?' Jesse said.

'Growths and degeneration. That part of her brain just . . .' He raised his hands, gesturing hopelessness. 'Disintegrated.'

'Jesus.'

We rolled through Westwood Village. Jesse glanced around. This was his old stomping ground, from his years at UCLA Law School. Off to the left I glimpsed the Medical Center through the semi-bohemian mishmash of falafel stands and movie theaters and crapola vendors that edged the campus. Jesse shifted his shoulders.

'Pain is nothing but a perception in the brain,' he said.

144

'Eliminate the perception and you eliminate the pain. You can do that by disconnecting part of the body from the central nervous system, or you can do it by altering brain chemistry.' His voice was dry as sand. 'Figure a vaccine would go for the second option.'

I thought of Valerie's unsteadiness, memory problems and paranoia. And of Ceci Lezak being given a postmortem skull x-ray in Wally's dentist's chair.

'Who else, Dad?'

'Some deaths are outside the pattern. A couple of kids, pretty clear their deaths were alcohol- or drug-related.'

'Chad Reynolds dying of exposure out in the desert?'

He nodded. 'Animals got to his body, but there was enough of him left for the coroner to find barbiturates in his system. And Billy D'Amato – the crash site reeked of whiskey.'

'Ted Horowitz?'

He shook his head. 'Pure tragedy, walking headfirst into that propeller.'

Jesse hadn't heard about that. His grip on the throttle wavered. 'Christ.'

'I know the CAG on the *Nimitz* – the officer responsible for carrier air operations. They investigated that accident six ways from Sunday. Teddy was a popular crewman and folks were looking for any way to explain what happened without blaming him. But he plain blew it.'

My head began aching again. The day was flashy. Cars were streaks of shine passing on Wilshire and trees waved dollar-green in the breeze. Around us office towers and penthouse apartments appeared. The boulevard curved, rolling like a river between rising cliffs.

'Then there's Dana West,' Dad said.

'The hospital fire?'

'It was arson.'

'Holy hell. How do you know that?'

'I called in a favor and—'

His cellphone rang. He excused himself and answered, speaking tersely and taking out a pen to write something on the back of an envelope.

My stomach was roiling. I pressed a hand to my belly. Nothing but a spark, and this little thing was already igniting my life physically and spiritually. Jesse pulled into the right lane. His hair fell over his collar. I wanted to push it aside and kiss him behind the ear and tell him the news before I burst into tears or flames. He stopped for a red light.

I doublechecked the address of Primacon Labs. 'Two more blocks.'

Dad hung up.

Jesse turned to him. 'If Dana West was murdered, then—'

'Hold that thought.'

He opened his door, jumped out and dodged away, weaving between cars and dashing across the intersection.

I gaped. 'What's he doing?'

'Damn.' Jesse smacked his hand against the steering wheel. 'He wants to talk to Swayze alone.'

And he thought that he could shortcircuit us because I would have to stay with Jesse to get his hardware from the back of the pickup. I jumped out.

Jesse pointed up the street. 'Forget it. Catch him.'

'No way.'

I fumbled with the bungee cords that lashed the wheel-chair frame to the truck. Dad was halfway up the next block. The light turned green and traffic began moving.

Jesse leaned out the window. 'Leave it. Go.'

Cars streamed past me. Horns blared. I yanked the frame free and chucked it into the cab. A Navigator rumbled by and the driver shouted 'Moron!'

I slammed the door. 'Meet me at Swayze's office.'

I ran after my father, across the intersection and down the street.

Argent Tower was twenty-five stories of smoked glass, shaped like a Celtic cross. In the sparkling plaza out front, purple sage and white jasmine gushed around an extravagant fountain. Above the entrance a banner advertised 200,000 square feet of office space still available. I ran down the sidewalk, seeing my father cross the plaza toward the entrance. My mouth was dry. How could he pull such a rude stunt?

By the time I shoved my way through the revolving door into the lobby, I was winded. I looked around. At the center of the building soared a spectacular atrium. Two mezzanine levels circled the lobby and for a dozen floors above that, walkways ran around the overlook. The elevators had Plexiglas windows from which to enjoy the view. This building was meant to be admired, and it was apparently brand new. On a tall scaffold near the entrance, two painters were lettering the name of a yet-to-open deli. And, given the banner outside begging for tenants, it was nearly vacant.

The gray man behind the front desk roused himself from his boredom and leaned forward in his chair. 'Help you?'

'Sorry. I'm running late. Evan Delaney to see Dr Swayze at Primacon.'

He had a face like a toad. He jotted on a clipboard and pushed it across the desk at me. 'Sign here.'

I scribbled my name on the sign-in sheet. He noted the time and lackadaisically tore off a square of paper that he affixed to a clip. 'Hand this back in when you leave.'

I clipped it on. 'Which floor?'

'Eight. Take the elevator on the far side of the lobby. The one behind my desk goes to the parking garage, and—'

'Thanks.' I strode away around the corner and saw elevator doors closing. 'Hold that.'

A hand stopped the door. I ducked in, wiping sweat from my forehead.

'Sorry I'm late. Traffic was horrendous.'

My father looked at me edgeways, pursed his mouth and let out a little *heh*. The doors closed and the elevator rose. The view soared up the atrium.

'Why don't you want me along?' I said. 'And don't tell me this is about having a security clearance.'

'I'll get more information out of Maureen on my own.'

'Information you'll filter as you see fit?'

'Are you questioning my motives?'

I turned to him. 'That was a dirty trick you pulled.'

The elevator stopped on Three and the doors opened. Nobody was there.

He pushed the Close button. 'Give Jesse some credit.'

'Excuse me?'

'He's smart as all get out, and he has guts. More than I ever imagined when I first met him.'

The elevator stopped on Four. Again it opened to an empty lobby. The doors half-closed, opened again, and finally crept shut. Dad punched Eight several times.

'Now, do you think someone so intelligent and so tough expects me to make allowances for him at a time like this? I don't.' He watched the numbers go up. 'So take it on the chin, and stop feeling embarrassed for him. This is deadly serious stuff.'

My face felt hot. Little muttering sounds popped around my mouth.

He frowned. 'You are madder than a hornet. Cool down.' His expression softened. 'I know you feel for Jesse. We all do.'

In his eyes I saw a sadness that nearly made me scream. Don't pity him. Don't you dare. I clenched my hands.

'Fine, Dad. But I'm coming with you.'

His mouth twitched, and he acquiesced. He watched the elevator rise through the atrium, eyes narrow, as though scanning the horizon for Comanches.

'Dana West was an Air Force nurse. Did you know that?'

'No.'

'She was posted to Blackfoot Depot when she died.'

'Where's that?'

'An alkali flat smack in the middle of Wyoming. It's a podunk place, and that hospital was barely more than a clinic. A gas explosion in the operating theater blew up half the structure. Fire took the rest of it.'

'Jesus. How do you know it was arson?'

The elevator lurched to a stop, bouncing on its cables. The doors cracked open on an unoccupied level: bare concrete and conduit hanging from the ceiling. We were two feet higher than the floor outside. We stared.

'This building has a few kinks that need working out,' I said.

Dad jabbed buttons. The doors pottered closed. We held our breath and felt the car move. When he spoke again, his voice was muted.

'Surgical fires are deadly. Light up a laser or electro-cautery tool around enriched O_2 and the results can be devastating. And generally it's the patient who gets burned.'

'So what happened to Dana?'

'Dana *was* the patient.'

The door thunked open. A woman's voice cut through the dire silence.

'Phil Delaney. Talk about a bolt from the blue.'

There in the sleek foyer of Primacon Laboratories, arms akimbo, knowing smile on her face, stood Dr Maureen Swayze. And she didn't look surprised. She looked like a woman who had long expected Phil Delaney to walk through the door.

He removed his hat. 'Sway.'

He smiled at her. His hand was out. She shook it briskly.

He gestured to me. 'My daughter Evan.'

She lifted her chin to peer at me through rimless glasses. From her squint, I might have been an intriguing retrovirus.

'You have that Delaney glint in your eye. Phil called it poise. Others labeled it mulishness.' She smirked at him. 'Did she inherit your taste for Jack Daniels and Patsy Cline?'

I almost squirmed. 'Yes, actually.'

'"Sweet Dreams" on the jukebox?'

'I'm more the "Crazy" kind.'

She laughed, brisk and clipped: a single *ha*.

Her hair was the color of tin mixed with copper. Younger, she had been one of those luxuriant redheads who looked at home striding into a wild headwind. Now, with a pencil jammed into her untidy ponytail and her blouse coming untucked from her skirt, she looked overworked and wonkish. The squint, I guessed, came from thirty years spent frowning into the lens of a microscope.

'It's China Lake, isn't it?' she said.

'Yes,' Dad said. 'Only now, it's more than that.'

'I heard on the news. Come with me.'

She gave the receptionist our names. As the girl jotted them down, Swayze swiped a passcard along a security strip by double doors and took us down a hall past offices and cubicles. The carpet was plush, the wallpaper soothing. Primacon looked busy. Purposeful men in shirt-sleeves were working at computers or conferring intensely, drawing diagrams of molecules on whiteboards.

'Quite a set-up,' Dad said. 'What's the focus of your research?'

'Enzyme de-aggregation of amyloid plaques as an approach to Parkinson's and Alzheimer's.'

She veered into an office. Papers were piled on chairs and shelves and a spider plant was dead on a credenza. On the bookshelf, a set of dogtags hung from a framed photo of a young Swayze arm in arm with an Army Ranger. She was in jeans and a tank top, wearing a beret. Wearing it like a commando, not a mademoiselle. I bet they spent evenings spitting bullets into the bedroom wall for fun.

Dad slapped his hat against his thigh. 'Word on the grapevine, these murders might have been committed by someone who was connected to the base back when you were working there.'

She cleared seats for us, dumping things on the floor. 'So why is it you're here, instead of the police?'

'The victims are members of Evan's high school class.'

She plopped down in her desk chair. 'Explaining why you dropped out of the sky like the Airborne, with offspring in tow. You think I can give you a name?'

'We're hoping.'

She took off her glasses, rubbed her nose where they'd left red marks and stared at my father. 'You're scared.'

'Damn right.'

'What information can you give me, beyond what I hear on TV?'

I sat down. 'I have a source who's told me the killer was attached to Project South Star.'

Her eyebrows went up. 'Goodness. How do you come to have sources who want to break security on a classified project?'

'They've told me the killer is known as Coyote.'

She drummed her fingers on the desk. 'And let me guess. Your source suggested that this killer was one of South Star's robo-grunts.'

'Excuse me?'

She glanced at Dad. 'What does she know?'

'What's in the open literature. Sway, you—'

'So this source played it up.' She peered down the length of her nose at me. 'Reducing soldiers' need for food and sleep on the battlefield? Keeping them from collapsing from pain? I was turning them into drones. Machines who kill without reason or remorse. Robo-grunts. Right?'

'Wrong,' I said. 'I have no complaint with giving our forces a physical edge on the battlefield.'

Dad gave her a conciliatory smile. 'Sway, we aren't here to argue.'

'She is.' She had heat in her voice. 'She thinks my project is responsible for killing her friends. Don't deny it.'

I didn't. I couldn't. I generally can't lie worth crap.

'I don't know how much propaganda you've swallowed,

but preventing pain and exhaustion in warfighters is not inhumane. It's life-saving.'

She reached for the dogtags that hung on the picture frame and tossed them on the desk in front of me.

'Those belonged to my husband Sam. When his unit was ambushed, he took an RPG blast to the gut. The enemy was closing in and he was in too much agony to aim his weapon, and his unit refused to leave him. So to keep his men from dying there defending him, he put the barrel of his rifle to his own head.'

The steel in her eyes discomfited me. I looked at the photo of the smiling Ranger. There was pride on his face, perhaps at having Maureen Swayze at his side.

'Did I want to keep that from happening to others? You bet. Preventing pain is a noble goal. So stop acting like you need to hold your nose around me.'

She returned the dogtags to the edge of the picture frame.

'Don't misunderstand,' she said. 'My work at China Lake was a martial enterprise and I knew it going in. The brain is the ultimate weapons platform.'

'Dr Swayze, that's what I'm afraid of. Some of my classmates have died from neurological problems.'

'And you think it relates back to that explosion near Renegade Canyon?' She eyed me. 'Yes, I remember it. You ended up shuddering on the floor in the gymnasium hallway. But it's not possible.'

'How can you be sure?'

'We monitored your health. There were no effects. Not even smoke inhalation.'

'What if this thing had a long incubation period?'

She held up a hand. 'There is no "thing". It's not possible. That's all I can say.'

I gestured at Dad, frustrated. 'Could you say more to him, if I wasn't here?'

Her phone rang. She answered, spoke two clipped sentences and hung up. 'Need to check on something in the lab. Come along, I'll give you the tour.'

Dad and I followed her out of the office and down the hall. I felt as though I was being sucked along behind a twister. She absentmindedly tucked her shirt back inside her skirt, nodding at people we passed.

'After I left China Lake, my research became focused on neurodegenerative disease.' She waved at the offices around her. 'Parkinson's treatments, reversing Alzheimer's by strengthening the body's defense mechanisms against rogue protein aggregations that can destroy the brain – the potential is tremendous. Absolutely mind-blowing. And we're on the bleeding edge of development.'

We passed a lab. I saw beakers and computers and two men scribbling equations on a whiteboard.

She eyed me, rimless lenses shining. 'I will not discuss my classified research with you. But I will say that if the explosion that day caused your class any lasting harm I will eat this laboratory piece by piece, down to the last petri dish.'

'If it comes to that, I'll buy the ketchup,' I said.

She gave a dry laugh. 'Fine. Now, brass tacks. You think somebody from China Lake has gone off the deep end. That was twenty years ago, so give me a prompt.'

Dad said, 'A young man, teens or early twenties. Probably white.'

'Neat. Compulsive. Mission-oriented,' I said.

She shook her head. 'I need more.'

'An unemotional loner. Maybe nocturnal,' I said.

She slowed and brought her thumb up to her lips.

'Someone comes to mind?' I said.

'I don't know.'

We reached a heavy door. She pushed it open and went through into a laboratory. Dad followed. I stood rooted in the hallway.

Dad turned, curious. 'Coming?'

On the door was a radiation hazard sign.

'I'm—'

Black and yellow and big as anything: WARNING.

'Sorry, I'm not feeling well.' I ran the back of my hand across my forehead. 'Could you point me toward the bathroom?'

Perplexity crossed both their faces. Swayze pointed around the corner.

'Just off the lobby. You don't need a swipecard to get out. Shall I go with you? Are you okay?'

I was backing away. 'Yeah, it's just . . .'

Dad stepped toward me. I shook my head.

'Get a name.' Turning, I rushed down the hall.

Damn. I needed air. I needed confirmation, absolutely, that I was actually pregnant. I needed to get out of this nightmare. It wasn't just my classmates at risk now, or me. It might be my child. Jesse's child. Oh, my God.

I shoved open the door to the lobby. The corporate wallpaper felt grating. The potted plants looked screechy. Two visitors milled in front of the receptionist's desk, waiting for her to get off the phone. I took four steps toward the women's room and heard what the receptionist was saying.

'Dr Swayze, Archie from security just called. A man's downstairs at the desk asking to come up and see you, third guy in a row, so Archie wants to doublecheck,' she said. 'This one's in a wheelchair.'

155

I reversed course. 'Tell Dr Swayze the guy down-stairs . . .'

The two men milling in front of the desk turned in unison. They filled out their suits extraordinarily well. One was Caucasian, late forties, with a sleek haircut and a scar that ran through his eyebrow. His gaze was weight-less. The second was African American, mid-thirties, with a shaved head and a goatee. They should have struck me as sales reps, men who spent off hours buffing up in the gym. But that's not how they carried themselves.

It was their hands. They kept them free at their sides, the way a martial artist does walking down a dark alley, or a cop does when it nears time to reach for a weapon. A noise ticked inside my head. *Federal government.* The white man was looking at my visitor's badge, reading my name.

They weren't wearing visitors' badges.

The receptionist said, 'Hang on, Dr Swayze,' and put her hand over the receiver to peer at me. 'Yes?'

The black man looked at his watch. 'We'll stop back later.'

Without another glance they strolled to the elevator.

The receptionist said, 'Miss?'

They weren't FBI. If they'd been with the Bureau, they would have asked me what I was doing here.

I walked toward them. 'Excuse me.'

They ignored me. The elevator chimed.

'Sir? Can you wait a minute?'

The doors opened and the men got in. 'Sir. Hey.' Scar pushed the button. 'Wait.' The black man stared at me and the doors slurred closed.

I turned to the receptionist. 'What did those guys want?'

'To join a meeting. They looked at my sign-in sheet to see who else was here for it.'

I crossed back to her desk. My skin prickled. The sign-in sheet had only three names: Swayze's, Dad's and mine.

'Call security back,' I said. 'Ask Archie who they were.'

'What's wrong?'

'Something's funny. They didn't have visitors' badges. Do it.'

She phoned the lobby. After a moment her expression sharpened. She eyed me.

'They did not check in with the desk. Archie doesn't like that.' Into the phone she said, 'Yeah, they're coming down.'

I gazed at the elevator. My palms were sweating. 'Stairs?'

Still on the phone, she pointed to the right.

'Have Archie tell my boyfriend to stay in the lobby and watch for these guys.'

I took off at a run.

Careering down the stairs, I heard my shoes pound on the concrete and my breathing echo off the walls. The elevators were erratic, so maybe I could beat the two men to the lobby. Gravity and adrenaline were working for me.

They were feds, I felt it like a rash. Why did they U-turn when I walked up?

I reached Three and kept going, feeling winded. It was no good. Even with fickle elevators I wouldn't beat them downstairs. When I hit M2, I slammed the bar on the fire door and bolted out of the stairwell onto the upper mezzanine.

A walkway ran around the floor. The lobby echoed below me and the atrium soared above. To my right, stairs descended to the lower mezzanine, which curved around to a broad staircase down to the lobby.

I ran to the railing and looked down. The painters were on the scaffold near the entrance. Archie was hoofing it toward this bank of elevators, hitching up his droopy gray trousers. He struck me as watchful but only intermittently alert, and I doubted that two federal agents had found it tough to slip past him. Jesse was on the far side of the lobby, waiting at the second bank of elevators.

'Blackburn.'

My voice echoed in the atrium. I waved and he spotted me. He raised his hands, gesturing *What the hell?*

Still leaning over the rail, I looked up. Here came the elevator. I caught the scenic view of two blue suits aboard. White face, black face. Salt'n'Pepa.

What the hell indeed? What did I plan to do – confront them?

Find out why they wanted to check up on Maureen Swayze and why they'd taken note of my name, that's what. I backed away from the rail and hit the elevator call button. The feds and I could ride down to the lobby together. Two floors wouldn't give me much time. But they apparently disliked conversation, so I could skip the pleasantries and boot them straight in the crotch.

Probably just verbally. I put myself in front of the doors. The elevator thrummed, approaching.

And kept going, right on past.

Damn. I ran back to the railing. One floor below, the bell went *ding*. The elevator stopped and the suits got out.

I ran for the stairs and headed down. Ahead, Salt'n'Pepa sauntered along the lower mezzanine toward the broad staircase that curved down to the lobby. Jesse called my name and I pointed at them.

I broke into a jog. 'Agent Mulder. Your fly is open.'

Pepa turned, bald head shining like a bowling ball. He spoke to Salt and they picked up their pace.

'Come back and join the meeting,' I said. 'We're serving donuts. With sprinkles.'

Below us a group of people came across the lobby, chatting loudly. Jesse was behind them, looking at me with confusion. Salt'n'Pepa reached the staircase and began jogging down, taking the stairs two at a time. I was about to do the same when I saw a janitor's sign: Caution, wet floor. Abruptly I pictured myself tumbling like Scarlett O'Hara down her mansion stairs and losing the baby. Grabbing the rail, I walked down carefully, placing each step so as not to slip.

Below us Archie came across the lobby at a trot, hitching his trousers. 'Hey, fellas. Don't go nowhere.'

People began filing through the revolving door out to the plaza. Salt'n'Pepa fell in with them. I reached the bottom of the stairs, hearing Jesse call my name, just as they pushed through the door and strode away surrounded by the crowd.

I hit the revolving door at the same moment as a couple of people coming in from the plaza. They blocked my view and I pushed around the door leaning sideways, trying not to lose the agents in the pedestrian crowd. I sensed the man on the opposite side of the door focusing on me. I glanced across. His face was turned away. I saw the back of a baseball cap on a blond head.

The sun flashed off the glass in the door and I rushed outside into heat and traffic noise. Where were the feds?

Wrong. Something was . . .

I turned and looked back at the building. The revolving

door was still spinning. The blond man in the baseball cap was walking into the lobby, his back to me.

I felt a disconnect.

He had been staring at me. I felt the remains of his gaze like a low-grade electrical buzz. A strange gaze, an old gaze, one that felt as though it had first fallen on me a long time ago.

Sound seemed to vanish. I saw the plate-glass windows reflecting the flash of passing cars. The revolving door spinning to a stop. The painters on the scaffold, lowering cans with a pulley. The stranger walking away, heading straight toward Jesse, who was angling for a side door.

Jesse frowned. Through the glass he mouthed, 'Ev?'

I blinked and put my hand to my forehead. The stranger walked past him. I pointed.

Jesse turned to watch him go. Gave me another glance, as if to say, You want me to do this, right? He called to the man. The stranger kept walking.

Jesse headed after him. Near the scaffold he came up behind the stranger, reached out and put a hand on his arm. The man stutter-stepped.

Mistake. I'd just made a mistake. Sound boomed back, cacophonous. I ran toward the revolving door.

The stranger yanked his arm away from Jesse. He darted toward the pulley, grabbed the paint can and swung it straight at Jesse's head.

'Oh, God.' I shoved through the door into the lobby.

Jesse ducked. The paint can flew past him and smashed into the plate-glass window. With a horrid *crack*, the glass spidered white. Red paint gushed over it like a wound.

A painter shouted 'Shit!'

The stranger grabbed Jesse by the arms and shoved.

He sailed backward and crashed into the scaffold. The painters lurched.

'Christ!'

'Hell—'

One fell, grabbing for purchase, and paint cans and rollers and trays crashed down. The painter caught the platform on his way down and grabbed hold, swinging below it, swearing wildly. Scarlet light rippled over him from the fractured window. Archie came running, and a uniformed security guard, and me. The glass wept paint. Below the scaffold debris littered the marble.

In the middle of it Jesse sat frozen, pressing the heels of his hands against the sides of his head, eyes squeezed shut. He was splattered red.

I ran up to him. 'Babe.'

He was panting for breath, fighting for air like a stutterer grasping for words.

The uniformed guard stepped forward. 'Is that blood?'

I grabbed Jesse by the shoulders. 'Are you hurt? What did he do to you?'

The guard pointed. 'Damn, he's bleeding.'

Helplessly I looked at the red mess splattering Jesse's sleeve and jeans. I wiped my fingers across it.

'It's paint.' In my voice I heard not relief but confusion and an edge of panic. 'Did he hit you, spray you with something, what?'

I looked around. The stranger was gone. I waved at the guard.

'Find the guy. Blond, baseball cap.' I pointed toward the far side of the lobby. I was nearly shouting. 'Don't just stand there. Come on, he's getting away.'

For a second he hesitated. Then he ran off, pulling a walkie-talkie from his belt.

Jesse battled for air. His heel began bouncing up and down. His right hand drew into a fist and began shaking.

The painter stared at him. 'Oh, man.'

Archie backed away. 'Crap. He's having a seizure.'

Jesse's hand was spasming. He seemed desperate to figure out how to breathe. The light bulb went on.

I looked up. 'Get me a paper bag.'

The painter said, 'Stick something in his mouth so he doesn't swallow his tongue.'

'A paper bag. Come on!' I put my hands against his cheeks. 'Slow down.'

He was hyperventilating. I leaned close to his face.

'Slow. Do it with me.'

Archie waved his arms. 'Put my belt in his teeth. No, lay him on the floor.'

Jesse squeezed his eyes shut. I felt him get a handle on it.

Archie backed toward the desk. 'I'm getting the paramedics.'

Jesse's eyes jumped. 'No.'

It came out as a cough instead of a word. His expression was pleading and shot through with embarrassment.

'No. It's okay,' I said.

Archie shook his head. 'He's having a fit. I ain't messing around with that. I'm calling nine-one-one.'

'Don't.' Jesse stared at his shaking fist. He breathed out, and in. His foot was still jittering. He pressed down on his knee, trying to stop it.

Archie waved at him. 'I don't want no lawsuit over him having a seizure in my lobby.'

Jesse grit his teeth. 'Do not. Call. The paramedics.'

He forced his fingers apart. His foot kept bouncing. I

remembered the same thing happening to me the time I hyperventilated. Too much oxygen, too little carbon dioxide: blood chemistry shifts and *bam*, muscle spasms.

I put my hands up appeasingly. 'Please. It's okay.'

'Then I'm logging this as your responsibility, lady.'

Jesse leaned on his knees. Pulled his elbows right back off, noticing for the first time that his jeans were sloppy with red paint.

I put my hand on his shoulder. 'What did the guy do to you?'

He shook his head. 'Sorry. That sound . . .' He drew a slow breath.

I looked at Archie. 'The man in the baseball cap. What the hell did he do to Jesse?'

He and the painter stared back blankly.

'Didn't you see him?'

The painter shook his head. 'Felt the scaffold jerk and then everything crashed down.'

Archie pointed at the revolving door. 'I was following them, guys walked out without answering my questions.'

I looked around the lobby. There was no sign of the stranger or the guard who had run after him. I nodded at Archie.

'Call the guard. See if he's found him.'

Archie took a walkie-talkie from the desk and clicked a button. 'Ramos?'

Jesse put his hand on my arm. 'Forget it. I'm okay.'

'You don't understand.' My nerves were crawling. 'It was him.'

My father's voice echoed across the lobby. 'Kit, what the hell's going on down here?'

He was striding toward us. Maureen Swayze was with him, frowning at the mess and the shattered window.

Archie clicked the walkie-talkie again. 'Ramos, come in.'

The hair on the back of my neck was standing up. 'I think Coyote's here.' I turned to Archie. 'The man's dangerous. Warn the guard.'

'The hell you talking about?' Archie said.

Swayze crossed her arms. 'My sentiments exactly.'

Dad looked only slightly less doubting. I grabbed his arm.

'You have to believe me.'

He looked at me, hard, and then at Archie. 'Call nine-one-one.'

Archie waved at me derisively. 'She told me not to.'

Dad stepped toward him, pulling out his cellphone. 'Then take your finger out of your nose and *shut down the building*.' He punched numbers and put the phone to his ear. 'I need the police.'

He spoke rapidly to the dispatcher. My pulse was jumping and gooseflesh was pinching my arms. I glanced nervously around the lobby. Archie huffed behind the desk, looking overtly miffed. Taking a key ring from his belt, he unlocked a cabinet on the wall and pushed a series of buttons on a control panel.

'I'm shutting the garage,' he said.

His face said, *Happy now?* He trundled toward the far side of the lobby, jingling the keys in his hand, and kept calling the guard on the walkie-talkie.

Dad, still on with the police, turned to me. 'What did he look like?'

'Blond hair. Slight. Pale.' I ran my hand into my hair. 'I didn't see his face, but he freaked me out, something about him . . .'

He put a hand on my arm. 'Focus and remember. How tall was he?'

'Maybe my height? But not huge. Slight.' My hands were cold. 'Ask Jesse. The guy grabbed him.'

Jesse looked up. 'The guy who swung the paint can? I just saw the back of his head.'

'What do you mean? He shoved you into the scaffold.' Dad stepped toward him. 'For christsake, it may be the killer.'

I put out an arm to block him. 'He stared you in the face for three or four seconds.'

Jesse looked as though a crushing weight had just landed on him. 'No. I don't remember seeing him.'

At the desk a buzzer went off. Dimly, we heard an alarm ringing. Swayze went behind the desk and bent over a control panel, frowning.

'It's the parking garage elevator.'

We heard a fire door slam open. Archie came stumbling around the corner, hands out, mouth wide. The buzzer and alarm continued ringing.

'What is it?' I said.

He stumbled to the desk and grabbed a phone. His hands were shaking.

'Ramos.' He stared at the phone as though wondering how the hell it worked. 'He's downstairs in the parking garage elevator. He's . . .'

His fingers hovered over the numbers. He was panting. He dialed 911.

Dad and I looked at each other and took off around the corner. We ran down the stairs to Level 1 of the parking garage, pushed the door open and looked around. The garage was an echo chamber of concrete. At the exit ramp a mesh grate had come down, sealing the way out. We ran to the elevator.

'Oh, shit,' I said.

The door was slowly opening and closing, like a pair of clapping hands. Ramos lay inside, with his head in the doorway. The doors closed, bumped his head, and slowly opened again. Dad jammed himself in the door to stop it. He hit a button inside, locking the door open. Bent down and put his fingers to the guard's neck.

'He has a pulse.' He looked around at the garage, and back at me. 'I'm sorry, Evan.'

He didn't doubt me any more.

Eighty miles east, the Riverside County Sheriff's Department helicopter hovered above the field. Two hundred feet up, rotors beating, it turned so the scene off the I-10 came into full view. Two sheriff's cars were stopped on the shoulder, a riot of lights flashing blue and red.

On the freeway shoulder an officer was interviewing the man who'd discovered it. He was sitting on the ground. From the radio chatter, he'd almost had a heart attack running back to the freeway and flagging down another driver with a cellphone.

Two officers were walking across the field, weapons drawn. The chopper stayed high to keep from flattening the grass with its downwash. Cutting through the yellow grass were tire tracks. They ran off the freeway and angled across the field for a hundred yards, ending at a copse of trees. From up here, the back end of the green Volvo wagon was visible. The officers approached the car.

14

Coyote strode down the alley behind Argent Tower, putting distance between himself and the underground parking garage. The security guard had dropped like an amateur. The mesh grate had rattled down far too slowly to keep him from running up the exit ramp.

What was going on?

The woman coming through the revolving door, she was China Lake. One of *them*. The man he'd shoved into the scaffolding as well. And they were trying to stop him. He stared at the sleeve of his button-down shirt. The man had touched him. He should not have done that. His lips drew back over his teeth. He pulled off the shirt and balled it up and shoved it into a dumpster.

He had seen the two agents striding across the plaza. They were nowhere near invisible.

This was *wrong*.

They wanted to get to Sway. He could not conclude otherwise. They wanted to interrogate her, suck out the information she could provide. And that would point them toward the mission. No. He could not allow that. Sway was *his*.

The China Lake people – they should not have been able to draw the connection between Sway and the mission. No, this was something that had to be fixed. Fast. Nobody could be permitted to stop him.

He walked down the alley. He heard police sirens. The baseball cap went into a dumpster. Shoving his hands into the pockets of his chinos to appear unhurried, he glanced back at the skyscraper. He had been close. So close he could smell it. It was like a taste on the wind, ephemeral. He lifted the lid off a trashcan and stuffed the blond wig inside.

He reached for the amulet, wanting to draw strength. His hand found empty air. He wasn't wearing it. Mr Hollywood Nebbish didn't wear dogtags. A howl began rolling up his throat. He fought it and felt it continue to rise. He stared at Argent Tower.

He had been denied. He put his left hand on the rim of the trashcan and slammed down the metal lid. He felt only pressure, squeezing, a twisting of the skin. He slammed the lid again. Nothing. He had no pain threshold. The vaccine had permanently removed his ability to sense, to feel.

Nobody could hurt him. He was impervious.

Breathing hard, he raised his hand and studied it. It was battered and bruised. This was his strength and power. This sacrifice was the price of invincibility. The howl tumbled deep in his throat. He could not have his own pain. He could only observe it when he took others. Again he gripped the trashcan and slammed down the lid, enraged at this weakness, this longing for rude physical sensation.

The sirens grew louder, keening, the sound warping between skyscrapers. He stopped and turned his face to the sun, looking east. Riverside. The child.

He began to run.

Dad came thundering back into the lobby through the revolving door. 'Nothing. No sign of him anywhere.'

Near the front desk a uniformed LAPD officer was talking to Jesse. The notes he was taking were as thin as Jesse's voice.

'I know the guy walked past me. I turned to follow him and the paint can came swinging at my head. After that . . .'

Dad crossed his arms. 'After that, what? *Think*, Jesse. You're good at that. Come on.'

Jesse's face was pale. Red paint striped his shirt, jeans and the wheelchair. He looked like a Jackson Pollock canvas. He glanced from my father back to the cop and began unbuttoning his shirt.

'Tag this as evidence.' He looked my way. 'Where'd the guy grab me?'

'Biceps. Both arms.' I held out my hands, showing the cop how the stranger had gripped him.

He undid the last button and took the shirt off, careful not to touch the sleeves. He held it out by the collar.

'Long shot, I know. But maybe your guys can lift a print.'

The officer called for a crime scene tech to bring an evidence bag. Jesse turned to Dad.

'Any chance I could borrow a shirt?'

Dad nodded. Jesse gave him his car keys and Dad went to get one from his garment bag. The tech bagged the shirt and asked Jesse and me to give him our prints for comparison.

Near the bottom of the curving staircase, Maureen Swayze stood chewing on her pencil. She looked shaken. I walked over.

'You believe me now, don't you?' I said. 'It was Coyote.'

'Yes. That's not only the logical explanation, it's . . .'

She took off her glasses and cleaned them on the tail of her blouse. 'Deeply disturbing.'

'Do you know who he is?' I said.

Her eyes were distant. She shook her head. 'No.'

'What about those two men who stopped by your office?'

'I have no idea.' She stuck the pencil back in her ponytail. 'Excuse me, I need to alert Primacon's security officer. Tell your dad I'll speak to him soon.' She jogged up the stairs.

The crime tech took my prints. When I finished, one of the painters walked up, holding out a rag. He nodded at Jesse, who was pressing his fingers onto the tech's print pad.

'He can clean up with this.'

'You can give it to him. He has ears and a voice.'

He looked stricken. I relented, taking it.

I walked over to Jesse. He finished with the fingerprinting and I handed him the rag. He thanked me and wiped it against his jeans. It only smeared the paint spatters into longer streaks.

I touched his shoulder. 'You scared me. I thought, I don't know, he—'

'Ev, for christsake.' He scrubbed with the rag. 'It wasn't the guy. It was that sound.'

'What sound?'

He looked up, eyes hot. 'The glass breaking, when the paint can smashed into it.'

The fractured glass sagged in the window frame. Where the can had hit, red paint oozed from a crack the size of a human head.

I lowered my voice. 'You had a flashback?'

He pressed his lips white, scrubbing with the rag. I exhaled.

He hadn't heard a paint can smashing a plate-glass window. He heard himself smashing into the windshield of the car that hit him. I knew what happened after that. The adrenaline rush ran out of control. He saw the car, the fall down the ravine, his friend Isaac lying dead. Eyes wide open, he didn't see Coyote.

'I fucked up,' he said.

'No you didn't. Jess, God – it's PTSD, not ineptitude.'

'I had hold of him. If I hadn't freaked, I could have kept him here.'

My stomach spun. 'No. It was Coyote. Christ, look what he did to the security guard. If you'd held onto him, that could have been you.'

'If I'd held onto him, maybe the guard would be okay.'

'No.' I felt dizzy. 'You can't even think about taking those kinds of risks.'

'Goddammit, Delaney. Stop mother-henning me. I'm not a child.' His voice echoed in the atrium. People glanced at him.

'No, that's not – you don't understand,' I said. 'Neither of us can take those kind of risks.'

He spread his arms. 'What risks? What are you talking about? Tell me.'

'It's . . .'

I looked up. Dad was walking toward us, carrying a black golf shirt. I ran my hands through my hair. Jesse glared at me.

Dad approached, his face studiously neutral. 'Here you go.'

'Thanks.' Jesse pulled the shirt on. It stretched tight across his shoulders.

Dad turned to me. 'You need to tell me why you came

down to the lobby in the first place. What the hell was going on?'

'I followed two men down from Primacon. They were government agents.'

He gave me a sharp look. 'You able to ID a federal agent from twenty paces?'

'These guys, yes.' I described Salt'n'Pepa. 'So what kind of federal agent doesn't show his badge, or push his power in other people's noses? Intelligence.'

He grunted. I took that as agreement.

A voice echoed across the atrium. 'Miss Delaney.'

I glanced around. Special Agent Dan Heaney, the FBI profiler, was striding toward us.

He worked at the nearby Federal Building, so it didn't surprise me to see him. But his pitted church pastor face looked drawn, and that did. His blue suit looked as though he had slept the wrinkles into it.

'You heard,' I said.

He nodded toward the plaza. 'Let's go outside.'

We followed him out into the sunshine. He jammed his hands into his pockets and led us over to the fountain.

'I've spoken to Detective Chang and he's in total agreement,' he said. 'We go proactive.'

Dad put on his hat, adjusting the brim. 'Buzzwords don't mean a whole hell of a lot to me, Agent Heaney.'

'We try to lure the killer into a trap.'

'How?' I said.

'Couple ways. The police could announce to the press that the killer has been sighted. That they have witnesses to the attack on the guard here today.'

Jesse shook his head. 'That means Evan. No.'

'And you,' I said. 'And Archie and the painters. And Ramos.'

172

'It's a ploy,' Heaney said. 'But it can draw a killer into coming forward to explain why he was near the murder scene.'

The breeze blew my hair across my face. I brushed it back. 'Coyote's an assassin personality. You really think he'd walk into the LAPD and try to make excuses? Or would he just track down the witnesses and eliminate them?'

Jesse picked at the tacky paint on his jeans. 'Evan's already a potential target. Don't give him an extra incentive to take aim at her.'

Dad nodded at Heaney. 'Other options?'

'A sympathetic journalist could write a story about the victims. Try to bring it home to the killer, promote some guilt.' He turned to me. 'Especially a journalist who could offer a personal remembrance.'

'And you think this would induce him to surrender himself?' Dad said.

'No. Lure him into the open. It might get him to visit the gravesites in China Lake. Or maybe—'

His cellphone rang. Excusing himself, he stepped away and answered.

Jesse continued picking at the paint. 'I don't like Heaney involving you, Ev.'

Dad crossed his arms. 'If you could give the cops a description of the killer we could short-circuit this whole process.'

Jesse looked away.

Heaney, talking on the phone, sounded terse. He drooped, his suit wrinkling further. I saw his face.

'It's bad news,' I said. 'Something's wrong.'

Tommy was standing in the break room at the China Lake police station, stirring a third lump of sugar into his coffee. The TV was tuned to a news channel. A red banner appeared behind the anchorwoman's hair: Breaking News. The visual switched to a news copter hovering over a freeway.

He set down his coffee and leaned into the hallway. 'Captain. You'd better see this.'

Across town, Abbie Hankins sat on her bed tying her Reeboks. Her hair was wet, but she didn't have time to dry it. She had fifteen minutes to get to work at the museum. Hayley was bouncing up and down on the bed, waving two My Little Ponys overhead, singing.

'Fly, ponies, fly, fly.'

The red banner flashed on the television screen. Abbie stopped tying her shoes.

'Hayley, shush.'

The sound from the news helicopter was poor. She grabbed the remote and turned up the volume.

'. . . a break in the search for Ryan O'Keefe. We can see flares burning on the freeway and the Highway Patrol directing traffic.'

Hayley bounced. 'Over the sky, ponies fly.'

'Girl, be *quiet*.'

Hayley stopped bouncing. She blinked, her bottom lip quivering.

Exhaling, Abbie pulled her into her arms. 'Sorry, baby.'

Hayley snuffled and started crying. Abbie held her.

The reporter shouted over the noise of the rotors. 'There's a copse of trees about a hundred yards off the freeway and there are a *lot* of law enforcement personnel over that way.'

Abbie watched, holding Hayley tight. Near the trees,

Sheriff's deputies loitered in an anxious circle. Abbie glimpsed a green Volvo wagon with its doors open. Photographers were snapping photos, crouching down for fresh angles. An ambulance was bumping slowly across the field toward it.

Hayley squirmed. 'Mommy, you're squeezing me.'

The ambulance stopped behind the deputies. Two EMTs pulled a stretcher from the back and rolled it toward the Volvo. They were walking slowly and didn't have any medical equipment in their hands. Something else was rolled up on the stretcher, something black and shiny, and then they stopped and unrolled it and unzipped it and Abbie knew what it was and what they were preparing to remove from the car and place inside it. She jumped to her feet, clutching Hayley, screaming at the screen.

I saw Heaney's face, and knew. 'No.'

'They've found Mrs O'Keefe's Volvo.'

I took a step back, putting a hand against my stomach. 'No. Stop.'

'The little boy—' He cleared his throat. 'He was in his car seat. He's been dead for some time.'

A wrench tightened around my temples. I heard ringing in my ears.

Dad's voice was almost inaudible. 'Did he suffer?'

Heaney looked at him and instantly away. Things went starburst yellow. I broke into tears.

'Kit, sweetheart.'

Putting up a hand to keep him back, I walked away. Past the fountain and the gushing flowerbeds, to the edge of the sidewalk by the street. I pressed the heels of my hands against my eyes.

I heard Jesse wheel up and felt his hand on my back. He didn't say anything.

After a minute I looked at him. Wiping the back of my hand roughly across my eyes, I turned to Heaney.

'We get this son of a bitch and we get him now. I'll do anything you want.'

15

In the hotel room, Coyote threw the suitcase on the bed. Into it he heaved clothes, toiletries, the computer, the yearbook. The child had been discovered. The news whores were hawking it on the TV downstairs in the hotel bar. He saw the footage, overhead shots from the news copters. They were like jackals in a feeding frenzy. And yet they had the audacity to hold him in contempt, these scavengers feeding off of his kill. He was their meat maker, their bread and butter. Not one of them had the skill or courage to see the mission through to completion.

Taking the child had not been a capricious act. It had been necessary. The child presented a danger to the world. He was a contaminant, with the potential to cause incalculable damage. Ryan was only the end link in a chain of events that had gone horribly awry. His fate had been ordained before his birth.

Coyote looked at the back of his hand. The bruising was severe. A hematoma was rising where he had slammed the lid of the trashcan on it. He squeezed and opened his fist. His fingers were swollen and his hand was stiff. Damaging the hand had been ill advised. It was an invaluable tool and he should care for it as meticulously as he cared for the weapons in their case. The hematoma was stretching the skin and tissue beneath. He took an

Exacto-knife from his medical kit. Holding his hand above the bathroom sink, he cut a slit in his skin an inch long. He felt the pressure of the knife, and a tugging sensation as he sliced through his skin, but no pain.

Becky O'Keefe had felt no pain either. Because of that, she had sealed the fate of her child.

He set down the knife and squeezed out the bloody, half-clotted bruise, working his fingers across the injury like a baker kneading dough. It glopped out and slid down the side of the sink into the drain. He cleaned the cut with antiseptic and closed it with two butterfly bandages.

He examined his hand, flexing and opening it. Range of motion was greatly improved.

Back in the bedroom he continued packing. He paused to flip through the journal, checking the notes he had recently added and the important elements he had highlighted in yellow marker.

Evan Delaney had clawed her hands into the knowledge stream and discovered Argent Tower. How?

Where had things gone wrong? It was imperative to walk back the cat and untangle that.

Not overall, of course – the origin of the problem was evident. Things had gone wrong twenty years ago, in the dry desert air under a ringing blue sky, when South Star went nova in the explosion. And since then they had been invisibly aggregating, until recently everything had begun to unravel. He took the amulet from the desk and put it around his neck. It would bring clarity of thought.

Walk back the cat. Walk it back, walk it—

A flaw existed. Agents should not have been at Argent Tower. The unclean unworthy should not have been there either, dipping her hands in the knowledge stream and trying to pull Swayze out. Sway was his, and the presence of these others would warn her that he was near. That was intolerable.

How did they get there? Somebody had talked.

Somebody who wanted to thwart the mission. Or somebody who was sloppy. Or greedy.

He had to think this through. And when he followed the ball of string back to the source of the error he would have to reconfigure the mission.

But first he needed a new lair. He grabbed his things and left the room.

The breeze lifted my hair from the collar of my shirt.

'I'll talk to Tommy and draft an article. Tell me what you particularly want me to include.'

'Emphasize the loss of your friends, the tragedy, what they meant to their families,' Heaney said.

'Twist the knife.'

'Right. Find out where the funerals are going to be held, and when. Make sure Coyote knows where his victims are being buried. The police will set up surveillance at the graves.'

'I have some media contacts who may run it,' I said. 'If we're aggressive about it we could possibly even get syndication, the Los Angeles market, widespread coverage. And if we can get it into an online edition, so much the better. You said Coyote's probably obsessing about media coverage. You want to bet he's searching for the story online?'

'Right.'

'Mainstream media is still probably the best bet to catch Coyote's attention, but I can also try and get it linked to by some influential blogs, really up the search hits.'

'Good.'

'Okay. I'll write it up and get you and Tommy a draft ASAP.'

Dad said, 'Something else. That phone call I got, while we were driving over here? It was a fellow I knew at China Lake. I'd asked him to try and track down any flight crews and paramedics who might have been on duty the day of the explosion.' He was grave. 'He found the helicopter crew. The pilot was killed last year, up near Whidbey Island.'

'Shit,' I said. 'Carla Dearing. Tommy told me about her murder.'

'Coyote's not just after the high school kids. He's going after other people who were connected to the explosion.'

He glanced up at Argent Tower.

'Swayze,' I said.

'That's what I'm thinking.'

Heaney said, 'You want to give me some names and phone numbers?'

'I've got a whole slew of stuff for you in my briefcase,' Dad said.

Heaney ran his hand over his pitted face and looked at the building. 'I need to speak with Dr Swayze.'

Jesse wheeled closer. 'Phil. You said the surgical fire that killed Dana West was arson.'

Heaney turned, startled. Dad nodded.

'Another of Evan's classmates,' he explained. 'Air Force surgical nurse who died after going under the knife herself.'

'Shit,' Jesse said.

'It happened post-op. An O_2 line had a leak, and a spark from an electrocautery tool set off a flash fire. The

O_2 line fed overhead back to the tanks, which were near some nitrous oxide tanks. The clinic went up like that.' He snapped his fingers.

'Get to the part about arson.'

'Dana was alone in the OR when it happened.'

Jesse's mouth went wide. 'No way. The surgical team left her alone?'

'Small-time clinic, the OR served as their recovery room as well.'

'Still, nobody was monitoring her?'

'That's not the shocking part. The doors to the OR were locked shut from the outside.'

'Oh my God,' I said.

'Somebody set it up. He managed to get access to a military facility and convince people he belonged there. And he knew how to make it look like a catastrophic accident.'

The sound of traffic grated against my ears. The implications sank in.

'Dad, that's not the shocking part. He didn't just want to kill Dana. He wanted that clinic eradicated.'

Dad nodded. A sick taste spread through my mouth.

'Because the place was contaminated with something,' I said.

'That's the conclusion I'm drawing.'

Heaney looked exhausted but intent. 'Can you get me that stuff now?'

'Certainly.'

We headed back inside. The crime scene techs were still working in the lobby. The painters and janitors were waiting for them to finish so they could clean up the mess under the scaffold.

I took Dad's elbow. 'How did you find out all this?'

'Called in some favors.'

'How many?'

'About all of them.'

He'd done an astounding amount of research in only thirty-six hours, apparently involving wheedling and coaxing brutal memories out of grieving parents.

'You always dig this hard and this deep?' I said.

His expression told me I'd asked a stupid question. Of course he didn't. He always dug deep, but he only clawed at a problem this hard when his family was involved.

He put his hand over mine. 'After I get the things for Heaney I have some work to do. You get going and I'll catch up tomorrow.'

'Okay.'

'You're not going to stay at home tonight.'

'No, I'll stay at Jesse's.'

His heels clacked on the marble floor. He leaned toward me and lowered his voice. 'Is he liable to have another one of these blackouts?'

Jesse answered, from closer than I'd expected. 'I didn't black out, and no. I won't let it happen again.'

He pushed past us, off balance and angry. I opened my mouth, but knew that words would be worse than silence. He disappeared around the corner. We followed, and stopped. I grimaced. He was in front of the parking garage elevator, reading the sign taped to the doors. *Out of Service*.

He gripped his pushrims. 'Ev, can you go get the truck?'

'Sure.'

He fumbled the car keys out of his jeans pocket. They fell from his fingers to the floor. He bent down to pick them up and Dad's golf shirt ripped open at the shoulder seam.

'Shoot. Sorry.'

He handed me the keys. He looked at the sign. And he hauled off, slamming the elevator control panel with the heel of his hand. The call button squealed.

For a moment he held his breath. Then his shoulders dropped. He laughed cheerlessly.

'Can't tell me this freaking building doesn't deserve it.' He spun and wheeled away. 'I'll meet you out front.'

For a second I watched his back. 'Wait.'

But he was already gone around the corner. I called again and went after him. He was halfway across the lobby.

'Jesse.' I ran and caught him from behind, wrapping my arms around his shoulders. We skidded to a stop on the marble.

'Evan, what are you doing?'

I circled in front of him and put my hands on his knees. 'I have to tell you.'

'What?'

I looked around for someplace where people wouldn't interrupt. One of the scenic elevators opened and a woman got out.

'Hold that,' I said.

She caught the door. Jesse looked bothered and baffled.

'Will you please—'

'Move. Now.' I gave him the death stare.

He backed up, fast, into the elevator. 'Delaney, what the hell is going on with you?'

I pressed the Close button. When the doors eked shut, I hit *Stop*.

He frowned with confusion. 'Did you drink some funky Kool-Aid up in Swayze's lab?'

183

'No, I'm pregnant.'

'And I'm smoking crack. Just tell me.'

'I'm pregnant.'

It was like sprinting to the edge of a roof and leaping blindly off, not knowing whether he'd be there to catch me. His eyes widened. His lips parted. As if he, not I, had just been thrown off a roof. Sweet Jesus, don't hyperventilate again. Don't hit the alarm bell. Don't ask for proof, or for a fire ax to smash the doors open and escape.

I dug my fingernails into my palms. 'Say something.'

He looked as though he was running ten scripts in his head, one after the next, boom boom boom. His expression was beyond bewildered, beyond shocked. It was unearthly. His gaze dropped from my face to my belly.

'Damn,' he said.

I grit my teeth.

'Damn.'

I wanted to swallow, but a sock was stuffed down my throat.

'You're sure?' he said.

I turned my face to the window. 'Not a hundred per cent.'

'You have to be sure.'

I nodded, staring furiously out the window at the lobby.

'Please,' he said. 'Tell me it's true.'

He took my hand. I looked. He was blinking as though his eyes stung. His grip was hard.

'Tell me this is real, because otherwise you're going to break me in two.'

My voice sounded disembodied. 'You're happy?'

'Hell, yes, I'm happy. This is . . .' His face fell. 'Aren't you?'

He couldn't hide the ache in his eyes. He was holding

joy in check, for fear that I'd give him an answer he didn't want to hear. I thought, in that moment, that I'd never loved anybody more in my life.

'I'm thrilled,' I said.

He pulled me onto his lap, held me tight and kissed me. And kissed me again. 'God, I can't believe—'

'Me neither.' I wrapped my arms around his neck. 'I never thought—'

'I know.' He clenched me to him, kissing me again. 'Especially—'

Again. Laughing. 'Impossible, yeah.'

There was a knock on the window. My father was standing outside the elevator with his phone to his ear. His face was set. He waved me out, mouthing '*Swayze.*'

I turned back to Jesse. 'This news is between you, me and the pregnancy test.'

His eyes cut to Dad, who looked as chilly as an iceberg. 'Fine with me.'

Dad rapped a knuckle on the window.

Jesse pressed his fingers to the corners of his eyes, pretending that he had something in them, and shook his head. 'I can't even . . . damn. It's— I don't . . .'

The loopy clown-grin painted my face. 'Jesse Blackburn, speechless. Oh, that I have lived to see this day.'

He gave me a cockeyed smile. I stood up and pushed the Open button. He pulled me back.

'Do you know how much I love you?'

I kissed him again. 'Yeah, daddy-o. I know.'

I walked out of the elevator with my hands up, showing I wasn't armed, so to speak. Dad waved me over.

'I agree with you, Sway. Scared the piss out of all of us.'

He gestured me closer. I put my ear near the phone.

'We need to talk.' Swayze's voice had a needly tension to it. 'Eller's Diner in Westwood Village, a block down from the medical center. I'm meeting the FBI agent there in forty-five minutes. Can you be there in thirty?'

'Certainly, but we can talk right now. I'm still here in your building.'

'I'm not. That place was giving me the creeps. I had to get out of there.'

'Maureen, what's this about?'

'You want a name? I have one,' she said. 'I know who Coyote is.'

16

Eller's Diner was bright and loud, and the coffee was bitter. I drank two swallows before the new reality hit: I needed to switch to decaf. Holy cow. Nine months without Java – and people thought my PMS was bad. In caffeine withdrawal I would be a screaming meemie. I pushed the cup away.

'Good idea,' Dad said. 'I think you're already het up enough for one day.'

'I'm not overwrought. And neither is Jesse. And things are fine with us.'

He ran a hand across his bristly white hair, watching the door. He had the gunfighter seat, back against the wall.

'That's between you two. Some things a father knows better than to enquire about.'

'Even if the father used to be in Naval Intelligence?'

He turned his head, slowly, to look at me. 'Sounds like you and your mom had a rip-roaring girls' night out last night.' His gaze panned back across the diner. He waved. 'Sway.'

She strode to our table, her face pinched, and sat down with a thud. Her feet stuck out coltishly on either side of her chair.

'Where's your boyfriend?' she said. 'Arranging to have himself put on exhibit in the Pop Art wing at the Getty?'

'Buying some clean clothes.'

'Why didn't you tell me you were a journalist?'

'It wasn't relevant, and how'd you find that out?'

'Instantaneous telepathic communication with the robo-grunt cabal.'

Monotone, I said, 'Right, the hive mind. I read about that.'

She smirked. 'Google. It took a tenth of a second. And your profession is extremely relevant.'

The waitress bustled up and poured her some coffee. Swayze waited for her to leave.

'Once I speak to the FBI, I'm afraid the press will get hold of me. I need some blockers to help me get down-field.'

'You want us to make you look good for the media if this all blows up?'

She made air-quotes with her fingers. '"Researcher Bred Supersoldiers." They'd show me walking out of the office in slow motion, with the *Jaws* theme playing in the background. I need you to be willing to tell them I didn't glorify the production of slavering killbots.'

'What do you expect me to do?'

'If it turns out that the name I have is the guy, be fair. And tell people that I'm the one who came forward.'

She glanced at Dad, eyes pleading. 'I can't let this damage the integrity of my current research. Primacon is doing fantastic work.'

He put a hand on her arm. 'Nobody wants to cut the legs out from under your current research.'

'I have to protect it.' She ran a hand into her ponytail, making it even more disheveled than before. 'If they start screeching that I cooked up a serial killer, will you tell them I don't have horns and a pitchfork?'

'I'll do that,' he said.

She nodded brusquely. Drank her coffee. Set the mug down, hard.

'I thought I had put China Lake to bed, permanently. Now this.' She blew air through her lips. 'That . . . *animal* was downstairs at my office building, scouting the premises.' Hands out again. 'Why?'

'Because South Star affected his health,' Dad said.

'And now the gal who made him sick is a target? But that's impossible. I couldn't have made him sick.' She gazed at him. Finally she exhaled. 'This guy scares me to hell. Can you tell? This is my scared-to-hell face.'

Dad patted her arm.

'Who is he?' I said.

'There was a youngster who joined our project. Early twenties. Ex-Army. Pale, slight, blond. Obsessively neat, very mission oriented.'

'Was he a test subject?'

'Yes. I never knew which agency he actually worked for and I didn't strive to find out.'

'What's his name?' I said.

'Kai Torrance.'

She spelled the first name for us, making sure we got it. 'Good luck to the cops and FBI finding him. He disappeared somewhere down the rabbit hole. Government, soldier of fortune, who knows. He could be working at Disneyland, operating the boats for It's a Small World.'

'That ride that could turn anybody into a serial killer,' I said.

'He wasn't physically distinctive. No major accidents or illnesses, no distinguishing characteristics except one.' She drank her coffee. 'He was nocturnal.'

Man. 'Because of South Star's insomnia research?'

'No. He claimed to have adopted the habit growing up on the street in Hollywood.' She leaned in. 'If you believed him, he and his mother lived in an awful apartment off of Franklin. She was a drug addict and when she got high he would spend nights up on the roof. I took his street-kid story as a self-created myth, but the nocturnalism was genuine. Then he began going out into the back ranges up by the petroglyphs, to be one with the ancients.'

'Uh-oh,' I said.

'He thought he was a reincarnated native spirit god. One of the shamanistic drawings brought to life.'

'Shit.'

'He spoke repeatedly about one carving, a coyote. The trickster, he said, very powerful. This is why I know he's your man. He must have adapted his own name into the code name. Kai Torrance. Kai T – Coyote.'

My heart was drumming. 'Did he get the pain vaccine?'

'Yes.'

'What happened to him?' Dad said.

'Nothing. The vaccine didn't work.'

'You're joking,' I said.

She turned in her chair. 'Yes. This is my joking face. Go ahead, laugh your head off.' Deadpan expression. 'The vaccine didn't work.'

'I'd say you're getting results right here, today.'

She pressed her lips tight.

'The day of the explosion at Renegade Canyon. Was Torrance at that cinderblock building when it blew up?' I said.

'Off the record?'

I nodded.

'Permanently off the record.' Her chin lowered. 'That

was supposed to be a controlled demolition. There were botched communications with the school district and . . .' She took off her glasses and pinched the bridge of her nose.

'You didn't know our class was going to be nearby?'

'Of course not.' She shook her head. 'It should never have happened. But we took all steps to ensure that you kids didn't suffer any ill effects.'

'But apparently we did.'

'No, it's not possible.'

'Coyote is killing us because of it. It isn't possible, it's fact.'

Her face was as tight as a cloth caught in a wringer.

'Was Torrance there that day?' I said.

'Yes.'

Across the diner, we saw Dan Heaney's rumpled suit filling the doorway. Swayze nodded and he began making his way over to the table. Dad and I stood to go.

She looked up. 'I don't have the slightest idea why Torrance is after any of us. But if it turns out that I had anything to do with it, I'll kill myself.'

Coming from anybody else, I would have taken that metaphorically. With Swayze I wasn't so sure.

We walked outside just as Jesse pulled up. He had on a new blue-and-white striped shirt and brown jeans. He lowered the window and handed Dad a bag from Macy's.

'Nearest thing to your black golf shirt I could find.'

'Appreciate it.' Dad gazed into the truck. 'Got room for Evan in there with all those roses?'

Jesse smiled inscrutably.

Dad put a hand to my cheek. 'I'll get to Santa Barbara as soon as I can.' He kissed my forehead and turned back to Jesse. 'Grow eyes in the back of your head, son. I'm counting on you.'

'Hey, honey. You want to party?'

The woman leaned her elbows on the window frame and smiled into the truck at Coyote. She was flabby and she was old, as far as whores go. Almost forty, he guessed, from the way her breasts sagged in the magenta tube top. Beneath the careless peroxide job, her roots mixed black with birdshit gray. She wasn't bitchy or hard or even disillusioned, like the runaways from Minnesota who would come out when the sun went down. She was simply tired. She was out on the street in the middle of the day.

He leaned across the truck toward her, Mr Horny Guy on a business trip to southern California. 'Depends. You have a place we can go?'

This was the crux of the negotiation. No hotels. No alleys. Not this vehicle. He had already driven away from three prostitutes who couldn't provide.

'My place,' she said.

'Close by?'

'Just up the road.'

He smiled and opened the door. She climbed in.

'It's fifty for the first hour, hundred for the afternoon. And I don't do anal.'

'Is it quiet? I don't want anybody interrupting our party.'

'Quiet as a tomb. That the kind of party you after?'

He signaled and pulled back into traffic. 'That's perfect.'

17

It was three p.m. when Jesse and I pulled into my driveway. The day felt cooler here than in Los Angeles, the sky bluer, the city more tranquil. The mountains shone green behind the house and children's voices burbled from the school playground up the street.

I hopped out. 'Half an hour and I should be packed and out of here. I'll meet you at your place this evening.'

He began grabbing his gear from the back of the cab. 'I'm coming in.'

'That's okay. I know you're dying to hit the mall and stock up on baby supplies. Jimi Hendrix CDs, Black's Law Dictionary, Beavis and Butt-head DVDs, all that good stuff.'

He unlocked the glove compartment. 'Put the Glock in your backpack.'

I looked up and down the street. Nobody was in sight. Nikki and Carl were both at work and there was no sign of Martinez and Sons or their truck. The breeze tingled against my bare arms. I put the gun in my backpack.

He lugged out his hardware, snapped the wheels on the frame, got out and came around the truck.

'And don't diss Beavis and Butt-head. They're cultural touchstones. We'll get a boxed set,' he said.

I got my arms around the three dozen red roses in the

back seat and we headed toward the garden gate. A smile entered his voice.

'Though the kid should start off with Bugs Bunny. Then Roadrunner, and The Simpsons.'

The kid. That disjointed heap of emotions jostled inside me again. Crazed, sweet, jumpy joy.

'As for music, Clapton needs to come before Hendrix. No, wait. Maybe Creedence.'

He was going like a runaway train. That was his method of handling uncertainty: talk, work, argue politics, swim three miles. Go. Keep moving. But never like this.

'But item number one is swimming lessons. Babies are natural swimmers, so we get the kid in the pool right off the bat. Oh, man – I've got it. We'll have a water birth.'

This was busting the speedometer.

'Though on second thought, getting you to relax in the water is like giving a cat a bath. And I have a bad feeling that when you go into labor, you'll be a biter.'

And in all his talk – of how do you feel, are you okay, do you need to stop and rest – there was one question he hadn't asked, hadn't hinted at. The huge stinking obvious question, the rhino snorting in the back seat.

Was it his child?

Anybody looking logically at the situation would have come up with two theories to explain how I became pregnant. One: that we'd defied expectation about his fertility by miles and miles. Or two: well.

But he never gave one breath of doubt. I saw nothing in his eyes, his words or his crooked persistent smile but complete belief in me. Not for the first time, I thanked the kismet that had brought him into my life.

I opened the gate and scanned the garden, seeing only the hibiscus and jasmine and the thick ivy pouring down the fence. Shade from the live oaks flurried on the lawn. At the door I peered through the glass. The living room was empty, the lights on in the kitchen. I turned the key in the lock and stopped still. The deadbolt was unlocked and the house silent.

'The alarm,' I said. 'It should be on but it's not.'

Jesse pulled me back from the door. 'Give me the Glock.'

I fumbled through the backpack and handed him the gun. He set it on his lap. Shit. Maybe I should hold it. He was a dead shot, but I could run and rack the slide simultaneously.

'Stay here.' Shoving the door wide, he went in. 'Hello?'

My vision was jumping. He cruised toward the center of the room, glancing around. At the dining table he slowed. He grabbed a piece of paper. Reading it, his shoulders relaxed.

'It's okay.' He spun around. 'Here.'

Tension poured out of my fingertips like rain. It was a note from Carlos Martinez.

2:45. Gone to Coast Plumbing Supply. Back half an hour.

I crumpled it up. 'Got to have a word with that dude.'

Jesse headed for my bedroom door. 'How did he get in to begin with?'

'That's part of the word I've got to have with him.'

He wheeled into my bedroom, craning his neck. I dropped the backpack on the coffee table, walked to my desk and hit *Play* on the answering machine.

My cousin Taylor's voice cooed at me. 'Hiya, hon. I dropped by some photo spreads for you to look over for my book project.'

A folder sat on my desk. I sighed.

'So sharpen up your editing pencil and—'

I pushed *Delete*. As I did, the phone rang. It was Abbie.

'Becky and her little boy. I want to vomit. A mother and her child, I can't—'

There was a broken pause.

'I know,' I said.

'Wally's dad's going to take the kids to his place up in Independence. I'll pack up their stuff and get school assignments and get up there this weekend.'

'Good.'

'Real good. He's an ex-Marine. He's the guy I want standing watch over them,' she said. 'Let me give you his address and phone number.'

I grabbed a pencil and paper and scribbled them down. In the background her kids squealed at each other. Abbie's voice sounded so ragged that listening hurt.

'Evan, this is the pit at the bottom of the world.'

'I know. You get your family someplace safe.'

She lowered her voice. 'Hayley thinks it's a special trip with Grandpa, but the older ones know something's wrong. Dulcie looks real tense. God*dammi*t, that look sends a pang through my chest.' She exhaled, hard, and gathered herself back under control. 'She's murmuring something to Travis, probably "Is Mommy wacko?" Yeah, he's nodding. But there's no way I can keep them from sensing it. I've never felt so afraid in my life.'

In the background, I heard, 'Mom?'

'Just a sec, kiddo.' She came back to our conversation. 'Listen, don't pass this information around. I'm only telling you and Tommy. This town leaks gossip like a sieve.'

'I promise. Watch yourself, Abbie.'

'Really. I'm thinking of trading in that big-ass van for a Hummer with a freaking gun turret on top.'

'You and me both. Seriously, be careful.'

We said goodbye.

Jesse came back into the living room. 'Bedroom's clear. Toolbox is open in the bathroom and Carlos left half a sandwich on the counter.'

I folded the paper with Mr Hankins's phone number and stuck it in my pocket. 'Let me pack up.'

The breeze blew the front door open and it knocked against the wall. Papers swirled off my desk. In the kitchen, something tipped over and rattled around. Jesse stopped, gazing at the tall kitchen counter.

I shut the door. 'Think we're safe. You can stand down.'

I headed toward my bedroom. He grabbed my arm.

'Wait.'

'What's wrong?'

He pulled me back. 'Sit down.'

His tone was anxious. I sat on the arm of the sofa. He tossed his head to flick his hair out of his eyes. He took a deep breath, opened his mouth to speak, and caught himself. Uh-oh.

He took off his gloves and set the gun on the coffee table. Tossed his head again and breathed deeper.

'Say it.'

He took both my hands in his. 'The whole drive up here, I've been struggling with how to ask this.'

My spirit cringed. Don't tell me he wanted to ask the huge stinking obvious question after all. He reached into his shirt pocket. Crap, what did he have in there, an instant paternity test?

'And last time I asked, things didn't end up where I thought they would.'

Wait. 'Last time?'

'So I'm just going to do this. Skipping the bit where I get down on one knee.'

In his hand he held a small black box. He opened it. I saw the ring.

'Marry me.'

The diamond was so big and brilliant that I feared staring at it could damage my eyes. I heard myself: the disbelief and laughter and nascent tears in my throat.

'You lunatic,' I said.

That had the wrong effect on him. He pulled the box back, wounded. I grabbed his hand.

Now I was laughing and crying. 'Certifiable, howling-at-the-moon lunatic.'

'Evan, please.'

'Can't I see if it fits?'

He gave me his wryest look. Taking the ring from the box, he slid it on my finger, clasped my hand and kissed it.

He started to speak again and I put my fingertips against his lips. 'Impetuous, gallant, wonderful lunatic. Come here.'

He swung onto the sofa and I kissed him. 'When on earth did you get this?'

'While you and your dad were talking to Swayze. Told you I was going shopping.'

I laughed, pushed him down and climbed on top of him. He grinned up at me.

From the kitchen came another rattling noise. And the high-pitched sound of my cousin's voice.

'I can't stand it. I cannot stand it any longer!'

Jesse flung his arms out and grabbed the back of the sofa. I jerked straight up, shrieking, '*Shit.*'

Taylor popped up from behind the kitchen counter.

'I heard.' She pressed her hands to her cheeks. 'Y'all are getting married. Oh, my Lord.'

I leapt all the way to my feet there on the sofa and clambered over Jesse toward her. 'What the hell are you doing here? Get out.'

'Wait till I tell everybody.'

She was pressing her hands against her cheeks as if she'd just been voted Miss America. I launched myself off the arm of the sofa and lunged across the living room toward the kitchen.

She put out her arms. 'Stay back.'

She was wearing an outfit from Dazzling Delicates' Weekend Fireworks range: a gray pinstriped push-up bra with lapels. A bow tie at her neck. I couldn't see what was below her waist because the counter blocked my view, but I doubted it was tap pants. In front of her lay a judge's gavel. I threw myself across the counter at her. She squealed and jumped back, knocking magnets and photos off the fridge.

'No, stay there,' she said.

I raked the air with my hands. 'I'm going to kill you.'

'Why? Don't you like my attorney outfit? You should adore this. It's "Love Court".'

That explained why she was wearing Atticus Finch eyeglasses. She kept her hands out, gesturing me back.

'It's for gals who want to show their men how conservative yet provocative they can be. Every lawyer should have one. And what's wrong with you anyhow? I'm *happy* for y'all.'

'This is not your news to tell. You leave my house and you keep your mouth shut.' I grabbed the gavel. 'Or I will shove this so far up your ass that you'll be spitting splinters through your teeth.'

'Evan, please. There's no call for potty mouth.' She stared apprehensively at the gavel in my hand and her grape-jam eyes widened with amazement. 'That is one honking huge rock. Where on earth did he get the money for that?'

I went stark still, stretched prone across the counter.

She stared mesmerized at the ring. 'Did he hold a fundraiser? Get sponsored in a marathon or something?'

'Jesse,' I said. 'Get the gun.'

Slowly I pushed myself back off the counter. Tater rolled her eyes.

'Y'all are such kidders.'

'Jesse?' I said.

Shooting a glance over my shoulder, I saw him sitting in his chair, pinching the bridge of his nose and shaking his head.

'I'm not touching this,' he said.

Hoisting the gavel, I crept toward the side of the counter.

Tater's hands shot out again. 'No. Don't. You have to stay there.'

'Why?' I crept another step.

'Because when you came in I was sentencing the prisoner.'

Brain burp. 'Sentencing . . .'

I leaned sideways, peering around the counter, hearing Jesse call out, 'Bad idea.' But I couldn't stop myself.

I jumped. The gavel flew out of my hand. 'Shit. Oh, crap.'

Tater put her hands to her head. 'I can explain.'

I turned in a circle, and another one. 'Damn. Carlos.'

On the floor behind the counter, squirming to pull up his knees, sat my bathroom contractor. 'No, Miss Delaney, you have this all wrong. I'm—'

'Get out. No! Cover up. God.'

But he couldn't cover up. His hands were manacled behind his back. I kept turning in circles.

'Taylor, cover him up.'

Carlos was a spectacular piece of manflesh, but from now on when I thought of him I wouldn't see his smoky brown eyes or bronzed chest and six-pack, or remember the slugger who knocked 'em out of the park for Santa Barbara High, or even recall the stunning male toolset he was fighting to conceal.

'Now, Taylor.' I stormed away from the counter toward the living room.

From this day forward, when I thought of Carlos Martinez I would see the message written in marker on his naked thigh: Doin' Hard Time. With an arrow pointing at his groin.

Taylor said, 'It's art, Evan. A-R-T. We were setting up for the photo shoot. For the B-O-O-K.'

The gun lay on the coffee table. Jesse saw my expression and put his hand on top of it, shaking his head.

Behind me Taylor's heels clicked on the floor, quick little steps like a miniature poodle's, *tick-tick-tick*. She came out from behind the counter. Jesse inhaled.

She had whipped on a trench coat and cinched it up, but not before we saw the bottom half of her ensemble: the fluffy white mules; the nightstick and little bullwhip hanging from her leather belt, for the chain-gang boss inside every lawyer. And the tiny G-string, in prison-guard blue. Too, too tiny.

Jesse slapped his palm across his eyes. 'I'm blind.'

From the kitchen floor Carlos whimpered, 'Taylor, where are you going?'

'The key to the manacles is in the bathroom.' She

tick-ticked past Jesse. 'And you, buster. Hope you can rely on that big old sense of humor to keep you entertained after the wedding, 'cause Evan is definitely not into warming up her audience. If you catch my drift.'

She huffed into my bedroom. A second later we heard her rattle into the bathroom.

Jesse drummed his fingers on his knee. He pressed his lips together. Pushing backward, he spun and headed after her through the bedroom door.

'Taylor, turn around,' he said.

From the bathroom came the sound of the door bumping the wall. Tater's voice, alarmed. 'Hey. What are you—'

A squeal. Clattering. Tater wailing like a teakettle: 'You freak, what in the Lord's name—'

Scuffling. Tater screeching, and two hard sounds, *slap, slap,* and her heels approaching double time. She ran tick-ticking out of the bedroom with her hands on her butt.

'He spanked me.'

Her Atticus Finch specs sat askew on her nose. Her eyes were bulging. Jesse wheeled out of the bedroom. She pointed at him.

'That psycho spanked me.'

He cruised past her. 'Shutting up would be an excellent idea.'

'What in God's name is wrong with you?'

He whirled around. 'Evan didn't tell you? I have CTIS.'

'Oh my word.' Her mouth was round. 'What's . . . ?'

'Intermittent severe CTIS, the worst kind. It makes me go batshit crazy.'

Carlos wobbled to his feet behind the counter. 'Taylor, the key. Please.'

Jesse advanced on Taylor. She backed away.

202

'Ass-whacking is stage one. From there it gets worse.' He gave her a zombie stare. 'I see dead people. In your hair.'

She backed around the sofa. 'Keep away.'

He pursued her. 'Stage three gets nasty.' He made a fist, thumb up. 'I get the uncontrollable urge to take this thumb and *phone your husband*. So I'd haul my ass the hell out of here. This second.'

We all heard the front door open. 'Taylor?'

Our heads turned in unison. In the doorway, plumbing supplies in hand, stood Miguel Martinez.

He beheld the tableau. His truck keys fell from his hand. The plumbing supplies fell from his hand. His head swiveled toward the kitchen and he gaped at his brother.

'Miguel, what is this?' he said.

As one, Taylor, Jesse and I looked at the man in the kitchen. '*Miguel*?'

He ducked back behind the counter, looking plaintively at his twin. 'Carlos, I can explain.'

The man in the doorway stretched his hands toward Taylor, beseeching. 'How could you do this to me?'

Her finger veered toward the kitchen. 'No, no – that's Carlos.'

Naked boy quailed, 'Chica, no. I'm Miguel.' He looked at me. 'And don't worry, Miss Delaney, I was never going to put this on the clock.'

That, in hindsight, is when I began feeling dizzy. I saw Tater push her *To Kill a Mockingbird* glasses up her nose. I heard Naked Twin tell her to check his tattoo, it had his home run total, and my head began spinning. Her heels clicked. She said, 'I'll be damned.' Carlos – fully dressed, heartbroken Carlos – bolted out the door. Taylor grabbed

203

a big box labeled 'Weekend Fireworks' and ran after him. Miguel dashed out from behind the kitchen counter shouting, 'The key!'

He was in full swing. That's when I fainted.

The room fuzzed back into being. The view was white and the floor lay hard beneath my back. I was staring at the ceiling.

'Lie still,' Jesse said.

My feet were up on his lap. I waited while color returned. Yellow came, and black shadow. The soprano hum cleared from my ears.

'Tell me they're gone,' I said.

'With a boot up their butts. One of yours. Hope you don't mind.'

Turning my head, I saw his shirt. Gray brightened to blue and white. His hand was squeezing my ankle.

'I put in a call to Dr Abbott,' he said.

'Okay.' Cautiously I pulled my feet down and sat up.

'Easy.'

The dizziness subsided. 'I'm all right. It's just everything. And I didn't eat all day.'

'You're going to the doctor anyway.'

Taking my hand, he pressed his fingers against the pulse point in my wrist. His face was fretful.

I squinted at him. 'Severe intermittent CTIS?'

He waited for a few seconds, counting my pulse, before he glanced down. 'Cousin Tater Intolerance Syndrome.'

I smiled. 'Did you fire Miguel?'

'Did you want me to?'

'No. I need him to lay the shower tile.' The zinging sensation faded. 'Twist his nuts off with a pipe wrench, maybe.'

'I got you something else. A fifty per cent discount on the remodeling.'

I held out my hand and let him help me to my feet. 'Reason number ninety-seven that I love you.'

18

The apartment building was a crumbling edifice overlooking the 101 where it slid down out of Cahuenga Pass into Hollywood. It reminded him of the place where he grew up. The trappings were as worn and tacky as the whore – dingy furniture, a hash pipe, and a set of Princess Diana commemorative plates from the Franklin Mint. He lowered the blinds and got to work.

He took out his cordless drill and installed the new lock on the door. The whore's life was lonely, but even lonely whores might have friends. And they always had a pimp.

He gave her corpse a final stare. Alive, she had been rotting flesh. Breathing, speaking, rutting meat. Saliva pooled at the back of his throat. And the Army had discharged *him*? Claimed that *he* was unfit to fight on behalf of meat like this – this . . .

I'm Wanda, honey. Hundred on the dresser, just put it right there and get undressed. Wanda's going to start the party.

But he refused to undress in front of Wanda, so she tried to undress him. She touched him. She should not have touched him.

What's this scar, baby? Ooh, looks like that hurt. Your necklace, that's kind of spooky. Why you wear something that ugly?

He had snapped her neck at C-1.

He bundled her body into a bedspread, duct-taped it

into a shroud and shoved it into the closet. He stripped and showered and toweled off, careful not to pull open the cut on his hand. He wiped the towel across the steamy mirror and beheld his reflection. His blown pupil stared back at him, black and wide.

He was not capricious and he was not wasteful. He only took those on the list. And he only tested them to determine whether they perceived pain, whether they continued perceiving pain under increasingly intense application of stimuli, and whether at some point their pain perception shut off completely. Most, of course, ended screaming. But those who stopped feeling pain, those worthless unworthy who didn't know the power and invincibility that could have been theirs – those ended in silent confusion.

He ran the towel around the mirror. He saw the scar, all the rest. He hated seeing it, this ugliness. He hated living with it. Some men, he knew, felt comfortable in their skin, proud and open, even if they were effeminate. The ladyboys back in Thailand would primp and priss, sashaying even if they were simply working behind the counter at their mama's dry-cleaning shop. And they were beautiful. The boy who saw him at the bar in Pat Pong had thought Coyote beautiful as well, the boy with the sleek black eyeliner who had kissed his ear and slid his hand along the crotch of Coyote's pants and laughed when he didn't respond, saying, You not want a ladyboy, cowboy, you want to *be* a ladyboy. Coyote had killed him.

Thinking of the boy caused him to fret. Things had begun going wrong when he saw the ladyboys. Their beauty, their silky movements and delicacy had upset him. Killing that boy had been beyond the mission parameter, but he had been compelled to do it. And he had been repulsed by those desires in himself. Herself. Whatever he was becoming.

He dressed and returned to work. Soon the apartment was transformed. The photos, printouts, x-rays and other recent data were thumbtacked to the wall. On the coffee table he set out the original source material from Bassett High.

Somewhere in here lay the error. He must find, correct and eradicate it, so that the mission could continue.

And he needed to do it quickly. Only four of them were left.

Dr Lourdes Abbott bustled into the examining room carrying my chart. Beneath her white lab coat she wore a gray wool dress and stethoscope. The furrow in her forehead had deepened since my last visit.

'Positive,' she said. 'You're pregnant. Very.'

I nodded. She crossed her arms over the chart and offered me a compassionate, noncommittal look. She knew I wasn't married.

'You've been under considerable stress, I understand. A pregnancy adds to that, especially if the news itself is upsetting.'

'No, this news is great.'

She looked doubtful.

'Really.'

Her furrow creased further. 'Despite what you see on soap operas, fainting generally isn't the first symptom of pregnancy. I want to check your blood sugar and do some blood work to make sure you aren't anemic.' She rested her hand on my arm. 'Get yourself seen by your Ob-Gyn as soon as possible. Till then rest, eat well and take prenatal vitamins. Drink plenty of water.'

'Yes ma'am.'

She patted my arm, saw the diamond on my finger and arched an eyebrow.

'Yup,' I said.

'Congratulations.'

'Thanks.'

Her hand remained on my arm. 'The young man out in the waiting room – he's the one who phoned about you?'

I indicated the ring. 'He's the one.'

Her eyebrow stayed up. Her expression reeked of curiosity.

'You're wondering how this happened?' I said.

'Frankly, yes.'

'Apparently we've been struck by lightning. We haven't had fertility treatment. It's pure, cosmic luck.'

Her face mellowed. The smile was in her eyes. 'Then I'm thrilled for you.'

'This kind of luck might only come around once in a lifetime. So I want to take the utmost care of myself.'

'Don't get over-anxious about the fainting. I'm cautious, not alarmed.'

'I went down on a hardwood floor.'

'Your body's designed to take that kind of bump. It's not as if you jumped off a building.' She eyed me. 'There's something else?'

'I just found out that I was exposed to toxic chemicals on a field trip in high school. I know this makes me sound like a hypochondriac, but a number of my classmates have died from neurological problems.'

Emotion guttered behind her eyes – concern, and perhaps skepticism. 'What kind of problems?'

'Varying. They start out with anorexia, paranoia,

obsessions, and loss of coordination. Then they just die. And another classmate has a terminal brain disorder. She says it's eating tunnels in her head.'

Dr Abbott stilled. 'How has she been diagnosed?'

'I don't know.' I realized that Valerie hadn't phoned me back. 'But she thinks it's tied to the chemical exposure. And no, I don't know which chemicals, and it'll be hell to find out.'

'Tunnels. That's the word she used?'

'Yes.'

She frowned and rubbed her ear. 'It almost sounds like she's describing a spongiform encephalopathy.'

'Mad cow?'

'Variant CJD, kuru . . . there are several varieties of transmissible spongiform encephalopathies, TSEs. She gave you no more information?'

'I'm waiting to talk to her again.'

She eyed me critically. 'You're awfully wound up over this.'

'Kuru and mad cow are prion diseases, right? Contracted from eating infected brains?'

'Yes. So, unless your school cafeteria engaged in ritualistic cannibalism, you should take a step back and calm down.'

'Can they be caused by exposure to toxic chemicals?'

She crossed her arms over my medical chart. 'Neurodegenerative diseases can be caused by anything from head injury to genetic mutations. You've extrapolated too far for the evidence you've been given.'

'You don't understand.'

At which point the spigot turned on. Sputtering tears, I told her about South Star's research into sleep deprivation and a pain vaccine. The explosion and the *Outbreak* treatment my class received afterward. Students from the field trip beginning to die after graduation. From propeller hypnosis, anorexia, drug abuse, a car wreck and now murder. Valerie Skinner and the brain-eating disease that was killing her.

Dr Abbott handed me a tissue. When I wiped my eyes, she put a hand on my shoulder.

'This is far more than I realized you were dealing with. But here's the bottom line. Your health is excellent. Correct?'

'Aside from this attack of the killer hormones, you mean.' I blew my nose. 'Yes. I've been fine.'

'Don't project your friend's illness onto your own life. If you speak to her, try not to apply every symptom she describes to yourself. You'll make yourself ill.'

I nodded. 'There's something else. One of my class-mates . . .' I cleared my throat. 'One woman died following childbirth. So did her baby.'

She sighed and fixed me with a cut-it-out glare.

'And no, I don't know why Sharlayne or her baby died. It's just godawful scary right now.'

Her hand circled my wrist, cool and firm. She took my pulse and apparently disliked the count. The furrow reappeared.

'How about I phone the hospital where Sharlayne was admitted and see if I can learn anything?' she said.

'Please. Yes. Thanks. God, thank you.'

I gave her the information about Sharlayne's Spirit and Le Bonheur Children's Medical Center in Memphis. I had a dozen more questions, but she was giving me a firm stare: conversation closed. She patted my arm. I wondered if she was holding back her thoughts so as not to terrify me.

'Let's get that blood work.' She squeezed my arm. 'You have another seven months to climb this mountain. Take it step by step.'

Back in Jesse's truck, we puttered through crosstown traffic. The sun was pulling the city into the kind of golden afternoon that beckons you down to the beach, laughing and splashing into the blue surf. Valerie didn't answer her phone. When we approached a dip in the road Jesse slowed to ten miles per hour and babied the truck across.

'You don't have to handle me like a Fabergé egg,' I said.

'The doctor wants you to take things slow.'

'Not this slow.'

Behind sunglasses his face was cool with concern. 'Watching out for you and the kid isn't just my top priority. It's my only priority.'

His protectiveness warmed me. 'Thanks, Galahad. But that old lady just passed you. The one on the sidewalk, riding the motorized scooter.'

'Did not.'

'She blew you a kiss and shouted, "So long, sucker."'

His mouth skewed. He swung around the corner onto Anacapa and eased the truck up to a more normal speed. His face remained tense.

'I let you down in LA. It won't happen again,' he said.

'You haven't let me down.'

The look he gave me was sharp. Admitting weakness took guts. And he hated it when people let him off the hook because of his disability.

'I know you won't let me down again,' I said.

He changed lanes. 'If you feel up to it I'll stop by work

and see what's brewing.' He checked the rearview mirror. 'Then – *fuck*.'

He braked hard. The tires squealed. He swerved to a stop, grabbed me, pushed me down and lay across me. He opened the glove compartment and grabbed the gun. I heard him rack the slide.

'Stay down.'

I grit my teeth, staring at the floorboards. Whatever was out there was behind us. There was no way he would get a good angle on it. He breathed *one, two, three* and sat up, throwing himself against the door and swinging his right arm to aim the Glock at the back window.

For an aching second, then two, I heard nothing.

'Shit,' he said.

'Jesse?'

'Fucking shit. Is that what I think it is?'

'I'm sitting up.'

When he didn't object, I poked my head up. He was flat against the door, gun arm rigid. I followed his line of sight.

A sound half-snarled from my throat. 'Lower the gun.'

He pulled his finger off the trigger and pointed the weapon at the floor. Sagging against the door, he ran a hand over his face.

'It looked like somebody was climbing on the tailgate.'

I ground my teeth so hard that my dental work creaked. 'Tater must die.'

I got out and stomped to the back of the truck where the Weekend Fireworks box sat with its lid half off. Panties and briefs and rubber toys lay strewn about. Looking up the street, I saw a red bra and a pair of fishnet stockings. I bet the love paraphernalia stretched back to Dr Abbott's office like Hansel and Gretel's trail of breadcrumbs.

Suzie Sizemore sprawled, partially inflated, against the tailgate. Her feet were still in the Weekend Fireworks box. From the ecstasy on her plastic face, she had climaxed from the thrill of flailing about in weekday traffic. I grabbed her, and the box, tossed them in the back seat and climbed into the truck, slamming the door.

Jesse sat staring dead ahead, hands tight on the wheel. 'That's twice today. Has anybody checked Taylor's scalp for the birthmark?'

'Which one? Sixty-nine, or six six six?'

'I can't take much more of this shit.'

I put my hand across his shoulder. He continued staring out the windshield, ignoring the traffic that flashed past and the bike that grumbled up and stopped outside his door.

All my adrenaline was depleted, so what I felt was the heat seeming to run out of my body.

'Boris and Natasha are here,' I said.

He looked at me, and out the window.

Jax Rivera was revving the throttle on the bike. Tim North, riding pillion, gave us his mutt's stare. Dangling from his index finger was a silver lamé jockstrap.

'Jesse, mate, this style's a bit tarty for you.' He nodded up the road. 'Follow us.'

19

'I don't like the vibe I'm getting here,' Jesse said.

He slowed the truck around a hairpin turn. Ahead, Jax curved smoothly up the hill. On the back of the bike Tim leaned with her, hewing to her movements like a shadow. La Cumbre Peak crowded the sky. Chaparral and drooping oaks congested the edges of the asphalt. Jax powered the bike over a rise and cut left onto a side road.

Jesse read the road sign. 'Knew it.'

The hill steepened past rows of eucalyptus and houses hunched back in the brush. Jax angled down a driveway with a For Sale sign, to a lot where the concrete foundation for a house was laid. We parked on a promontory overlooking the city and followed them up onto the concrete slab, Jesse popping a wheelie.

Tim's bearing was Army. He moved with the economy of a snake. He admired the two-million dollar view while we approached.

Trying to maintain a cool façade with a paid killer wasn't simple. 'You're carrying the British love of irony too far.'

'Coyote Road. I suppose so.'

'Kai Torrance. I need to know if that's Coyote.'

He continued taking in the panorama. 'What's brought you to this juncture?'

'A typhoon named Maureen Swayze, plus two goons who move like they have the same sniper training as you.

215

And a guy in a baseball cap who sent Jesse on a whirl around the dance floor. It was a regular fiesta. All we were missing was the piñata.'

Jax approached. 'I imagine Coyote had you penciled in for that role.'

My flesh crept. 'We saw him. Blond, slight, mister inconspicuous.'

'Don't rely on physical appearance,' Tim said. 'Next time Coyote may turn up as a fat cop or an old woman.' He turned his head at last, taking us in. 'Even I don't know what Coyote looks like, and I've met the bastard.'

Shit. 'Took you long enough to tell us.'

'It was in Colombia, during one of the more robust interludes in the War on Drugs.'

He glanced at his wife. She was strolling to the edge of the slab, admiring the view. Even wearing shitkickers and motorcycle leathers, she might have been gliding through a *pas de deux* in *Swan Lake*. Colombia, to hear Jax tell it, was where she hit the end of the line as a CIA operative. It was impossible to know whether she was remembering the final act in Medellin: the lover who betrayed her to narco-traffickers, the heroin she doped him with, the 9 mm round she fired into his temple.

Tim said, 'In the field you sometimes work with peers from other intelligence services. I was occasionally part of Coyote's supply chain, providing logistics.'

Jesse put his hands on his pushrims. 'Thought you were at the top of the chain, behind the night scope.'

'Even rock stars occasionally take day jobs.' Tim smiled a rough smile. Considering that he was the scariest man I might ever consider trusting, it was a disarming look.

'Of course Coyote was using a cover identity. But you've nailed him. Kai Torrance.'

I let out a breath. 'He was CIA?'

'I never saw who signed his payslip. I only know that in his prime he was terrific. Quiet, effective and reliable,' he said. 'Later I crossed paths with him in Thailand, and he'd changed. He was edgy, almost brittle. His methods had become eccentric.'

'How so?'

'He'd taken to slicing claw marks into the bodies of his targets. Signing his work like he was bloody Zorro. Needless to say, a signature spook is an oxymoron.'

Jesse was grim. 'Who are we up against?'

'He's trained in sabotage and demolition, and he's adept at vigorous interrogation.'

Demolition. Jesse and I glanced at each other, thinking of the explosion at the Air Force clinic that killed Dana West.

A bitter taste filled my mouth. 'He's a trained torturer?'

'He was trained to withstand torture. His methods of inducing pain were of his own devising.' He turned to me. 'Covert ops deal with the most malign thugs on the planet, and it's not your average agent who leaves his air-conditioned office in Virginia to face violence and dysentery in the armpits of the world. I'm telling you he's one vicious cat with an unholy level of devotion to his mission.'

The sun felt harsh. I sat down on the edge of the foundation slab.

'What happened in Thailand?' I said.

'Drugs, whores of various flavors – devotion to mission doesn't exclude the usual appetites.' He took a pack of cigarettes from his shirt pocket. 'Something split inside him and the wheels came off, at high rpms.'

I ran my hands through my hair. 'He killed somebody?'

'A transvestite in Bangkok.'

Jesse glanced over. 'Is he gay?'

'Gay, bi, a goat shagger, I don't know. But this *katoy* – this Thai ladyboy, it wasn't a simple murder.' He shrugged. 'Huge city like that, ordinarily a whore dies and few people take notice. But the trappings of this death were, well, it was . . .'

He stared at the ground.

Jax mimed a knife slicing flesh. 'Coyote used a Ka-bar. Took 'em off mid-wank.'

Jesse flinched. So did Tim.

'After that Coyote turned into smoke,' he said. 'Out of play, dead, who knew?'

'Why,' I began, and had to clear my throat. 'Why did his mission change from sorting out thugs in Southeast Asia to killing my classmates here at home?'

Jax sat down beside me. 'You've made the leap, then.'

'That he never went off the government clock.'

She nodded. 'In a manner of speaking.'

'Is Project South Star still active?'

'No. This seems more like an after-effect. South Star died out but Coyote burns on.'

The sun felt hot on my face. 'If you walk back the cat, the tangled ball of string unspools to China Lake. Things went wrong when my class got too close to that explosion out in Renegade Canyon. We were exposed to something that's causing my classmates to get sick and die. And now it's leading Coyote to kill them.' I looked at her. 'Are we the error that somebody's trying to correct? The flaw?'

Jax eyed me. 'Get sick and die? Is that why you were coming out of a doctor's office?'

I should have known they'd been following us from Dr Abbott's. 'No, I'm fine. Are you telling me that you didn't know about that?'

Jesse raised a hand. 'Before you ask any more questions, I have one.' He waved at Jax and Tim. 'Why do you want to help track down Coyote? Tell me how come you give a shit.'

They didn't answer. Tim lit a cigarette.

'Cross off altruism or a desire to atone for your own sins. That leaves money or a vendetta.'

Tim's expression didn't change. 'Nobody's paying me to kill Coyote.'

'So it's a freebie?'

Jax stood up. 'It's neither. What matters is that I will not lie to Evan or put her in danger. That's all you need to know.'

'The hell it is.'

Tim dragged on his cigarette. 'Jax went to Evan with information intended to shut down this bastard before anybody else died. So maybe you could dial it down, mate.'

'Don't tell me to cool it.'

'Twenty minutes ago you pulled a gun on an inflatable toy. Cooling it is precisely what you need to do.'

Jesse closed his eyes and put up his hands. 'Fine.'

Jax sat down beside me again. 'Summarize what you've learned.'

I gave them the short form: South Star, explosion, death, death and death.

She scanned the view of the harbor. 'It almost ties together, but not quite. We're missing something.'

I looked at her. 'He killed the helicopter pilot last year near Seattle.'

'Dearing? I didn't know she had a China Lake connection.'

'Do you know about any other murders?'

219

'There was a car wreck in Cincinnati that's suspicious.'

'Hell,' I said. 'Marcy Yakulski?'

'That's it. The paper reported that the gas tank caught fire when they flipped. It didn't report that somebody watched the car burn.'

'A bystander?' Jesse said.

'This was a dispassionate observer. He stood by while two people burned inside the vehicle. But the driver ignored the flames and managed to get her child free and carry her down the street. The observer followed. When the driver collapsed he stood over her, staring. He was there when the fire department arrived. Before he fled, one of the firefighters saw him squat next to the driver, touching her. The autopsy showed marks in her flesh.'

Jesse's voice was low. 'Holy fuck.'

'That was Marcy,' I said. 'Did he rig the crash?'

Jesse came up behind me. 'No, I mean that Coyote was observing the effects of South Star. He watched Marcy burn to study the effects of the pain vaccine.'

From the hillside below us a vulture swooped up into the sky, black wings a hole in the blue. I closed my eyes, trying to shut out all but the evidence. Trying to make the string untangle.

'We weren't vaccinated against pain. We were contaminated with something, and so was Coyote. And now he's trying to get rid of us.'

'It's a cover-up,' Jesse said. 'Coyote isn't out there running amok. He's on assignment.'

Tim dragged on his cigarette. 'A comment from one who toiled in the bowels of government. If an agency wants something covered up, they may outsource the work so that they can keep their hands clean.'

'Covering their asses?' I said.

'They're bureaucratic weasels. They like their comfy offices in Whitehall and Langley. They like their projects to look like successes in the after-mission reports. One gets promoted by running clean, successful projects.'

'So they're going dirty as hell to clean up a messy project from way back?' I said.

Jax shrugged. 'It's conceivable.'

I ran my hands through my hair. 'Then Coyote's using the serial killer profile to distract attention from his real agenda.'

Jesse rubbed his palm along his leg. 'Problem is, some government agency may have outsourced the cover-up of a toxic chemical exposure to an actual psychopath.'

'If that's what's going on,' Jax said, 'then Coyote has backers, funds, and possibly contacts who provide him with information to target his victims.'

'Salt'n'Pepa?' I said.

'I'm not sure who those men might have been. But right now we don't know who you can trust. Presume that somebody is feeding Coyote information. Watch yourself.'

Jesse looked at me, bleak. Above us the vulture lazed in the sky, riding the late afternoon thermals.

I stood and began pacing. 'It still doesn't scan.'

Jesse echoed me. 'For the government to try to kill every kid in a class that was exposed to toxic chemicals – for what? You're right. It's overkill.'

'We still haven't put it together. Something else is going on.'

Jax said, 'You need additional information. Who else can you talk to about this?'

I jumped. She was right behind me.

'I need to talk to the classmate who's ill. And maybe

the doctor back in China Lake who advised the high school.' Looking toward Jesse, the sun spun into my eyes and I put a hand up to block the glare. 'Tully Cantwell, you met him at the reunion.'

Jax took hold of my hand. 'Oh, my.'

She turned it so the ring flashed in the light. Her eyes narrowed.

'Colorless, excellent clarity, superb cut.' She looked at Jesse. 'Mister, you have taste.'

Her feline gaze assessed me. She smiled as though enjoying the answer to a private riddle and brushed the back of her hand across my cheek. I swallowed, dry-mouthed.

Tim stubbed out his cigarette. 'Here's the thing. Coyote likes knives and fire. And he's after you.'

He crossed the concrete, hands loose at his sides. 'There's an adage. First rule of a gunfight? Bring a gun. First rule of a knife fight? Bring a gun.'

My mouth was still dry. 'What's the first rule of a fire-fight?'

'Be someplace else.' He stepped closer. 'Get out of Dodge.'

That wasn't an adage but a directive.

'I'm working with the cops and the FBI,' I said.

'Then do it on the fly. Keep moving and keep your head down. Coyote has no limits. Even if some government agency is sponsoring him, these killings are deeply personal. You can't stop him, you can only stay ahead of him.'

They turned and headed back to the bike. Overhead, the vulture soared in a figure eight, drawing a sign in the sky. Eternity.

222

20

I heard the keycard flip the lock. I hiked the bath towel around myself just as Jesse pushed open the door. He came into the motel room with Mexican food, and it smelled great.

My hair was wet and the air conditioning was up high. The South Coast Inn had what we needed for the night: a hot shower, a king bed, high-speed Internet access and privacy. This was called getting out of Dodge.

I pulled on a white T-shirt and jeans. Jesse set the food on the coffee table.

'Rudy's taquitos. Babe, this is reason ninety-eight.' I took the fork he offered, grabbed the plate and started wolfing. 'Thank you.'

Green chile salsa, fried tortillas, guacamole and sour cream: the start to my pregnancy diet. I was eating for two, and right then I didn't care if the second person was Marlon Brando.

Jesse got his own plate and dug in. He looked at the notes and printouts slung across the coffee table.

'How's it going?' he said.

'Sally Shimada's taking the feature idea to her editor.'

Sally was a reporter at the Santa Barbara *News-Press*. She was charming, dogged and ambitious, so with luck I thought I might get my feature on the reunion killings published within a day or two. After that I could work on spreading it to other papers and online.

'At a minimum she'll interview me for a piece of her own. And I left a message with Dr Cantwell's office in China Lake. Still no answer on Valerie's number, though. That worries me.'

He eyed me. 'You need to set that aside. Eat up, stretch out on the bed and rest. No worrying tonight.'

'Sure. Flip that switch on my back, would you? I can't reach it.'

He glanced at my computer. 'Making progress on the writing?'

'Excellent progress.'

I took my plate to the desk, sat down and scrolled through my document. He backpedaled to get a look.

'What is this?' he said.

My smile felt pleasingly evil.

He read the screen. 'You're not serious.'

'You don't think Taylor deserves it?'

Setting his plate on his lap, he pulled the computer to the edge of the desk. He read aloud.

'"Dear Mrs Boggs: Thank you for your proposal for *Pants on Fire: Weekend Fireworks for Couples*, which your cousin submitted on your behalf."'

He looked incredulous.

I gestured at the screen. 'Didn't I mock up a first-rate publisher's letterhead? I'm lethal with fonts.'

'"Your photographs have a gritty, *verité* quality. And we agree that pants on fire are essential to the nation's physical and spiritual health. Regretfully, however, your book does not fit with our current list. Photo essays are expensive, and the dimensions . . ."'

He blinked.

'Okay, I need a better adjective there.' I deleted *vast*.
'Colossal? Thundering?'

'Gargantuan.'

'Now you're talking.' I typed.

'". . . the dimensions of your gargantuan ass preclude us from publishing it as a coffee table book. Even an over-sized one. We have forwarded it to our sister publication, *Cattlemen's Quarterly*, where bovine proportions are *de rigueur* and . . ."'

'Scratch "bovine".' I backspaced and retyped.

'"Heiferlicious", that's evocative.' His jaw had gone slack. 'How are you going to pull this off? You've given the publisher a New York address.'

'Manhattan Area Code, that's all she needs to see on the fax header. Think your cousin would send it? The practical joker?'

'I'll phone him.'

'Excellent.'

He took over the keyboard and added a final line.

'"In closing, may we compliment you on your impeccable proofreading."'

I kissed him on the cheek and stood up. He snagged my hand.

'You never lose your equilibrium. Did you know that?' he said.

I gave him a puzzled look. 'What do you mean?'

'You handle everything and you never capsize. Granted, you might handle things aggressively, but you always keep your feet underneath you.'

'I'm told it's either poise or mulishness.'

'You even cope with a sarcastic hothead proposing marriage to you.'

I smiled. 'I think of you more as a spirited wiseass.'

He held onto my hand. 'Thank you. For everything.'

The words, his lopsided smile and the humility in his voice hit me like a skillet in the face.

'Babe.'

I drew him to the bed and he swung over to sit next to me. I put my hand against his cheek.

'I'm the one who needs to thank you, for this tremendous gift,' I said.

'You're welcome. But I want you to know that I mean it.' He pulled me down and we lay facing each other. 'Thank you for taking me as I am. Thank you for taking this ride with me.'

'Taking each other as we are, I think that's what marriage has to be about.'

He brushed my hair back from my face. 'Fearsome idea, isn't it?'

'Bloodcurdling.'

His lopsided smile remained. He rolled onto his stomach and propped himself up on his elbows.

'Our genes, wrapped up in a new package. Unbelievable.' Giving me the once-over, he said, 'I predict freckles.'

I eyed him back. 'Blue eyes. Long legs.'

'Your imagination.'

'Your relentlessness.'

'The comical way you cry at the end of movies.'

'That's not comical, it's warm-hearted. Your misguided fashion sense.'

'*Terminator* turns on your waterworks. It's comical. What's wrong with my fashion sense?'

I pulled up his shirt. His shorts showed above the waistband of his jeans. 'Krusty the Clown boxers. You're right, that's not misguided. It's tragic.'

'Your mouth.'

226

'Your mouth.'

We stared at each other. He broke out laughing.

'God, what a nightmare,' I said.

He laid his cheek on my belly and whispered, 'Hello, baby. It's your dad.'

It's the sweetest of memories.

When the stars came out, Coyote climbed the fire escape to the roof of the whore's apartment building. It was a cheap California roof, tarpaper covered with gravel that scrunched beneath his feet. Squatting down in the dark, he lifted his face to the sky and let the noise of the nearby freeway flow over him. The air carried the metallic taste of auto exhaust. He knew what he had to do.

He had to take the four who were left. He would take others as well, but those four were the crux of the project. Taking them would stop the leaks. Taking them would balance the scales. It would cleanse and rectify. And he knew how he had to make his approach.

One name came back to him. She was a pivot point. She was one of the original group, the ones who set his life on the path to disorder. The documents contained more than enough information about her to help him focus his hunt. Valerie Skinner would be beyond valuable.

He put his hands on the gravel roof and scratched his fingernails back, drawing claw marks. The shamans knew, the Shoshone and Paiutes of the Neolithic high desert. You draw your hunt, you carve it into the stone as his fingers had carved into Becky O'Keefe's burnt flesh, and you bring good fortune upon yourself.

He looked down. In front of the building a car stopped, a blood-red Camaro, and a man climbed out. He had a rat's twitchiness. The pimp was here.

He rushed down the fire escape to the apartment and began packing up his work. Footsteps climbed the stairs in the hall and the pimp pounded on the door. He ignored it. When the man left, he would get out. He didn't need to go far, but he wanted to be away from this site when the stench of Wanda began wafting out. He knew where he would go. He gazed out the window, down toward the crawl of Hollywood. It had been many years, but it was time to go home.

Angie Delaney pulled into the driveway after dark, feeling weary. Work had been a total loss. All she could feel was a grinding worry about her daughter. But she knew that Phil was taking things in hand, and that alone made her feel more secure. Phil was a son of a bitch, but he was her son of a bitch.

She grabbed her purse from the passenger seat and saw the crumpled bits of paper littering the floor. She picked them up and realized they must have fallen out of Evan's backpack.

She sighed. The visit had been too short. Blow in, blow out, the human hurricane. But that was her girl: Evan was her father's daughter.

Loneliness swept through her. Damn, she missed her kids sometimes. The fact that they grew up and moved away was not fair, not at all. She uncrumpled the bits of paper, pressed them to her skirt and smoothed them out.

She smiled to herself, seeing Evan's handwriting. A grocery list. A legal sheet scribbled with court case citations. The receipt from the pharmacy.

She saw the itemized list of purchases and felt as though she'd been slapped in the head. *Early Pregnancy Test*.

She ran inside to call her ex-husband.

The ocean shone electric blue, lit from below. I swam nowhere. The surf roared and breakers hurled themselves up the sand. Jesse was standing on the beach.

Wind rakes his hair across his eyes. He's waiting for me. I have to get to shore but I can't kick.

Behind me comes a ripping sound. I turn. Three gashes are tearing toward me along the surface of the water. Strike fighter speed. They're talon tracks but the creature, whatever huge thing is slicing the ocean, is invisible.

Hey. My arms won't swim. I call to Jesse but the surf swallows my voice. The gashes race toward me. Where they rip the water it turns translucent, veined a bloody blue.

Do you have a message? I'm yelling. And Jesse sees. He runs into the surf, dives through a wave and comes up sprinting. Head down, thresher kick, barreling toward me. The tracks are bearing down, roaring, and now in their wake the water is black. *Laughing, wildly.* I stretch my hand toward Jesse. He's right there, inches away, when the talons slice the water on top of him.

I jerked awake. My hands were clutching the covers and I felt as though a concrete block was laid across my chest. The glow from the television flickered on the ceiling. The dream hung in my mind, sharp as a scream. I rolled over and reached for Jesse.

He wasn't in bed. I blinked my eyes into focus. A news channel was on TV, showing footage taken from a helicopter: overhead shots of a freeway, a copse of trees, Becky O'Keefe's Volvo. A photo flashed onscreen, showing Becky holding Ryan on her lap. He was nestled against her chest, wearing a smile that knew neither pain nor fear. I lay still, feeling small.

Jesse was at my computer. I got up.

'Can't sleep?' I said.

He hit a key. 'It's six a.m. You've been out like a light.'

Now that I looked, gray daylight was leaking under the foot of the drapes. I ran my hands around his shoulders. His skin was warm. His hair was going in ten directions. I kissed the top of his head, saw the computer screen and froze.

'Where did that come from?'

'Your dad.'

'Shit.'

He lifted his hands off the keyboard. 'You'd better watch. But brace yourself.'

I sat down. He reset the video to the start of the stream. Giving me a sidelong glance, he pushed Play.

In jerky, home-movie style, the camera crossed a room. A living room, a starter home, Ikea-blond furnishings blurring past. Light bled in from a window, overwhelming the lens, and the picture whited out. When it came back the cameraman was standing in front of an easy chair, centering on a woman sitting there.

'Dana.' The man's voice was gentle. 'You want to say hello?'

I gripped the edge of the desk. 'Jesus Christ.'

Jesse put his hand on my back. 'Her husband took the video. He forwarded it to your dad.'

The camera zoomed in, focusing on her face. It was Dana West. Or what was left of her.

She was crumpled in the chair. The camera held steady on her shoulders and face, but that couldn't hide the spasms that pulled at her limbs. She was wasted, her head little more than a skull with skin. She couldn't have weighed more than eighty pounds. She looked like a malformed toy. She was laughing.

230

Her lips drew back, her teeth protruded and her tongue came out like a slug. Her hand writhed past the camera.

'Hey,' she shouted.

Her voice was slurred, pitched like a cat caught in a trap. Her hand came back across the view, fingers twisted. I realized she was waving.

Behind the camera her husband said, 'Honey, do you have a message?'

Her gaze roamed over the ceiling. One of her pupils was normal size. The other was dilated wide. It looked wet and black.

This was the frame where Jesse had paused the video. Now it kept going.

Dana continued laughing. The sounds coming out of her throat seemed entirely unconnected with her thoughts, movements or emotions. I clawed the edge of the desk.

Gently the man said, 'Dana, remember what we practiced?'

For a second I thought she had gone incoherent. But it became horrifyingly clear that she was lucid. Her eyes stopped roving. She stared straight at the camera. Though she continued writhing and the laughter blurted from her throat, she fought inch by inch to bring her balled hand up to her face. Her mouth widened and the trapped animal voice cried out.

'Hi little girl.' She groped for breath. 'Mommy loves you.'

She bumped her fist to her mouth and blew a kiss. The camera zoomed out, in time to see Dana drop her hand to a stomach swollen with pregnancy.

21

I came out of the bathroom after being sick. Jesse was sitting with his eyes closed, rubbing his fingers across his forehead.

'You may not want to watch the second video,' he said. 'Play it.'

I sat down. Sludge was running through my veins. He queued up a new file.

It was low bandwidth streaming video, sent from a webcam. A man in the uniform of an Air Force officer sat at a desk talking to the camera. He looked spent, my age but dust inside. His was the gentle voice behind the video of Dana.

'At first I thought she was depressed. Her first trimester she got really, really down. She didn't want to eat and she couldn't sleep.'

He blinked. 'But then the panic attacks started, and she began hallucinating. Like she was dreaming, wide awake. I knew something was horribly wrong. She lost her coordination and started slurring her speech. Then it ate her up.'

He looked into the camera. 'That video I sent? That was two weeks before the baby came. By then I knew Dana wasn't going to make it. We'd had the MRI. When I took the video, she hadn't slept in eight weeks. Period. Total insomnia.' He clawed his fingers through his hair.

'We made the video so the baby would – so that when she got old enough, she'd have something from her mother, to know her by. Even with Dana like she was at the end . . .' He closed his eyes. 'It was going to be for our baby girl.'

He reached out and hit his keyboard. The video blanked. When it came back a few seconds later, he looked more composed.

'The baby lived three hours. She had – profound neurological abnormalities.' He pressed his lips together. 'Her name was Clare.'

I didn't move a muscle. Jesse didn't seem to be breathing.

'She was delivered by Caesarean and that night Dana started bleeding. They couldn't stop it. Finally the next morning they opened her up again and performed a hysterectomy. I mean, there wasn't much point in trying to salvage anything. They just ripped everything out to stop the hemorrhaging.'

Now he looked at the camera. 'Post-op, that's when the fire happened. And I've always known that there was no good reason for those doors to be locked.' He shook his head. 'Why? I know she was dying, but to kill her like that . . . to start a fire that blew up the OR and then burned down the place?'

He leaned toward the camera. His voice remained gentle.

'Captain Delaney, find out who did this to my wife. Because I'm going to kill the motherfucker.'

Coyote stood by the window, amazed and apprehensive to be here. Everything felt familiar: the light, the traffic, the heat and the smell. The halls were still ratty, the carpets

233

just as moldy, the hallways as tainted with scuzz and urine as ever. Once, back in the days of silent movies, this had been a middle-class apartment building. Now, it was the last refuge of the decrepit and despondent. Home.

The clothing nest was long gone, but it was home nonetheless. She locked the door and undressed. Off came the eyeglasses and frumpy blazer and frowsy gray wig. They went in the suitcase with the photo ID that Mrs Public Health Nurse wore when visiting elderly shut-ins, such as the crone who occupied these rooms with her croaky voice and shuffling slippers and eagerness to open the door to a face who would listen to her complaints. Coyote pulled on fatigue bottoms and a white wifebeater T-shirt and felt himself return. He sucked in a lungful of dusty air, tasting success like a promise on his tongue. It was time for the final push.

He turned the journal to a new page and began annotating. He felt himself revving up. He had an email: holy cross china lake, thurs 10 am. tc. It was good timing. He hung the amulet on a candlestick and got down to planning.

Dr Abbott sat at her desk watching the video of Dana West on my computer screen, fingers steepled in front of her lips.

'Anorexia, complete insomnia, ataxia and myoclonus. That's the slurred speech and jerking movements.'

She lifted the printout. Dana's husband had emailed her medical reports.

'The MRI confirms that she had a transmissible spongiform encephalopathy. Her brain was riddled with holes.'

'How about the baby?' I said.

'I don't know. I don't have any medical data on the infant.'

I watched her, practically begging her to give me absolution, a free pass, to wave her doctor's wand and sing Bibbity Bobbity Boo and tell me I was okay.

She said, 'I spoke to the doctors in Memphis about Sharlayne Jackson. She died from intracranial hemorrhaging after a fall. She was at twenty-five weeks' gestation.'

'The baby?'

'Was delivered, but was simply too small to survive.'

I sank in the chair, saddened. 'So Sharlayne's death was unconnected?'

'I don't know about that. The doctors found it perplexing. She had fallen down some stairs and hit her head, hard. But afterward she said that she felt fine. She was covered with bruises but insisted that she didn't feel any pain at all. She went on with her day at work. Then that afternoon she went into premature labor. She didn't feel the contractions. She gave birth in the middle of her school classroom.'

I felt frozen. 'She had it. The pain vaccine. It killed her.'

She didn't quite acknowledge that. 'If I had to venture a guess, this is a variant form of Sporadic Fatal Insomnia.'

'Lack of sleep can kill you?'

'Patients generally die from secondary infections, often pneumonia. The primary problem is a prion infection that spongifies the brain.' She sat forward. 'The major strain of the disease is genetic – familial fatal insomnia. But your classmates seem to be suffering from a TSE that arises from infection. Inhalation may be the transmission mechanism in this case.'

'What are you going to do?'

'Get more information. And you should speak to your friend who's ill – Valerie? Also, talk to that doctor back in China Lake who handled the medical waivers after your class was exposed. If this is a new TSE, I'll notify the CDC's emerging infections division.'

All I could think about was peak soldier performance: Project South Star's work with sleep deprivation and pain control. It had gone wild.

'I think this has infected the killer, too,' I said. 'But . . .'

'But the killer can't possibly be as ill as Dana West.' She looked at the computer image again. 'If he's infected, either he isn't end-stage, or something's keeping him going.'

This wasn't making sense.

I forced myself to look at Dr Abbott. 'Can people with these diseases pass it along to their children?'

'Some forms can be inherited. Not all.'

The walls in the office constricted. 'I think this form can be passed on. I think that's why Coyote killed Becky's little boy.'

I stood up, ready to run for the door before the walls closed on me.

'Evan.'

Dr Abbott was standing behind her desk with my lab results in her hands. 'All your blood work came back normal. And you're showing no – I repeat no – signs of neurological instability.'

'I'm close to having a panic attack right here on the carpet. That's a symptom, right?'

'To be absolutely safe, I'm going to recommend that you get an MRI—'

'Schedule it.'

Hands up. 'Once you're past your first trimester.'

Six, seven more weeks. Could I handle that before the other symptoms made me insane? Panic. Paranoia. Uncontrollable laughter and tears.

'Okay, okay.' I swallowed. 'Okay.' Another swallow. 'Are there tests for these diseases? Can you check to see if the baby's okay?'

She shook her head. 'You're going to have to wait.'

I tore out of the doctor's office and went ripping up the street in the Mustang, punching the number for Sanchez Marks. Damn if I wanted to tell Jesse, but we were in limbo. However, I didn't get to break the news. His PA sounded breathless.

'He's on his way to court. The Dieffenbach case, hell broke loose and he's trying to get a TRO.'

'Which judge?'

'Rodriguez. By any chance do you have a decent shirt and a tie for him?'

I didn't. When I crept into the back of the courtroom, he was arguing for the temporary restraining order and Judge Sophia Rodriguez was looking like vinegar. Opposing counsel wore pinstripes. Jesse's T-shirt sported a picture of Darth Vader and the caption 'Who's your daddy?'

But when Rodriguez clacked her gavel, he had the restraining order.

'Thank you, your honor.' He pushed back, turning to leave.

'And Mr Blackburn, never again. Understood?'

'Yes, your honor.'

He came down the aisle looking chastened rather than victorious.

'Did she hold you in contempt?' I said.

'One-time exemption, because she wants to get her grandson a shirt like this.' His eyes shone with worry. 'What did Abbott say?'

I told him on the way out, walking along the corridor toward an archway that opened onto morning sunshine. We could say nothing to comfort each other. As we walked outside tourists strolled past, listening to a guide describe the Moorish architecture.

I turned. At the back of the tour group, looking like Cossacks on vacation, were Salt'n'Pepa.

'I don't believe it.'

Jesse turned. 'Son of a bitch.'

I strode toward them. 'Hey.'

They looked up from their courthouse brochures. Salt was decked out in a white Izod shirt and chinos, Pepa in a Notre Dame sweatshirt and Yankees cap. With the smoothness of dance partners they turned and headed for the street.

'No, you don't.' I tossed Jesse my bag and ran toward them.

'Ev, wait.'

They jogged across the street, beating the light. Traffic stopped me. They sped out of sight beyond the library, cutting toward State Street one block over.

Jesse caught up. 'What are you doing?'

The light changed. 'This is about equilibrium. I'll take Victoria. You cut through the arcade.'

Pointing down the street, I broke into a run. These guys were bugging the hell out of me, and with everything out of control I was damned if I was going to let one possible chance for information or clarity escape. Again. I ran, seeing my reflection in the tall windows of the library.

I passed restaurants and shops and stopped on the corner of Victoria and State. I looked down State in the direction of the beach. Palms shrugged in the breeze. The street was shiny with traffic, the sidewalks dense with shoppers. Down the block Jesse came out from the pedestrian arcade onto the sidewalk, glancing around. He saw me, waved and pointed across the street.

I bolted across the crosswalk and ran down State. There were Salt'n'Pepa powerwalking amid the crowd a block ahead. I dodged a clump of teens playing hooky from Santa Barbara High. They wore piercings and *life sucks* expressions. A surly lass blew smoke at me. Yeah, chem class is harsh. It's a tough-ass world. I bumped her aside, saying, 'Grow up.'

Salt'n'Pepa crossed Carrillo and fuzzed into the crowd. I worked to keep them in sight. Across the street Jesse slalomed around disconcerted tourists and jumped a curb to keep from getting stuck at the light. I kept running.

When they cut into the wide promenade at the Paseo Nuevo mall, I figured they might know we were on their tail. Damn. If my father had really worked as a spook the least he could have done was teach me some tradecraft. Instead, Jesse and I were dogging these two like a couple of fans chasing a rock band. And hey, what do you know, Salt headed into Mel's and Pepa kept going. Splitting up, that was probably Undercover 101. I heard Jesse whistle and caught sight of him coming around the corner. Pointing him after Pepa, I veered through the door into Mel's.

Gloom, Formica and whiskey: everything the committed drinker wants at eleven-thirty in the morning. Salt stood at the bar. The bartender took his five and slid a Budweiser across to him. He gazed at his reflection in the mirror along the wall behind the bottles of Maker's Mark.

I hopped up on a stool. 'If you're investigating crop circles, the courthouse tour's the wrong place to find them. Check behind the Old Mission. But be prepared, it's a crop triangle.' I smiled sourly. 'And your iPod's missing one earpiece.'

He continued staring at the mirror, ignoring me and his beer and the wireless radio receiver in his ear. The bartender rang up his Bud and slapped change down in front of him, giving us the eye before wandering away.

'What are you doing here?' I said.

He didn't respond.

'Coyote? South Star? The pain vaccine that's killing the people Coyote doesn't?'

He kept gazing at his reflection.

'These are my classmates and their kids, you jackboot SOB. Tell me.'

He stared at the change on the bar, shifted his shoulders and finally spoke.

'I'm tracking down the conspirators who assassinated JFK.' He thumbed a quarter and slid it at me. 'There's a pay phone back there. You spot anybody lurking on the grassy knoll, give me a call.'

Call it a draw. I wasn't going to get anything from him. I stood up.

'Hope your buddy picks you out something nice from Victoria's Secret.' I poked him in the shoulder with my index finger. 'Tag, you're it.'

Outside in the sun, I looked down the mall past chic stores and restaurants hung with wisteria. Jesse was cruising toward me shaking his head, indicating that Pepa was gone. While he was still some distance away, my phone rang. He pulled it from my purse, answered it, listened a moment and threw it to me like it was a live snake.

I caught it but heard a dial tone.

'What's wrong?' I said. 'Who was it?'

'Tater.'

I stared at the phone, and again at him. 'What did she say?'

'She . . .' He looked like he was about to gag. 'She called me Spanky.'

My skull nearly exploded right then. The phone rang again. I flipped it open.

'People claim we're related by blood, but I fully believe that you were birthed by a hyena and switched in the crib at the hospital. And if you ever, *ever*—'

'He's killing kids now.'

I cringed. 'Valerie?'

'Becky's little boy. I'm so fucking scared,' she wheezed. 'I can't stay here. I have to get away.'

'Valerie, is anybody with you?'

The wheezing intensified. 'Some weird shit is going on.'

I looked at Jesse. 'Define weird.'

'Phone calls where nobody's there. Hang ups,' she said. 'And they're messing with my email.'

'Messing how?' I said.

'I can't explain, I don't have the words anymore. Catching it?'

'Intercepting your emails?'

'I'm not imagining this. I've seen a car driving past. Four or five times, then parked down the street.'

'Val, I think you should call the police.'

'No.'

'If things are this weird, and you're this scared, do it.'

The wheezy frailty evaporated and her voice came out strong. '*No*. The police are watching me. They'll try to touch me.' She coughed. 'They put a camera in the mailbox.'

My blood pressure pumped higher. 'Listen to me. You need to call a neighbor or a friend and get somebody to come over and help you out, right now.'

'No. Don't you understand? There's nobody.'

I didn't care that I was on the cellphone. 'Valerie, where are you?'

'Canoga Park.'

That was the west end of the San Fernando Valley: an hour-fifteen in a fast car.

'Give me the address.' I pulled a pen from my back pocket.

'What are you doing?'

'Coming to check on you.'

There was a moment of dumb silence, and then a sob that sharpened into another bout of coughing. 'Thank you.'

'Give me your address.'

'It's . . .' Dead air. 'I don't know it.'

My stomach clenched. 'Try.'

'I can't remember.'

'Val. Do you know the street name?'

'Northridge Road.'

'Good. Can you look out a window and see the number out front?'

'It's an apartment building. I can't see it.'

'Neighbors?'

'They're men. They won't help.'

'How about your driver's license? Get it and read me the address.'

'My license has an old address.' The tears were coming back into her voice. 'I have to get out. I'll go someplace public. I can walk to Kimo's. It's a big coffee shop on Northridge Road.'

'No, Val – going outside alone doesn't sound like a good idea.'

'Kimo's on Northridge Road.'

'Valerie—' But I was talking to silence. 'Damn!'

Jesse looked grim. 'She's being stalked?'

'Maybe. She sounds paranoid. She's afraid of the police and afraid of men.'

'You really want to go?'

'She can't defend herself. She can barely function. I can't leave her there alone.' I clenched my jaw. 'Besides, I've been trying to talk to her for days. And maybe I can get hold of her doctor. Or if nothing else, Social Services.'

I weighed the phone in my hand. Jesse glanced at it.

'You going to call the police?' he said.

'FBI. Heaney can get the police there faster than I can.'

Northridge Road was a shopworn thoroughfare jammed with pet shops, thrift stores and mattress showrooms. A police car sat at the curb outside Kimo's. I'd made it here in an hour and three minutes.

One police car. Please tell me that's a good sign.

Inside, the hostess looked at me apprehensively and pointed across the restaurant. In a booth at the back, hunching into a corner as far from the female police officer as she could, was Valerie. She was huddled inside a black hoodie, looking like a cornered rabbit.

'Val.'

243

Her eyes lit, feverish and needy. 'I don't believe you actually came.'

I slid into the booth next to her. When I put a hand on her forearm, she shied as though I'd set a hot iron to it.

'Sorry.' She rubbed her arm, giving me a surreptitious glance. 'People touching me creeps me out.'

'Val, you okay?'

She looked at the table. 'I'm fine. I'm just a jackhole.'

'No you're not.'

'Yeah, I am. Nobody's tapping my email. The mailbox isn't spying on me.'

'Glad to hear it.'

That brought a smirk. 'It's spying on you and Chariot Boy.'

I relaxed. If she could cover mortification with humor, she still had strength left.

The cop beckoned to me. I excused myself and followed her out of Valerie's earshot.

'She showed up about half an hour ago, disoriented and toting that little suitcase.' She nodded at a case on wheels parked next to the booth. 'She refuses to go to the hospital. Won't let me touch her. A waitress got close enough to read her Medic Alert bracelet and get her doctor's number so we could page him. We're waiting for his call.'

'Okay. Good.'

'I've gone out on a limb here, holding off on calling the paramedics.'

I lowered my voice. 'She isn't crazy. She's terminally ill.'

'Obviously.'

'But I don't know whether this is a crisis that calls for taking her to the ER.'

'After I got here she took some pills and she's calmed way down. Seems more embarrassed than anything else.'

Behind us a phone rang. Valerie took a cell from her purse and answered it.

'Yeah, I did. I had an episode.' She sat straighter. 'No, it was stress, I'm okay now. I doubled up on my dosage.' Her brassy wig glared under the lights. 'No, no aura . . . Dr Herron, *no*. I don't need to go to the hospital.'

The cop looked worried. *Sotto voce*, she said, 'Word came down from above, she's being stalked.'

'It's possible.'

I explained. The cop's lips pursed.

I said, 'She told me a car was driving back and forth in front of her apartment building.'

She looked at her notes. 'Green, late model station wagon. A family car.' She gave me an assessing look. 'What do you think?'

I thought it sounded like Becky O'Keefe's Volvo, which had been shown two hundred times on television in the last twenty-four hours. 'Let me talk to her.'

I returned to the booth.

Valerie set her phone down. 'Nothing changes, does it? The diva makes herself the center of attention by acting like a nutjob. But still I got myself an audience.'

'Do you want to go to the doctor?'

'No. I want to go home.'

'I don't think it's wise for you to be alone.'

Her face looked even more pale than at the reunion. Her hands were covered with band-aids and had the casual bruising that very old people's skin sustains.

'Not home to my apartment. China Lake.' She met my eyes. 'You understand?'

I understood.

I turned to the cop. 'I'll take it from here.'

The Mustang crawled through late lunchtime traffic. Above the power lines, the sky tended toward brown. The temperature was in the seventies but Valerie huddled in her sweatshirt, hands stuffed in the pockets.

'Do you need to stop by your apartment?' I said.

She shook her head. 'I never unpacked after the reunion. Everything I need is in my suitcase.' She smiled sardonically. 'Benefits of paranoia. You're always ready to run.'

'Can you get on an airplane?'

'Yeah.'

'Can you afford a ticket to China Lake from Santa Barbara?'

'No problem. It'll be one way.'

I let that conversational spitwad lay there, signaling and turning up the onramp onto 101. The freeway was cream of traffic soup, rush hour at one p.m. Los Angeles bites.

'Do you still have family in China Lake, Val?'

'And here the curtain of lies comes crashing down.' Her shoulders rose, birdlike, and fell again. 'That stuff I said at the reunion, about bygones? It was bullshit. I haven't talked to my mom in a year. I went to China Lake to make up with her, but I weaseled out. I didn't even see her.' Color rose in her pale cheeks.

I drove. After thirty seconds she said, 'No comment?'

'No.' I checked the rearview mirror. 'Do you mind if we talk about your illness?'

'I haven't slept in fifty-six nights.'

'Damn.'

'I'm like a shitty night crawler or something.' She stared

246

out the windshield. 'But I have dreams when I'm awake. I get this aura.' She held a hand up to the side of her head. 'Like a red sunrise at the side of my vision. And then I hallucinate.' She sighed. 'It's not so bad. Sometimes I'm a movie star.'

'You always wanted that.'

'I did get a job with a microphone, you know. I got to yell, "Cleanup on aisle two."' She snickered. 'And the box boys jumped when I said it. I was the bitch diva of the supermarket checkstand. So the movie star delusion is okay. Too bad the paranoia and weird compulsions take the fun out things.'

When I looked at her, she gestured at the wig.

'You thought it was because I was having chemo.'

'I did wonder.'

'No, it's trichotillomania. Compulsive hair pulling. I turned myself into a cue ball, strand by strand.' She rested her voice a moment. 'And I can't feel pain. My brain's going to shit and I'm falling apart and it doesn't hurt. Nothing hurts. Hit me with a brick and I wouldn't bat an eye.'

She dug her hands deeper into her pockets. 'Why do you think I wear long sleeves? I'm not just cold. My arms are covered with cuts and bruises. Burns. I'm not careful because I can't feel it.' Her voice was as dry as fallen leaves. 'That's why I can't stand to have people touch me. They could hurt me and I wouldn't know it.'

'I'm sorry.'

'They did an MRI. It found evidence of amyloid plaques and spongiform encephalopathy, and the doctors freaked. This thing is like BSE and they're afraid of getting infected by it. They had a conference on how to handle their implements after they examined me. They'd already

247

done a lumbar puncture and were flipping because the way they sterilize them doesn't kill this kind of disease.'

She glanced at me. 'Am I freaking you out?'

'No. A week ago you would have, but not now.' I took a breath. 'Dana West died of the same thing, Val.'

Her mouth opened.

'Shannon Gruber, too. Linda Garcia. Phoebe Chadwick. Sharlayne Jackson, I think.'

She blinked repeatedly. Her chest rose and fell, sparrowlike. 'Tell me. Tell me everything.' Quizzical, she turned to me. 'Wait. Santa Barbara to China Lake?' As if only now noticing that we were heading out of LA, she scanned the surroundings. Car dealerships and fast food outlets and a pet cemetery. 'LAX or Burbank's closer.'

'Yeah, but I need to pack, and all my stuff's in Santa Barbara.' I punched the accelerator. 'I'm going with you, Val.'

We reached Ventura before I finished telling her about the illnesses, the accidents, the fire killing Dana West.

Traffic had emptied out. We flew through Ventura, passing orchards and malls, rolling along beside the surf. Valerie's face was white. Truth, in my view, is generally for the best. But maybe it had been too much.

'You all right?' I said.

'I'm about to fudge my pants. I need a bathroom.'

I hit the next exit and pulled in at a busy gas station. It had a minimart and looked clean and safe. Valerie opened her door, got halfway to her feet and sat back down.

Her voice was dim. 'Little help?'

'Need me to come in with you?'

'Sorry.'

I opened my door and a feeling passed over me, akin to bug wings brushing the back of my neck. I looked around. The gas station was bustling, but my inner voice said *Watch it.*

Grunting, Valerie gripped the door for balance and hunched to her feet. I opened the glove compartment and pulled out the Glock. She saw it and gaped.

'Christ, what's that?'

'It's me listening to the voices in my head.'

My own, and Jesse's. *You don't stop on the freeway, even if somebody hits you. You drive to a police station. And you keep a round chambered.* I shoved the gun in my purse, got out and walked around to her side.

'Is that thing loaded?' she said.

'Absolutely.'

She hung in the doorway of the car. One of her hands was twitching.

'Come on. Let's find the women's room,' I said.

She didn't move. Her gaze lengthened. Her hand continued trembling.

'Val?'

Cars whined past on the freeway. Her eyes began clicking back and forth, fast. The twitch climbed her arm to her shoulder. Oh, man. Drool slid from the corner of her mouth. My pores opened, adrenaline flooding me.

'Valerie.'

For a second I thought it was a seizure, until I recognized what I was seeing: REM dreaming. Except that she was wide awake and standing up. I called her name again and shook her arm. She blinked and stepped back, bumping the door of the car.

She gazed around, breathing rapidly. 'Did I go out?'

'Apparently.'

She put a hand to her head. 'Shit.' She looked at me, and my purse. 'Did I dream that fucking gun?'

'No.'

Sticking her hands out for balance, she began walking toward the minimart, taking baby steps. I reached to support her elbow.

'Don't touch me.'

She sounded as much frightened as angry. I opened the door and followed her back through the minimart to the women's room. My little voices were still nagging at me, so I went in with her, closed the bathroom door and put my back against it.

'I didn't mean to scare you,' I said. 'But this is a serious situation.'

'I hate guns. The police have guns.' She pointed near the sink. 'Put your purse down on the floor.'

'No. Listen to me. Coyote's a chameleon. He changes his appearance to suit the situation. We have to be careful.'

'It might go off. I don't want it around.' She peered at me, looking equally hurt and suspicious. 'Maybe I don't want you going to China Lake. I want to go there to be safe, not to have somebody following me around with a gun.'

I sighed. 'Full disclosure. I don't think China Lake's any safer than Canoga Park or Santa Barbara. In fact, other people are getting out of there.'

That brought her up short. 'You're kidding. Who's that scared?'

'Abbie, for one. She's taking her kids on a trip.'

'Are you saying I shouldn't go?'

'I'm saying other people are leaving town.'

'How far out of town?'

'Real far.'

'Where?'

'Never mind. The point is—'

'Someplace else is safer? Should I meet my mom there?'

'Forget that. I'm just trying to make the situation clear to you.'

'If China Lake's dangerous then how come you're going?' she said.

Because I'm *compos mentis*, and healthy, and armed.

'You know a safer place? Abbie knows a safe place and told you?'

Calming a paranoid is like putting out a fire by throwing matches at it. Every remark merely provides more fuel for their fears. I was starting to think my Good Samaritan act had been a bad idea.

'Why are you guys trying to keep this from me?' she said.

Because not only had I promised Abbie, but I didn't think Valerie could control her tongue. And she was lucid enough to know that. She looked offended.

Then she rolled her eyes. 'I get it. You'd tell me, but then you'd have to kill me.'

I exhaled. Every time I thought she was going to skid over the edge, she managed to pull it back.

'Something like that,' I said.

'You won't take the gun on the plane,' she said.

'No, Val. Of course not.'

She nodded and went into a stall. 'Okay then.'

I didn't tell her that I planned to stick close to Tommy. He would have a gun. Plenty of them.

Back in Santa Barbara I stopped by Jesse's office to return the Glock. He met me in the parking lot, knowing better than to let a weapon cross the threshold at the law firm. Sanchez Marks was jokingly called the Militant Wing because of his boss's leftist leanings, but in fact her politics were solidly anti-gun. Jesse was glad to see me, and concerned.

'You look kind of ragged,' he said.

I accompanied him to the truck, glancing over my shoulder to make sure that Valerie was out of earshot back in the Mustang. She was staring at the mountains. She hadn't spoken to me since Ventura.

'No good deed goes unpunished. Richard Nixon was less paranoid than she is,' I said.

'Get her on a plane as soon as possible.'

'About that. I'm going to China Lake too.'

I told him why. He took it in, grim but understanding. 'I'll drive up tonight.'

'Great.'

I ran my index finger over his new blue tie. It matched the button-down shirt he'd bought.

He nodded. 'Yeah. Tragic fashion I can handle, but contempt of court gets expensive.'

I checked out of the South Coast Inn and drove home to pack some extra clothes for the trip to China Lake. Mr Martinez was in the bathroom grouting the new floor tile. In the afternoon light the house glowed red with roses. Valerie lay down on the sofa in the living room and I turned on the television and gave her the remote.

'Thanks.'

That was the first word she'd spoken to me in an hour. I went outside, sat at the table in the dappled shade under the oaks, and phoned Tommy.

He sounded brisk. 'Your article, it's good stuff. You really know how to hit the emotional angle hard. I think we can go with this and get some mileage out of it.'

'I need to know something. Was Kelly Colfax pregnant?'

The stark silence at the other end provided the answer.

'That's in the autopsy report but hasn't been released to the public. How did you know?' he said.

'Playing the odds.' Woman's intuition. Terror.

I told him about Dana West and Sharlayne Jackson, and about Valerie: they apparently had a transmissible spongiform encephalopathy, and I suspected the others had it too.

'Holy shit,' he said.

There was another long pause. 'Tommy?'

'I'm just digesting all this.' His voice picked up steam. 'How would Coyote know about people from our class who are sick?'

'My mother told me something. After the explosion, parents were asked to sign waivers allowing the Office of Advanced Research to access our medical records.'

'You think they're using that? That Coyote has access to our records? Today?'

'I think he has a source. Somebody's feeding him information.'

'Targeting information.'

'Tommy, I don't think this is a cover-up. I think it's a cleansing operation.'

'So he's wiping us out 'cause, what – we're the dirt they left behind?' He was wound up now. 'Do you think that's why he killed Ryan O'Keefe?'

'I do. I'm really afraid Coyote's killing women who are having kids.'

'Shit.'

'I need to talk to Dr Cantwell,' I said. 'He would have

been involved with the medical waivers. And he kept tabs on half the families in town.'

'You think he's the source?'

'Stranger things have happened. And I've called his office six times but haven't heard back. I think he's avoiding me.'

'This isn't the kind of thing you should discuss on the phone.'

'Damn straight. I want to go with you to talk to him.'

He almost said something, but just let the air hang. I held back the reason I wanted to see Dr Cantwell. My own doctor couldn't tell me if my baby was in danger. Maybe Cantwell could.

'Good. That's just what I was going to suggest, because the *China Lake News* is going to run your piece today. I want you to add one item before you submit it. Kelly's funeral is tomorrow morning. Holy Cross, ten a.m. You should come. There'll be photographers and news crews. If we're going to draw Coyote out, we want to pull out the stops.'

I was in my bedroom zipping my suitcase when I heard someone knock and open the front door.

'Kit?'

I hauled my suitcase off the bed and out to the living room. Dad was standing by the door, *Abraham Lincoln* cap in hand, his white hair bristling in the sun. I hugged him and pulled him toward the couch.

'I've been trying to get you. I'm going to China Lake,' I said.

We approached the sofa. Carefully, Valerie sat up.

'Dad, do you remember Val Skinner?'

She was shrunken inside her black sweatshirt. 'Mr Delaney, it's been a long time.'

'It certainly has.'

He held out his hand but she merely crossed her arms. His posture was slide-rule straight, his mouth tense. He looked disconcerted. He looked, in fact, horrified at the sight of her.

I returned to my suitcase, fighting to close the zipper. 'We're on the three-thirty flight. Want to come?'

He didn't answer. He was watching me, his expression disconsolate.

'What's wrong?' I said.

Valerie stood up. 'I'm going to go sit outside in the shade. Let me know when you're ready to go.'

When the door closed behind her, he said, 'My Lord. She looks like one of those little dried apple dolls.'

'She has it.'

'God almighty.' He kneaded his hat in his hands. 'It's like Dana West.'

'I know.' I tugged at the zipper of the suitcase. 'I took the video and Dana's MRI to my doctor. She agrees, it's what they call a TSE. Transmissible spongiform encephalopathy.'

'Your doctor?' he said.

I straightened. 'Is this what's got you so worried?'

Unexpectedly he swooped me into his arms and hugged me tight. 'How am I going to keep you safe?'

A bright silver fear ran across me. My father might occasionally admit to worry, in a cool and distant way, but he never showed dread like this. I held onto him.

'Dad, I'm going to be secure. Tommy's picking me up in China Lake and I'll have police protection the entire time. And Jesse's driving up tonight.' I rested my face against his chest, smelling Old Spice, the scent I associated with him from earliest memory. 'Please don't make me more scared than I already am. I have to do this. If there's any way I can help bring this to an end, I have to do it.'

'It's more than that. This is something I never thought I'd have to face, and now . . .'

I looked up, and felt myself wilting. He was gazing at me in a way I hadn't seen in forever. As if he saw me eight years old in a white dress and veil, processing to the altar to receive my First Holy Communion.

Inside, my joy and gratitude and fear for the baby turned momentarily to shame. My throat tightened. He might, eventually, think my pregnancy a blessing. But he would never think it had come about the right way. I couldn't imagine telling him, not without begging his forgiveness and understanding.

Easing out of his embrace, I turned to the suitcase and wrestled with the zipper.

'Let me,' he said.

He reached for the zipper and his gaze froze. He was looking at the ring.

'Evan, is that what I think it is?'

Shoot.

He lifted my hand. 'Jesse gave this to you?'

My face felt tight. I knew my cheeks were candy-apple red. 'Yesterday, after we got back from Los Angeles.'

'That helps explain the truck full of roses.' He held onto my hand. 'Have you told your mom?'

'Not yet. Jesse and I wanted to tell you together.'

He looked worn and worried. My stomach was aching.

'Dad, I'm happy.'

'You don't look happy.'

'Because I didn't want you to find out this way.'

And because he looked miserable.

Jesse and I had gotten halfway to the altar once, before

seeing that we weren't ready for it. When we called off the wedding it took me a week to tell my father, because I knew what I would hear in his voice, no matter how sympathetic he tried to sound: relief.

The heat in my face leached down my cheeks. I pulled away from him.

'I love him like nobody's business. That's what counts.'

'Evan, please don't.'

Turning to the desk, I slammed my computer shut. 'Don't what? Don't say I love the man I'm going to marry? Why don't you say what's really on your mind?'

'You're jumping to conclusions here. I just – you took me by surprise just now, that's all.'

'Let's figure this out. What's got your goat? Jesse's honest and brave and trustworthy and . . . he's kind to children and small animals.' I jammed my computer into its case. 'And he loves me. None of that's the problem. So what is?'

'Stop.'

My face was hot and my heart was thumping. This couldn't be good for me, but I couldn't seem to help myself.

'Stop what? Talking about the real issue?' I said.

In the bathroom, Mr Martinez turned up his Mariachi station. Dad lowered his voice.

'Fathers find talking about their daughters' love lives painful.' He wrung his hat in his hands. 'Excruciating, truth be told.'

'Say it, Dad. Why don't you want me to marry him?'

God in heaven, sometimes I am the most moronic woman on the face of the planet. As a lawyer, I know never to ask a hostile witness the 'why' question. No way, baby. It's cross-ex hell, the opening of Pandora's box.

He stilled. 'Because I don't think you've thought through what your life will be like.'

'I've been living this life day in and day out. You're the one who doesn't know what it's like.'

'Marriage is a far different endeavor than dating, Evan.'

'What a shock.'

'Today everything seems exciting, the right decision, even if it's impulsive. You're thirty-three, it's a stressful time, and he's here for you. I'm talking about what happens ten or twenty years from now.'

I felt sick, not physically but spiritually. 'No. Oh, God. You think I'm settling.'

His dark eyes pinned me. I knew I was right.

On the television, the caption *Reunion Killer* appeared behind the news anchor's hair. I grabbed the remote and turned up the volume, tearing away from Dad's gaze.

'. . . authorities are seeking to question a former soldier attached to the Naval Air Warfare Center in China Lake. Described as white, of slight build and approximately forty years old, he may be going by the name Kai Torrance. Anybody with information about this person is asked to contact the LAPD or FBI,' the anchor said. 'The security guard attacked at a Westwood office building remains in guarded condition this afternoon at UCLA Medical Center.'

I watched the TV to avoid looking at Dad. 'Let's hope this leads somewhere.'

'Indeed.'

Heart still drumming, I gathered my things. Dad put on his hat.

'I'll give you a lift to the airport,' he said.

The ride was tense, spattered with superficial chitchat. When we pulled up to the curb, he helped Valerie and me get our things out and wheeled her small suitcase inside to the check-in counter.

'Sure you won't go with us?' I said.

'I have some things I need to take care of here.'

I hugged him goodbye, but when he turned to go I felt wrong about the argument hanging between us. I caught him on his way out of the terminal.

'I don't want to fight,' I said.

He put his hands on my arms. 'We're not fighting.'

'No?'

'I know not to engage in a battle I can't win.'

I sighed. He hugged me again.

'Stay safe, and don't do anything rash.'

'Like get married.'

He kissed me and got back in the car.

An hour later, taxiing to the runway in the tin can airplane, Valerie leaned back and turned her head toward me.

'You and your dad seem close.'

Outside the windows, scrubland rolled by. 'Yes.'

She was quiet a long moment. 'Back in school, I never really knew you.'

'Even though you stole my journal and read it cover to cover?'

'Even though.'

I made a *heh* sound. Twenty years I'd wanted that confession, and now vindication felt flat.

'What you wrote was sweet and funny. You really liked your parents and your brother.'

'Are you saying you actually thought I was okay?'

'No. You were a hopeless geek.' Traces of a smile. 'But then, I was an asshole.' Her voice faded. 'Thank you for all that you're doing today.'

She closed her eyes.

The plane turned, held at the end of the runway, and powered into its takeoff roll. Lifting off the tarmac, I glanced down. The ground swooped past. At the end of the runway beyond the chain-link fence, I saw Dad leaning against the hood of his rental car. He raised a hand and waved. I put my own hand to the window and pressed my face close to the glass, watching him as long as I could.

Only when he passed from view did it cross my mind. What did he have to take care of in Santa Barbara?

22

Climbing down the narrow steps to the tarmac, I pulled out my earplugs. The plane glinted in the sun like a silver mirror. Valerie eased her way down the stairs and we walked slowly to the terminal. Heat swarmed off the concrete. I glanced up at the endless blue sky and down again, overcome by its brilliance.

Tommy was waiting. He had on shades, his pork-pie hat and an Aloha shirt, and was chewing gum behind lips drawn tighter than a guitar string.

'You look worn out,' I said.

'Ditto.'

'At least you're not smoking.'

He pulled open the collar of his shirt. A dozen patches clung to his chest like leeches. He smiled at my expression, revealing a wad of gum the size of a golf ball.

'Nicorette.' He took Valerie's suitcase and handed me the *China Lake News*. 'Page one.'

Once he had pulled out onto the highway in the unmarked department car, I unfurled the paper.

GONE BUT NOT FORGOTTEN

By Evan Delaney
Special to the News

Crappy headline, but I didn't have a say over that.

Saturday night Ceci Lezak stood before a memorial display at Bassett High's reunion and told me, 'We don't need to add any more names to the list.'

Those were the last words she spoke to me. Twelve hours later she was dead.

'Is this in their online edition?' I said.

'Yeah.'

'Good. I put in as many keywords as I could. Figure Coyote might be trawling the web for news of himself.'

The wind gusted and sand danced across the road. Tommy accelerated, revving the car up to seventy.

'Forensics has come up with some strange stuff.'

I looked up from the paper. 'On Coyote?'

'Both murder scenes were wildly clean. No fingerprints, no hairs, no skin under the victims' fingernails, no bodily fluids.'

'So you're saying this is a careful cat. We already knew that.'

'We got a partial boot print from the Colfax scene. Size ten, but our techs say the depth of the print indicates the killer may have been wearing extra large boots to make himself appear taller and heavier than he is. The one other interesting thing we've picked up is a hair from a wig.'

'Whose wig? Coyote's?'

'Blond, two inches long. Short hair, maybe a man's wig.'

'He had blond hair when I saw him in LA,' I said. 'Any more information about Kai Torrance?'

'We're waiting for Military Records to come back to us. It's a tedious process even for law enforcement.' He glanced at me. 'And in this case it seems that the records clerks are always out to lunch. Nobody really wants to dig this stuff up.'

We sped along the highway in the dazzling sunshine. On one side of the road trees struggled in the wind and a trailer park hunkered under the heat. On the other, cyclone fencing and razor wire scrolled past, interspersed with warnings to KEEP OUT. Beyond the wire, the base unrolled across fifty miles of sand and rocks and bruised mountains that chewed the horizon.

'There is one piece of potential luck. They found a dental implement outside Wally Hankins's office, called a curette. We sent it to the Kern County crime lab over in Bakersfield.'

'What are they hoping to find? DNA?' I said.

'DNA, his blood, Ceci's blood, anything helps. We also sent the bodies and evidence to Bakersfield. But that lab's underfunded. They're backlogged even for a high-profile case like this. And after you told us this might be a prion disease, the doctors went apeshit. They had to lock down the lab where the autopsies were performed and institute strict decontamination protocols. They freaked but good.'

From the back seat, Valerie said, 'Welcome to my world.'

He looked in the mirror. 'Is it cooling down back there?'

She gave him thumbs up. He turned up the volume on the police radio and focused on the road. Whatever else he wanted to tell me, he didn't want Valerie to hear.

'Where we going, Val?' he said.

'The Sierra View Motel.'

'Not your mom's house?'

'She works at the motel.'

We pulled in a few minutes later. Tommy got Val's suitcase out of the trunk and I got out to tell her goodbye.

I was extremely relieved at getting her off my hands, but seeing the expression on her face made me feel guilty. She stared at the motel looking stoic, almost hopeful.

'Will you be okay?' I said.

'Fine. If it doesn't work out, I'll get a room. Order champagne and whatever passes for caviar in this town, trash the place like a rock star.'

'Good luck.'

Tommy said, 'Kelly's funeral is tomorrow morning. Do you want us to pick you up?'

'No.' She looked rueful. 'I'm only going to attend one more funeral. You know me, the diva. If I'm not the star, I ain't going.'

She walked toward the office. Tommy waved goodbye, looking sympathetic, but he couldn't peel out of the parking lot fast enough.

'What didn't you want her to hear?' I said.

'Kelly had this same neuro thing Valerie has. Her brain was eaten up with holes.'

'Ceci?'

'Early stage.' He grimaced at the road, chewing his giant wad of gum.

'He's killing people who were exposed to the pain vaccine,' I said. 'It's more than an obsession. It's a cull.'

He nodded, grim. Fumbling in his shirt pocket, he pulled out a pack of Nicorette and shook two more pieces of gum into his mouth.

'You know how hard it is to get rid of prions? At a forensic laboratory? Places like that reek with formaldehyde. It kills most infectious agents, but it only makes prions stronger.' He shook his head. 'This is fucking scary.'

'Does heat destroy them?'

'If it's real hot.'

'Like the fire that killed Dana West.' I waited for him to look at me. 'Or the explosion we witnessed at Renegade Canyon.'

'Which is why we're going to see Dr Cantwell right now.'

Frowning, he reached over, popped the glove compartment and fished out a pack of cigarettes. 'Excuse me.' Rolling down the window, he hawked his gum across the road.

'I know, littering's a five hundred dollar fine. You can turn me in for the reward when Coyote's under arrest.'

He shook a cigarette out of the pack and punched the lighter. 'Guess I picked the wrong day to stop sniffing glue.'

Dr Tully Cantwell's office was bright and dreary. The receptionist looked as though she spent her time tut-tutting about the maladies patients brought upon themselves and then dragged into her waiting room. She was the doctor's Chief of Staff and she didn't want Himself to be disturbed.

Tommy flashed his badge.

'No appointment?' she said.

I leaned on the counter. 'He's been waiting for us for twenty years.'

An office door opened. Dr C nodded us in.

His white coat hung limply on him. His belly slurped over the waistband of his slacks, his tie riding the swell. He slumped into his desk chair and smoothed his combover.

'I can't say I'm surprised to see you, detective. But Evan, this is unexpected.'

Tommy spoke conversationally. 'How soon after the

265

explosion did Maureen Swayze ask you to start tracking the health of our class?'

'Quickly.' Cantwell fingered his *Go Hounds* tie clip. 'Glad we're skipping the blarney. Dr Swayze contacted me a week or so after the explosion. She asked me to work with the school and parents to track any health problems that developed. She was concerned.'

'Who got access to the medical data, exactly?'

'The high school and the Office of Advanced Research out on the base.'

'In other words, you and Swayze.' Tommy reached in his shirt pocket for his cigarettes, and stopped himself. 'You got permanent access to all the health records for our entire class.'

'No. Not all parents signed the waivers.' Cantwell looked at me. 'Your mother particularly refused. And we only had legal access until you reached majority. After that, you could withdraw consent.'

'Could. How many actually did?' Tommy said.

Dr C looked at his desk blotter.

'So, you what? Kind of forgot to remind people of that when they turned eighteen?'

Cantwell blushed.

'Is Swayze still getting reports on our health?'

'No, of course not. Her project wrapped up and she moved on. I haven't heard from her in almost twenty years, and nobody from the base has asked for information in nearly that long.'

'So if she's not providing our medical records to Coyote, who is? You?'

Cantwell froze.

'You were the doctor for the high school. That means you got access to all our records, not just those kids whose

266

families were your patients. Did you give the information away, or sell it?'

'What are you talking about?'

'Coyote is being fed information about our class. I think that information originates in this office.'

'My God. No. I wouldn't do that.'

'Then who? Your receptionist? Your file clerk? Do you have computer firewalls, so nobody can access your system from outside? Does your office link to the records department at China Lake Hospital?'

Cantwell flushed. His chumminess had disintegrated.

Tommy inched forward on his chair. 'That's okay. I'll be coming back with a search warrant, and we'll question your entire staff. When did you realize that our class was getting sick?'

Cantwell's eyes defocused for a moment. He attempted his jolly helpful confessor smile, and abandoned it. His fingers worried the tie clip.

'Doctor,' Tommy said.

Cantwell sat unnaturally still, saying nothing. I spoke quietly.

'Phoebe Chadwick, Shannon Gruber, Linda Garcia, Dana West, maybe Sharlayne Jackson. We know they all had some form of TSE. And now Valerie Skinner has it too.'

'When did you know, Dr C?' Tommy said.

Cantwell stared at his desk blotter.

'Funny thing,' I said, 'at the reunion Valerie avoided you because she didn't want to face an unhelpful doctor.'

I waited for him to flinch, and he did.

'But she's been talking to me. She has complete insomnia. She's covered with bruises because she can't feel pain. Her brain is riddled with holes and her own doctors are afraid to perform invasive tests. She says they talk about amyloid plaques and spongiform encephalopathy.'

His voice was little more than a mumble. 'I suspected with Shannon Gruber. The panic attacks and insomnia.'

My blood pressure spun up. 'Did you know it was a TSE?'

'Not for several years. Linda Garcia was a patient of mine. The anorexia was secondary to profound total insomnia and sensory deficits. That's when I knew.'

Tommy looked incredulous. 'And you did nothing?'

'They were my patients. I cared for them.'

I performed a gut check. My throat was dry. 'When did you know that this disease could cause birth defects?'

Few things are more awful to watch than a man breaking inside. He stared at the green blotter on his lovely desk, and he crumbled. His head sank forward until his chin rested on his chest. He held very still for a moment, and then, heaving in a breath, he cracked into sobs.

Tommy sat stunned. So did I.

'I didn't mean for this to happen. I didn't know. You have to believe me.'

Cantwell slapped a hand over his face and turned away in shame. 'Linda Garcia. She got sick after she lost the baby.'

Tightness in my throat. 'What baby?'

'It was born nine weeks early, with profound neurological deficits. It died shortly after birth,' he said, and spun around, red-eyed. 'And you have it wrong. It's not birth defects. It's worse than that.'

I gripped the arms of my chair. Tommy watched me with concern.

'Teratogenesis. You know the word?' Cantwell said.

Though it sounded familiar, I shook my head.

'From the Greek *teras*, meaning monster. Literally translated, monster-making.'

Tommy was clenching his fists. 'What?'

'The pain vaccine,' I said.

Cantwell nodded. 'It can cause fatal congenital malformations, but that's not all it does. It's not only teratogenic but mutagenic.'

'It causes mutations?' Tommy said.

The lights in the room seemed to pop with little bites of color.

'It causes chromosomal mutations in the host. I never had access to the pharmacological formula and I don't know the exact mechanism by which it operates. But I suspect that it affects mitochondrial DNA, so that it becomes embedded in the genetic code and is passed on to an exposee's children.'

'Son of a bitch,' Tommy said. 'How long have you known this?'

Cantwell shook his head. 'I wasn't sure until very recently.'

I put my hand to my forehead. 'But some of us are healthy and have healthy children. Not everybody who was exposed has become infected.' The colors nipped at the air around my face. 'Have they?'

'I don't think so but I can't be sure. Prion diseases can take decades to manifest.' He caught my eye. 'You don't have children, do you?'

Tommy's face was stark. 'I do. Five kids, you bastard.'

Cantwell looked at him. 'Don't you see? I know next to nothing about this. Just that this prion is potentially a million times worse than BSE, fatal insomnia, kuru, any of those TSEs.'

'Why?' I said.

'Those diseases are hard to get. Variant Creutzfeldt-Jacob disease, a couple hundred cases after repeated exposure to contaminants, and the epidemic slowed down when infected meat was removed from the food chain. Likewise kuru. The epidemic spread like crazy over the course of a few decades, coinciding with the rise of ritual cannibalism among the tribe in Papua New Guinea. Once missionaries convinced the tribe to stop the practice, the epidemic diminished radically.' He spread his hands. 'But kuru wasn't genetically transmissible. This is. Easily transmissible.'

He raked his fingers through his stringy hair. When he dropped his hands to his lap his combover stuck up like a bunch of frightened threadworms.

'It can infect the genome. That's what you don't understand. It can get *loose*.'

'This is science fiction,' Tommy said.

'How do you think mad cow got started? Feeding ground-up sheep brains to cattle that should have been grazing on green fields. *That's* science fiction. And South Star was a top secret government research project. What they were doing out there with genetic manipulation and enhancement – who knows?'

My voice sounded weak. 'You're saying this thing could spread like wildfire.'

'Do you know how prions work? They're not like viruses or bacteria. Prions are the only known disease agent that have no DNA. They're pure protein. So they don't replicate. They turn other proteins into prions.'

Science fiction. A memory scythed across my mental landscape.

'Prions are deformed proteins. When one touches a

normal protein it deforms too, converting into another prion. And then those new prions touch other proteins and convert them, until they clump together in the brain.'

He worried his tie clip like a rosary. 'Amyloid plaques, those are protein deposits. The brain has defense mechanisms, but prion diseases build these clumps too fast to fight. They turn the brain to mush, and the body's defenseless.'

'How do you kill prions?' Tommy said.

'You can't. They aren't alive,' Cantwell said.

'Destroy them, then.'

Cantwell's eyes were red. 'They're virtually indestructible. Normal sterilization measures are futile. Autoclaving at high temperatures, exposure to ultraviolet light or high power x-rays, cold, drying, organic detergents – they're all useless.'

He looked at us, hopeless. 'The pain vaccine – it's made you exposees dangerous. You can spread the prion agent and infect human DNA.'

I felt nauseated. 'It's like ice-nine.'

Cantwell nodded. 'You aren't the first person to draw the analogy.'

I glanced at Tommy. '*Cat's Cradle*, Kurt Vonnegut. A scientist invents an alternate form of water called ice-nine. It crystallizes every drop of H_2O it touches and turns it into more ice-nine.' I felt distraught to see Cantwell nodding in agreement. 'It's what prions do. They touch normal proteins and turn them into more prions, setting off a chain reaction. Until they eat out your brain.'

'So what?' Tommy said.

'In the novel, ice-nine eventually gets into the water supply. It freezes all the oceans.' I slumped back. 'We're

271

the oceans. People. These things could get loose and corrupt the human genome.'

'That's nuts.'

'Maybe. But that's what Coyote believes. And he's trying to stop it,' I said.

'So how do *we* stop it?' He waved his hands. 'I mean, these prions turn on. How do we turn them off? Reverse this thing?'

Cantwell fussed with his tie clip. 'You can't.'

Tommy stood up, looking as though he'd taken a 100,000 volt hit. 'I don't believe you. There has to be some way to stop it.'

'Stop breeding.'

'What else?'

Flat stare. 'Coyote's solution. Get rid of the breeders and their children.'

Tommy lunged at him across the desk. He grabbed him by the tie and yanked him forward onto his green desk blotter.

'I have kids, you asswad. Why didn't you tell us? What if they're going to get sick? What if Coyote goes after them?'

I jumped to my feet and grabbed the back of Tommy's shirt. 'Stop it.'

He twisted Cantwell's tie. I yanked on his collar and he whipped around, fist cocked.

'Don't hit me.' I leapt back, one hand in front of my face, the other over my belly.

Tommy let go of Cantwell and put his hands up. 'Done. I'm done.'

The doctor slumped back, breathing heavily. The door burst open. The starchy receptionist stood in the doorway, aghast.

'Doctor?'

Cantwell raised a hand. 'It's all right, Helen.'

She looked doubtful, but he straightened his tie and finger-combed his thready hair. He reassured her again and she left, beady-eyed, closing the door behind her.

Tommy sat down. 'Sorry.'

Cantwell shook his head. 'No, I deserved that.' He laughed, and the laugh turned into another bout of sobbing. 'I deserve everything I get.' He looked at us. 'You've completely forgotten, haven't you? My family's at risk here, too.'

'What in hell are you talking about?' Tommy said.

'My wife. Antonia was with you on the field trip that day. She's as much in peril from this disease as any of you kids.'

Turning the key in the lock, Jesse opened his front door and scanned the entryway, the living-room and, outside the plate-glass windows, the deck and the blue surf rushing up the sand.

This couldn't be good.

He tossed the keys on the table, loosened his tie and wheeled over to unlock the door out to the deck.

'Evan's not here. She flew to China Lake,' he said.

Phil Delaney tipped the front legs of his chair back to the deck and glanced around slowly, taking him in from under the brim of his hat.

'Yes. I drove her to the airport.'

The man's stare had a *High Noon* quality. It was disquieting as hell. Jesse nodded him in, turned and headed for the kitchen. Phil's boot heels barked on the hardwood floor behind him.

'I'm going to change and hit the road. If I push it I'll get up to China Lake by eleven,' Jesse said.

273

He opened the fridge and took out two Cokes. Leaned back and grabbed the opener from a drawer, popped off the bottle caps and one-armed his way over to the kitchen table where Phil was standing.

'Obliged.' Phil took the bottle, drank, and stared down at him again. 'I know she's pregnant.'

That stare fixed him. He heard the fridge humming and the surf crashing up the beach and the static inside his head, hissing *Dude, you're toast*.

'There's something you have to do for Evan,' Phil said.

'I'm going to marry her.'

'No.'

Son of a bitch. 'Yes, I am. Absolutely.'

'That's not what I mean.' Phil set the Coke bottle on the table. 'Though we'll talk about the constancy of your intentions another time. This is something else.'

He took off his hat. The look on his face was brooding. 'Are you as tough as I hope you are?'

'Man, just spit it out.'

'Evan cannot have this baby.'

Jesse stared at him, numb.

Phil's voice was flat. 'You have to convince her to terminate the pregnancy.'

23

'**G**et out,' Jesse said.

Phil's eyes were hard in the sunlight. 'It's an appalling thing to ask. I know that.'

Slamming his Coke bottle down on the kitchen table, Jesse crossed the living room, threw open the front door and spun around.

'Get the hell out of my house.'

'You have to listen to me,' Phil said.

'*Now.*'

Phil walked toward him.

'Coyote wants to cleanse the gene pool. He's killing women who are having children.'

'So we protect Evan. You don't ask her to abort the baby.'

'This pregnancy puts her at the top of Coyote's kill list. What do you want to do, take her to Australia? The Himalayas? That's not enough. He'd hunt her down.'

'No. It's unconscionable.'

'Jesse—'

'You're Catholic. What is fucking wrong with you?'

Phil's stride was slow and heavy. 'You could hide out on the moon and having this baby could still kill her. She has to end the pregnancy.'

A cold white pain, like electricity, ran through him.

275

With horror, he realized that Phil wasn't angry with him.

'Could? You want her to have an abortion on the basis of *could*? This is your grandchild, my . . .' The white electricity spread along his arms. 'My child.'

'Dana West wasn't the first to have a terminally ill baby. It's happened to others and it could happen to Evan too.' He stopped in front of him. 'Son, this child might not survive. If it has the same neurological abnormalities as some others, it won't live more than a few hours.'

Electricity crawled across Jesse's chest. 'Might not. Don't you hear yourself?' His voice had gone; he could barely hear himself. 'Kill the baby, on the chance it might not survive? That's unspeakable. The baby might be fine. No. *No.*'

'If the baby's born too sick to live, Evan will die inside. You and I both know that. She'll consider herself responsible.'

The conviction and pain in Phil's voice were all too real. Jesse closed his eyes.

'Don't ask this.'

'We don't know what triggers this disease. Maybe pregnancy itself ignites it. We can't take that chance, not with Evan's life.'

'You don't know . . .'

'You saw the video of Dana West.'

'This is wrong. And if . . .' Electrical hiss in his head. 'If pregnancy triggers it, then Evan's already . . .'

'We simply don't know. Hormones increase over time as a pregnancy develops. The endocrine system adjusts, the body's metabolism shifts. It could be a case of reaching a tipping point, a saturation level. Some kind of point of no return.'

Jesse shook his head. 'There has to be a way. Ask Maureen Swayze. She developed the pain vaccine. She knows what it is and how it operates.'

'She won't divulge that information. She's bound by the National Security Act.'

'Then fucking make her divulge it. Christ, *think*.'

'No. She's even more implacably cussed than I am. Besides, telling anybody else about the pregnancy would be dangerous. Once that news gets out, there's no way to prevent it from reaching Coyote.'

Jesse clutched his pushrims. 'I won't do it. There has to be another way.'

'There isn't. I've spent the past twenty-four hours sweating bullets to come up with another solution and there isn't one. And while you're sitting here, the odds are going against Evan. Every single second that you wait she's in greater danger.'

All the air had gone from the house. He yanked at the knot in his tie and pulled it off.

'You're telling me it's Evan or the baby.'

'My daughter's life is on the line. Why the hell else do you think I would ask such a terrible thing?' Phil took one step closer. 'I'm a hardass, because life demands hard choices. I'm asking you to make one now. If you love Evan anywhere close to the way I do, you'll think about it and understand.'

His vision spiked gold with fear. He wheeled to the plate-glass windows, wanting to jump up and run across the sand and dive into the water and swim, go, put his head down and kick through the waves, sprinting out into the Pacific until Phil's demand and this nightmare and the possibility it might be true sank and drowned.

Phil's boots tolled behind him again. 'You have no

idea who you're dealing with. Coyote is a professional killer and he apparently has backing. You cannot imagine how these people think, how little ordinary morality affects them or how far they'll go.'

No. Jesse shook his head, clearing it. What was he thinking? Grab Evan and hold her tight, that was what mattered. Keep her from all of this, her and the baby.

He felt Phil standing behind him. 'I know you want to protect Evan. I'd expect no less from you. If you want to marry my daughter, it's essential that I know how deeply you'll commit yourself to doing that.' He stepped into view. 'But you can't do it by yourself. Not with all your fast talk and determination. Not even with your Glock.' He loomed over him. 'Jesse, face it. You can't equalize things.'

Phil was staring at him, not at the wheelchair, but he got the message. He was never going to take down a killer like Coyote. He held Phil's gaze.

'Have you already asked her yourself?' he said.

Phil glanced out at the beach. 'No. I shoot straight and most of the time she'll take that from me. But I can't ask Evan this. She would turn against me.'

'You son of a bitch. And you think she won't turn against me?'

'I tried. I stopped by her house before I took her to the airport. But we got off on the wrong foot and I . . .' He looked regretful. 'Never in a million years could I convince her to end it. She's every inch as pigheaded as I am. Especially when the subject concerns you.'

He looked worn. 'You're the only person who can possibly persuade her. You're the man she loves.'

'It would drive a stake through her heart.'

'I know you want this child, but the pregnancy might

278

kill her. Are you going to take that gamble with her life?'

Fucking shot to the head. He leaned on his knees, his vision pounding.

'Do whatever it takes, but get her to have a termination. I mean whatever it takes. Tell her you don't want it. Threaten to break up with her. But get her to do it *now*, before Coyote finds out.'

Phil looked out the window. 'She can get the abortion pill. She can do it quietly, in a doctor's office. It's still early enough.' Weariness came over his face. 'Son, I'm sorry. It's simply not meant to be.'

'She'll refuse.'

'She'll resist. And you know why? Because of you.'

Jesse looked up. Phil walked back to the kitchen, pulled over a chair from the table and sat down. Leaning forward, he clasped his hands between his knees.

'The reason she won't listen to anybody else about the baby is because of you. She thinks this is your one shot at fatherhood, and she won't give it up.'

The electricity spread and sank through his skin.

'It may never be safe for Evan to have children. But for you she'll risk South Star burning her up, and Coyote coming at her like a wild dog. Unless you stop her.'

Phil's voice dropped. It sounded sad and genuine and deeply frightened.

'So I need to hear an answer from you. The most honest truth you've ever told.'

Jesse looked at him.

'How much do you love my daughter?'

Jesse heard the front door shut. He heard Phil's rental car start up and pull out. He sat at the kitchen table. Sunlight stretched across the house, screeching off the windows and the Coke bottles in front of him. The waves crashed outside, relentless, effortless, mindless. So fucking simple. He stared at nothing.

He backhanded the bottles to the floor and put his head in his hands.

24

The priest was florid with the heat and the weight of it all. At the altar inside Holy Cross church he stood and spread his arms for the final blessing.

'The Lord be with you.'

The stricken and angry family and friends of Kelly Colfax lumbered to their feet. The television camera at the back of the church focused on the pallbearers taking their places, Kelly's brother and Scotty Colfax's burly friends from the high school football team. The priest raised his hand and gave the final blessing. I made the sign of the cross, hearing him say *Go in peace* and replying *Thanks be to God*.

The organ rang out, a tender melody played full-throated, and Kelly's casket was carried past. Scotty struggled down the aisle after it, supported by his parents.

Never had celebrating mass left me so desolate.

Walking outside, I shielded my eyes from stark sunshine. TV news vans lined the curb, sprouting satellite dishes and antennae. The crowd was dense. Tension bled into the air. I looked around.

Where was Jesse?

Milling through the crowd, I turned on my cellphone and checked voicemail. There was nothing new, just the one message.

'Ev, I'm not going to make it to China Lake. Something's, it's . . . I'll, ah.'

His tone sounded so thin.

'Tonight's just screwed. In the morning . . . yeah, I don't know. I'll have to call you back.'

Hesitancy was not one of his traits. People bumped their way past me. I replayed the message. The frayed edge in his voice was unmistakable.

Abbie swarmed through the crowd. 'Woman, you're a sight for sore eyes.'

She wrestled me into a hug. Behind her Wally wedged his way between people. He was crammed into a brown suit and looked like a dog that had been run hard and left in the heat without water. Dark circles rimmed his eyes.

'Your article made me cry all over again,' Abbie said. 'Just like this funeral.'

Putting the phone away, I kissed Wally's cheek. 'How you doing, chief?'

He sort of shrug-nodded. 'Yeah, well. But it's good to see you.'

Abbie pushed her glasses up her nose. 'You going to the cemetery?'

I nodded, scanning the crowd for Tommy. He and his colleagues were among the congregation. They would conduct surveillance at the graveside service as well. They had arranged for Kelly's family to leave mementoes on her grave: photos and a teddy bear. They were hoping that Coyote wanted to collect further souvenirs of his work.

Abbie linked arms with me and swept me toward the sidewalk. I leaned close to her and lowered my voice.

'When are you leaving?'

'This afternoon, when I get that piece of Detroit crap metal back from the auto shop.'

I glanced around again. Abbie frowned.

'Who are you looking for?'

Jesse. But I knew he wasn't here. I put on my sunglasses.

'Tommy. He wants me front and center.'

We walked a few more steps, pulling away from Wally. Abbie's voice dimmed.

'Wally's close to a heart attack. The state his office was in after the police finished – seeing where Ceci died, it's just too much. I don't know what he's going to do about the practice. He can't bring himself to set foot in the building.'

I looked her over. 'It's more than that, isn't it?'

She held her breath for a moment, standing straight, and then slumped. 'Yeah. He's scared shitless for me and the kids. Once I get up to his dad's place, he'll be able to ease down a little.'

'Good.'

She looked at me. 'Sometimes I think you're lucky, not having kids to worry about.'

The wind raked my face. It was dry and hot, and I felt weak. Abbie froze.

'Evan, I didn't mean . . . shit, sorry, I'm a blundering idiot sometimes.'

'No, that's not it.' Should I tell her? Keeping it in was killing me. This was supposed to be joyous and instead it was an ache, a secret that I couldn't bear hiding away. The throng flowed around me, a stream of sober suits and best dresses.

'What?' she said.

'I can't stand this anymore. I—'

283

Ten feet away, moving like a sharp stick among the meandering and spaced out, I saw a familiar figure with silver spiky hair.

'Mom?'

She turned. Pulling off her sunglasses, she came toward me at blitz speed, arms out.

'There's my girl.'

'You should have told me you were coming.'

Her embrace felt abrupt and rigid. She smoothed my hair off my forehead, leaning back and gazing at me with overt apprehension. She looked elegant in a dark suit and turquoise blouse, but she was all elbows and nerves.

'It seemed the worthy thing to do, to honor one of your classmates under these circumstances.'

She glanced blankly at Abbie. Abbie was probably an inch taller and sixty pounds heavier than when Mom had last seen her. Then it clicked.

'Well. Look at you.'

Back in high school Abbie had not been one of Mom's favorite people. Thanks to an ounce of dope in Abbie's pocket when I was pulled over on a traffic stop, I got busted for possession and earned a juvenile record. Mom drew up like a prickly plant.

Her protectiveness annoyed and touched me in equal measure. 'Water under the bridge, Ma.'

She pursed her lips, glancing at me sharply.

'Abbie's now a civic and cultural booster. She even drives a van. She has a lovable husband and three freakishly intelligent kids. We would all do well to emulate her.'

Mom's expression tightened. Her eyes went both bright and dark, and for a moment she seemed to look right into me. Boom, like thunder. I felt it through and through. She knew.

Abbie tossed her hair out of her eyes and waved to Wally. 'Walls, over here.' Her expression brightened. 'Mrs D, you have nothing to worry about. I'm no longer a bad influence on Evan.'

I couldn't break from my mother's gaze. A coruscating pain took me, not in body but spirit. This should have been the happiest moment imaginable, to share with her the joy, to see her light up at the news of my pregnancy. But the look on her face, the tension in her grip, sank me.

I felt blood pouring down my nose and running onto my upper lip.

'Ugh.' I pressed my hand to my nose.

Mom put her hand on my shoulder. 'Tilt your head back.'

Abbie fished a wad of tissues from her purse. Muttering thanks, I pressed them to my face.

Mom took my arm. 'The heat and dry air always did this to you. Let's get you out of the sun.'

'It's okay.'

She looked at Abbie. 'Did you drive?'

'Yeah. We're going to the cemetery, do you—'

'Let Evan sit down.'

Abbie's expression turned to alarm. 'Is something wrong?'

Through the tissues I barked, 'No.'

For a long moment my mother and I stared at each other. Her brittleness seemed more than worry or even disappointment. It seemed like a kind of grief.

Tommy's voice cut through the crowd. 'There you are. We're going to head out.'

He walked up and saw the tissues shoved under my nose.

'It's nothing,' I said, adding, absurdly, 'You remember my mother, don't you?'

With equal absurdity he shook her hand, all gracious formality, before gesturing toward the parking lot. 'Come on, I have a first-aid kit in the car. We'll put a cold pack on the back of your neck.'

But he didn't turn to go. He stared straight at my hand, his expression mixing surprise and chagrin.

Abbie's eyes went round behind her specs. 'Holy smoke.'

I mumbled through the tissues. 'Yes, it's a bloody engagement ring.'

'Did they dig that out of South Africa with a backhoe?' she said.

Tommy smiled. 'Some damned detective I am. Congratulations, Rocky. Don't punch anybody with that hand.'

Abbie grabbed me and laughed too loud for the mood of the crowd. 'My hell, you lucky girl. Mrs D, isn't this the best?'

She and Tommy turned to my mother, and shut up. Mom didn't look happy. She looked harrowed. I felt the bottom dropping out of everything.

The vehicle crested the rise and rolled down the hill outside China Lake. The road was a black arrow in the heat. Mountains sliced the horizon, cutting earth from cyan sky. The wind, buffeting the truck, called a welcome. Coyote licked his lips.

He would not miss this opportunity.

Opportunity had slipped away from him in Canoga

Park. He ran it through his head again, assessing the cause, walking back the cat. He had set it up with care. He had frightened the target out in the open, drawn her into range and been prepared to take her. He had put Valerie Skinner in that coffee shop, waiting and alone. And then Delaney had called the police.

Wild card – that's why opportunity had eluded him. His chance evaporated because he had failed to account for the wild card. A China Lake woman had outflanked him. That would not happen again.

He touched his chest, wishing for his amulet. The nature of the hunt, the urgency of the mission, had required him to leave it back at base. He longed for the reassurance it gave.

Sage and yucca sheared past the truck. Delaney was a wild card, but he could turn that to his advantage. She could be useful to him. Her newspaper article contained sufficient facts to tell him that she was still dipping her hands into the knowledge stream.

According to the China Lake school district's online attendance records, the Hankins and Chang children were absent from class. They were beyond his reach. But Delaney, he felt certain, knew where the children were.

He needed that information. He would not take Delaney until she provided it to him. And once she did, he would take them all. He would seize the opportunity, today.

Mirages writhed across the highway. The sky vibrated blue. A sound, a thirst, built in his throat.

Coyote sings here. Coyote was born here. South Star, god of the underworld, had spit him forth bleeding and burned, breathing the smoke, impregnated with shrapnel, and had sent him out to hunt.

And now he was back, for the last time. The people who caused his pain, his alienation and disavowal, would finally die here. *Carpe diem, canis latrans.* Coyote would seize the day, by the throat.

25

The cemetery was ratty. A row of eucalyptus trees formed a leaky windbreak against the encroaching desert. A groundskeeper riding a lawnmower tossed his cigarette butt onto the lawn. That did it. Two hundred years from now, I don't want crabgrass and sand crawling across my name. I don't want visitors glancing idly at a neglected marker, wondering, who was that? Scatter my ashes on the wind. Find a mountaintop and sing 'The Dance' by Garth Brooks and send me back to the earth as dust.

We followed Abbie and Wally across the grass to the gravesite. He put his arm across her shoulder and she leaned against him for a moment, resting her head. The sun bore down like a weight; wearing a black suit had been ill considered. Tommy was eyeing the graveyard like a hawk. Excusing himself, he veered away to the edge of the crowd.

I took Mom's arm. 'You know, don't you?'

For a second she gazed at the pallbearers carrying Kelly's casket toward the grave. Her pace slowed and she looked at me with suppressed anguish.

'I found the receipt for the early pregnancy test,' she said.

My throat tightened. 'I didn't mean for it to happen this way.'

She turned to me. 'Sweet girl, I'm not angry and I'm not disappointed.'

She hadn't called me that since I was about fourteen. The tightness in my throat worsened and my eyes began to sting.

'Mom, I know it's a shock, but this baby is an extraordinary gift.'

She looked as though she couldn't begin to find the words to explain how many things were wrong with what I had just said. I fought the tears away.

'What happened to saying that I should hold onto Jesse?' I asked. 'To telling me I should give him your love and that you think we're building something strong and—'

'Evan, that's not it at all.'

'It kills me that you aren't happy.'

She took hold of my arms. 'I'm frightened out of my wits for you.'

I blinked against the bright sunlight. 'That's it? Oh, Mom, I'm scared too. Some of my classmates . . .' My voice caught. 'They had pregnancies that . . .'

I couldn't bring myself to say it, not here in a graveyard, not in relation to a life I was creating. Mom's eyes were full of pain.

'You know about those children, don't you?' I said.

'I talked to your dad about all of this.'

'All of this?' I stepped back. 'God, he knows I'm pregnant? What did he say?'

'Ask him yourself.' She nodded across the scraggly lawn. 'There he is.'

Beyond the grave and the assembling crowd, I saw my father striding toward us. I shrank inside.

'You two have been tag-teaming me all week long,' I

said. 'What are you going to do, tell me not to rush into things? That's what Dad said yester—'

Yesterday.

I exhaled. No wonder I'd felt as though he was picturing me walking up a church aisle in an immaculate white dress. *Don't do anything rash.* He didn't just mean marriage, he meant *Don't jump into a shotgun marriage.* Damn him and all his unspoken subtext.

Rounding the mourners, he walked up, touched Mom's elbow and pecked her cheek. His face looked as strained as hers: dry, windblown and tough as cactus.

'Angie. You're looking great.'

'Philip.'

He spread his arms and waited for me to step into his embrace. I hugged him, feeling nervous and outmaneuvered. At the grave, the priest adjusted the purple stole around his shoulders and beckoned to stragglers.

'Come on,' I said.

I avoided Dad's eyes. Linking arms, we walked together to the grave.

The priest raised his hand to offer a final blessing. In the front row Scotty Colfax sat slumped like a sack of rice. At the edge of the crowd Tommy stood watchfully. I saw other police officers among the crowd, people I recognized from the station. I held onto both my parents, feeling rough.

None of us spoke. We didn't need to. The tension was a choking vine.

At the final *Amen*, people began heading to their cars as fast as decorum allowed, eager to escape the heat. Dad led us toward the parking lot, shading his eyes to peer at the horizon. Hazy with distance and altitude, the Sierras thrust into the sky.

Mom followed his gaze. 'Been a while, hasn't it?'

'Town feels different. Though that may be the circumstances.' He glanced at her, his expression oblique. 'But the mountains look the same as the day we arrived.'

We approached his car. Tommy walked over, looking as alert as a cat, and shook Dad's hand.

Dad brightened. 'It's been a long time. Good to see you, son.'

'Sir.' He lowered his voice. 'After the casket's interred, Scotty's going to place the flowers and the teddy bear. From that point we'll have officers surveiling the cemetery twenty-four/seven. Then we see if we draw Coyote to the bait.'

He scanned the crowd, already looking for him. Then, remembering himself, he shot Dad a smile.

'Congratulations. You must be a proud papa.'

'Excuse me?' Dad said.

'Father of the bride. Even if her dude does live to take on The Man.'

He winked at me. Excusing himself, he left to talk to another officer, pulling out a pack of cigarettes as he went.

The wind flicked against my hair. I asked the heavens for courage.

'Dad, Mom told me you know about the baby.'

He gave me his slow gaze and opened his mouth to speak. I stopped him.

'This is unexpected but it isn't unwelcome. It's serendipity, like catching gold dust in my hands.' I swallowed. 'If I've let you down, I'm sorry.'

His face softened and he clasped me to him. 'Kit, you haven't let me down. I don't give a rip about all that. Your health and happiness are what matter to me.'

'Please understand. Please.'

God, again with the tears. At this pace I was going to dehydrate. Luckily, in a cemetery nobody considers an outburst of crying out of order. Dad hung on, rocking me back and forth, trying to calm me.

'Ssh.' He put his lips near to my ear, whispering, holding me tight. 'It's all gonna be okay. You'll get through this.'

I scrubbed a knuckle across my eyes. 'Damn straight. And then we're throwing the biggest, in-your-face wedding bash this side of ancient Rome. Later when we pull out the albums, we'll just hope the kid can't count to nine months.'

His breathing slowed, and the rocking stopped.

'What?' I said.

His arms were tight around me. 'If you want a big wedding, that's . . .'

I looked up at him. 'What is it?'

'Nothing. That all sounds wonderful.' Loosening his grip, he began leading me toward his car. 'Let's get you out of this sun.'

I wiped my eyes. He kept his arm around my shoulder.

'Where's Jesse? I thought he was going to be here,' he said.

'So did I.'

'Didn't he—' He exchanged a glance with Mom. 'Didn't he drive up?'

At his tone, disquiet wormed around me. He gazed straight ahead. Mom was peering strenuously at the Sierras.

I slowed. 'What's going on?'

'He said he was going to join you. Given the circumstances, I would expect him to hold to that.'

The air thickened. I stopped. 'I can't get him to answer

his phone. Something's wrong. What do you know that I don't?'

They looked at each other.

'Dad?'

I felt as if I'd just been hit in the face with a pie. One made out of hammers and ball bearings. *I have some things to take care of here.*

'You didn't go and talk to him, did you?'

He didn't need to answer; his face said it all. Mom's too.

'Oh, God. What did you say to him?'

Caution came into his eyes. 'Just spoke about your future.'

'Just. *Just* about our future?'

And, oh, the look that crossed his face with that possessive *our*. I had misunderstood him. I knew then how awful the talk with Jesse had been.

'Not our future. My future.' I blinked, dizzy. 'You don't see a future that's ours, do you?'

Mom stepped forward. 'Phil. Tell her.'

For a minute he held still, ruminating. 'We talked about the pregnancy, yes.'

'Tell me you didn't shoot him,' I said. 'I need to sit down.'

I walked to his rental car, opened the back door and plopped down.

'What did you say to him?'

'We talked about . . .' He frowned, and it looked to me as though he was questioning his own resolve. 'We talked about you having this baby.'

All at once I wasn't hot anymore. I was ice cold.

'You did what?'

And a deeper chill seeped through me, biting and vile. 'You don't think I should have the baby?'

My parents stared at me. Pins and needles danced in my fingers.

'You want me to end the pregnancy?'

Dad crouched down to eye level with me. 'Honey, I know the idea seems excruciating, but—'

'How dare you?'

Mom leaned into the doorway. 'Ev, calm down for a second and listen to reason.'

I shrank from her. 'You agree with him?'

I turned away, crab-crawled my way across the back seat, opened the far door and climbed out. I stared at them over the roof of the car.

'You went to Jesse and told him I should get rid of his child? You wanted him to go along with that? How the hell – Jesus Christ, how could you?'

Dad's face was sad. 'He understands how dangerous this pregnancy is.'

'Dangerous?'

'Kit, you saw the video of Dana. You heard her husband. And you know that's why Coyote killed her and eradicated that clinic.' He continued giving me that sad look. 'Jesse understood that. That's why I asked you where he is. I expected that he'd already talked to you about it.'

That cut me through and through. The ripping sound, the one from my dream, tore through my head.

'Are you telling me he goes along with this?'

Mom looked sad now, too. 'Sweetheart, don't think badly of him. It's an awful thing for him to have to face.'

The noise in my head got louder. I walked away from the car, across the parking lot under the sun, feeling short of breath. This wasn't happening.

My eyes defocused until all I saw were the Sierras chaining the horizon. Beneath those mountains Jesse had spoken to me in the moonlight, telling me he would not let my life become a compromise. He had promised. He said he would fight.

For a moment I stood with the wind slapping my hair. I turned back around.

'You're lying.'

Mom's face pinched. I walked toward my parents.

'That's not what happened. Jesse fought you, didn't he, Dad?'

Dad tried to cover it, but I saw a flicker in his eyes.

'He refused even to consider it. I know he did.'

Mom looked at Dad. Dad looked at me.

'What did you use on him? Lies? Guilt?' That elicited a twitch near his eye. I strode closer. 'How did you phrase it to him? Make him think I was having this baby out of pity? Make him feel he was saddling me with not only a child but with . . .'

I had to grit my teeth to keep from spitting or shouting. 'You didn't. Tell me you didn't take away his pride.'

I clenched both fists and raised my hands and stepped right up in his face. I was so close to hitting him that I didn't know if I could stop myself.

His voice was steady. 'This is life and death. I'm not proud, but I couldn't hold back. Nothing is more important than you. Not even Jesse, no matter how much you care about him.'

'What did you say to him?'

He didn't reply.

'Tell me.' I stared him in the eyes and refused to look away. 'He hasn't shown up and it's because of what you said to him. Tell me what you said.'

Slowly, painfully, the resolve ebbed from his eyes.

'I asked him to dig deep inside for the most honest

296

truth he could find. I asked him how much he loved you.'

'What did he tell you?'

He had one last moment of hesitation, gazing into the distance, as though he was taking not only Jesse's measure but his own.

'He said he loves you more than his own life.' His eyes met mine. 'I told him it was the right answer.'

The chill ran down to my bones. Jesse wouldn't choose death for me or the baby. He would choose something else. The dream flashed in my mind and I saw him sprinting toward me through the surf, only to be ripped away. In that instant, I had never hated anyone as I hated Phil Delaney.

Dimly I heard my name being called. Tommy was striding toward us, phone pressed to his ear. Captain McCracken was with him. His face was flushed.

'There's a break. LAPD was able to lift a print from your boyfriend's shirt. They got a hit on it,' Tommy said.

'Oh.'

'We have a lead. Come on, we need you over at the station.'

The house and yard were noisy. Chimes, clanging, and metallic ringing surrounded him. It was the tinning of the windmills and mobiles and rickety sculptures in the back yard, some kind of art garden.

Through the kitchen window Coyote saw the woman scurrying around. She was stuffing clothing and vitamin supplements into a duffel bag. Then prescription bottles and about five ounces of what looked like Colombian weed. She didn't look like a woman preparing to go back to work after a funeral. She looked like a woman getting ready to bug out of town.

He tapped on the window. It sounded like a tumble-weed scritching at the glass. She turned around. Jumped.

He waved.

Hand pressed to her chest, she crossed the kitchen and unlocked the door. 'Christ, you startled me. What are you doing at the back door?'

'Admiring your sculpture garden. What do you call that, junk art?'

Antonia Shepard-Cantwell waved him in. 'Bricolage. It's art made from objects at hand. Robin, you should know that term.'

Hanging garbage was the term that came to his mind. The tinsel in the scrawny trees mimicked the garish earrings tangled in her long hair. Fortunately, the neighbors wouldn't mind the trash menagerie. There were no neighbors. The house was ten miles outside of town.

She returned to the duffel bag, jamming in tie-dyed skirts and a pair of Birkenstocks and a sketchpad.

'Where are you going?' he said.

'Taking a little vacation. I have plenty of sick leave stored up with the school district. This is all getting too close for comfort.'

'Why?'

She packed. She couldn't look him in the face. She felt uncomfortable with his bitch-princess smile and queer androgynous voice. She always had. From the beginning he had presented her with a surface that discomfited her. Not only did she never look beneath it, she never looked directly *at* it. She never saw him at all.

She only saw the money.

'People are beginning to figure out that your friends in the government have been keeping tabs on the exposees. It's a bit hot for me right now.'

'Who, Toni?' he said.

'Tommy Chang and Evan Delaney went by my husband's office. They were after information from him. They're on to the connection with the explosion. Chang went bonkers and grabbed Tully.' She kept packing. 'I know you were planning on the usual amount. But for this information I think I deserve more.'

'That's abrupt of you.'

'Listen.' She wiped her hair back from her face. 'It's getting harder and harder. Back when Tully's office ran on paper records, it was easy to slip the information to you. Now that everything's computerized, things have tightened up. Only a few people have access to his system, and even fewer have his passcode to get past the firewall. If the police start looking, it won't take them long to come looking for me.'

'And if I remind you that this is a matter of national security?'

'Baloney. The exposees are part of some experiment and you're harvesting information so you can control them. This is a matter of power.'

But Toni Cantwell liked power. She liked excitement. That's why she had agreed to their cloak-and-dagger act all those years ago. And she liked money, enough for her to wangle Little Mister Faggot a temporary job in her classroom as a student teacher so that he could keep tabs on the exposees. She liked it enough to betray her husband by providing the man she knew as Robin Klijsters with unlimited access to the exposees' medical records.

If she still thought he was working for the government, then he would leave her illusions intact.

'I see. How much were you thinking?' he said.

'Two thousand. And I'm in a hurry. Tully's coming to pick me up. He'll be here any minute and I don't want him to find you here.'

He smiled. 'You can't honestly think he'd be jealous of a queeny little thing like me.'

She looked at him at last, with distant curiosity. 'One question, Robin. All these years you've been working for Uncle Sam, didn't they ever complain about a flaming gay in their midst? Or in your department is it Don't Ask, Don't Tell?'

'In my department, such a question might be the last one you ever asked.'

'Right.' She zipped up the duffel. 'You don't know who it is, do you?'

'Who?'

'Coyote.' She looked at him. 'I don't want to sound paranoid, but I have to wonder if the government knows who he is but doesn't want it to get out.'

'No, Toni, I have no idea who Coyote really is.'

'If you knew, you'd tell me, right?'

'You would find out immediately.'

She nodded, reassured, and held out her hand for the money.

'One question of my own,' he said. 'The day of the explosion. You were in sole charge of the children, weren't you?'

'Yes.'

'So the four who ran off and wandered into range of the explosion were your responsibility.'

'I was leading the discovery of the petroglyphs. I didn't see them run off.'

Her hand was open, palm up. He unzipped his fanny pack and reached inside.

'Did it never occur to you that insufficient security could lead to unforeseen consequences?' he said.

Toni frowned. 'They were thirteen, fourteen years old. Their lives were nothing but a series of unforeseen consequences.'

'Their lives are irrelevant. I'm talking about my life.'

'What?'

He pulled the Taser from his pack and fired. The darts hit her in the chest. Her head snapped back and her earrings flickered in the light. So did the knife.

26

I slumped in the back seat of Dad's rental car. We barreled along the road behind Tommy and McCracken, heading for the police station. Dad gripped the wheel, talking low and fast at Mom as though giving her a mission briefing.

'South Star got out of control. The pain vaccine proved to be an infectious agent and they had to shut down the project.'

'By blowing up the lab?' she said.

'We'll never find any paperwork confirming it, but you bet your butt.'

'Wasn't that overkill?'

'They must have needed to sanitize the site.'

'Didn't it occur to them that an explosion would spread the vaccine agent into the air and contaminate anybody who came in contact with it? Jesus, who was running that project, the Three Stooges?'

'We can assume it was a controlled explosion that didn't go as planned. I imagine they needed extreme heat to destroy the South Star agent. They couldn't just put a flamethrower to the place. And remember when this happened.' He glanced at me in the mirror. 'Kit, Russian satellites overfly the base. If Moscow had downlinked photos showing hazmat teams and flamethrowers dismantling the lab brick by brick, it would have raised their suspicions. Whereas a building out in the back ranges at China Lake blowing up, that's just SOP.'

Standard Operating Procedure. I looked out the window at the ragged desert. Jets howled overhead, shredding blue sky. Dad was trying to bury our argument by putting the discussion on crisis footing, and I wasn't having it. I took out my phone and tried again to reach Jesse. I couldn't.

Dad forged onward. 'For whatever reason, the explosion didn't go to plan and your class was exposed to the vaccine. And Sway was wrong. South Star was effective. It worked.'

Mom crossed her arms. 'Corrosive fuel additives, my ass. I told you Swayze was a stone liar.'

'It was a classified project, Angie.'

'I know. So you lie about it. SOP.' She tightened her arms against her chest. 'Swayze's still lying about it. She told you Coyote couldn't have been infected and that South Star couldn't possibly be making people sick.'

'She may actually believe that.'

'Phil, do you think my bullshit detector has gone offline? The explosion turned Evan's class into guinea pigs. And it took twenty years, but now the test results are coming in and somebody's decided to shut down South Star all over again.' She ran a hand over her spiky hair. 'I goddamn wish Coyote had shut Swayze down all those years ago.'

'Can it, Angie.'

She smiled. It was an acid smile, lips drawn back, eyes corrosive. My brother and I can do it to perfection. It's called the Delaney Fuck You.

'Yeah, she's Albert fricking Schweitzer nowadays. Too

bad her defense research created a monster who's killing mothers and children.'

'Coyote's stalking Maureen, so bite your tongue. If anything happens to her, you'll feel pretty damn lousy.'

I raised my hands. 'Shut the hell up, both of you.'

Dad glanced at me again in the mirror. Mom stared out the window. The town rushed by.

At the Civic Center, a van with the call letters of a Los Angeles TV channel was parked outside the police station. The reporter sat inside freshening her makeup. By the time we pulled up, Tommy and McCracken had already gone inside. When Dad parked, I jumped out and headed for the door without speaking to either of my parents.

'Kit, wait.'

I kept walking. Dad caught me by the arm and I pulled free.

'Leave me alone.'

He stepped in front of me. 'I know you're angry.'

'Angry? You think this is as simple as anger?' I shoved my hair out of my face. 'Yesterday, did you come by my place planning to tell me to have an abortion?'

'I meant to broach the subject. But damn, Kit . . .' He looked like scoured wood, eroded by time and care. 'Look, I knew this would happen. You would turn into a wall. I knew the only possible way to get you to understand would be for Jesse to talk to you. It was a tactical decision.'

I stepped back from him. 'No, Dad. It was cowardice.'

I might have taken an ax to his chest. His shoulders drooped. I pushed through the door into the station.

Mom hurried after me. 'Wait.'

I kept walking across the foyer. She caught up.

'We should never have gone behind your back. We're

just damned scared, and we panicked. I'm sorry, Evan. I'm an ass.'

I turned to her. I was so furious, I thought my hair might ignite.

'Did Dad have an affair with Maureen Swayze?'

'What?'

'Adultery. It's like flirting, only immoral.'

She stiffened. 'Did somebody tell you that?'

'Nobody had to tell me anything. All I have to do is listen to you and Dad snipe at each other.'

Her cheeks reddened. 'For christsake, no. It's bad enough they were friends. That's sufficient to piss me off.'

A watery sensation washed over me, relief splashing my anger. 'It's revealing that you presume somebody told me so. China Lake's like a bowl of carnivorous fish. Falsehoods as SOP, rumors wafting like perfume. Is this where you and Dad learned to plot behind people's backs?'

'Evan, please.'

'Lie and manipulate and put the screws to Jesse and hope he'd cave in?'

'Can we save this for later? What's going on now is about keeping you alive and well.'

She put a hand on my elbow. I shied away. My head was pounding.

'No. You think if we stop talking about it you'll get absolution. You won't.'

Dad walked up looking deflated. Across the station, Tommy stuck his head out of an office and waved us back. I walked ahead of my parents, unwilling to see their faces, and tried once again to call Jesse. No luck. Where the hell was he?

*

305

In the parking garage below Argent Tower, security lights eradicated the shadows. CCTV scanned the exit ramp and the elevator. 'Paint it Black' was pounding from the truck stereo.

Jesse drove along empty acres of concrete, hunting for the car. The garage was nearly as vacant as the office building. He had no luck on the first two levels and cruised down the ramp to Level 3.

'Gotcha.'

Of course Maureen Swayze would park her silver BMW 540i as far from other vehicles as possible. She didn't want such a beautiful car to get dinged. It and a Range Rover were the only cars on this level. He stopped next to it, doublechecking. Yeah, it was the car he'd seen the other day outside Eller's Diner in Westwood when Swayze went to talk to Phil and Evan, with the Argent Tower parking sticker in the window. It had to be hers.

He circled back to the elevator and parked. The security camera was bolted to the wall above the elevator door. Ten feet high, he estimated. He got his crutches from the back seat.

He got the chair out, set the crutches between his knees and wheeled over. Make the camera eleven feet. He was six-one. When he stood up he would have to stretch, and stretching wasn't his strong point.

Stopping beneath the camera, he listened for cars or the elevator approaching, but heard only the building's ventilation system. Taking a breath, he stood up. He leaned against the wall to brace himself and reached up with one of the crutches. Not far enough. He checked his balance, reached up a bit more, and shoved it against the bottom of the camera. It swung toward the ceiling. Yes.

He threw the crutches back in the truck. It might only

306

be a minute before the guards noticed that the camera was screwy. Even that sluggish Archie up at the desk might spot it and jump. He wheeled to Swayze's BMW. He hoped the prissy German alarm would squeal at the slightest twitch. He didn't want to smash the window.

He slid the end of the tire iron between the window and the doorframe and he muscled the glass, just half an inch. The car's lights flashed and the alarm shrieked like a cheerleader.

Yanking the tire iron free, he spun and made for the Range Rover parked further down the garage. The pillars supporting the roof were too narrow to hide behind, but an SUV would work fine.

Two minutes later a uniformed guard ambled out of the elevator, fingers in his ears. He walked around the BMW and took note of the license number. He radioed upstairs and headed back to the elevator.

Jesse pressed his hands over his ears. This would work or it wouldn't. If it didn't, he would end up under arrest. But screw it, he was in all the way. He could show Evan and the kid his mugshot. But he had to have Evan and the kid to show it to.

Four minutes later, Maureen Swayze came hurrying out of the elevator, keys in hand, a scowl on her face. She was wearing a white lab coat and a disheveled ponytail. Her little glasses glittered under the fluorescent lights. She clipped over to the BMW, pressed the key fob and disarmed the alarm. In the sudden, blessed silence she stopped cold.

'Remember me?' Jesse said.

She didn't answer. She simply stared at the Glock resting in his hand.

*

Tommy waved a printout. 'The fingerprint hit on your dude's shirt. It was a partial that LAPD matched to a complete print they pulled off the revolving door at that office tower.'

'Is it Kai Torrance?' I said.

'Robin Klijsters.'

He led us into Captain McCracken's office overlooking the parking lot. McCracken was weighing down his desk chair, talking on the phone.

It took a second for the name to match the memory. 'You're joking.'

'No, that's the name. Robin Klijsters. LAPD got the print from State Records. An old file, years back.'

McCracken hung up the phone. 'They get an address?'

Tommy handed him the printout. 'Here. House on the west side, out past China Lake Boulevard. I have two units checking it out, but the records file is almost twenty years old.'

He didn't recognize the name, I realized. 'Tommy, don't you know who Robin Klijsters is?'

'Who?'

'Our old student teacher.'

He stopped dead. 'Holy shit.'

We gaped at each other.

'That makes no sense,' I said.

But holding his brown-eyed gaze, I knew it all made sense somehow. We just weren't seeing the connection.

'Klijsters was our student teacher in art class.' I said. 'The skanky little weasel who told Ms Shepard I was imagining things when Valerie stole my journal.'

McCracken's chair creaked. 'Klijsters worked at Bassett?'

'With Antonia Shepard. Shepard-Cantwell. She's still there.'

308

McCracken pointed at Tommy. 'Call the high school and get the art teacher on the phone. And contact the school district about records. Get all the background you can on Klijsters.'

I looked at Mom. 'Oh, God. Ms Shepard.'

Tommy shot toward the door. I grabbed him.

'Ms Shepard. Could she be the one who's been funneling information to Coyote?'

He held in the doorway, wound like a top. 'She could have accessed all Dr C's records. Shit, if she got his password she could have used his computer system to get past the firewall at China Lake Hospital.' He looked like he wanted to smack himself in the head. 'We blew it with Cantwell. It may not be him, but his wife.'

McCracken leaned forward. 'Detective?'

Tommy explained. I listened, running it all over in my head. Again I looked at Tommy.

'This still doesn't scan. Klijsters wasn't a super-soldier, he was . . .'

'Boy George. I know.'

The springs on McCracken's chair wailed. He stood, raising his huge hands in the air. 'Hold your horses, right there. What do you mean, he was Boy George?'

Tommy shrugged, working out how to phrase it. 'More effeminate than the Homecoming Queen.'

'Hey,' I said.

He gave me a winsome look, contrite. 'No, Rocky, you were a real princess. I mean that he was—'

McCracken waved a sheet of paper at him. 'I'm talking about this. We got the report from the County crime lab. That dental implement we recovered near Wally Hankins's office.' He handed the sheet to Tommy. 'The curette.'

Tommy read. 'Prion contamination.'

309

'From Coyote?' I said.

McCracken said, 'Keep reading.'

'They recovered blood evidence and DNA. It didn't belong to Ceci Lezak. It's an unsub.' Tommy looked up. 'Then it must be Coyote's. If we can match it to Klijsters, we have him.'

McCracken took off his scratched glasses. 'You don't have him. Klijsters isn't a him at all.'

Tommy read further, and looked up in shock. 'What the hell?' He looked at me. 'The blood on that dental implement came from a woman.'

27

Breathless, Coyote swung the knife in the close confines of the kitchen. The teacher was fighting.

She clawed at him. 'Bastard! Stop it!'

He pinned her left leg and slashed the Achilles tendon. She screamed. The decibel level indicated that she was experiencing hideous pain. He cut the hamstring tendons and moved on to her right leg, severing the Achilles there, disconnecting the muscles from the bones.

Flipping her onto her back, he dove on top of her. She windmilled her arms and scratched his face. Her teeth were bared.

A tremendous thrill shot through him. She was magnificent. Why had none of her students been inculcated with her spirit? She smacked him in the face. If only he had been able to embrace the pain. He grabbed her wrist. She saw the knife, seven inches long, serrated, forged with a channel along the blade that let blood sluice from penetrative wounds in a clean, quiet run. She didn't flinch, she didn't freeze or withdraw mentally. She was engaged in the battle, flesh and soul.

In legend, Coyote and Woman fought, trying to outwit each other. Was this Woman, at last?

He changed tactics. Forcing her into mechanical compliance by severing tendons or nerve groups was not as challenging as forcing her into pain compliance. He lay atop her, pinned one of her hands to the floor, pried her fingers open and ran the knife clean through the tendons in her palm. She screamed.

'Bastard. Fucker!'

He lowered his face, his mouth inches from hers. 'New information. I need it right now.'

She spat at him. He wrestled the knife around and pushed the tip against her cheek.

'New information.'

She stared straight back at him, willing to brave his gaze. At last, a superb animal, embracing the dynamic of hunter and hunted. Unwilling to concede.

'I can blind you and peel your face off. I can flay you and leave you spread across this floor like pig slop spilled out of a bucket. And I'll save your tongue until the end, so you can give me the information.'

Still she held his gaze. He hovered close above her like a lover.

She moved her lips. 'Chang and Delaney.'

'Yes?'

Her breath hissed out and in. 'They know about the others. The pregnancies. Evan was frightened.'

'Frightened. Of course.' He lowered his lips closer to hers, beginning to see. 'Pregnancy?'

'I think so.'

'Think harder.' He took her lower lip between his teeth and began to bite.

Reaching up, she grabbed the handle on the oven door and slammed it down, hitting him in the back of the head with it.

The blow knocked his head down hard on hers and the back of her skull hit the linoleum. He bit through her lip and the pain finally broke her. She fell limp in agony.

He roared and lunged up, ripping her bottom lip in half.

The knife was lodged in her cheek. He pulled it free and sliced her across the face, drawing claw marks.

She raised her functioning hand, trying to protect her face. He knew he'd found her fatal flaw. She was an artist, concerned with appearance. Vanity: a woman's weakness.

She grabbed his hair.

The wig was on securely but she clawed her fingers into it and pulled. Perhaps she thought doing so would hurt him. Then, using what leg movement remained to her, she brought her knee up under him, hoping to get him in the balls. No way was that going to happen. He held stiff and took the blow.

In her eyes shock and knowledge fought with the intense pain she must be experiencing. She was drenched in blood and the floor was becoming slippery. It was time to finish this, but he wanted to observe how she faced the certainty of her taking. A worthy opponent deserved that.

At the front of the house came the sound of a door opening. 'Antonia.'

The teacher roared an animal wail. With one last effort she swung her arm and smacked him in the face. He blinked, grabbing his face, feeling the contact lens slide off his eye.

Footsteps came running, and a man cried out. 'Toni?'

Coyote drove the knife into her trachea. He bore down with both hands while the blade sank through her throat, pushing until it hit the bones of her spinal column. She became silent and still.

She had pulled the wig off. He disentangled it from her dead fingers.

The noise came from behind him: shoes scuffing on

tile. He turned and saw the man fleeing for the front door. Coat lapels flapping, bald head trailing strands of hair from a combover. The doctor.

Coyote pulled the knife from Toni Cantwell's throat. The doctor was a coward, leaving his wife to the dogs. He would die a coward's death.

I looked at McCracken, taken aback. 'The killer is female?'

Behind his scratched eyeglasses, he appeared equally perplexed. 'Yes. Are you telling me Klijsters *isn't* female? Robin, I was presuming it was a woman's name.'

'No, he was a man.' I glanced at Tommy. 'At least I thought he was.'

McCracken took off his glasses to reread the results from the crime lab. His beefy features were flushed.

'The crime lab definitely found two X chromosomes. Whoever got stabbed with that dental pick is female.'

I thought back to the moment at Argent Tower when Coyote passed me in the revolving door. Short blond hair and a baseball cap and men's clothing. Jesse had seen a man go by, too.

No, we'd seen the back of a head.

Jax and Tim's depictions came back to me – the perplexing change in Coyote's demeanor as the years passed; the fascination with transvestites and gays; the castration and murder of the male prostitute in Bangkok. The sexual fluidity and love of disguise. And the rest: Robin Klijsters, the simpering, theatrically camp student teacher working in Ms Shepard's classroom.

'Christ, Tommy. He treated our school classroom like an animal lab.' And I cleared my head. '*She* did. She's had us in her sights ever since.'

Though the Glock was aimed at the ground, Swayze went rigid when she saw it.

'Walk around the far side of that Range Rover,' Jesse said.

She stood immobile. 'Have you lost your mind?'

'I'm batshit crazy and prone to spasms. So don't make me angry, because if I lose it, we're going to get hurt.'

She blinked.

'Don't expect the guards to come charging down, either. I put the security camera out of commission.'

She looked up at it. The surprise on her face said *How the hell?* Her resolve seemed to slip.

'And if I have to go to jail for this, I will. So you're shit out of arguments. Walk.'

She walked.

'My colleagues are going to notice that I'm gone.'

'You don't want your colleagues to hear this. Give me your lab coat and car keys.'

She did so with a sneer. He took the keys, patted down the white coat, removed a cellphone from the pocket and tossed the coat back.

'Sit down with your back against the wall.'

She settled herself on the concrete, squinting at him as though considering the best way to put his eyes out. He kept back. Phil trusted Swayze's motives, but Jesse wondered if his warning about Coyote applied to this woman, too: *you cannot imagine how little ordinary morality affects these people, or how far they'll go.*

'What do you want?' she said.

'You're going to help bring Coyote in.'

'Coyote? I have been helping. For heaven's sake, I'm the one who gave a name and description to the FBI.'

'No, you've been lying for twenty years. You lied to the

315

parents after the explosion and you lied to Phil and Evan the other day. That means you damn well lied to the FBI too.'

She shook her head.

'You knew from the beginning that the pain vaccine was lethal. You know that it's killing Evan's classmates and their children. You know that anybody South Star doesn't kill, Coyote will, because South Star spawned Coyote.' He leaned forward. 'And you like it that way.'

Her glasses shone at him. 'You're off your lithium. Let me call your shrink.'

'You want South Star and its aftermath to go away for good. By your lights, Coyote's cleaning up your mess.'

'You did black out the other day, didn't you? Coyote was here, casing the building.'

'Maybe you're betting on him leaving you for last. Once he kills all the exposees and their kids, then you'll call the police with new information you've suddenly remembered. Because I think you know much more about who he is and how to find him than you've told anybody.'

He took a breath. 'But you're going to tell me.'

'There's nothing to tell.'

'When you lied to Evan and Phil, they didn't try to force the truth from you. They drew a line. I won't.'

Swayze looked quizzical. 'Why are you willing to go to these lengths? This is . . .' She waved at the Glock.

'Assault with a deadly weapon? Not yet.'

He lifted the gun and racked the slide. It made a solid, serious noise.

'Maybe now it is.'

Her shoulders twitched. 'Capturing Coyote won't solve your problem. Even if he's arrested, Evan remains at risk from South Star.'

He didn't move, but he felt it: lie number one, abandoned. For the first time, she had just admitted that South Star was dangerous.

'If Evan is infected, then you're powerless to stop it,' she said. 'There's no cure. You can kill me, but you can't change that.'

'Then tell me how to test for it.'

'MRI.'

'You didn't MRI your test subjects back at China Lake.'

'I don't get this. You wouldn't shoot me just to find out if she's going to get sick. You'd shoot me if you found out she *is* sick.' She eyed him critically. 'You're afraid that she'll give it to you.'

'No. How do you test for it?'

'She can't infect you. It's only transmissible by—'

'Blood test, genetic analysis? Tell me.'

'It's only transmissible by inhalation or inheritance. There's no way she could infect you.'

She was so focused on the Glock, she hadn't been paying attention to anything else. He raised the tire iron in his hand.

'I won't break anything, I'll just hit you where it hurts. Tell me.'

She lifted her chin. 'You don't have the brass.'

God, he hoped he was right about her. He swung the tire iron against her shoulder.

Pain shone bright and loud in Swayze's eyes. She grabbed her arm. 'You son of a bitch.'

Jesse clenched his teeth, biting down the disgust he felt at himself. 'Do you get how deeply invested in this I am? Tell me.'

'Son of a bleeding bitch. You're safe, you imbecile. She can't infect you.'

317

His pulse was pounding. He wanted to throw up. He hit her again.

She flinched this time, but the tire iron connected with her elbow. 'Dammit!' She swung her head toward him, grimacing. 'You cannot be infected. South Star only affects women.'

He held still, tire iron in his hand, realizing what she had just said.

'Coyote's a woman?' he said.

Her lips parted. Lie number two, abandoned.

'You told Evan and Phil that Kai Torrance was a man,' he said.

She stared at him, her lips puckering. 'Kai thinks of himself that way.'

His mouth hinged open. 'And thanks to your sensitivity training, you respect the wishes of the headfucked robo-grunt community?'

She sneered. He sneered back.

'Sorry, I mean sociopathic crossdressers affected by Total Badass Syndrome.'

She was breathing heavily and her tin-colored hair was falling out of the ponytail. 'Now are you satisfied? Even if Evan is infected, she could not possibly transmit it to you.'

'Can you test her?' he said.

She looked disbelieving. 'What *is* it with you? She could never infect you. It's—' Behind the glasses, her eyebrows rose. A clearer light shone in her gaze. 'She couldn't infect you, but she could infect any children you have together.'

If he flinched now, he would be deeply fucked. He held the tire iron ready to swing again.

Her expression cleared. She laughed. 'You want to have

children, is that it? The male imperative to spread your seed triumphs over all else.'

The pain receded from her eyes and she gave him an analytical stare. 'Yes, Evan can be tested. If she's serum negative, you'll be fine.'

He wasn't sure he believed her. He knew now that she was a deep and thorough liar. And he knew that she didn't appreciate how serious he was.

'After you help track Coyote down, you'll get Evan that test.'

'Very well.'

'And you won't weasel out.'

'Fine.'

'No, really. Because before I drove down here, I put together an email. It's queued up to be delivered to my boss tomorrow morning. It's on the law firm's server so you can't find it and delete it.'

'What are you talking about?'

'It details all your work with South Star, your plans to create supersoldiers, the explosion going wrong, your desire to kill all the people in Evan's class, your being in cahoots with Coyote, the whole thing. It includes a video of one of the China Lake victims, along with her MRI. Combine it with all the forensic evidence the China Lake police have gathered about the most recent victims, and you'll be toast.'

She blanched.

'I know you want to continue your current research. You see yourself on stage in Stockholm accepting a Nobel, and you don't want South Star spoiling your chance at that. So this next part is up to you.'

'What?' she said.

'The email instructs my boss to take it to Fox News,

CNN, the *Washington Post* and *LA Times*. And she will.'
He shifted. 'I work for a firm called Sanchez Marks.
Around Santa Barbara they call it the Militant Wing,
because my boss is one of those old peacenik lefties who
hates anything military. She's like a Jack Russell terrier.
Once she gets her teeth into you, she doesn't let go. And
this is the case that would make her career.'

'But that would . . .'

'Destroy you. I know.'

She looked shocked. 'You'd destroy Primacon as well.'

'Do you see any sign that I care?'

'We're working on catastrophic diseases of the brain
and central nervous system. For God's sake, it's research
that could one day lead to treatments for spinal cord
injury. You'd crush that hope?'

'And if professional ruin won't persuade you, the email
also suggests that you have a treatment for the South Star
agent but are withholding it until Coyote dies. It should
give her an extra incentive to track you down. As soon
as possible.'

'You're bluffing.'

'You stopped thinking that several minutes ago.'

Her eyes clouded. She seemed at a loss. Somewhere
in the far recesses of the garage, tires squealed.

'This stops, now,' he said.

'And if I do it? What will you do in return?'

'I'll delete the email. But I have to be around to do
that.'

'That's not enough.'

'If you manage to have Coyote eliminated, I won't
complain. If you want to call your old buddies in the
government and arrange for some of their enforcers or
outsourcers to take Coyote down quietly, that's fine.'

Her sneer stayed in place.

'And when we find her, I'll go in first, ahead of you,' Jesse said. 'But you have to help me. Otherwise, the game is up for you. Period.'

Swayze pressed her hands to the concrete floor. 'How can I be certain you'll keep your bargain?'

'Yeah, I don't trust you either. But I'll have the email. You'll have that sore shoulder and you can always turn me in to the cops. Psycho crip attacks researcher for failing to cure SCI. You could probably get a felony warrant on me.'

She eyed him. 'Fine.'

'How do we find Coyote?'

She stood up. 'We go to Hollywood.'

The doctor slammed the Lexus into reverse and floored it backward down the driveway, screaming. The car door was wide open.

'Antonia. Oh, Toni. Oh, God.'

He hit the mailbox and it flew into the air. The car bounced into the street and across it onto the dirt. His hands floundered around the dashboard and gearshift. He closed his door, looked through the windshield and saw Coyote standing on the front porch, observing. He screamed again.

Coyote stepped off the porch and walked toward him. The doctor grabbed the gearshift, banged it into Drive and flew out into the street, spinning the wheel. The car fishtailed and he drove off one side of the road and then the other and finally screeched down the hill.

Coyote jogged down the street behind him. He had parked the vehicle past an outcropping of rocks, a heavy pickup truck with offroad tires, hunting lights on the roof and a bull bar on the front. He had presciently garaged it in China Lake the previous week. In ninety seconds he was belting down the road, catching up. The Lexus was heading down the hill toward US 395, four miles ahead. The doctor was trying to reach help.

He would fail. Coyote narrowed the gap, the truck eating up ground across this enormous empty sinkhole, this secret and dirty place that stretched everywhere in all directions, even up. Where the jets flew with heavy armaments and wouldn't notice one craven doctor taking flight.

The Lexus zagged and recovered. The doctor must have checked his rearview mirror and spotted the truck. Coyote accelerated.

The Lexus zigged again. He saw the doctor fumbling with a cellphone. Coyote closed on him.

28

McCracken seemed to swell in height, girth and purpose. 'Chang, find out if those uniforms have found Klijsters' address. And get on the phone to Military Records again, see if they can't goddamn pull up a print of this Kai Torrance person and compare it. Hell, wait. I'll call the FBI and see if they can't tear some ass.'

He grabbed his phone, shooing us out of his office. My parents and I followed Tommy to his desk. As he picked up the phone, a uniformed officer came rushing down the room.

'Detective. Line two, it's Dispatch.'

Watching a friend do his job, when you've known him since childhood, is always eye-opening. All Tommy's laid-back cool had annealed to calm focus.

'Yes?' He listened for a moment. 'Who's responding? Okay. Hang on, I'm putting you on speaker.' Eyeing me, he hit the speaker button. 'Terry? Play it back from the start.'

The dispatcher's voice distorted over the speaker. 'One second.'

Tommy said, 'Nine-one-one call. Listen and tell me if you recognize the voice.'

The dispatcher returned. 'Okay, detective.'

'Nine-one-one emergency.'

'For godsake, help me.'

I looked at Tommy, alarmed.

'*He's coming, he's after me. Please for the love of Christ send somebody.*'

'*Sir, slow down. I can barely understand you.*'

More than static was crackling through the speaker. It sounded as though the caller was on a cellphone in a car. From the noise of his engine, he was barreling along.

'*I'm on Eagle Pass Road, heading toward the highway. Hurry.*'

There was a squealing sound, like tires screeching.

'*He killed my wife and he's after me in this giant truck. Oh my God.*'

The dispatcher asked who.

'*Coyote. He's chasing me. Jesus, hurry.*'

My pulse leapt. I looked at Tommy. Mom and Dad crowded around the desk.

'*Sir, who is this I'm speaking to?*' the dispatcher said.

'*Tully Cantwell. I'm trying to outrun him in my car. Blue Lexus.*'

'*Dr C?*' Her voice spiked. '*Hold on, doctor.*'

Tommy looked at me. 'Sound like him?'

'Yes.'

The dispatcher. '*Dr C. Tell me again where you are.*'

'*Coming down the hill toward three ninety-five, south of town. Godsake, get the Highway Patrol out here. He's gaining on me.*'

Tommy stared at the speaker. 'I know where he is. That's way the hell out of town, but it sounds like he's only a couple miles from the highway.' Breath. 'CHP's on the way.'

From the look in his eyes, I knew he was picturing the narrow asphalt road, Cantwell's car sliding onto the shoulder and skidding off on the sand, the doctor racing for US 395, thinking if he could make it there he'd be okay.

Noise sheared from the speaker. Cantwell grunted with effort. Tires squealed.

The dispatcher again. *'Dr C, did you say that your wife is . . .'*

He sobbed. *'Toni's dead. I saw her on the floor, he was . . . clawing her, like an animal.'*

Mom hissed and put her hand over her mouth.

'Where, sir?'

'My house. Call Detective Chang.'

Tommy stared hard at the speaker.

'Coyote's small. Wearing black. His hair, he was wearing a wig but Toni pulled it off. He has a buzz cut, Vin Diesel thing, like he shaved his skull with a hunting knife.'

'Is this the suspect?'

'Yes! And his outfit is covered with . . .' He choked. *'With blood.'*

Loud noise barked from the speaker, a hard metallic thwack.

Dad put his hands on the desk. 'Jesus, Coyote's ramming him.'

The sound of Cantwell's engine grew louder. He was flooring it. The horrid loud sound of metal crunching metal. We heard Cantwell over the roar. He was whimpering.

'Dr C? Sir, are you there?'

'Oh God, he's right behind me. Right there, his grill's in the mirror—'

More whimpering. *'Tell Detective Chang. Coyote, his eyes, they're wrong, they're—'*

Whump. The tires shrieked. The phone clattered, as though Cantwell had dropped it. The sound went muffled.

The whining sound accelerated to a wail. Cantwell cried a long anguished cry. My skin shrank and my nails pressed into my palms.

'He's close,' Tommy said. 'The highway's gotta be right there. He just has to get across the tracks and down to the bottom of the hill.' Though Cantwell couldn't hear him, he leaned toward the phone. 'Hang on, doc, the Highway Patrol's on its way.'

Distantly, Cantwell regained his voice. *He's falling back. I'm outrunning him.*

But we heard the deep growl of the truck, approaching fast. Cantwell wasn't outrunning it at all. Coyote was taking a hard run at him. Mom grabbed my hand. The noise of the two engines blended into an almighty howl and though I turned away, I still heard Cantwell scream.

The pickup rolled through smoggy sunshine, east through Hollywood. Jesse ran a red light, the third one, keeping the truck moving so Swayze wouldn't be tempted to jump out.

Swayze watched the surroundings with the alertness of a hungry owl. 'Kai was a street kid from Hollywood before enlisting in the army. Her mother was a drug addict. They lived in this awful apartment off of Franklin Avenue.'

'How do you know?'

'One time she disappeared from China Lake. We found her on the roof at this place. Her mother was dead but she went back there anyway, treated the apartment almost like a nest. She might again.'

Jesse kept her in his peripheral vision. She was acting out of pure self-interest. Her only hope of staying out of trouble was to keep Coyote from falling into the hands of the police, and she would use him to that end.

'You didn't tell the FBI about this apartment?' he said.

Her expression said: Don't be an imbecile.

'Why haven't you gone to this place before?' he said.

'I've driven by the building. But I can't knock on the door. I'm a familiar face.' She looked at him. 'You can knock on the door, though.'

'I'm a familiar face to Coyote too.' He glanced at her. 'You think she'd kill you?'

'In a second. Kai's becoming psychotic. From the evidence I can glean, we're talking about total insomnia, REM dreams erupting into the waking world, lack of pain destroying her conscience and her ability to restrain herself. She has no off switch.'

'So she'll want to kill me, too.'

'I presume that gun is loaded.'

He turned onto Vine, heading toward the hills. 'Who outsourced this cleansing operation to her?'

Swayze checked her fingernails.

'Are you her project manager?'

She picked at a cuticle.

'Why has she gone on this rampage?' he said.

'She was at the lab the day of the explosion. She saw the four kids come out onto the hillside. She ran back to the lab to stop the detonation, but it was too late. She was exposed to unheard of concentrations of the vaccine, in a wholly uncontrolled manner.'

'So was Evan's class.'

'No. They got less of it. And Kai had already been vaccinated. The effects were different on her.'

He kept the truck rolling around the corner onto Franklin. 'Does she blame those four kids?'

'That's a logical assumption.'

He felt hot. 'She's saving them for last, isn't she? She has something special planned for them.'

'I imagine so.' She crammed some loose strands of hair back into her ponytail. 'South Star could become a viciously dangerous new disease vector. No matter what you think about me, you must understand that it needs to be stopped. I want to do what I can to assist that.'

Traffic gleamed along. He checked the speedometer.

She glanced at him appraisingly. 'And you . . . has Evan agreed to attempt a pregnancy, is that it? Are you planning IVF?'

He watched traffic.

'Not that I object. Presuming that Evan is clean of infection, I think you two should have a litter of children.'

His nerves slithered at her tone. She cut her eyes at him.

'I've seen your physical and psychological profile from the US Olympic training camp at Colorado Springs. You should have been a gold medalist.'

Mouth open, he turned to her. 'You did what?'

'Your psych profile shows intense competitiveness and dedication. You earned your spot on the US national team despite several disadvantages. Your mother smokes and she's an alcoholic. You worked to earn a swimming scholarship to the University of California so you could get away from the house and make something of yourself.'

'How the hell did you—'

'Though I must say, today you've surprised me with your ruthlessness.' She rubbed her arm. 'And Evan – well, look at her. She's one of the prime exemplars of her class.' A thoughtful expression on her face. 'It should be a brilliant combination.'

The slithering sensation increased. 'What's your point?'

'You should consider it. Seriously.'

She pointed up the street. 'Turn here. This is it.' She eyed him again. 'You sure you're ready for this?'

'Yes.'

He hoped he was right.

Steam hissed from the radiator of the Lexus. The doctor biinked, regaining consciousness, and cringed in apparent pain. He listened to the rumbling engine and reached out to turn off the ignition.

Coyote stood on the roof of the car, observing.

The doctor realized that the steering column wasn't there. He focused and saw that he was on the passenger seat.

Gingerly he straightened his head and looked about at the yucca trees and rocks and the interior of the car. He seemed to be figuring out that his head had created the crack in the windshield. He put his right hand to his forehead. It was streaming blood. Scalp wounds truly bled prodigiously. He jerked a breath.

'Toni . . .'

He looked around again, searching perhaps for the police or for his wife.

Coyote jumped from the roof onto the hood of the Lexus, landing loudly. He spun, crouched and gazed at the doctor.

Cantwell recoiled. Perhaps from the sight of his clothing, glinting wet with blood. Perhaps from the distortion of the cracked glass. Perhaps from seeing Coyote's eyes, one blue and the other black, the pupil blown. It would be like looking down a hole.

He spoke loud enough for the doctor to hear through the windshield and over the rumble of the engine.

'I took Toni.'

The doctor whimpered.

Cur. Gutless dog. Coyote stood and kicked at the shattered windshield. It sagged but didn't break. The doctor flinched, attempting to raise his hands to his face. Coyote kicked again, ferociously, and glass collapsed with a sick chiming sound into the front seat of the car. It covered the doctor like snow, gleaming in the light.

Coyote crouched down again. 'Do you hear that sound?'

He paused, waiting for the doctor to focus on the rumble.

'That is a freight train. If I estimate correctly it will arrive in approximately two minutes.'

The doctor glanced around in panic. While he was unconscious Coyote had shoved him into the passenger seat and driven the Lexus right here, to the center of the railroad tracks. The doctor jerked toward the passenger door. He got nowhere. His left hand was handcuffed to the steering wheel.

'I threw away the key,' Coyote said.

He held up the Ka-bar. The doctor cringed. Had the man never held a scalpel? Did he not recognize a tool?

'If you work at it, you should be able to free yourself with this.'

The doctor stared at him in horror, the realization dawning on him. Coyote leaned in and stabbed the knife into the plastic of the dashboard. It stuck.

'That's your wife's blood on the blade. If you mix the two, perhaps you'll gain some of her courage.'

He stood. The train was louder now, coming closer to the bend.

'You have sixty seconds. If you have the fortitude, take the decision.'

Sauntering to the front of the car, he hopped down. When he looked back the doctor was staring at the knife. He strolled out of the way of the impending impact. The train would not have time to stop when it rounded the bend.

The doctor stared up the tracks. And he stared at the knife. He yanked on the handcuffs, hoping to pull them loose. The noise of the train drew near.

And at that moment his cellphone rang. The doctor looked around, hearing the sound, patting his jacket.

Coyote held up the phone. 'Looking for this?'

He read the display: 911 emergency dispatch. 'It's the police. Did you contact them?'

Cantwell's lips moved. 'They're coming.'

'I think not.'

He flipped open the phone and lowered his voice to the doctor's middle-aged timbre. 'Doctor Tully Cantwell.'

The dispatcher spoke with the mechanical even tones of the professionally dispassionate. It was an admirable quality in a woman's voice. She asked him to reconfirm the information he had given her before they were cut off earlier. He listened to her, eyeing the doctor and shaking his head.

'No, none of that's true. I apologize for this, but one of my patients got hold of my phone and I'm afraid he made that call to stir up trouble for me. He's—'

The dispatcher began sounding dyspeptic.

'He said what? For the love of God. My wife is fine. Unfortunately he's mentally unstable . . . That's correct. No, I can't give you his name. Doctor-patient confidentiality. No, I'll deal with this.'

He flipped the phone shut. His hands were sticky. He needed to change and shower. He had the change

331

of clothing in the truck. He could shower at his next stop, when he retrieved the weapons he had cached the last time he was in China Lake. The train rumbled closer.

In the half-smashed Lexus the doctor pulled the knife free from the dashboard. He was sobbing. He held it over the tendons of his wrist.

The noise of the engine grew louder. Coyote gazed toward China Lake. It was time for the final work of the project, the progenitors. Abigail Johnson Hankins, Thomas Jian Chang, Kathleen Evan Delaney and, first of all, Valerie Ann Skinner. The doctor screamed, raised the knife and plunged it into his wrist. The locomotive thundered around the curve. The horn blew and the brakes shrieked. The roar of the engines vibrated through him.

What a *satisfying* sound it is, metal shredding metal.

Outside the police station, sirens blared. I looked out the window and saw three fire engines roaring south. The fan began flinging shit.

Another detective called out to Tommy. 'Major MVA out past the college. Car versus train.'

Tommy sagged. I pressed my fist over my mouth. Mom turned to Dad and he held onto her elbow.

McCracken's voice rocked the station. 'Chang.'

He was standing in his office doorway, calling to his detectives and uniformed officers, ordering patrol cars to check out the motor vehicle accident and the reported murder at Dr Cantwell's home. Tommy jogged down to McCracken's office. When he came back a minute later he unlocked a desk drawer, took out his service revolver and shoved it into his shoulder holster.

'You stay put. You'll be safe here.'

'What about Valerie?'

He was pulling on a windbreaker to cover the holster. He stopped. 'Where is she?'

'I don't know. Most likely at her mom's.'

'Find out. I'll send a unit.'

I pulled out my phone. 'She won't open the door to the police. She's paranoid.'

'Shit. Will her mom?'

'I presume so, but she may be working at the motel.' I dialed Valerie's cell and heard it ring. 'I'll go with the unit.'

Dad stepped up. 'I'll go with you.'

I stood stiffly, not wanting to look him in the eye, feeling dry and coarse. Valerie didn't answer. I nodded to Dad.

'Fine,' Tommy said.

He waved a uniform over, a young officer with a serious, eager face. Tommy told him to call the Sierra View Motel and the Skinner residence and to take us wherever Valerie was.

Tommy put his hand on my shoulder. 'You rule, Rocky. You always have.'

'Take care,' I said.

'All right, all right. I'll quit smoking.'

In the patrol car, the young officer fired up the engine and backed out.

Valerie's mother, Alma Skinner, was not on duty at the motel and there was no answer at her house or on Valerie's cell. I buckled up as he drove toward the exit, and saw Abbie's van pull in.

'Wait a moment,' I said.

I got out. Abbie and Wally were walking toward me.

She waved. 'I'm heading up to Independence and wanted to tell you goodbye.'

'Coyote's here.'

I told them and their faces became stricken close to panic. She grabbed Wally's hand.

'The kids,' she said.

'Go talk to Tommy.'

Clutching hands, they rushed into the station.

I jumped back in the patrol car. 'Let's go.'

Grime and heat covered the Hollywood neighborhood like a tramp's stinking coat. Dogs had been at garbage cans overnight. Jesse set the Glock on his lap and covered it with his jeans jacket. Inside the apartment building, a funky scuzz gummed the baseboards. The elevator smelled of urine. On the top floor, Swayze hung back out of sight and he knocked on the apartment door. Nobody answered.

'I'll go see if the super will let us in,' she said.

'No, I'll go.'

She turned her head. She kept that chin so far in the air that he could see up her nostrils. 'I'm not going to run out on you.'

'I know. But I can be charming.'

The superintendent had one eye and breath like a dog on gin. He hated being pulled away from the Dodgers game, and he really hated hearing that Mrs Kazanjian wasn't answering the door. She was frail. Also mean as a cockroach, so he definitely hated the notion of barging in on her. So he guessed it was okay if Jesse took the key. He could see the concern on Jesse's face, yeah, real honest concern, even if his business card said he was a lawyer.

334

Right. And the guy probably thought he would get a reward if it turned out they were averting a crisis. Be right back, Jesse said.

Upstairs, Swayze was waiting. She looked alert and wary, and when he neared the door she retreated down the hallway. Watching her back away, he remembered that Coyote was trained in demolitions.

'Do you think she might have booby-trapped the door?' he said.

'It's possible.'

Angling as far back against the wall as he could, he jangled the lock and pushed the door open, turning his head and leaning away.

Quiet.

Yellow light slanted through the windows. Dust motes rode the air. The smell was fust and lavender and, in the stuffy heat, another odor creeping along the edges of the walls. The punk of bad meat.

Jesse hung in the doorway, hands on the frame for mental balance. 'Oh, fuck.'

The walls and kitchen table were covered with documents. Photos, notes and charts were pinned to the walls. Books and a computer were set up, volumes and volumes of notes, he could see that. The apartment had been turned into a war room.

Swayze shoved past him and strode in.

'Don't. Come back,' he said.

She strode briskly down a hallway. She stopped at a door, stared in with dispassionate calm and returned to the living room. 'She's dead.'

Adrenaline flooded him. 'Coyote?'

She examined the photos on the walls. 'Mrs Kazanjian. Broken neck, quick and efficient.'

He hung in the doorway. 'This is a murder scene. Get out before you contaminate it.'

He got his phone. He had to call the LAPD. He stared at the phone but it was throbbing in front of his eyes. Hell, not now, don't lose it here.

Swayze went to the kitchen table and began pawing the papers.

Forcing his eyes to focus, he dialed. Swayze peered through the things on the table and gathered notebooks into a stack. Going into the kitchen, she returned with a basket on wheels, the kind old ladies use to bring their groceries home from the store. She began dumping papers into it.

'Stop that,' Jesse said.

The emergency dispatcher came on the line. 'I need the police.'

He told her what was happening. Swayze loaded the grocery cart. In went notebooks, charts and receipts.

'Cut it out,' he said.

He didn't want to cross the threshold. The apartment was contaminated with depravity. But Swayze was going to take the evidence and dispose of it to keep her name clear. He went in, wheeled to the table and grabbed her arm. She shook him off.

'You don't understand. If you really want to get Coyote, this is how. I can use this to bring her in. She'll want it all,' she said. 'Don't lose your nerve now.'

And then he saw, amid all the painstakingly detailed notes and charts on the table, several familiar items. There was a Bassett High School yearbook. And the *Dog Days Update* they'd handed out at the reunion. And – Jesus.

He could feel the rush at the back of his head, chasing him, about to erupt.

In the center of the table was a weatherbeaten blue journal. It was evidence and he knew he shouldn't touch it. He took a pen from his pocket and used it to flip open the cover.

'Oh, no.'

The name was written right there inside the cover, in a girlish teenage hand. *Property of Evan Delaney.*

29

Jesse flipped the page with the cap of his pen.

October 8th. Tommy Chang said hi today in the hall. It's the first time he's spoken to me since the field trip. Those brown eyes of his look so mournful. He is so, so sweet.

How the hell did Coyote get hold of this? It had disappeared what, eighteen years back?

Swayze continued loading documents into the grocery cart. Getting everything she wanted from the kitchen table, she moved on to the living room. He gave up worrying about contaminating the evidence. He grabbed the yearbook and opened it up.

Damn, it belonged to Valerie Skinner.

He called Evan's cell. It made sense to him now. The four of them who were left. The original group of troublemakers.

Come on, ring. Pick up, pick up.

Coyote knew everything about all of them. And they didn't know how close the killer was.

The phone rang, on and on.

The China Lake patrol car sped along the asphalt west of town. The sun glared off the hood. The young officer at the wheel, Will Brinkley, drove with singleminded concentration. Dad sat in the back seat behind the mesh screen. If Brinkley had noticed that I wasn't speaking to my father, he wasn't commenting.

A thought was nagging me. If Coyote was female, Maureen Swayze was either wrong about Kai Torrance, or she was less than truthful. The asphalt ran out and we were blowing dust behind us, heading toward the tired group of houses near the end of Jimmy's Ranch Road.

The houses had originally been built to house people who worked at Jimmy Jacklin's ranch. A couple were now abandoned, and the house belonging to Alma Skinner looked close to derelict as well. We pulled into the gravel driveway and a line of crows took flight off the peak of the roof, buckshot black against the blue sky.

An old Chrysler New Yorker was parked out front, paisley with bird shit. Brinkley stopped and a bolus of dust rolled over the cruiser. We walked to the front porch. A thin arm of crabgrass was nudging the cracked concrete. A wind chime banged off key.

Brinkley pulled open the creaking screen door and knocked. As he did, my phone rang. I read the display and my heart bounced into fifth gear. *Jesse.*

When I answered it all I heard was static.

'Jesse. Are you there?'

Dad glanced at me sharply. Brinkley knocked again.

Behind the static, I heard Jesse's voice. 'Ev, can you hear . . .' Fading to a hiss.

Brinkley knocked a third time, stepped back and glanced at the windows, perhaps thinking to walk around the house. I shook my head at him and simply turned the doorknob. The door opened.

Jesse's voice came back. '. . . in Hollywood, Coyote's been . . .' Warping out.

'Babe, it's a bad connection.' I checked. I barely had a signal. 'I'm going to lose you.'

The static thickened. Behind it he was shouting. '. . . found your . . . watch out for . . .'

Dead line buzz.

Brinkley leaned through the doorway. 'China Lake Police. Anybody home?'

Punching Jesse's number, I leaned through the doorway after him. 'Valerie? Mrs Skinner? It's Evan Delaney.'

I could hear a television droning. An air conditioner rattled. Somewhere in the back of the house it sounded as though curtains were flapping against the walls in the wind.

The warning had been in Jesse's voice. I had heard it. I punched his number and got nothing. *No Service.*

Brinkley hesitated in the doorway, unsure about whether to go in. But I had no legal limitations on my behavior, and no such compunctions.

'Val.'

I crossed the minuscule entryway into the living room. The air conditioner was going full blast. In the kitchen a television was playing on the counter. Talk show hillbillies whined and pointed at each other while a therapist pursed her lips.

The faucet was dripping. I turned it off. The smell in here was one I associated with slobbish college boys negotiating their first apartment: rancid food. On the stove a can of Campbell's chicken noodle soup was congealed and moldy.

Brinkley came in.

'Something's not right here,' I said.

Mom was in the lobby at the China Lake police station when Wally and Abbie pounded through the door. Wally was gripping Abbie's hand and talking on a cellphone to his father.

Abbie pushed her glasses up her nose. 'Tell him to put the kids on the sofa and sit his butt on a chair with his shotgun leveled at the middle of the door.'

Her cheeks were red, her blonde hair windblown. She looked like a Viking about to swing her sword.

Across the station Tommy was zipping his windbreaker, preparing to head to the Cantwell murder scene and complaining that all the department's cars were checked out. Abbie barreled toward him.

'Chang. Coyote's killing entire households, and my kids are out in a cabin near Independence with one tough old man standing between them and what's out there.'

Tommy stopped, brown eyes alarmed. 'Address?'

Wally gave it to him. Tommy told the officer on the front desk to contact the Inyo County sheriffs and get a unit out to Mr Hankins's house until the parents got there. The desk officer nodded and picked up the phone. Then the switchboard stopped Tommy from leaving.

'Detective, you'd better take this. We're putting through a call from a motorist out on the rim road north of town.'

Tommy grabbed the phone. 'Yes?'

A woman's voice, talking rapid-fire, came at him. 'She won't get in the car. She's a real mess, you need to get out here.'

'Slow down. Back up,' he said.

'I said, we saw this woman jump out of a pickup truck onto the highway. The truck was a big black thing with a bull bar and lights on top.'

'You got the plates?'

'I gave them to the nine-one-one dispatcher. We tried to help but the woman wouldn't let us. This woman, she's weaving along the shoulder of the highway on foot and screaming at us when we try to get near. She's asking for her friends. Says she wants Abbie and Evan.'

Tommy glanced up sharply.

'What?' Abbie said.

The motorist sounded edgy. 'This gal, she's like a cancer patient or something. Every time I try to get close to her she acts like she might attack me. Somebody's gotta get out here, like right now.'

Tommy glanced at Abbie. 'It's Valerie.'

He explained. She looked at Wally.

'You meet the sheriffs at your dad's. Tommy and I will get Valerie.'

'We'll have to wait for a uniformed officer to get back here before we can take a black-and-white,' Tommy said. 'When she sees it she may get aggressive.'

Abbie held up her keys. 'Big-ass van to the rescue. Come on.'

Jesse hit her number again. 'Answer, Ev. Answer.' He looked at Swayze.

'Coyote's in China Lake, isn't she?'

In the living room, Swayze continued pawing through Coyote's things. She tossed items off of the coffee table and dumped out a backpack.

'I don't know.'

The phone didn't ring. He heard static and clicks and blank air.

Swayze let out a sound halfway between surprise and triumph. In her hand she held a necklace: a silver chain from which hung a set of dogtags and a strange, corkscrewed shard of gray metal. It swung, clinking in the sunlight.

'We've got her. It's her talisman. She'll have to get this,

more than if she was a junkie and this was her fix. She thinks it's her power.' She looked astringent with victory. 'Come on, we're getting out of here.'

He heard the thin wail of sirens in the distance. 'That's the cops. I can't leave.'

Evan's phone was out of service. He hung up, found the slip of paper with Phil's number, but couldn't get through on that either.

Swayze walked to the kitchen table. 'If you stay here, you'll be arrested for wrecking a murder scene. At this point, your only chance of getting what you want is to come with me and help draw Coyote in.'

Maybe, maybe not. He only knew one thing for certain: he had to get hold of Evan, or somebody who could put her under armed guard. All of them. Now.

'We have a bargain. I get Coyote, you delete that email.' Clutching the talisman, she shook it in his face. 'I'm keeping my part. Keep yours. Move it.'

Swayze grabbed Coyote's computer from the table, shoved it into the grocery cart and headed for the door.

'Last chance. Once the LAPD rolls up you're spending the afternoon under interrogation. No phone, no way to get hold of Evan, no way to help her.'

She walked out the door. The sirens were clearer now.

He had to call the China Lake Police Department, but he didn't have the number and getting it would take a minute he didn't have. The sirens were virtually down the block. He heard Swayze's heels and the grocery cart creaking down the hall.

'Shit.' He went after her.

Officer Brinkley and I left the kitchen. In the living room, table lamps were on and an ashtray sat full of cigarette butts. Last week's issue of *People* magazine was open to a story about the celebrity adoption *du jour*. Dad was standing in front of the mantel, examining some framed photos. The air conditioning was raising goosebumps on my arms.

Brinkley paused at the top of a hallway. The doors were closed and music was playing. His right hand went to his holster. Unsnapping the latch, he began walking down the hall. I followed him, step by slow step. Again I heard a beating sound, like heavy cloth batting against the walls.

'I think there's a window open back here somewhere,' I said.

Brinkley put his hand on a doorknob. 'Hello?'

He knocked and opened the door. Inside was a tidy bedroom filled with porcelain dolls and fluffy pillows. We kept going. The music got louder. A second bedroom revealed an unmade bed and a suitcase open on the floor, full of women's clothing. Brinkley continued down the hall, toward the door at the end. I moved to follow him, stopped and turned back around, looking at the suitcase on the floor. The clothes inside were bright and blowsy.

The music played, singsong. Once more I heard the beating sound. It seemed busy, multilayered, eager.

Brinkley knocked on the door at the end of the hall. 'Police.'

The beating sound became frantic, swelling to the same level as the radio. Brinkley put his hand on the doorknob. My stomach went hollow.

'Officer, don't—'

He opened the door.

The window was broken, the drapes swirling. The beating sound turned frantic and the birds, the flock of crows that carpeted the bed, rose in flight. The air shattered black with wings. Cawing, clawing, they flew at us. I screamed. Brinkley slammed the door. They filled the hallway and crashed against the wood on the other side and I kept screaming.

'Evan!' Dad came running. 'Hell on earth—'

Wings, beaks, claws and stink caromed around the hallway. I dropped to the floor in a ball, heard them fly overhead and got to my knees and crawled for the living room. Behind me came the sound of Brinkley discharging his gun into the door. A wall of sound shrieked from the bedroom, crows cawing like banshees.

My glimpse inside the bedroom had only lasted a second, but I had seen. The birds were feasting. They were fighting each other in a pile three feet deep, ripping chunks of flesh out of a carcass on the bed.

The rim road paralleled the edge of the base north of town, a black strip running through bare desert in tandem with the razor wire. Fifteen miles out into the emptiness Abbie saw Valerie staggering down the center of the asphalt.

Tommy put his hand on the dashboard. 'Oh, crap, look at her.'

She was limping away from them, trying to run. Abbie pulled to the side of the road behind her and opened the door. Tommy grabbed her arm.

'Wait.'

'What?'

He scanned the view in all directions. 'Something's off. Where's the motorist who called in about this?'

Abbie looked around as well. At every turn there was nothing but sand and scrub.

She waved at Valerie. 'Then let's get her and get out of here.'

Valerie turned to face them.

'Oh my God,' Abbie said.

Her hair was a mess, her wig askew. Her face was worse, bright red with scratches, as though she'd hit a cactus. Her blouse was torn. A patchy streak of blood ran diagonally across it.

Tommy took his gun from the holster. They got out and walked quietly toward her, Tommy holding the revolver at his side, barrel pointed at the ground. Heat swelled off the asphalt. As they approached Valerie began backing away.

'No,' she said.

Her eyes looked at Abbie without recognition. One was blue, pinprick pupil. The other was dilated wide open, deep and black. She raised her hands to fend them off. Abbie stopped on the center line of the road, ten feet from her.

Valerie waved her arms. 'Keep back.'

Abbie raised a hand. 'Val, it's me. It's Abbie.'

Val pointed at Tommy. 'Look out, he has a gun. Put away the gun, put away that fucking gun.'

Tommy calmly holstered it. 'Val, it's cool. Come on, it's just us.'

She looked around wildly. 'Where is he? Is he gone?'

Abbie gave Tommy a sidelong glance and spoke quietly. 'We have to get her to the hospital ASAP.'

'I know.'

Valerie backed away from them. 'Where's Evan? Evan was with me before. I want to see Evan, get her out of the car.'

'Evan's not with us, Val.'

'Where is she? What's wrong? Why isn't she here?' She pointed at them. 'She ran away to the safe place with your kids, didn't she? Why won't you tell me where everybody's going?'

'What happened to you, Val?' Tommy said.

'Jumped out of his truck.'

'Coyote?'

'Opened the door and jumped out.'

'Where'd he go?'

She pointed west, toward the long miles of slope heading toward Highway 14.

Sweat creased its way into Abbie's eyes and tickled its way down her back. She inched toward Valerie, wiping her hand across her forehead.

'Val, we have to get you in the van. It's cool in there. We have a first aid kit. Come on, you're safe now.'

Valerie turned, tried to run and fell. They ran to her side. When Abbie put her hand on her back, she flailed a hand around. She fell back to the asphalt, chest heaving.

Tommy said, 'Come on, let's get her in the car. This whole scene reeks.'

'What do you mean?'

He kept looking around, but there was nothing to see but sand and rocks and the road.

'Val escaping from Coyote, in this condition?' He shook his head. 'I have a bad feeling. Like Coyote let her go.'

'To . . .'

'Yeah, to draw us out here. Come on.'

Working together, they lifted her to her feet. Abbie tried to support her elbow but she said, 'Don't touch me,' and tottered to the van. She flopped into the back, collapsing on the bench seat like a broken toy.

'Why isn't Wally with you?' she said.

347

'He's gone to take care of the kids.'

'Take me there.' Her voice cracked. 'I want to be safe. That's safe.'

'No, we're going to get you to the hospital.'

'I don't want to go to the hospital. Why won't you take me to where the kids are? Nobody will take me there.' She lifted her head. 'Tommy, where are your kids? Can you take me there?'

Abbie got behind the wheel and fired up the engine. 'Everything's going to be all right.'

'Why are they all safe and you're out here with that fucking gun? Abbie, how come you won't help me?'

'Val, we're doing that, right now.'

She U-turned and put the pedal down.

The siren was blaring nearer. In the pickup Swayze snapped her fingers at Jesse.

'Faster, come on,' she said.

He tossed the wheel over his shoulder into the back seat and hauled the frame of the chair into the truck. He pulled his feet in and slammed the door. Twenty-five seconds, pretty damned fast. He yanked the disabled placard off the rearview mirror and stuck it in the glove compartment.

An LAPD black and white came hauling up the street, lights flashing.

'What are you waiting for? Go,' Swayze said.

'Chill.'

Two cops got out and strode to the apartment building. When they walked through the door he signaled and pulled away from the curb. Swayze's forehead was creased, a line digging between her brows.

'Well played.' She sounded grudging. 'But you said you

wouldn't expose me to the police. You're breaking your bargain.'

'I said no such thing. I said if you help bring Coyote in I would delete the email.' He glanced at her. 'Anything I can do to keep Coyote from getting close to Evan and her friends, I'm going to do.'

Accelerating around the corner, he stuck his phone in the hands-free set and called China Lake information, to get the number for the police department. Waiting for them to put him through, he headed into central Hollywood.

'Back to your office?' he said.

'Yes. Can you access your email and delete it from there?'

'When Coyote's out of action.'

He hit Hollywood Boulevard and headed for Westwood. Over the speaker, the China Lake police switchboard came on the line. They told him that both Detective Chang and Captain McCracken were out. He tried not to yell at the operator.

'Take this down and get the message to Tommy and McCracken. It's crucial.'

He told her what he'd found at the apartment. She sounded perplexed, and repeated it to make sure she had it right.

'Yes. Get the information to them *now*.'

Ending the call, he looked anxiously at the phone. Who could he call to explain why he'd left the crime scene? He didn't know anybody at LAPD. The District Attorney's office? They passed the Chinese and the Egyptian theaters. Tourists thronged the sidewalks under the postcard-blue sky. Swayze unbuckled her seatbelt and turned around, kneeling on the seat and leaning into the back.

That alarmed him. 'What are you doing?'

She came back with Coyote's laptop. 'Figuring out how to contact Kai and draw her in.'

He nodded at Coyote's necklace. Swayze was wearing it around her own neck.

'With that?' he said.

'And this.' She held up a plastic case with a cross on it. 'Her medical kit.'

'What's in it?'

'Anabolic steroids and stimulants, looks like, prepped for intramuscular injection. Kai must consider it a treatment to keep the prion under control.' Her smugness was almost radiant. 'She's going to want it back.'

He hoped she was right. The talisman and medical kit would be more powerful draws for Coyote than a teddy bear placed on a grave. If they could pull her away from China Lake, the sooner the better.

Swayze opened the computer and it came to life.

Jesse nodded at it. 'At the apartment I read an email. The address it came from was bassett.cl.edu. Somebody at Bassett High School is emailing her.'

She opened the email program. 'A friend? Or a contact, perhaps.'

He had too much to think, too much to do, and was nowhere close enough to protect Evan the way she needed protecting. The message he'd left for Tommy and McCracken would sound insane, he feared. Coyote, this woman Kai Torrance, had possession of Evan's high school journal and Valerie Skinner's yearbook. She could only have obtained them from Valerie herself. And when she got them, she wouldn't have left Valerie alive.

Reaching for the phone, he punched Evan's number.

★

I grabbed Dad as I ran, pulling him along, flinging open the screen door and hearing it bang against the wall and bang again when Officer Brinkley came streaking out behind us. Crows were swooping up over the peak of the roof, landing on the chimney, screaming as though maddened. I pitched toward the cruiser and dove in the nearest door, the driver's. Dad and Brinkley thudded into the back seat. We slammed and locked the doors.

'Jesus H. Christ,' Dad said.

'The fuck was all that?' Brinkley said. 'Fucking shit.'

'Did you see? Did you see it?' I said.

'I saw it, yeah.' Brinkley ran his hands over his face as though wiping off slime.

A crow swooped, black and mean, wings spread, talons out, and landed on the hood of the car. It opened its mouth and cawed at us.

Brinkley and I screamed, a loud stupid shrieking *agh*, and flung ourselves back against the seats, hands in front of our faces.

'God. Shit.'

The bird's black eyes glared at us. A piece of meat hung from its beak. I hit the horn and held it down. The bird flapped away.

'There's a body on the bed,' Brinkley said. 'The place was covered with those birds, did you see it?'

I saw it, heard it, smelled it and felt it as though that wall-to-wall carapace of shining black wings was covering my own flesh.

'I have to call the station,' he said.

To do that he needed to get in the front seat. He put his hand on the door handle and two more crows landed on the trunk of the car. Their claws scratched on the paint. Brinkley pulled his hand off the handle.

'Put the radio transmitter up against the mesh.'

He told me which buttons to hit and he spoke through the screen into the mike. His voice was loud, no longer eager but verging on panic.

'Possible homicide,' he said. 'Send detectives and the crime techs and an ambulance.'

The image of shivering black wings and feasting mouths wouldn't leave me. And something else.

I replaced the radio transmitter. 'The feet on the bed. Did you see them?'

'Yes. God*damn*, that's the worst thing I've ever seen in my life.'

'What did you see?'

'That bird perched on the shoe, picking at the toes.'

'The shoe.'

'Sandal, I mean. A woman's sandal.'

I turned around and looked at his pale eyes. 'The other shoe was a cross-trainer.'

There were two bodies on the bed.

'Kit.'

Behind the mesh screen, Dad was holding up one of the framed photos from the mantel. My vision was thumping. For a second my brain locked up, before I understood.

'Coyote got them both,' I said.

He pointed at the date stamped in the corner. 'Taken last month. Easter.'

'What the hell are you talking about?' Brinkley said.

The photo showed the woman who must have been Alma Skinner, a parched gal in her sixties with a cigarette in her hand. She was arm in arm with Valerie. It was the Valerie I remembered from high school: fleshy, voluptuous, with that imposing nose and a look of injury and entitlement in her eyes. She was the picture of robust health.

She was not the terminally ill girl who had baby-stepped into the reunion, not the woman I had picked up in Canoga Park, not the woman who had flown up here with me on the plane. However, she looked much like her – the hair, the eye color, the posture. Subtract seventy pounds, give her a nose job and a supposedly fatal illness, and she could have passed. She *had* passed, showing a driver's license as photo ID to the airline.

Valerie was dead. She'd been dead before the reunion. Coyote had assumed her identity.

The radio squelched, the dispatcher calling to tell Brinkley that backup was on the way. I held the transmitter up to the screen and pushed the button so that Brinkley could talk.

'We have two DBs here,' he said, 'and a possible ID on them. Valerie and Alma Skinner.'

The dispatcher said, 'Valerie Skinner? Did you say you're at the Skinner residence?'

'Affirmative.'

'Detective Chang went with a citizen to help a Valerie Skinner.'

Oh my God. I spun. 'Who?'

Brinkley asked her.

She came back. 'Detective Chang went with a Mrs Hankins to assist Valerie Skinner. She's apparently wandering along the edge of the rim road north of town.'

'Tell her to get Tommy on the radio,' I said.

Brinkley relayed that. The dispatcher came back. 'Negative. He's in Mrs Hankins's vehicle. We don't have radio contact.'

I was feeling panicky. 'What's his cellphone number?'

Brinkley looked confused. 'What is it?'

I started the cruiser and threw it in reverse. 'We have to find Tommy and Abbie. They think they're going to pick up Valerie. They're wrong.'

'Hey—'

Brinkley slammed against the screen as I spun the tires backing down the drive.

'Stop. Immediately,' he said.

I threw the wheel and the car slewed around. 'They can't get Valerie. She's dead.' Jamming the gearshift into Drive, I floored it. 'If it's not Valerie, it's Coyote.'

They were heading straight into the hands of the killer.

30

Turning into the underground garage at Argent Tower, Jesse tried one last time to get Evan on her cell. Nothing. The high desert had swallowed her and he didn't know if the China Lake Police Department would get his message to Tommy and McCracken in time. He needed to do more. He pulled into a parking spot and Swayze once again knelt backward on her seat, packing up the stuff she'd taken from Coyote's lair.

He stuck the phone in his pocket, opened his door and stopped. His nerves felt like they'd been scraped raw with a cheese grater. He took the phone out again.

'What are you doing?' Swayze said.

'Calling the FBI.'

He scrolled through a list of stored numbers. The phone fell out of his hand.

A ringing sound came into his ears. He tried to lift his hand and couldn't, couldn't even close his fingers. He felt dizzy. His arms buzzed and his face felt numb. The lights were spangled. He turned his head and saw Swayze, calm and vicious and pleased, and now the view was spinning. He fell forward against the steering wheel.

'Wha'd you—'

His tongue refused more than that. Noise now, loud ringing. He fought to focus his eyes and saw his right leg, a hypodermic syringe sticking into his thigh like a tranquilizer dart. He fell sideways into white oblivion.

In the back seat of the cruiser, Officer Brinkley slapped his hand against the mesh screen. 'Pull over. Let me drive.'

Dad shook his head. 'That's not going to happen, son.'

I kept my foot down, fumbling for the radio with one hand. 'Can I use this to make contact with a cellphone?'

From the description the radio dispatcher had given, Tommy and Abbie were driving up the rim road along the edge of the base, ten or fifteen miles north of us. No other China Lake police units were in their vicinity. A Highway Patrol Car was near the Isabella turnoff on Highway 14, but we were several miles closer. Everybody else from the department was busy south of town at the train wreck and Shepard-Cantwell murder scene.

We reached the asphalt road. The car gained traction and leapt forward. It had a huge snarling engine and though it boated like the Exxon Valdez, all I cared about was getting hold of Tommy.

'Forget calling a cell from this radio,' Brinkley said.

I pushed the transmit button and held the handset to my face. 'Somebody, come in.'

The police dispatcher answered. Aiming the car up the road, I yelled at her to contact Tommy's cell. 'And call this number, too. Jesse Blackburn.'

Brinkley shouted through the screen. 'The China Lake Police Department is not a call forwarding center.'

'I don't care. If they can get Jesse, *he* can try to raise Tommy on the cell too. The point is, we have to get hold of him.'

But I had a bad feeling that Tommy's cellphone was

356

as useless right now as mine was. We were going to have to catch them in person.

'Don't you get it?' I said. 'Coyote came into town dressed as a man, this guy Robin Klijsters. Only that's probably an alias.'

'Kai Torrance,' Dad said.

'Yeah. Tommy's still waiting for confirmation from Military Records, but that's my bet.' I glanced at Dad in the rearview mirror. 'If Coyote's a woman, then Maureen Swayze was either wrong about Torrance, or she didn't tell us all she knows.'

I saw him exhale, heavily.

I held tight to the wheel. 'Coyote killed Valerie and her mother. She did it before the reunion and hid the bodies in the back room. Then she disguised herself as Valerie. It's all been a ruse.' I shook my head. 'That suitcase on the floor in the spare bedroom isn't the same one that Val brought on the plane.' For the fourth or fifth time I had to correct myself. 'Coyote, I mean.'

And didn't I feel like an idiot. 'She got us all divulging everything we had learned about South Star.'

Dad nodded. 'And because she seemed so ill, everybody overlooked the drastic change in her appearance.'

'None of us had seen Valerie for fifteen years. We didn't know. Shit, Dad, she even told me she'd gotten a nose job.'

My head was ringing. How the hell did she even know about that? About all our high school memories? I could see her stealing Valerie's driver's license, but the rest was beyond me.

'She killed Valerie to get access to the rest of us,' I said.

And Tommy and Abbie still didn't know. Coyote was going to get them if we didn't get there first. The road

357

stretched on and on. I jammed my foot harder against the gas pedal.

Abbie turned up the AC, trying to cool the interior of the van. In the rearview mirror she could see Valerie lying huddled on the back seat. Once more Tommy checked his phone, and once more he shook his head. They couldn't call the paramedics. They had to get to the hospital.

'Where do you think he went?' Abbie said.

'Coyote?' Tommy said it uncertainly.

She gave him a nervous glance. 'Still have that funny feeling?'

He ran his hand over his head, gazing at the asphalt road and blazing blue sky. 'Couple more miles, we should have cellphone coverage. Keep it at the limit.'

The road topped a rise and rolled down a long hill. At the bottom it curved onto Rock Creek Bridge, the spot that locals called 'the plunge'. She eased off the gas, lining up for the turn, and became aware of a presence, a rising behind her. The mirror darkened.

In the back seat, Valerie was sitting up.

But it wasn't Valerie. It was someone else pulling off the brassy wig and tossing it aside to reveal brown stubble. The bulky coat came off. The billowy blouse came off.

The frail dying woman was gone. In the mirror Abbie saw firm alabaster skin, cut musculature, a scar like a set of claws running down across one shoulder and under the fabric of a skintight wifebeater undershirt. Braless, nipples poking through the fabric in the chill of the air conditioning.

Abbie's mouth opened. 'Tommy—'

The knife glinted into view.

Abbie swerved. The blade sliced Tommy's seatbelt and jacket and she saw a burst of blood. She braked, jerking the wheel. The van fishtailed off the road onto the dirt. The knife swung again. She gripped the wheel, fighting to control it, saw the bridge and saw they were going to miss it. She heard the back door of the van slide open. She braked, turned hard, trying to keep the van out of the gorge, and felt the wheels catch. The view flipped sideways. She saw sand and sky and air and shadow. They rolled over the lip of the ravine.

Ahead, dawdling along the rim road, was a Jeep. We'd come eight miles up this road and it was the first vehicle we'd seen. On the far side of the cyclone fencing, the scrub and sand ran uninterrupted across the basin all the way to the wine-red ridges of the mountains.

'How do I turn on the lights and siren?' I said.

'Just go around him,' Brinkley said.

Fine. I hit the headlights and swung into the left lane, roaring around the Jeep. Any other time, the look on the driver's face would have been priceless. I pulled out my cellphone one more time, as though flipping it open could hex a signal into existence. No service.

I gazed at the shotgun that was locked upright next to the dashboard.

'I don't know what kind of weapons Coyote has,' I said.

Brinkley said, 'Besides that twelve-gauge I have my sidearm and another pump action in the trunk.' He glanced at Dad. 'You experienced with any of those?'

'Yes.' Dad leaned close to the mesh. 'Evan, you'll stay in the car if there's the slightest hint of trouble.'

I angled back across the white line. 'Does this cruiser have bulletproof glass?'

'No,' Brinkley said. 'So stay down.'

I nodded. The car ate up the highway. We crested a humpbacked hill and swung over the Rock Creek Bridge across a ravine. The highway spread out again like a black whip, cracking on into the empty distance. Where were they?

Abbie heard the radiator hissing and smelled the tang of gasoline. She lay still. There was sky above, filling the V at the top of the ravine. She could see the bridge high overhead. She was only beginning to perceive the depth of the pain.

The van was upside down on top of her. She saw the open driver's door and the splintered windshield, but she couldn't see anything of herself below the hips. She was a big gal. How come the van seemed to be laying flat on the ground even with her under it? Fucking Detroit family values piece of crap. Top-heavy ass of a vehicle.

High above, tires whined across the bridge and faded away. Pebbles tumbled down the side of the ravine.

Where was it? That thing from the mirror? She lifted her head and pain cleaved her, as if a machete had gone through her forehead.

She lay back against the ground. After a second she whispered, 'Tommy?'

Behind black agony she heard a bubbling sound. She had blood in her mouth but that wasn't it. The sound came every time she drew breath. She moved her arm and her hand flopped. Her left wrist was broken. She put her right hand against her chest and felt the blood, not the drip of a cut but the wet slurp of a sopping diaper. She lifted her hand so she could see it. The blood was dark red, almost brown.

360

Within the van something creaked, and the frame of the vehicle pressed on her hips. She cried out.

'Abbie.'

It was Tommy. The van creaked again and she groaned.

'Stop,' she said.

Slowly, agonizingly, Tommy's head appeared above her in the open doorway of the van. His eyes were black, swollen shut, and his nose was smashed. Blood was trickling out of one of his ears.

'Sorry,' he hacked. 'Where are you?'

'Down here. Where's that thing?'

'Don't know. Can't see.'

'Get off me.' She hated sounding rude. 'Please.'

'Gotta come out this way. Sorry.'

She steeled herself but still the pain deepened. He was slithering on his back, pushing with one leg, trying to get purchase with his heel to push himself out the doorway. Now she saw Tommy, lying on the cracked windshield above her. She understood that one of his legs and both his arms were shattered. He wasn't going anywhere.

'Where's Valerie?' Abbie said. 'Is she in the van?'

'Don't know.'

She swallowed and tasted blood. 'Where's your gun?'

He tried to move one of his arms, in the end only bumping his biceps against the shoulder holster he wore under his jacket. His voice was broken.

'Gone.'

More pebbles came rolling down the escarpment. Abbie turned her head, trying to see what else was coming. A sub-sonic ache rang through her.

High above, near the bridge, Un-Valerie stood watching them. She was dusty and her skin had been scraped red from shoulder to elbow. Her face was a shimmering apparition, translucent white. She began walking down the ravine toward them.

Bighorn Flat, Shoshone Creek – the cruiser bore past places whose names crawled at me from my youth. Mirages snaked above the asphalt road. Doubt pitted my stomach.

'We should have seen them by now.'

In the rearview mirror Dad's lips were pressed white. 'Agreed.'

'Where'd they go? Did we miss them?'

'Pull over, Kit.'

This time I did it. Brinkley jumped out of the back, opened the trunk and grabbed the second shotgun and a box of shells. He handed them to Dad. I slid across the bench seat and Brinkley took the wheel, turned the car and began backtracking at eighty miles per hour.

'There aren't any turnoffs, no junctions, no gates through to the base or even cuts in the fence that I've seen,' he said. 'They're either offroading *way* off track, or—'

'The plunge,' I said.

He nodded. The plunge was the ravine beneath the Rock Creek Bridge, where every year some teenaged hotrodder or drunken trucker managed to get his vehicle airborne. I scanned the empty expanse of rocks and sagebrush. The plunge was probably ten miles back this way.

Brinkley punched the accelerator. 'Do you know how to load a pump shotgun?'

I tossed him a glance. Either my driving skills had turned me into a junior police cadet, or he was scared freaking out of his mind.

'Yeah,' I said.

He gave me a key. 'Shells are in the glove compartment.'

His hands were heavy on the wheel. 'Detective Chang is a dead shot. If this guy's taken him, then . . .'

I unlocked the shotgun and found the cartridges. They felt solid in my hand. 'Then we'd better be ready.'

'Load the weapon.'

Un-Valerie picked her way down the ravine. Her sleeveless undershirt was torn, exposing one breast. Her pale skin gleamed in the sun. She looked unearthly, with those Renaissance features, that frail Madonna's mouth beneath those freaky eyes.

Abbie whispered. 'Tommy, it's coming.'

She felt him struggle to move, saw him twist his head around to get a view. He managed to work one eye open. He inhaled sharply.

'Abbie, you gotta get out of here.'

That's when it sank in how truly screwed they were. 'The van's on top of me. I'm pinned.'

Un-Valerie sidestepped down the slope, now about fifty yards away. Tommy again pushed with one heel, trying to get some purchase. Abbie tried to get enough air to speak above the bubbling sound.

'Tommy. Before we crashed, it kept talking about our kids.' She saw him raise his head and look around the interior of the van. 'It wanted to know where our kids are.'

Un-Valerie tripped on a rock and stumbled, falling to its knees.

'It wants to kill us, and Evan,' she said. 'And it wants to kill our kids.'

Tommy groaned again. It was a sound of despair.

'It's coming to find out from us where they are,' she said.

She heard the chill in her voice. It came from beneath the pain. It was a still and excruciating note of truth.

'Abbie,' he said, strained, 'her weapons are here in the van.'

Her pulse surged. 'Get them.'

He moaned with effort. The van rocked, pressing on her. The pain slammed down and a goblet of blood poured up her throat. She vomited and lay coughing.

Tommy's one good foot knocked around the interior. 'Almost.' Metal sang against the frame of the van. 'Can you see what's there?'

She tilted her head and spotted the weapons that Tommy was trying to kick out the door to her. Her vision, chill truth, grew sharper.

His voice was soft. 'Coyote tortured Kelly and Ceci. She took her time. You understand?'

She stretched her hand toward the weapons. 'Not close enough.'

He groaned again, inching with his shoulder, trying now to use his splintered arm to scoop the weapons out the door to her.

'Abbie, understand? I don't have the strength.'

'Yes you do.' She stretched her fingertips. 'Come on, I almost have the knife.'

He grit his teeth and let out a hard moan and shoveled the things out the frame. Abbie gasped and slapped her hand down. She managed to stop the grenade that came rolling toward her.

'Got it. You did it, Tommy.'

A knife lay near the grenade. She fumbled it into her hand, feeling how heavy it seemed.

More rocks came spinning down the hillside. Un-Valerie was back on its feet, dusting its hands on its pants and coming on again, picking its way down the uneven slope.

Tommy let his head fall against the roof of the van. 'That's not what I meant.'

'I've got the knife. Tommy, I've got it.'

'Abbie.'

She looked at him. He looked back, and she understood. Above her, Un-Valerie came on.

Brinkley slowed the cruiser at the top of the hill. Two hundred yards down the slope ahead, the road curved onto Rock Creek Bridge.

'Oh, my God.' I leaned forward, gripping the shotgun in both hands. 'Do you see it?'

Skidmarks. Brinkley gunned the engine.

'We missed it before.' My eyes were stinging. The gun felt heavy in my hands. 'God.'

Skidmarks were plentiful on winding desert back roads and, heading the other way looking for Abbie's van, we hadn't noticed them. But these, I could tell, were sharp and fresh and led to tire tracks that spun off into the sand and disappeared into the plunge.

From behind me, Dad said, 'Lock and load.'

I pulled the action back and shoved it forward again. The first round chambered with a hard crack.

Brinkley hit the brakes.

Abbie felt the knife wobbling in her hand. Her palm was so slippery with her own blood that she could barely grip it. She had to get a better grip, had to get ready.

'Abbie,' Tommy said.

'I have the knife.'

'I don't have the strength. It could kill me before I'd tell it where my kids are. But . . .'

His voice sank, and with it Abbie's heart.

'But I don't have the strength to keep from telling it where your kids are,' he said.

The knife wobbled again. She saw Un-Valerie above her, thirty yards away. It was moving out of kilter, limping. It looked damaged, like a machine with a broken element.

'Abbie.'

Un-Valerie's face stayed utterly calm. Its foot was twisted into an unnatural position but it walked without flinching. It held a knife, a long thick serrated blade, and it held it confidently. Its strength was undiminished.

'Could you keep from telling?' he said.

She watched it. The thing paused, breathing in, and glanced at its exposed breast. Disgust crossed its face. It lifted the torn undershirt over the nipple. Enough blood was spread across its chest that the fabric stuck, staying put. It turned its head and stared at Abbie, its expression unhurried and ravenous.

A sob spurted from her throat. 'No, I couldn't.'

Tears filled her eyes. Coughing more blood, she dropped the knife. They had only one chance now.

'Can you get the grenade?' he said.

'Yes.'

She would. She had to. Un-Valerie began making its way across the final twenty yards of the slope, picking her way cautiously among the loose rocks. Abbie stretched her arm, and stretched again. The grenade was solid green, lying on the sand an inch beyond her fingertips. She breathed in, hearing that sucking sound from her chest, and shoved herself at it. She grasped it in her hand and dragged it back to her side. Feeling how heavy it was, and how weak her arm was, she had no doubt.

'I can't throw it.'

'I know.'

She closed her eyes.

Tommy's voice was weak but pure with meaning. 'You have to time it absolutely right. Pull the pin and let go of the striker lever.'

Opening her eyes, she stared at the sky. 'How long once I let go?'

'Three, four seconds.'

Un-Valerie reached the dry bank above the sandy creekbed. Its face was greedy and almost luminous with longing.

Abbie weighed the grenade in her hand, making the final calculation. She felt its potential energy. She heard Un-Valerie jump down into the creekbed and footsteps scuffing across the sand toward the van.

'Get ready,' she said.

Brinkley stopped the cruiser, unbuckled, and climbed out with his hand on his sidearm. Dad leapt from the back seat.

'Get behind the car and stay down, Evan.'

I threw open my door. Dad leveled the shotgun and advanced toward the lip of the ravine.

Abbie held the grenade in her good hand, clasping the striker lever as best she could. She slopped her bad arm into the van, finding Tommy's shoulder. She let it rest there, feeling his chest labor up and down. A second later he dropped his own broken arm on top of hers.

'Now,' he said.

Wally, I love you. She put the ring of the pin between her teeth. *Dulcie, Travis, Hayley. My world.*

Coyote stepped into sight behind the van, the blade in her hand flashing with sunlight. Abbie pulled the pin.

31

I ran around the patrol car, shotgun aimed at the sky. Ahead of me Dad and Brinkley charged toward the lip of the ravine.

The explosion roared out of the gorge, echoing off the hills and bridge and rocks around us. Dad dropped to one knee, aiming the gun. Black smoke threaded up from below.

I heard flames crackling. The smoke boiled thicker. I brought the barrel of the shotgun level with the ground and ran at the edge of the ravine.

Dad jumped up and grabbed me around the waist. 'No.'

The echoes dimmed. The smoke thickened and a chill ran through my marrow. I strained against him, trying to get to the edge and see down to the bottom.

'Abbie,' I yelled. 'Tommy.'

Dad clutched me tight and lifted me off my feet and hauled me back from the edge.

'Don't look.'

'*Abbie.*' I kicked in his arms, throwing my head back, knowing and refusing to know. 'Let me go. They're down there.'

'No, Kit.' His voice was broken against my cheek. 'They're gone.'

*

The flashing lights were garish. The area near the bridge crackled with China Lake patrol cars, Kern County sheriffs' cruisers, a Shore Patrol Jeep, County fire trucks, and a Search and Rescue team that had nobody to rescue, only remains to recover. Under the hot wind I sat in the back of Officer Brinkley's cruiser. Outside, Dad drank coffee from a Thermos that Captain McCracken had wangled from one of the firefighters.

McCracken was grave and pale. He spoke in undertones to Dad, trying to shield me from the information that was gradually coming in. Dr Tully Cantwell had been crushed by a freight train. Antonia Shepard-Cantwell lay murdered in their home. Valerie Skinner and her mother were both dead from knife wounds at the house on Jimmy's Ranch Road.

'The Skinners,' Dad said. 'Nobody knew they were missing?'

'Mrs Skinner worked two weeks on, two off, at the motel. She was off this past week so nobody suspected. Sounds like she was a bit of a loner. And Valerie—' McCracken glanced in my direction. 'Told her co-workers at the Vons down in Canoga Park she was taking a week off and going to her high school reunion. Nobody had a reason to think she was missing.'

Dad shook his head. 'No husband, no friends . . .'

'Apparently not.' His weight seemed to hang heavily on him. 'She lived alone. Not even pets.'

There was a flurry of movement at the edge of the ravine by the bridge abutment. The Search and Rescue team was winching up the basket holding the first body.

When I got out of the cruiser, Dad put an arm around my shoulder and we trudged over. For now, at least, I had lain down my anger at him. The cops and paramedics and Shore Patrol officers fell quiet. Almost as though we'd rehearsed, we wandered ourselves into a row, standing sentinel.

The sun was so sharp above the Sierras, about to drop and touch the high peaks, that I felt pain behind my eyes. And I had to turn my head away for a moment when they hauled the rescue basket over the slope onto the sandy ground. The black bag was thick and shiny, aggressively zipped and strapped into the basket. I pressed my face to Dad's chest. The Search and Rescue team handed duty over to the EMTs, who lifted the bag onto a gurney and rolled it toward the back of an ambulance.

'Do they,' I began, and had to clear my throat. 'Do they know who?'

McCracken was close by, his jowls sagging. 'Tommy.'

I watched them load it in the ambulance, wishing for words to offer, some consolation or farewell. But faced with that black shroud, the finality, the absence, the barrier, was absolute.

Over my shoulder I heard one of the rescue crew say, 'The next one's on her way up.'

There's no way you can watch your oldest friend dragged dead up a hill in a body bag. I closed my eyes and listened until I heard the gurney roll into the back of the ambulance. Dad gently turned me toward the patrol car.

'No.' I tugged him with me to the back of the ambulance.

'Kit, honey, don't put yourself through this.'

'Tommy and Abbie shouldn't be alone.' I glanced at the EMT. 'Is this . . .'

McCracken approached. 'They're sure it's Mrs Hankins.'

I nodded, standing there blankly trying to offer some witness, a moment of worthiness, something besides silent helpless grief.

Officer Brinkley came up to McCracken, accompanied by a firefighter. 'That's it. They lifted the vehicle. There's nobody else.'

It was confirmation, not news. For the past two hours the cops had been talking about two DBs. Two dead bodies, not three. They'd found a trail of blood leading away from the van up the dry creek. Footprints showed that a person had climbed out of the ravine half a mile upcreek, out of sight of the bridge. But this, the verification that Coyote had not died with Abbie and Tommy, drilled home our unmitigated failure. It was the worst outcome possible.

Brinkley shifted, gun belt creaking. 'Fire captain served a hitch in the Marines. He's seen scenes like this before. He says it looks like the vic, the woman, she may have been the one who blew the grenade.'

McCracken looked up sharply. 'What?'

'Maybe attempting to kill Coyote when she got close enough.'

I turned back to the ambulance and with every reverence I could muster, I touched my fingertips to the black plastic of the body bag.

My eyes were dry. My voice came back to me. 'This isn't the end. I swear it to you, Abbie.'

I walked away, calling to Dad. 'Let's go.'

McCracken dropped us at the hotel. When Dad opened the door into the lobby, I saw Mom hurrying toward me, arms out. I fell into her embrace. The desk clerk stared, riveted, until Mom gave him a glare. I felt numb and aware that this wouldn't last, that the weight and darkness would arrive soon. But for the moment I lay my head on her shoulder and knew that she was holding me up.

She spoke softly to Dad, touching his hand. He told her he'd be along in a second. Pulling some change from his pocket, he went back outside to get a cold drink from the vending machine.

She led me across the lobby. 'Nothing for it now but to pray.'

'I can't.'

'Not for them, Ev. Your friends, what they did out there, the courage it took—' She clutched my shoulder. 'They're already home. There's no pain, only welcome. Pray for Wally and for all the kids.'

I nodded.

'Miss?' The desk clerk was leaning across the counter, holding out message slips. 'These came for you.'

I glanced at them. They all said *from Jessie*.

Outside, tires squealed. Mom and I turned and saw a beige car pull up next to the vending machine. The door swung open. Out jumped federal agent Pepa. Salt was behind the wheel.

'Uh-oh,' Mom said.

I froze. 'They're feds.'

I felt a real need to run. Pulling Mom's arm, I backed across the lobby, wondering if we could get out the other side before they came through the door.

Outside, Pepa walked up to my father and put a hand on his elbow. He stuck him with a flat stare and words I couldn't hear. Dad stiffened. Salt jumped from the car, came around and took Dad's other arm. They led him to the car and shoved him into the back seat.

Mom and I ran outside.

The agents hopped in the car and pulled out. Dad turned, looking out the back window. The resignation in his eyes was utterly unfamiliar. But he wasn't looking at me, he was looking at Mom. They shared a connection that said: long time coming, but it's finally here.

32

Mom dropped the phone back onto its cradle. 'He's on the base.'

'Why'd those goons take him out there? He's not in the Navy anymore.' I paced in the hotel room. 'And why won't you tell me who you were talking to?'

'The men who grabbed him – who do you think they were?'

'CIA? FDA? Mormons?'

'Naval Intelligence.'

It should have set me burning with curiosity and anger, but all I felt was a quiet *click* at the base of my brain.

'Why'd they grab him?'

'They're undoubtedly investigators.'

'What do they think he has to do with Coyote?'

'Evan, they've never been after Coyote. They've always been keeping an eye on your dad.'

'Why?'

'Best guess, they keep watch on cleared personnel who've raised a red flag. Like Phil did, running around asking everybody questions about South Star.'

'And now they've arrested him?'

She looked at the phone. 'No, they haven't. But black projects are supposed to stay black, and he was shining a bright light on this one.'

'So if he's not under arrest, then what?'

'They're questioning him. They're going to hold him on base for twelve hours.'

'Shit.'

I rubbed my forehead, staring at the message slips the clerk had handed me. They left the taste of anxiety in my mouth.

'These types like to show off. But they're also exceptionally serious about their job.' Her eyes were knowing. 'And they may actually think they're doing him a favor, getting him out of trouble with the China Lake cops over this matter of a hijacked police car.'

That left me feeling cold. 'How do you know so much? If you tell me you're a spook, I will . . .'

'You don't think a stew could be a spy?' She crossed her arms.

'No, Mom, that's not what I mean.'

'For your dad to get his security clearance, they effectively had to clear me as well. Let's just say that if I ever want a job with the NSA, I'm set.'

'And you're not going to tell me who you spoke to just now?'

'No.'

She put her hand on mine, trying to lessen the sharpness of the response, and frowned. 'You're cold.'

And when I held out my hands, my fingers trembled. 'I'm scared for Dad.'

And I was off balance about the messages from Jesse. I stared at them as though trying to decipher runes. *Call. Urgent. Vital.* But I couldn't find him. Sanchez Marks said he'd taken a personal day, and he didn't answer at home or on his cell.

Mom patted my hand. 'How about a club sandwich?'

I nodded and she ordered room service. I changed out

of my suit into jeans and, feeling grubby, went to the bathroom and rinsed the dust from my face. I heard my phone ring. When I walked out of the bathroom Mom handed it to me.

'Lavonne Marks,' she said.

She was Jesse's boss. 'Lavonne?'

'Where is he?'

'What's wrong?'

'If that's a feint, I'm not having it. Put him on the line.'

'I don't know where he is. I've been getting alarming messages from him.'

'I'll bet. I just received a call from the Los Angeles Police Department. They say Jesse trashed an apartment in Hollywood, and ran before they arrived. It was a murder scene. They've issued a warrant for his arrest.'

Lightheaded, I sat down on the bed. 'That's . . . no. That's wrong. I—'

'Moreover, the blockhead actually left his business card with the building super, so the LAPD knew exactly who he is and how to hound my keester. Find him. Tell him this is no laughing matter. Not only could he lose his job and his law license, he could go to jail.'

I hung up, blank with fear, and the room phone rang. Mom got it. Alarm crossed her face and she turned on the TV. I took the phone from her.

'You watching the news?' said Captain McCracken. 'Here I walk in the station and find a message from your fella, wanting to give me evidence about Coyote. Very angst-ridden, very good-citizen. Only problem, he contaminated a crime scene and the LAPD thinks he's in on a murder.'

I put my head between my knees.

'His prints are all over Coyote's apartment. So LAPD's

377

wondering how that partial of Coyote's they lifted from Jesse's shirt a few days ago actually came to be there,' he said. 'And by the way, Coyote's prints from the apartment match Robin Klijsters. Only the name that popped up for the LAPD was Kaija Torrance. There's your gal.'

'Ev.'

Mom was watching a news bulletin. It showed police cars in front of a dilapidated apartment building, paramedics bringing out a body bag. A man with an eyepatch, probably the building super, looking unkempt and distraught. Old lady, he was saying. Dead, unbelievable. Guy in a wheelchair.

Mom held my forehead while I leaned over the toilet and retched.

When I finished, I sat bunched on the bed and let her wrap a blanket around my knees. I called Jesse's house and cell and got no answer. I dialed his parents' number and hung up before putting the call through. *Arrest warrant* and *your son* were words that had already cut them to the bone thanks to Jesse's drug-addled brother. I called his former advisor at UCLA Law School and his old roommate who worked in downtown LA. Neither had heard from him. I sank down on the bed, spent and spinning with dread.

Mom brought me a glass of water and sat beside me, brushing her fingers through my hair.

'You know that he was trying to do the right thing,' she said. 'Whatever happened, he did for the best of reasons.'

'I know. And he's screwed.'

Wound like a top, I picked up my phone again and called Mr and Mrs Blackburn after all. His mom might drink herself into a stupor at the news, but I couldn't let them hear it on television. After that, I drew my knees up and stared at the wall.

It was about half an hour later when my phone beeped. A message had come in. Grabbing it, I fumbled my fingers across the keypad, seeing *From Jesse*.

'Oh, God.'

Need U. Westwd

Westwood. My vision thumped. I punched his number and dammit, he still didn't answer. I redialed. He had to be there, had to. A new message beeped.

Pls Hu

What? Please hurry? I shook the phone as though that would knock the rest of the message loose onto the display.

I clambered off the bed, searching for my shoes. The phone beeped yet again. I read the message and a moan broke from my throat.

Hurt

The last plane for LAX left China Lake at 7:15. The crew slammed the door while Mom and I were still threading our way down the narrow aisle to our seats. I had the phone to my ear. The young flight attendant asked me to turn it off and I nodded and continued listening to it ring in LA. The engines began spooling up before we buckled our seatbelts. I hunched down below the seat in front of me, hiding.

Finally, a voice came on the other end of the line. 'Swayze.'

I spoke under my breath. 'What's happened to Jesse?'

'Who . . . Evan?' Her voice gained an edge. 'Jesse took a tire iron to my shoulder. Then he put a gun to my head.'

I closed my eyes. The trembling was coming back strong. 'What have you done to him?'

'Huh.' Longer pause. 'He threatened to ruin me. He forced me to go with him to that apartment in Hollywood. Let's stop talking about what I did.'

'Tell me.'

'I treated him like the animal he is. I chased him off. Without involving the police, I add, for which you should be pissing with gratitude. Where he is now, I couldn't care less.'

'I don't believe you.'

Even with the engines blaring I heard her huff with indignation. 'I'm finished with this whole affair. It's in the hands of the authorities and I'm out of it. However, if you or your rabid dog show up here again, I'll call SWAT. I mean it.'

My trembling was gone. I felt rigid. 'Liar.'

I hung up.

The flight attendant was bleating her safety lecture over the PA. Every nerve was already stretched thin. One more time, I tried the number Special Agent Heaney had given me.

And God bless the FBI: he answered.

'Affirmative. Your boyfriend fled the scene of a murder, just ahead of the uniforms. LAPD is after his rear, big time.'

The turboprop engines blared. I put my finger to my ear.

'Agent Heaney, I'm desperate.' I told him about Jesse's text message. 'Can you help me?'

'You're the one who can help. He needs to surrender himself to the police. You can advise him to do so, promptly.'

'This is not Jesse. You have to believe me. Something's screwy.'

'Yeah, him. I don't know what sent him off the deep end, but he gave his business card to a witness before running from the cops.' His voice rose over noise in the background. 'I'm coming to China Lake with an FBI response team. If you decide you can help, you'll find me at the police station.'

The little plane taxied out, bumping over the tarmac. I leaned against the seat in front of me as though in brace position for a crash.

Heaney's voice dropped. 'I'm sorry about your friends, Evan. I truly am. Tommy was one of the good guys.'

'I know.'

'Listen, here's a name at the LAPD. Lieutenant I know in Robbery-Homicide. She won't be involved in this investigation, but she can put you in contact with the people who are. Use my name and hers, maybe you can get Jesse a more sympathetic hearing. Anyway, it might give them a reason to keep their weapons holstered when they make the arrest.'

I wrote down the name, thanking him profusely. The evening sun panned through the windows, gold light making the passengers shade their eyes. I dialed the number for the Robbery-Homicide Division and they put me on hold.

What sent Jesse off the deep end? I leaned back in my seat, staring at mountains silhouetted black in the distance. My father sent Jesse off the deep end. I tried to fight down the anger and couldn't. This was a disaster in the making, and Dad had sparked it by attempting to manipulate Jesse. What the hell did he think, telling him there was no choice but to terminate the pregnancy? Telling Jesse something was impossible was like taunting a mountain lion with a sharp stick.

Robbery-Homicide answered the phone. Heaney's contact was out of the station, so I reeled off my name and number and said it was urgent that I speak with her about Jesse Blackburn. I peeked up above the seatback. Urgent that someone meet me in Westwood to—

The flight attendant stood there with her hand out. 'Ma'am, give me the phone.'

I shrank from her. 'I'm speaking to the LAPD.'

'This is the third time I've asked you to stop talking. Give me the phone.'

'Thirty seconds. Come on.'

The pilot turned at the end of the taxiway and held.

'Surrender the phone or we'll return to the terminal and you'll be removed from the plane.'

I turned away from her but she was grabbing for it. Mom put her hand on me. Her voice was matter-of-fact.

'Give her the phone.'

Slumping, I handed it over.

'You can retrieve it in Los Angeles,' said the flight attendant.

The smirk on her face made me want to smack her. She tucked it in her pocket and flounced back to her seat.

I knocked my head back against the headrest. 'Stormtrooper.'

Mom patted my hand. The engines revved and the plane surged down the runway. Now all I could hope was that the text message I'd sent to Jax and Tim would be received.

Primacon Labs. Help.

Fortune favors the bold. It was not a warrior who said that, but an ancient poet. But though Virgil understood the workings of the world, he didn't know about wild cards.

Coyote drove through the encroaching dusk, assessing the op. She had been nothing today if not bold, yet fortune had sneered at her. Drawing Valerie Skinner on her own face, drawing Chang and Hankins out to the rim road, had not brought success upon the hunt. Today was an intolerable failure.

Chang and Hankins were gone, but she had not taken them. The moment she stepped around the van and saw the grenade in Abbie's hand, she knew what Abbie intended to do. It had been like reaching a river only to watch it dry up before she could drink. Furthermore, Delaney and the children remained beyond her reach.

Her patience was running thin. When the grenade detonated, Delaney had been close on her heels, armed and accompanied by the police. Upcreek by the truck afterwards, Coyote had seen her through the binoculars, watching the recovery operation. She supposed that Evan was honoring the dead.

Bravery: Abbie Hankins had it, she had to admit. Pinned beneath the van and unable to flee, she chose to fight. Abbie had meant to kill her. But the grenade had a four-second delay, and when Abbie pulled the pin, she ran. Still, two women in one day with uncommon courage; this was a sign.

The truck rolled through the darkening evening. The freeway was a river of traffic, taillights and tire drone, a soothing welcome back to Los Angeles.

She moved her shoulder. She had taken shrapnel. By putting Abbie's van between herself and the grenade, the vehicle had taken the brunt of the explosion, but even so, she had sustained blood loss and minor penetrating wounds. She rotated her left arm. She couldn't achieve full range of motion and muscle strength was diminished, perhaps ten percent. That was within mission parameters but nevertheless a concern. And her shoulder was significantly abraded from jumping out of the van before it crashed into the ravine. She would need debridement and a stiff injection of antibiotics. Her fractured tibia was strapped with a makeshift splint, but needed to be more securely immobilized. She had to get back to base.

Her cellphone chirped with the sound of a message arriving.

She glanced at it and the red flame ignited around the edges of her vision. It was a photo of her amulet. The sound grew in her throat. Somebody had stolen it. They knew. They'd found the apartment.

But this was not in the possession of the police. This . . .

Sway. She recognized the phone number. Sway had taken this. Why?

She drove, trying to comprehend. Sway was *hers*. Sway had given her everything. Why would she take the amulet away?

Another beep: a second message had arrived. When she saw it, the sound subsided in her throat. Power and prey, alpha and omega. The hunt was going to draw to a successful conclusion after all. Sway had taken the amulet, but she was going to give it back, along with the thing Coyote sought.

She crested the top of Sepulveda Pass and flowed down the hill with the river of traffic on the 405. Where the city poured out at the bottom of the hills Coyote caught a glimpse of Westwood. The towers along Wilshire Boulevard stood out like steel trees along a stream bank. Soon. She put down the window and smelled Los Angeles, that familiar metallic jazz in her nose. Car exhaust and greenbacks. And sweat, blood, garbage, all the things she'd known as a child, all the things Sway had helped free her from. Now drawing her back.

Her arm was stiff. She could feel dried blood on the back of her undershirt. She had to complete the mission before her physical condition degraded any further. She glanced once more at the words illuminated on the phone display.

Evan Delaney.

She drove through the electric night toward Argent Tower.

33

Jesse felt metal digging him between the shoulder blades. The buzzing sound ebbed and swelled in his ears. His head pounded and his mouth felt like sand. He really, really had to take a leak.

He opened his eyes and saw the plastic face next to his, grinning obscenely.

He batted it away. It flopped into the air but its big round O of a mouth didn't change its expression. Shit. Taylor's inflatable doll.

He was on the floor in the back seat of the truck.

Light pissed through the windows. His shoulders were wedged between the front and back seats and his legs were jackknifed and whatever he was lying on was drilling him in the back.

Swayze had drugged him and dumped him back here. Goddamn, he hadn't watched her closely enough. She must have found the syringe and sedatives in Coyote's medical kit.

He looked around for some way to sit up. The passenger-side shoulder belt hung from the doorframe. Stretching, he grabbed it and pulled himself up.

Christ. His head banged like a snare drum. He unjammed himself from between the seats and hauled himself up, gritting his teeth. His back was going to spasm, his legs were going to spasm if he didn't keep calm. He breathed, waiting for the cymbals to quiet down inside his skull.

After a minute he took stock. The truck was parked in a dim corner of the garage beneath Argent Tower. Level 5, bottom of the garage. There were no other cars. He was alone.

It got worse. His cellphone was gone. The keys were gone.

The Glock was gone.

Feeling a bruise on the inside of his elbow, he saw blood clotted over a needle mark. Shit, Swayze had jammed the first hypo into his leg and then given him an intravenous dose to keep him out. Sodium thiopental, probably, from the way his head was racketing. He looked at his watch. It was 8:10 p.m.

Swayze wanted him out of commission. Why?

Pain hammered down his back and into his legs. He forced himself to breathe slowly, leaning forward, trying to stretch out the spasm. Getting out of here was paramount. Swayze thought she'd marooned him here, but there was something she didn't know: he had a spare set of keys. They were in a magnetic case stuck under the frame of his chair. He straightened, slowly. On the floor he saw what had been jabbing him between the shoulders. It was the quick-release axle for one of his wheels. The buzz in his ears swelled again.

One wheel was in the back next to him, but the frame and second wheel were gone. So were his crutches.

For the longest moment he just stared. His head was about to implode.

Slinging himself toward the front seat, he reached and hit the horn.

The sound echoed in the garage. He held it for almost

a minute, his heart drumming, but got no response. He lowered his hand and slumped between the seats.

He couldn't wait around hoping for somebody to come along and find him. Swayze was playing out some kind of endgame. He had to get out of here and find out if Evan was all right. Pushing himself up again, he glanced down the long dim expanse of the garage. The elevator was at the far end. There was no camera above the elevator door on this level. He fell back against the seat.

And looked again.

Dumped outside the elevator was his hardware. Fucking Swayze. He opened the door.

Outside Argent Tower I paid the cabbie and strode with Mom across the plaza toward the entrance. It was 8:30.

'Stormtrooper,' I reiterated. 'Eva Braun.'

'Let it go.'

But I kept seeing that snotty smirk on the flight attendant's face when we landed at LAX, and instead of my phone she handed me a form. 'Fill this out and apply at our Customer Service counter for the return of your property.' Twitching lips. 'They'll be open tomorrow at nine.'

Mom didn't have a cellphone, so on the way out of the airport I stopped at a payphone and tried one last time to reach Agent Heaney's LAPD contact. She wasn't available and I didn't know if she had received my earlier message.

Lights were firing up in the skyscrapers along Wilshire. But Argent Tower, nearly empty, reflected the last embers of sunset, scarlet and orange multiplied a thousand times. On the lower stories a few office lights were burning.

The top two-thirds of the building were dark. Only one floor in the building was brightly lit. I counted: eight. Primacon.

We approached the revolving door. The cracked plate-glass window had been replaced. In fact all the plate-glass windows had been replaced. They were crosshatched with packing tape labeled 'Ultraglass'. Argent Tower, it seemed, didn't want any more mayhem.

I took Mom's elbow. 'We stay downstairs if at all possible. Okay?'

'Fine by me.'

'If it turns out that the only way to do this is to go up to Swayze's lab, then I'll go and you stay in the lobby.'

Her face was severe, the laugh lines deep and tired around her eyes. 'You're not going anywhere by yourself. That's why I came with you.'

'This is protection. You stay with the security guard down at the front desk. If I'm not back down here with Jesse in five minutes, call nine-one-one.'

'They'd arrest him.'

'If it gets to that stage I'd rather take our chances with the police. I don't trust Maureen Swayze.' I attempted a lighter expression. 'You taught me that.'

'Glad it sank in.' She looked into the lobby. 'Let me take point on this.'

The doors were locked. Inside the towering lobby, Archie the Gray sat behind the desk looking bored to wood. Beyond him the atrium soared into gloom. Mom knocked on the glass.

Archie sat up as if he'd been poked with a trident. He trundled across the lobby, suspicion in his eyes, and called to us from beyond the glass. 'What do you want?'

She gave him her most dazzling Welcome Aboard smile. 'Angie Delaney to see Maureen Swayze.'

Five more yards. His shoulders ached and his shirt clung to his back. His hands hurt like hell. He was wearing his gloves, so his palms weren't getting torn up, but his backside was going to be in a sorry state, and there went his goddamned jeans *again*. He stopped and hitched them up.

The ventilation system droned. The fluorescent lighting hummed and flickered. He drew a breath and kept going, tossing his wheel alongside him. Four more yards. Someplace above him tires squealed around the entrance ramp and he stopped again, hoping. And he picked up the tire iron from his lap, just in case. But the building was virtually deserted. Nobody was going to bother driving all the way down to Level 5.

He wiped the back of his hand across his forehead. Swayze had dumped his gear near the elevator either because she thought he wouldn't make it this far, or she truly didn't expect him to wake up from the sedatives. He kept going. She had no idea that dragging his ass across the garage didn't just wear him out, it fucking infuriated him. She thought she'd seen him ruthless. She had no idea.

Two yards. One. He grabbed the frame. Under the seat cushion he found the car keys. He got to work.

Archie frowned, his toad's mouth drawing down, and unlocked one of the side doors.

'Thanks,' Mom said, leading me in. 'Could you phone up to Primacon and tell Dr Swayze that I'm here?'

Our footsteps echoed on the marble. The atrium was spooky in the deepening light. The painters' tall scaffold had been moved next to the railing for the mezzanine. It looked like a bizarre museum specimen, a spindly dinosaur skeleton.

I said, 'How's the guard who was injured the other day?'

Archie shook his head. 'Still in intensive care. It ain't looking too good.'

We followed him to the desk, and he grabbed the phone to call Primacon. I crossed my arms, feeling chilly and anxious. On Archie's side were a computer and a monitor for the building's closed circuit television cameras. I saw hallways, a back door, the entrance to the parking garage on Wilshire and the exit around the corner on the side street.

'What's that?' I said.

Archie looked up from the phone. I was pointing at one of the monitors. It showed only – concrete?

He gave the monitor a passing glance. 'Parking garage. It's been out of whack all day. Sometimes the cameras slip on the mount. Maintenance is scheduled to get on it in the morning.'

I looked at the other monitors. Cameras covered levels 1 through 3, though I knew the garage went a couple of levels deeper than that. Unease lowered across the back of my neck.

'The morning?' I said.

Archie's gray face crunched with confusion. 'Look, we only got a skeleton crew, and this building's still getting the final tweaks. Construction ain't even finished yet.'

'That camera's pointing at the ceiling so you can't see what's happening in the garage. Doesn't that make you uneasy?'

He peered, his toad mouth pursing.

'Who else is on security tonight? Do you have an armed guard? Get them down here,' I said.

He glared at me. He didn't like being told his job, but he didn't seem to be doing it.

'Please,' I said.

Mom tugged on my elbow and pulled me away from the desk, out of Archie's earshot. 'I'm getting a funny feeling about this.'

'You never get funny feelings.'

'I know. That's why I think we should leave.'

My radar was lighting up as well. Nothing specific, but a vague collection of miscues overlaid with the big drumming fact that Jesse had to be here, someplace nearby, in deep shit.

'No,' I said. 'I can't leave him here. But it's time to call the police.'

Jesse fired up the truck and backed it out. His arms were tired to the point of shaking. Long time since he'd been that tired, maybe after doing sets of 200 fly in the pool. He turned the truck around and headed up the exit ramp. He never thought he'd be so damn glad for all his wheels.

On Level 4 he swung into the garage, checking to see if Swayze's BMW was there. He didn't know what she was up to and he intended to find out. But the only vehicle on 4 was a dusty pickup with monster tires and a bull bar on the front, parked near a maintenance room. The door to the maintenance room was open and inside he saw pipes and heavy equipment. He U-turned and went up to the next level.

There was the BMW. He cruised past, feeling the urge

to key it, to write something obscene in German along its gleaming flanks. He stared for a moment. No. Swayze would come later. Right now he had to get to a phone and reach Evan. And he didn't trust anybody in Argent Tower as far as he could throw it. He had to find a payphone.

He gunned the truck up to Level 1 and across the garage toward the exit at the far end. There was a gas station a couple of blocks up Wilshire, and it had to have a payphone. He punched it up the exit ramp, clanking over the one-way spikes, and out onto the street. Behind him the bleak office lights of Argent Tower shone in the dusk like clown teeth. He watched the building recede in the rearview mirror, relief growing with every foot it fell behind him.

Mom and I headed back to the desk. Archie was staring at the CCTV monitor, scratching his nose. He picked up a walkie-talkie.

'Atkins? You there?' he said.

A voice fuzzed back. 'Ten-four.'

'Where are you? Need you to check out the camera in the garage.'

'Garage? By myself?'

He was probably thinking of the guard lying in ICU because he'd gone down in the parking elevator to look for Coyote. The phone rang on the desk, a light blinking.

'I'm coming down,' blurted the walkie-talkie. 'I'm up in the Sky Bistro, give me a minute.'

Archie picked up the phone. 'Yeah, Dr Swayze. Lady to see you here, name of . . .' He looked at Mom.

'Angie Delaney.'

He repeated it and listened. 'Yeah, that's what she says. Angie.' Now he glanced at me. 'You Evan?'

I nodded. My radar was pinging louder now. Needles and pins were tingling along my palms.

With a huge thunk, the sound of a big electrical switch being thrown, the lights went out.

34

The lobby went dark and the air conditioning shut down. Out on Wilshire, headlights streaked by. Protectively Mom took my hand.

The walkie-talkie fuzzed. 'Archie, we got a blackout up here.'

'Here too.'

I pointed at Archie. 'Call the police.' I pulled Mom away from the desk. 'Let's go.'

The phone at Archie's desk rang again. He answered it, saying, 'Yeah, Dr Swayze.'

I tugged Mom toward the door.

Archie called out: 'Hey. You ain't going nowhere.'

I pushed the bar to open the side door out to the plaza, but it didn't budge. Archie had locked it behind us when we came in. I turned. Through shadow I saw that he was still on the phone with Swayze, nodding intently.

'Let us out.'

Emergency lighting kicked on, spot floodlights casting eerie light from corners and high angles in the atrium. The painters' scaffold reared toward the mezzanine, bony and reptilian. Deep in the bowels of the building a generator whined into action and skeleton power returned. The closed circuit television monitors swelled back to life.

Archie, uplit in the light emanating from the screen, glared like a spooked frog.

He hung up the phone. 'Get away from the door.'

My heart was skipping like a record needle. 'Let us out, *now*.'

He came around the desk. 'I said, move away from the door.'

He was coming at us. Incredulous, I said, 'Nine-one-one. Three numbers. Jesus, do it.'

His eyes had the dead shine of a sledgehammer. 'Nobody's getting out. Security protocol. We lock down, so that way nobody else gets in.'

'What did Swayze tell you?' I said.

'Not to listen to you. That whatever you're pulling, not to fall for it. Get away from the door.'

'I'm not trying to let Coyote in. Don't you understand? If the lights and power have been shut down, that means Coyote is *already* in.'

He grabbed my arm. Mom jumped at him.

'Hands off my daughter.'

She snatched hold of his hand and pinched. Archie howled and let go of me. Mom and I ran.

The gas station was brightly lit, and outside the minimart there was a payphone. Jesse pulled up next to it.

He had a bunch of change in the cup holder, enough, he hoped, to call Evan in China Lake. His second call would have to be to the LAPD. He figured he was in trouble up to his armpits. Leaving a murder scene, at the lair of a serial killer – the cops must be going nuts, and he bet everything that Swayze hadn't called and squared things up for him. He glanced over his shoulder at the office tower. Finding out what her game was, that was item number three tonight.

He stopped still, coins shining in his palm. Argent Tower had gone completely dark.

He started the truck and pulled up to the front of the minimart pounding the horn. Inside, the clerk stared out from behind the counter, frowning. He waved to her but she shook her head. She wasn't allowed to come out. He grabbed the disabled placard and held it up so she could see and kept waving to her. Finally, reluctantly, she stepped out from behind the counter and opened the door.

'Call the police,' he said.

He was still trying to explain to her even as he pulled away, screeching out into traffic, thinking of that big dusty pickup with the bull bar parked next to the maintenance room down in the garage. Horns honked around him. He gunned the truck back toward Argent Tower.

We ran into the gloom, past the desk and across the soaring lobby.

'There's a back door. I saw it on the TV monitor.' I glanced at Mom. 'What did you do to Archie to make him let go?'

'Pressure point. Takes down the meanest unruly drunks, so be glad for stormtrooper stewardesses.'

We turned down a hallway and found ourselves confronted with locked double doors. We turned back. Archie stood in the center of the lobby, waiting for us. I veered past one bank of elevators, aiming for the mezzanine stairs.

The elevators pinged and the doors opened. I skidded to a stop, heart bouncing. A uniformed security guard stepped out, walkie-talkie in hand.

Archie shouted, 'Grab them.'

Simultaneously Mom and I blurted, '*Assholes.*'

The guard was a scrawny guy with fuzz for a mustache. His face pinched and he stalked toward us. Mom pawed through her purse.

'I'll mace you,' she said.

I yanked her off in another direction, toward the stairs that led down to the garage. Slamming the bar on the door, I pulled her into the stairwell. Ice-hot emergency spotlights turned the walls white.

We burst out of the stairway one flight down on Level 1. The garage was empty. Forty yards away, the entrance ramp led out onto Wilshire. We hurried toward it.

'We have to get to a phone. We can't just leave Jesse here, and if . . .' Catch in my throat. 'If he's hurt bad . . .'

A grinding noise obscured my voice. My eyes bugged. 'Oh no. Mom, run.'

Up at the top of the entrance ramp, a metal grate was cranking down. We ran. And damn, my mother was in good shape. She pumped her arms, sprinting beside me. The grate clattered further down, six feet from the ground, five, four.

'Shit,' she yelled.

She lunged toward it, bunching herself to dive and roll for freedom.

'Mom, no!'

We weren't going to make it. I grabbed her arm, pulling her up short. The grate hit the ground. She sank her fingers into the mesh and tried to haul it back up.

'Dammit.'

She shook it, hot with frustration, and threw her purse to the ground. I looked around. The exit ramp, a hundred yards back at the other side of the garage, was still open. The mesh grate was just beginning to crank down, much more slowly than this one had. I pulled on Mom's arm.

'Come on.'

'No.' She resisted. 'Look.'

Out on Wilshire a horn honked. 'Evan.'

It was Jesse. The truck was in the middle of the street and he was leaning out the window waving. How the hell he got there I had no idea, but the First Cavalry, the Seventh Fleet or even the Four Freaking Horsemen of the Apocalypse couldn't have looked more welcome.

I pointed, yelling. 'The exit.'

He accelerated away, tires squealing, heading around the corner for the side street. Mom grabbed her purse and we turned and ran. Icy light and shadow slid over us. Above the elevator the security camera glared. I gave it the finger. With both hands.

At the exit ramp the grate continued cranking down. We were about eighty yards away. Ten, twelve seconds if we sprinted like hell.

'Faster,' I said.

We closed on the ramp. I heard the truck coming. Headlights swelled, the brakes screeched and it swerved into sight, the back end sliding around, rubber smoking off the tires.

Mom was breathing hard. 'Christ, does he always drive like that?'

The truck held at the top of the ramp, blocked by one-way spikes and a sign warning of severe tire damage. Through the glare of the headlights I saw the grate coming down.

We were too far away.

'No,' Mom said. 'No.'

For another second the pickup idled outside, and then Jesse gunned it down the ramp. I yanked Mom out of the way.

He hit the spikes and the tires blew. The wheel rims shrieked against the concrete, sparks jumping red, and he slammed on the brakes, skidding down, approaching the grate.

Mom gaped. 'What's he doing? He'll never get out again.'

He knew. The truck slewed, slowing, the hood and roof sliding under the grate. The noise was ridiculous. The cargo bed slid under the grate and the truck shuddered to a stop. The grate cranked down and hit the tailgate.

And kept cranking. Metal groaned and the back end of the truck began crunching down. Mom and I ran toward it.

Jesse opened his door. 'Come on.'

The grate labored down. The back end of the truck moaned under the pressure. The tail-lights shattered. The latches for the tailgate gave way, it sprang open, and the grate thunked down onto it and kept cranking. The front end of the truck seesawed up. The grate clunked and groaned and with one last shriek, finally stopped.

The tailgate was bent out of shape, the shocks, tires and rims shot. The grate had stopped a bit more than a foot off the ground. Jesse hung in the driver's doorway.

'My insurance agent's going to kill me,' he said.

Running to the door, I threw my arms around him. 'Jesus, this is reason number ninety-nine. Are you okay?'

He braced himself to keep from sliding out of the door. 'Fine.'

'I got your text. What happened? How bad are you hurt?'

'I'm not hurt. And I didn't send you a text.'

We stared at each other. He exhaled.

'Swayze took my phone.'

'Shit.'

'And the gun.' His eyes were alight with apprehension. 'Coyote's here. Her truck's parked outside the maintenance room down on Level Four.'

Slowly, with dread, we all looked back into the garage.

He lowered his voice. 'You have to get out. Swayze used the text messages to draw you here. And she used you to draw Coyote here.'

Mom's voice dropped to a growl. 'The bitch. The lying, shit-eating bitch. She's the one who outsourced Coyote's killing spree, isn't she? And now she wants to get rid of you.'

'And then maybe get rid of Coyote,' Jesse said. 'All clean and quiet, here in this empty skyscraper. She may have a clean-up crew on standby, waiting to sanitize it afterward.'

We looked at the grate. There was room for us to slither under it, but there was no way to get the frame of the wheelchair out.

'I'm not leaving you,' I said.

He shook his head. 'You have to get yourself and the kid the hell away from here.'

Mom raked her fingers into her hair, looking up the ramp. 'If Coyote's definitely the one who shut down the power, she may have done it so that people would evacuate. She could be waiting for you outside.'

'I doubt it,' I said. 'I think she's going to be up at Primacon.'

Faintly, through layers of concrete, we heard police sirens.

'Thank God,' I said.

Mom put a hand on my arm. 'I'll go up to the lobby and get the cops down here.'

'Not alone,' I said.

She pawed through her purse and handed me a canister of mace. 'If anybody tries to touch you, press this button. They'll grab their eyes and shriek like little girls.'

'What about you?'

'I've got pepper spray. And a lighter.' She peered into the bag. 'And a screwdriver.'

'Mom.'

'Also a Nutri-grain bar, but I wouldn't rely on that.'

'How the hell did you get all that on the plane?'

'Checked it on the tarmac for storage in the hold. You didn't notice, you were too busy arguing with Eva Braun.' She squeezed my arm. 'I'll stand by the front windows and get their attention. It's the safest way.'

She looked at Jesse. I knew what she was thinking. The cops were going to storm in with guns drawn, and they didn't just think Jesse had trashed an apartment, they thought he was Coyote's accomplice. One of us needed to talk to them and try to convince them he wasn't dangerous. The LAPD wasn't known for its bashfulness in apprehending suspects.

'When we come upstairs,' I said, 'I want to see Archie and Atkins pepper-sprayed and squealing like beauty queens.'

'On the slightest pretext.'

The siren got louder. 'Hurry.'

She ran to the stairwell. Jesse began snapping the

wheels on the chair frame. He looked stark and sounded exhausted.

'What was that about?'

'LAPD has a warrant on you. You'd better start thinking about how you're going to surrender yourself.'

'I was afraid that's what you meant. How screwed am I?' He tossed his hair out of his eyes, watching my face. 'Shit.'

'Don't worry, we'll make it go away.' I put my hand on his cheek. 'You've also got me, and I'm a lot harder to get rid of.'

His gaze was grateful, melancholy and deeply anxious. He pulled me in and hugged me.

'Thank you for showing up,' he said.

For a moment I almost let everything go. I felt tears and grief and gratitude beginning to well. He didn't know what had happened, and all I wanted to do was stay wrapped in his arms and tell him. But once I started I wouldn't be able to stop. I straightened.

'Ditto,' I said.

He pulled the chair close, boosted himself on board and spun around, exhaling. He put the tire iron on his lap. It and the mace weren't the best of weapons, but better than nothing. We crossed the garage to the elevator.

His voice was quiet. 'Never thought I'd say this. It's great to be in this wheelchair.'

I hit the call button and put my hand on his shoulder, hoping he wouldn't feel how shaky I was. The elevator hummed. The call light flicked off and the doors pinged open.

He stared. I clutched his shoulder and covered my mouth with my free hand, willing myself not to scream out loud. I had to keep the shrieking in my head.

Inside the elevator, plumes of blood were sprayed across the floor, walls and ceiling. Collapsed on the floor, dead from a slash across the throat, lay Archie.

35

Breathless, I reached the top of the stairs. The door led out to the lobby. I grit my teeth and eased it open a crack.

The lights were flickering as though damaged. It looked like lightning had broken loose inside the atrium. I crept out into shadow. If I could get past the elevator and around the corner, I'd be able to see the desk, the front windows and the street. And please, God, let me see Mom waiting for me. My heels racked on the marble floor. I took off my shoes and padded barefoot, hearing every step, every breath.

The parking elevator dinged and the door gaped open. Archie's desanguinated body glistened at me. The gash through his throat looked like a red grin. I turned away. Ahead I saw only the lightning flicker. I saw no candy-colored police lights, heard no sirens.

I approached the corner. Peered around.

The lobby was empty.

The crazed lighting and streaking headlights out on the boulevard turned the scene into a sci-fi set. And – oh, no. Out at the curb sat an LAPD black and white. I ran across the lobby to the doors. They were still locked. I slammed a fist against one of the plate-glass windows. The cop was getting back in the car and closing the door. He couldn't hear me. I looked around. The potted plants were all king-sized, too big to lift.

The desk. I sprinted around it and grabbed Archie's chair.

I froze. Stuffed under the counter was the scrawny security guard, Atkins. His eyes were crossed and his lips were blue. His tongue was oozing from between them. His head lay at an angle like a sock puppet. And beyond being dead, he was undressed. His uniform shirt and pants and hat were gone; he was lying there in his briefs. Pulling the chair behind me on its casters, I ran back to the windows. The police car was still there but now its headlights were on.

With an almighty roar I swung the chair into the air and flung it at the plate-glass window. I turned my back and shielded my face with my arms.

Thud.

The chair bounced off the glass and clattered to the marble. I gaped. There was no more than a pea-sized crack in the glass. The nonbreakable, tough as hell, stupid goddamned new Ultraglass. I was kicking and beating on the window, watching the patrol car signal and pull out into traffic and cruise away out of sight down Wilshire.

'No. No.'

I leaned my head against the glass, straightened and spun around. Turning my back on this building was as stupid an act as I could imagine. I ran to the desk, leaned over and grabbed the phone.

The receiver came free in my hand, the cord springing with it, neatly cut.

I dropped it. Thought twice and picked it up and held it like a club while I peered around the lobby and up at the mezzanine levels and walkways that ascended around the rim of the atrium.

I had to find my mother. I had to get out with her and

Jesse and I needed help right this damned second. What did I have? Mace. A telephone receiver. My wits, what was left of them. My lover, who had plenty of wits and a tire iron and wheels for feet. And there had to be other people in this freaking tower. A janitorial crew, the odd wonk who couldn't leave his desk. Somebody who would have a working cellphone and could redial the police.

The voice of fact and necessity tinned at me, far back in my thoughts. *There's a key to unlock the doors.*

The fire alarm. I could pull the fire alarm. *Archie had a set of keys.* The fire alarm would get plenty of attention here, fast.

Get the keys.

Deep down, I moaned. Even when I pulled the fire alarm, it would take five to ten minutes for an engine crew to get here. Jesse and I could slide under the grate, but once he did he'd be stuck. The fastest and safest way to get out of here was to get Archie's keys.

Psalm 91, is that the one about not fearing the darkness of the night? Slowly, reluctantly, I tiptoed back toward the stairwell, feeling the marble cold beneath my bare feet, clutching the mace and the phone. There would be a fire alarm by the elevator. The lights spasmed above me. I turned the corner.

Maureen Swayze was waiting for me.

I screamed and jumped and brought up the canister of mace.

Just as quickly Swayze brought up a gun, no, something else – and I shouted, turning away, putting my arms over my head.

Pain engulfed me. Outside, inside. Electric shock. I was rigid, falling, biting my tongue. The pain was unbelievable. I hit the marble and couldn't move, couldn't scream.

407

Swayze grabbed me by the arm and dragged me into an elevator.

The walls of the elevator whirled like a fairground ride. Tears leaked from my eyes. I lay twisted on the floor with Swayze standing above me, appraising me as though I were a frog pinned to a lab tray. She held the stun gun in her hand, and she looked eager for a repeat performance. Head to toe it felt as if straight pins were sticking into me. My legs and arms were floppy clubs. My tongue was bleeding, blood running out the side of my mouth onto the floor of the elevator. The car lurched to a stop and the door pinged open. Swayze dragged me out into a half-lit hallway.

Even with the walls spinning I could tell this wasn't the slick corporate lobby of Primacon Labs. We were on one of the building's unfinished floors.

Concentrating, fighting for some tiny use of my body, I hung my head and spat blood on the floor. As she pulled me along I dragged my hand through the blood. It left a trail like fingerpaints. I fought, slowly bending my knees.

She stopped, dropped to one knee and jammed the stun gun against my belly, right at my panty line.

'The Taser is a nonlethal device. Usually.' Her eyes, behind her glasses, were remote. 'I'm not current on the research as to its effect on a first-trimester fetus.'

I stopped breathing. Swayze's face lit with satisfaction.

'As I suspected.' She stood. 'Get up. Crawl.'

With effort I pushed up onto my hands and knees. They shook like bamboo sticks beneath me.

Her voice was self-congratulatory. 'I couldn't understand why your boyfriend was so desperate to be sure that you're healthy. But then I recalled how you turned tail and ran the other day when we approached the door with the radiation warning. And I got to thinking.'

From the angle of the emergency lights and the echo off the walls, I could tell we were on one of the floors overlooking the atrium. I saw dropcloths, paint buckets and sawhorses, drywall and conduit hanging from the ceiling. She grabbed the back of my collar and jammed the Taser against my shoulder as I inched along.

'Faster.'

I crawled toward the exterior windows. Outside, skyscrapers glittered with lights and Wilshire Boulevard snaked toward the Pacific. I felt my coordination returning. If I bunched myself I could roll. I didn't know if I could get to my feet but perhaps I could knock her off balance. I took a breath, testing the strength in my arms.

'No you don't,' she said.

She shocked me again.

When I came around, I knew I'd been drooling bloody saliva out both sides of my mouth. The lights outside spun like stars. I was groaning. I'd wet my pants.

The ripping sound was painful in my ears. My head began to clear and I understood that she was securing my hands with strapping tape to a steel pillar. Her face, half-shadowed above me, was purposeful.

'Believe it or not, I consider this an unfortunate turn of events,' she said.

I moved my legs but couldn't get any purchase. I was lying on my back with my hands above my head. Swayze was whipping the tape around my crossed wrists and the pillar, tighter and thicker. My hands ached and began to lose feeling.

'I wish it were possible to keep you alive.'

So stop. I tried to say it but my tongue and lips wouldn't cooperate.

'But this is much bigger than you or I.' She slung the tape around and around my wrists. 'Your father would understand that.'

No. I moaned it.

She worked with imperious detachment. In the pale light coming through the plate-glass windows I could see sweat shining on her face.

'You've inherited a terrific genetic base from him. Presuming that you're serum-negative for the prion, you and Jesse could have half a dozen high-caliber children.'

I swallowed and tasted blood.

She dropped the tape and yanked against the bindings, checking that they were secure. She had wound it a quarter-inch thick. I pulled and felt layer upon layer digging into my wrists. I couldn't budge them from the pillar.

She stood up, wiping the back of her hand across her forehead. 'You wouldn't be the first. A number of your classmates have borne superior children. Abbie Hankins in particular.'

At Abbie's name I felt a welt of pain in the center of my skull. I squeezed my eyes shut, smothering a cry.

'Her daughter Dulcie tests at an IQ of a hundred and fifty-two on the Stanford-Binet scale and her pre-schooler shows signs of savant-like genius.'

I heard her shuffling around, and opened my eyes. She was at a makeshift table, laying items out on the work surface, including Jesse's Glock. I recalled Tim North's advice.

First rule of a gunfight: bring a gun.

First rule of a knife fight: bring a gun.

She glanced at me. 'Do you know the etymology of the word *teratogenesis*? The usual translation is monster-making. In medical usage it refers to substances that cause malformations in the fetus.' Brushing her hair back from her face, she crossed to me. 'But the Greek prefix *terato* doesn't only mean monster.' She crouched down at my side, her eyes shining. 'It means wonder.'

Her gaze ran down my body. I tried to bend my knees.

'You thought this was a cover-up, didn't you? That Coyote was killing women because they were exposed to the prion. Big bad government trying to sweep its dirt under the rug.' She sneered. 'How pedestrian.'

She pulled up my shirt, exposing my skin. I tried to squirm away but couldn't get my legs to follow instructions. The Taser had fried my nervous system.

'No, if it were at all possible to start a breeding program under controlled conditions, this would be spectacularly exciting. Imagine, true teratogenesis. Wonder children.'

She put her hand on my stomach. It was warm.

'My remit is to return the situation to one of safety. The infected exposees present a risk to the genome. Once the epidemiological evidence started coming in, there was no alternative.'

She stroked her hand across my stomach. 'They were doomed, you understand? And they were breeding in an uncontrolled manner. Their children would have become a danger if left loose. Those who survived would have become Coyotes, but without the guidance or training to perform as warriors. They would be feral.'

Her hand lingered on my stomach, dry and warm.

'But as warriors . . .' Her voice sounded awestruck. 'If only you could have seen Kai at the height of her abilities. She was a magnificent creation.' She shook her head.

'But she's gone far beyond her mission brief. I need to pull her in, and this is the best way to get her here.'

You don't want the police to get hold of Coyote. You don't want her to talk or to go on trial.

My voice slurred, but I managed to get the words out. 'You're protecting yourself and the people who set you up to this.'

Her sneer returned. 'You don't understand at all, do you? You have too much of your mother in you, I think.'

She removed a necklace from around her neck. It jangled and caught the light. I saw dogtags and a piece of shrapnel. She stroked the shrapnel across my stomach, unzipped my jeans and tucked the necklace into the top of my panties. Standing up, she took a cellphone from her pocket, flipped it open and snapped a photo. The flash momentarily blinded me. I heard her thumbing a phone number and then a beep as she sent the photo to somebody.

My vision returned. She was at the table. She picked up a hypodermic syringe and turned to me.

Fear jumped into my voice. 'No. Don't.'

Puzzlement in her eyes. Then she huffed. 'This is not for you.'

She put it in the pocket of her white lab coat. If it wasn't for me then it must be for Coyote, and I didn't think it was a vitamin shot. She put the Glock in her other pocket and picked up the Taser.

'I'll scream,' I said. 'Somebody will hear me.'

She gave me a final glance. 'Yes. When you scream, *I'll* hear you. That's how I'll know when it's time to come back.'

She walked away.

In the dark, with the megawatt glitter of Los Angeles coming through the plate-glass windows, I understood.

This was an ancient game. I was the goat staked in the clearing to lure the wild predator into the trap. Meanwhile, the hunters hid and waited.

Back in the darkness, the stairwell door clicked shut.

I jerked my hands against the tape. Nothing. I tried to slide them up the pillar. No way. I wrestled my legs under me and tried to turn over and sit up. I couldn't.

I listened to the sounds of the building, and I began to cry.

My breath caught and choking sounds worked their way to my lips. I tried to stop myself. I heard the traffic down on Wilshire, immensely distant, a metallic rush. I heard the sounds of the building, creaks and clicks and machine groans. And a humming sound.

The elevator.

I squeezed my legs together, trying to curl myself up into a tiny, baby-sized ball. I bit my lip to keep from screaming or sobbing. I thought of Kelly Colfax, gutted like a deer carcass on her kitchen floor with knife wounds sawn into her legs and genitals. My stomach was exposed. Coyote's necklace lay jammed in my panties, hissing with starlight. The humming sound ebbed. The elevator pinged. I heard the doors slide open.

Pain, please don't let the pain go on and on. Please, give me the courage to hang onto my dignity. Don't let me die begging and whimpering. In the eerie light, I saw a flash of metal. Spinning spokes.

'Ev.'

Then I was crying, hard, and trying, harder, to keep quiet. Jesse was at my side and I was saying, 'Quiet, gotta be quiet. Swayze's in the stairwell.'

He pulled against the tape, trying to find the end and unwind it.

413

'She's waiting for me to start screaming. She expects Coyote to be here any minute.'

He circled to the other side of the pillar and clawed his fingernails into the tape. He was wearing his half-fingered gloves and his hands looked filthy. Under his breath he said, 'Shit.'

'Jesse, did you hear me? Swayze's out in the stairwell.'

He looked at me, and back in the direction he'd come. Without a word he spun and headed away. A moment later I heard keys rattling in a lock.

Then came the sound of pounding on the stairwell door.

Jesse came back. He made one more attempt to peel the tape loose. I could see fear in his eyes.

'What did you do out there?' I said.

He gave up with the tape. 'I locked the stairwell door so Swayze can't get back in here. The elevator door's jammed open with a potted plant. I didn't want to have to wait around for one.'

'How did you . . .'

He held up a set of keys. They and his hand were smeared dark, and I knew with what.

'Archie's?' I said.

He was looking around the floor. 'Yeah.'

'How did you find me?'

'Blood trail.' He backed up, to a collection of paint cans near the windows. He looked around, went to the work table, pushed over to a pile of stuff a few feet away. He bent and pawed through it. I saw paint brushes, rollers, paint trays, more rolls of packing tape.

'Come on, there's gotta be . . .' He kept pawing. 'Scissors, a box cutter, something. Shit.' He straightened and peered around, searching for something that could cut me loose.

Out by the stairs, I heard a humming sound again.

'Jesse.'

He wheeled back and clawed his fingernails into the tape again. He took the tire iron from his lap and put the end against the tape and scraped. It would work, eventually, but the tape was wound so thick that it would take a long time. He was barely making a dent. The humming sound continued.

'Jesse, that's the elevator.'

'I know.'

There were four elevators on this level, the two just around the corner and two on the opposite side of the atrium walkway. He had only blocked one.

'Cut me loose.'

'I'm trying.'

He sawed the end of the tire iron against the tape.

'That's Coyote in the elevator. Jesse.'

He stopped sawing and swung the tire iron at the pillar like Tiger Woods walloping a ball. Metal sang but the tape stayed stuck. The elevator hummed. He looked over his shoulder toward the stairs and the elevators. He was breathing hard.

He glanced down and the truth in his eyes nearly broke me. He couldn't cut me loose. Hope drained. I lay there, cold.

Then he looked at my belly. In one swift gesture he grabbed Coyote's necklace and put it around his neck.

He pushed back, hard, skating backward across the floor. 'Don't make a sound.'

I raised my head, his name on my lips. He whirled and disappeared toward the walkway around the atrium, out of sight.

Air gulped in and out of my lungs. No. What he was doing was suicidal.

An elevator call button rang. I heard doors slide open.

And echoing across the building from the far side of the atrium walkway, Jesse's voice, and dogtags chiming against shrapnel.

'Looking for this, bitch?'

36

The amulet swung from Jesse's hand. Across the building on the far side of the atrium walkway, Coyote turned around.

Come on, bitch. Come and get it.

She had features like a Raphaelite Madonna and skin as pale as marble, with blue veins snaking beneath the surface. Her eyes were out of synch, one pupil blown wide and black. Her hair was shorn and she was wearing a security guard's uniform.

Her lips drew back, and the bitch came on.

She strode toward him, limping. He hit the elevator call button. She rounded the walkway and he saw that her leg was broken. She had strapped the fracture with a makeshift splint but with each step her leg sagged above the ankle. She was keeling toward that side, her shoulder hanging low. She held a hunting knife in her left hand.

The elevator came and he pushed inside. She moved. Fast.

He hit Close and grabbed the tire iron. She broke into a run, coming with canine assurance and fury. He backed up. She lunged but the doors slid shut.

Jesus.

The elevator headed down, the view out the window dropping toward the schizoid lighting in the lobby. How could she run like that on a broken leg? He passed Five,

Four, and the bell chimed for Three. Shit, somebody had called it. Swayze?

He gripped the tire iron. The doors opened and a janitor pushed his cleaning cart into the doorway.

The guy stopped, staring at him in shock. 'Crap, man, you scared me.'

'Christ, am I glad to see you.' He saw a cellphone hooked to the guy's belt. 'Call the police and get the SWAT team over here. Tell them Coyote's in the building.'

'What? Why do you have those keys?'

'Do it now. Then get the hell out of here.' He looked at the cleaning cart. 'A knife. Do you have a knife on your cart? Scissors? Anything big and sharp?'

'Dude, what the hell?'

Jesse shot him a look. 'The security guards are dead. So call for help, and then fucking *run*.'

The janitor stared at Jesse's bloody hands and the tire iron. He began backing away.

'Come on, I need a knife. And get this cart out of the door. Please, if you leave it here I'm stuck.'

The janitor backed up one more step, turned and fled. The stairwell door slammed shut behind him.

All right, dumbass, any more bright ideas?

Above in the atrium he heard Coyote running. Her footsteps halted and two floors above him, that deathly pale face leaned over the railing and stared down. She pulled back and he heard a door being thrown open. She was coming down the stairs.

The elevator doors slid shut, bumping the janitor's cart. He tried to push it out onto the walkway, putting his shoulder into it, but the cart was too heavy. He heard the stairwell door bang open. Grabbing a broom from the cart, he backed against the rear wall, jammed the brush

418

against the cart and shoved. The cart skittered out onto the walkway. He tossed the broom against the window and pushed Close. Fast. A bunch of times.

Here she came.

She stared at the amulet around his neck, her teeth bared. He hit Close again and the doors inched toward each other. She lunged.

The doors shut. Coyote's arm was jammed between them. The knife was out, the point ten inches from his face. With every ounce of strength, he swung the tire iron.

The sound cracked in the air and her wrist and hand skewed, deforming at an angle below her elbow.

Through the slit in the doors, she glared at him. She continued trying to push the doors open, using her upper arm. Her hand and wrist sagged but she held onto the knife. The door began wedging wider. Oh, shit.

He slammed the tire iron against her arm again and again. She growled, now trying to wedge her shoulder in the doors. He hit her again, bringing the iron down like a sledgehammer. The knife dropped from her fingers. Her hand retreated out of sight. The doors closed.

Holy fuck.

The leg, the arm, none of it mattered. She was impervious. Unless he killed her or fried her central nervous system, she would simply keep coming.

He hit the control panel and the elevator began to rise. Outside the window, Coyote's translucent face appeared. She watched the elevator pull away, her head tilting back, freaky eyes following him.

She opened her mouth and wailed.

The sound made his skin shrink. He turned his head, trying to swallow, and saw the floor.

'Yes.'

The hunting knife lay in front of him. He grabbed it and pressed Six. Leaning back, he tried to catch his breath. Outside, the view soared over the atrium.

Oh, God. He slapped his hand against the glass.

Leaning over the walkway railing to see who was howling, was Angie Delaney.

He pounded on the glass. 'Angie.'

She looked up, spotted him and her mouth opened in surprise.

He pointed upward, yelling, 'Evan's on Six!'

He slapped his hands to the window again: five fingers and one finger. She disappeared from his view. The elevator continued rising.

Two floors above Angie, staring down over the railing, her face knotted with anger, stood Maureen Swayze.

37

My hands throbbed, numb. The tape bit painfully into my skin. But what was unbearable was the quiet.

All the sounds I'd heard earlier had been overcome by jagged sobs and the words whispering from my lips. *Our Father, who art . . .*

Hell, what was the rest of it?

In heaven. Hallowed . . . If I could recite the rest of it, I wouldn't go insane. If I could get to that part about *deliver us from evil*, then maybe . . .

I heard Coyote wailing.

I cringed my knees together. Come to me, prayer. Come on. *I'm on a highway to hell . . .* The elevator call button chimed.

I looked and saw Jesse come around the corner.

All my defenses evaporated. I erupted in tears. 'Oh my God.'

He had a knife in his hand. An enormous, serrated knife. He was winded and his hands were shaking. He began sawing at the tape that bound me to the pillar.

'What happened?' I said.

'Got this from her.'

My voice was wracked with tears and astonishment. 'Got it? Simple as that?'

'Broke her arm with the tire iron but that won't stop her. She'll be coming.'

Concentrating, he fought the trembling in his hands and sawed into the tape above my wrists.

'Your mom's downstairs. She's okay,' he said.

He kept sawing as I broke into another bout of tears. He looked at me, ragged.

'I hope.'

With one last shove of the knife, he cut through the tape. I swung my arms down and he helped me sit up. Blood and sensation flooded painfully back to my hands. I struggled to my knees and fell against him.

He clutched me. 'Can you walk?'

'Don't know, she Tasered me twice.' My voice dropped. 'I wet my pants.'

'Join the club.'

I couldn't tell if he was joking. I tried to get my feet under me and stand up. I wobbled and stayed put on the floor.

'Not working yet,' I said.

'Climb on.'

He jammed the knife and tire iron behind his back and pulled me onto his lap. He was joking about the pants, I realized. He was simply spooked half out of his head. With me slumped against him he turned and carted us back toward the elevator, swerving around paint buckets and sawhorses. My limbs felt weak and tingly. Working at it, I made a fist. Control was returning but strength was still distant. We rounded the corner and I saw the elevator door jammed open with the potted plant. Jesse wheeled in and muscled the plant out of the way. His shirt was clinging to him and he was breathing hard. He pushed the button for the lobby.

'Anybody out there's going to be able to see us coming down,' he said. 'Can you hold the knife?'

I squeezed my hand again, wondering if I could grip it. The doors began to chug closed.

Ding, next to us the second elevator stopped. When we looked we couldn't see anybody inside, but then the doors opened, and we heard them.

A woman was shrieking. 'Shit. Fuck.'

'Get off—'

Thudding sounds and a slap and a loud crash racked out of the elevator, and a cry of shock, pain and surprise. Mom and Swayze rolled out onto the floor in the walkway.

They were grappling, clawing, pulling hair and kicking and biting each other. Swayze's glasses were gone and one side of her face was red, her eye swollen shut. Mom's forehead was bleeding and her blouse was ripped open.

I jumped off Jesse's lap, lunging for them, and fell smack on my face. Jesse shoved his way around me out to the walkway.

'Stick the broom in the door,' he said.

'Swayze has the Glock.'

I sloshed around, got my hand on the broom and tipped it into the doorway so the elevator couldn't leave without us. And so that Coyote couldn't get up here in it. Fighting to my knees, I crawled out of the car.

On the floor ten feet away, Swayze punched Mom in the mouth. Mom clawed at Swayze's face. It was so swollen on the right side that I knew Mom had pepper-sprayed her. Swayze kicked Mom and rolled away, scrambling to her feet. I saw Jesse swing the tire iron, hard, and Swayze drop. She howled and grabbed for him. Mom pulled at Swayze's lab coat and Swayze wriggled out of it, twisting free. I saw the Glock slide out of the pocket and Swayze swing at Jesse and Jesse trying to get the knife from behind his back and to keep control of the tire iron and not get

423

dumped on the floor. And I saw Mom come up with the Taser.

She jammed it against Swayze's shoulder, yelling, 'Jesse, clear.'

He raised his hands. Mom fired.

Nothing happened.

They held still for a second, looking at the Taser.

Swayze backhanded Mom into Jesse and turned, looking for the gun. I crawled toward them.

'Pocket,' I said.

They didn't hear me. Swayze fell toward the Glock.

'Mom, her lab coat. The pocket.'

Swayze came up with the Glock. 'The Taser's out of power from making Evan piss herself. There's not enough juice left for you to shave your legs with.'

Mom was on Swayze's right side. Swayze couldn't see Mom stick her hand in the pocket of the lab coat and discover the syringe.

Swayze racked the slide on the Glock. Clutching the syringe, Mom jammed her in the calf and pushed the plunger.

She stared, appalled, gasping. She dropped the gun and pulled the syringe out. Grabbing her leg, she fell in a ball on the floor, screaming. Mom staggered back.

Crawling to Jesse's side, I pulled myself to my feet. My legs held. I reached out.

'Mom.'

She seized hold of me. On the floor Swayze convulsed. Her head jerked and her eyes rolled back to whites.

Jesse backed into the wedged elevator door. 'Come on.'

I faltered after him, clinging to Mom. 'I can't believe you did that.'

Mom stared at her. 'She set Coyote loose on your class.'

She pulled me toward the elevator, but I hesitated. The Glock lay on the floor beyond Swayze, just outside the door of the second elevator. I needed to get it but I didn't want to get close to her. Her face was blue. Bloody foam frothed from between her lips. Her limbs were slamming the floor.

If I stuck close to the wall I could pick my way around her. Letting go of Mom, I took a step.

The bell for the second elevator chimed. The door yawed open, and out stepped Coyote.

Even with her hair shorn, her face scratched and her arm grotesquely broken, she was striking. Androgynous, and wounded, and intent.

'Ev.'

Jesse pulled on the back of my shirt, dragging me into the elevator. Coyote attacked.

Her shin crunched and slipped when she put her foot down. She fell to her knees. I tangled with the broom handle and stumbled, landing on my butt in the doorway. I crab-crawled backward as the doors began to close, but Jesse and my mom were behind me and there wasn't room. Hands in, butt in, left foot in.

'You.' She crawled toward me and grabbed my right foot. 'You belong to me.'

The door closed, hit my calf and came open again. Coyote sank her nails into my ankle. With her one usable arm, she began hauling me out of the elevator. She was wickedly strong.

'Jesse, help.'

He grabbed my collar but Coyote was pulling, and that meant she pulled him along with me. I tried to clear the broom from the door but only managed to get it upright.

The door shut on my leg again and this time it stayed closed. Outside, Coyote's voice rose.

'You took my life. You're mine.'

'Jesse, I'm stuck.' I put my other foot against the door and pushed.

The elevator lurched downward, dropping two solid feet and jerking to a halt. The broom handle, jammed upright in the door, shattered.

Coyote held on. My leg was stuck.

'Jesse, this is urgent.'

'I don't have any leverage. Ev, push.'

'I am pushing. Shit. Shit.' I put everything I had into shoving with my left leg. The door squeezed my shin. Outside, Coyote growled.

Mom climbed around Jesse and braced herself, foot up on the wall of the compartment, hands hauling on the door, trying to open it.

'The tire iron,' I shrieked. 'Use it. Leverage.'

She grabbed it from Jesse and wedged it in the two-inch space between the doors and yowled and threw her all her hundred pounds against it. The car dropped again. The doors began crawling open.

Yes. I saw my leg. I saw the carpet outside. I saw Coyote's face. And her good hand, wrapped around my ankle like a bear trap. The doors gradually spread wider and she looked at me as if I were the meal she'd been waiting for all winter, and she pulled.

'No, no.' I began sliding out again.

Jesse grabbed me with one arm, hanging onto his wheel with the other. 'Angie, help.'

The doors closed again, on my knee. Above me Jesse and Mom pulled, groaning, trying to get me back inside the car.

426

Coyote's hand tightened on my ankle and the car shuddered, the cables groaning. I screamed, knowing what was going to happen in a few more seconds. If my leg stayed stuck I would be mangled to bone meal.

Jesse yelled. 'One, two, three!'

He and Mom pulled, one last almighty effort, and hauled me back. My knee appeared. My calf. My ankle, with Coyote's hand still gripping it. The car went down. My foot appeared. In Jesse's hand, the knife appeared.

I shut my eyes. 'Do it.'

I felt the blow, the huge momentum behind his swing. I felt blood and pain. I pulled myself back into the elevator.

The car lurched and motored downward with a long hard drop, as though a gallows door had fallen open. It bounced and danced on the cables and kept going down, the motors humming. Opening my eyes, I kicked and squirmed and pulled my knees up, panting. My ankle was slashed and bruised but still hooked to my leg.

Jesse pushed back. Mom shrank against the window. I inched back to the wall. We all stared at Coyote's severed fingers.

They lay glistening in a row on the floor, still attached to the knuckles, blood pooling around them. Jesse had taken off the end of her hand. He put the back of his wrist against his mouth as though suppressing his gag reflex.

'Holy shit,' I said.

They had nothing to add to that.

'Thank you. Both of you.'

The lights flickered. The elevator stopped humming, started again and slowed. We looked at the numbers and saw Three, M2, M1. The car stopped with a thunk and bounced on the cables. The call button pinged and the doors stammered part-way open. We were on the mezzanine, and the car was three feet higher than the walkway outside. We were stuck.

I pushed Close, Open and Lobby. Neither the doors nor the elevator car budged an inch.

'Go,' Jesse said. 'Get out and start running.'

'What are you going to do?' I said.

He nudged forward. His wheels just fit between the doors. 'Jump.'

'Then what?'

He shot me a glance, frazzled. 'Find another elevator. Bump down the stairs or let you piggyback me. Anything but hang around here.'

Mom scooted around the edge of the car, staying clear of the severed half-hand, and leaned out.

'Clear. Let's do it.' She jumped out.

My heart felt thready. I stepped around the gory fingers and followed her, thumping down onto the wide walkway of the mezzanine. Below us in the lobby the lights were still spasming. Jesse handed me the hunting knife. I backed out of his way, watching him wheelie and balance himself in the doorway. Three feet was no piece of cake. He was going to land damned hard.

'Sure you don't want to—'

'I'm sure.' He rocked his feet up, inching forward, gauging it.

Something warm sprayed my cheek, a mist. The gunshot echoed around the atrium. Mom fell to the floor.

'Ev,' Jesse yelled. 'Get down.'

Mom lay crumpled on the carpet, eyes wide, gasping. I dropped to her side. My horror was airless and jagged.

Jesse shouted at me. 'Evan.'

I looked up. Coming down the stairs from the upper mezzanine was Coyote. She was gimping along, her foot turned on its side. The remnant of her right hand hung soaked in a bloody strip of fabric. She had ripped her shirt and wound it around her palm to stanch the bleeding. In her left hand she awkwardly gripped the Glock.

Mom stared up at me. The pain in her eyes looked as though it had come at her from a direction beyond our experience. She opened her lips but didn't speak.

Coyote balanced her way down the wide mezzanine staircase. Her face was deathly pale but impassive. She appeared less a woman than a zombie eking its way across rough terrain. She wasn't flinching, wasn't cringing. Though desperately injured she obviously felt no pain. Only purpose.

'You took my life. You four.'

She worked to raise the Glock again. It weighed a couple of pounds and with her arm fractured by the tire iron she struggled to control it. Her hand drooped. She began raising her entire arm from the shoulder.

First rule of a gunfight: bring a gun. First rule of a knife fight . . .

A rasp rose in my head, the sound I'd heard when I saw Coyote walk past me through the revolving door, and when I knew that Tommy and Abbie were dead, the hollow roar caused by certainty kicking the base out from under my world.

I could run. And the day after tomorrow I would bury Jesse and my mother.

If I didn't run, I had to get close. All I had to put between them and Coyote was my own body. Now, before the gun came up.

The rasping disappeared. Truth rang through me like a

bell. I could not let Coyote get down the stairs. If she did, we were lost. No matter what happened, I had to stand.

Raising the knife, I ran at her. The sound coming out of my throat was wild. She could not get down the stairs. Could not.

Behind me I heard Jesse screaming at me to stop. I saw Coyote brace her torn right arm beneath her left hand, supporting it and working the Glock up to firing position. I charged her, knife out, seeing the gun aimed at the rug, at the air, swinging around.

She dodged and the knife went through her shirt. She grabbed me, wrapping her damaged arms around my chest. And she pulled me back, off balance, toward the railing. Jesse screamed, I screamed. Clasping me like a lover, Coyote flung herself backward and together we flipped over the rail.

We fell. And hit the painters' scaffold.

I landed on my back on the rickety wooden platform. Coyote whammed down on top of me. Her uneven eyes hovered inches from mine. Her right arm was wrapped beneath me, pinning my left arm to my side. Her left arm, in which she held the Glock, pressed on my right hand. She had the knife pinned to the platform. I couldn't wrest it free.

'You took my life,' she said. 'That day. South Star, I tried to stop it.' Teeth bared. '*Stop it*. You were downwind, I knew you were.'

I tried to get my arm out from under her. No good. I swung a leg around and kicked her broken ankle. That did worse than nothing. It didn't hurt her but the scaffold wobbled beneath us. It was only a couple of feet wide. Falling the next twenty feet to the marble floor of the lobby would be easy as anything. She bared her teeth.

430

'I ran back but it detonated. I got it full force. And this is what I've become.'

Over her shoulder, on the mezzanine above, I saw Jesse wedging his arm around the rail and giving it every effort he had to stand up. He was at least six feet above us. He couldn't possibly reach me. The scaffold trembled again. Coyote wrapped her legs around me and the platform, holding on as though riding a wild horse bareback. Frantic, I tried to brace myself. The knife slipped from my fingers. It dropped and dropped, and it was a long time before I heard it bounce on the marble.

Inches from my face, Coyote's mouth lost its sneer. Her lips quivered. For a second I saw Kai Torrance, the street kid holding her tragedies inside, the woman who so hated herself that she no longer believed she was a woman. The animal that couldn't feel pain except by inflicting it on others.

'My life,' she whispered.

Groaning with exertion, she brought up her left arm. The Glock came into view. She had wedged her index finger deep into the trigger guard so that she had a secure grip.

'You took.'

She aimed the Glock at my face. I grabbed her hand. She was still strong but with her arm broken she had only the barest ability to resist. I pushed and bent her broken bones and twisted her hand around to an angle it could never naturally have reached, and I shoved the gun against her temple.

Her gaze cleared. It seemed to burn with startled recognition. 'Woman. You.'

Staring her in the eyes, I squeezed her trigger finger. The roar was deafening.

Everything flew. The gun, Coyote and me. The recoil slammed me sideways and the scaffold shuddered again and though I grabbed for the platform, the whole thing went over like an animal brought down. I rolled off the side, over and over in the air, spinning with Kai Torrance to the floor below.

38

Fragments remain. Memories like shards of colored glass, flashing with light every now and then.

The fall. Air and darkness, the clear thought: Fuck, this is going to hurt.

Lying on the marble. Still, broken somewhere, Kai Torrance's body underneath me. Hearing Mom's voice. Seeing Jesse bump backward down the stairs, hanging onto the rail, calling my name over and over.

Spinning lights, blue and red. LAPD commandos breaking the front windows with a battering ram.

Jesse's face next to mine after he dropped onto the floor beside me, his hand on my cheek. Mom on the other side, holding me.

Reaching up, my fingers touching her, hearing her say she was all right. Shock and pain.

The rest of the night, and the next two days, are nothing but shadow. I spent them under heavy sedation at UCLA Medical Center. When I regained coherence, Mom was standing at the window in my room with her arm in a sling, looking pale and seraphic, her spiky hair a halo in the afternoon sun. Dad was dozing in a hard chair with *HMS Surprise* open on his lap. By my bedside Jesse was frayed and silent, his head and shoulders resting on the bed, his hand clasping mine. He had spent one night in jail before Captain McCracken and Special Agent Dan

Heaney combined their leverage to convince the Los Angeles authorities that he was one of the just. No charges had been filed against him.

Kai Torrance was dead before we hit the ground.

Maureen Swayze was on a ventilator in the ICU. The doctors didn't know if she would survive. The poison in the syringe was a genetically engineered variant of tetrodotoxin, the neurotoxin found in puffer fish. Primacon was researching its potential as a Parkinson's and epilepsy treatment. She was cardiac and nerve-damaged, partially paralyzed and in excruciating pain. And cogent. When they asked her if she could write down the name of her next of kin, she took the pen and scrawled *Kill me.* Mom sounded calm when she described it.

After that, I slept like a baby.

The next week, after I was released from the hospital and the truck came home from the body shop, Jesse and I drove up to the high desert. My left arm was in a cast. My pelvis had a hairline crack, but there was nothing for that except rest. I'd had an MRI and a dozen blood tests that all indicated I was free from infection by South Star. Jesse rested his elbow on the window frame. Trisha Yearwood was on the stereo, true aching country music, a generous offering on his part and yet another reason why I loved the man so much. The sky was lacquered blue. A hawk soared overhead, riding the thermals, searching for prey.

Far north of China Lake, he turned off the highway and followed the old road up the slope into the sage and scrub. It was late afternoon and the sun was angling down. Thunderheads boiled above the mountains. He stopped and we worked our way across the rocky ground to the overlook. Across the valley the Sierras soared to meet the blue.

In my hands I held an armful of white roses. I chose one.

'For Kelly.'

I tossed it to the wind.

I chose another. 'For Ceci.'

And so it went, one for each of them. I felt calm, until the last few.

'For Valerie.'

I flung the rose in the air. Seven remained. I bunched three and raised my hand. My voice had a fissure in it.

'For Tommy.'

They arced out over the rugged terrain. Three more. Her name wouldn't come easily, and so I breathed and said it in a whisper.

'For Abbie.'

The wind caught them and they soared for a second, and were gone. Jesse took the final rose from my hand. His voice was quiet.

'For the baby.'

Heat ran through me and the wind brushed my back. Above the Sierras lightning rippled, flashes in the clouds so far distant that the thunder died before it reached us. Emptiness didn't begin to explain how I felt.

'I'm so sorry,' I said.

'No.' His face was grave. 'That's not what you say to me. Not ever.'

I felt pain behind my eyes. I blinked, trying to hide my tears and confusion. But he pulled me onto his lap and took my face in his hands.

'I'm in this with you. All the way.'

'I only wish . . .' I closed my eyes. 'If only—'

435

Fingers against my lips. '*If* is a word that will eat you alive. Believe me, I know.'

He smoothed my hair out of my eyes and kissed my forehead. We held each other and watched the daylight sail away.

'You ready?' I said.

Dad nodded. He squared his shoulders and smoothed down his bristling white hair. I straightened his tie. My hand lingered.

'There's no turning back,' I said.

'This day has been far too long in coming. It's time.'

Mom stepped up and took his hand. We walked through the courthouse archway. Jesse was waiting outside.

The day was sunny and the television cameras were gathered on the sidewalk. Lavonne Marks was reading to them from a prepared statement. Reporters were taking notes. Dad shook Jesse's hand.

'You don't have to do this, Phil,' Jesse said. 'Not for me.'

'Yes, I do. Not just because I took the coward's road with you.'

I could hardly bear to look at my father's face. I was already frightened over what was coming. Seeing the regret in his eyes when he looked at Jesse was almost more than I could bear. Dad knew he was wrong for asking him to have me terminate the pregnancy. He wanted to undo things, make up for this, redeem himself.

But it was more than that.

He wanted to atone for twenty years when people from my class were suffering and dying because of the explosion at China Lake. He couldn't have prevented the blast or stopped us from being exposed. But, he had come to believe, he could have done more. Pressed harder. Taken chances and dug deeper. But he hadn't, and my friends had died.

He stepped to the microphone.

'My name is Philip Delaney. I'm a retired captain in the US Navy, a veteran with twenty-five years of military service. I'm here today to talk about an operation called Project South Star, and how agencies working supposedly to protect this nation instead hired an assassin to murder a group of civilians from China Lake, California.'

He was falling on his sword.

'You in the media have been covering the Coyote killings. What you don't know is that this killer was made, not born. And she was set loose to execute classmates from the high school in China Lake, my daughter among them.'

I watched the reporters and cameramen. They were attentive. Did they understand what he was doing? He was blowing it all away. He was going to lose his security clearance, his job, his reputation. He would be discredited, shamed within the military and intelligence communities to which he had dedicated his life. He would probably be prosecuted. He was betraying his oath of secrecy for the sake of me, my classmates and the idea that the nation deserved better than what Maureen Swayze and the black world of government ops had given them.

I was proud of him.

He spoke with dignity and assurance. Beyond the reporters, a small crowd of onlookers was gathering on the sidewalk. I wanted to make sure they listened, closely, and appreciated. I tried to make eye contact with each of them, willing them all to stay and hear him out.

Abruptly, my vision prismed. At the back of the crowd, still, hard, and conspicuous as hell, stood Jakarta Rivera. Her face was somber. I shot a glance at Dad.

He didn't stop talking or break the rhythm of his statement, but his eyes settled on her and his voice slowed for a moment. He lifted his head, just an inch. In the back of the crowd, Jax did the same. Their eyes held for a second. She turned and walked away.

It took me the whole drive home to work up the courage. Swinging the Mustang around the corner onto my street, I finally turned to Dad.

'I saw Jax.'

He gazed at the live oaks and oleander, the kids playing basketball across the street, the leaves in the gutter, everywhere but at me.

'Dad.'

'I'm going to have a lot of time on my hands. Maybe you can come down to Key West. We'll take the boat out and do some fishing.' He loosened his tie. 'Fishing trips are an excellent time to talk.'

He was gazing into the distance. I slowed the car. When I put my hand on his, he took his time before looking at me.

I nodded. 'It's a deal.'